Praise for *Faithful*

"*Faithful* by Kim Cash Tate is not only beautifully written, it is a novel that changes you, that makes you question your heart and attitudes. I can't recommend it highly enough!"

— Colleen Coble, bestselling
author of *Lonestar Homecoming*

"Kim is a wonderful storyteller. As she paints the picture of the women in this book they don't seem like characters from a novel, they sound like you, like me. When they wrestle with their faith, we wrestle with them and find out, as they do, that God is always faithful."

— Sheila Walsh, international
speaker and bestselling author

"Three friends. Two husbands. One Romeo. All are shaken to the core as author Kimberly Cash Tate peels away layers of lies and self-deception to reveal the rotten core of infidelity and its tragic consequences. But this novel is also about hope and healing as her well-drawn characters discover the freedom of being FAITHFUL."

— Neta Jackson, author of the Yada
Yada Prayer Group and Yada
Yada House of Hope novels

"Good fiction has to grab me, knock me around, and make me care about what is happening to the characters. But great fiction inspires me. Kim Cash Tate accomplishes it all in *Faithful*."

— Marilyn Meberg, Women of
Faith speaker and author of *Tell
Me Everything*

"Kim Cash Tate's enjoyable novel is true to both the realities of life and the hope found through faith in Jesus. Romance meets real life with a godly heart! Hooray!"

— Stasi Eldredge, best-selling
author of *Captivating*

faithful

KIM CASH TATE

THOMAS NELSON
Since 1798

NASHVILLE   DALLAS   MEXICO CITY   RIO DE JANEIRO

Published in Nashville, Tennessee, by Thomas Nelson. Thomas Nelson is a registered trademark of Thomas Nelson, Inc.

Author is represented by the literary agency of The B&B Media Group, Inc., 109 S. Main, Corsicana, Texas 75110. www.tbbmedia.com.

Thomas Nelson, Inc., books may be purchased in bulk for educational, business, fund-raising, or sales promotional use. For information, please e-mail SpecialMarkets@ThomasNelson.com.

Publisher's Note: This novel is a work of fiction. Names, characters, places, and incidents are either products of the author's imagination or used fictitiously. All characters are fictional, and any similarity to people living or dead is purely coincidental.

Scripture quotations are from the NEW AMERICAN STANDARD BIBLE®, © The Lockman Foundation, 1960, 1962, 1963, 1968, 1971, 1972, 1973, 1975, 1977, 1995. Used by permission.

Library of Congress Cataloging-in-Publication Data

Tate, Kimberly Cash.
    Faithful / Kimberly Cash Tate.
      p. cm.
    ISBN 978-1-59554-854-2 (pbk.)
    I. Title.
PS3620.A885F35 2010
813'.6—dc22   2010020396

Printed in the United States of America

10 11 12 13 14 RRD 5 4 3 2 1

To Quentin and Cameron,
may you always be strongly aware
of God's faithfulness in your lives.

One

CYDNEY SANDERS JUMPED at the ringing of the phone, startled out of slumber. She rolled over, peeked at the bedside clock, and groaned. She had twenty whole minutes before the alarm would sound, and she wanted every minute of that twenty. Only her sister would be calling at five forty in the morning. Every morning she called, earlier and earlier, with a new something that couldn't wait regarding that wedding of hers. Not that Stephanie was partial to mornings. She was apt to call several times during the day and into the evening as well. Everything wedding related was urgent.

Cyd nestled back under the covers, rolling her eyes at the fifth ring. Tonight she would remember to turn that thing off. She was tired of Stephanie worrying her from dawn to dusk.

Her heart skipped suddenly and she bolted upright. *The wedding is tomorrow*. The day seemed to take forever to get here, and yet it had come all too quickly. She sighed, dread descending at once with a light throbbing of her head. She might have felt stressed no matter what date her sister had chosen for the wedding. That she chose Cyd's fortieth birthday made it infinitely worse.

She sank back down at the thought of it. *Forty.* She didn't mind the age itself. She'd always thought it would be kind of cool, in fact. At forty, she'd be right in the middle of things, a lot of life behind her, a lot of living yet to do. She'd be at a stride, confident in her path, her purpose. She would have climbed atop decades of prayer and study, ready to walk in some wisdom. Celebrate a little understanding. Stand firmly in faith. Count it all joy.

And she'd look good. She was sure of that. She'd work out during her pregnancies, and while the babies nursed and sucked down her tummy, she would add weights to the cardio routine to shape and tone. As she aged, her metabolism could turn on her if it wanted to; she had something for that too. She would switch up her workout every few weeks, from jogging to mountain bike riding to Tae Bo, all to keep her body guessing, never letting it plateau. Her husband would thank her.

He would also throw her a party. She wasn't much of a party person, but she always knew she'd want a big one on the day she turned forty. It wouldn't have to be a surprise. She'd heard enough stories of husbands unable to keep a party secret anyway. They'd plan it together, and she would kick in the new season in high spirits, surrounded by the people she loved.

Now that she was one day away, she still had no problem with forty. It was the other stuff that had shown up with it—forty, never been married, childless. Now, despite her distinguished career as a classics professor at Washington University in St. Louis, she was questioning her path and her purpose and dreading her new season—and the fact that she was forced to ring it in as maid of honor in her younger sister's wedding . . . her *much younger* sister.

She was still irritated that Stephanie kept the date even after their mother reminded her that October 18 was Cyd's birthday.

"Why does that matter?" Stephanie had said.

The only thing that mattered to Stephanie was Stephanie, and if she wanted something, she was going to make it happen. Like now. She cared not a whit that she was ringing Cyd's phone off the hook before dawn, waking Cyd and the new puppy, who was yelping frantically in her crate in the kitchen.

Cyd gave up, reached over, and snatched up the phone. Before it came fully to her ear, she heard her sister's voice.

"Cyd, I forgot to tell you last night—*stop*," Stephanie giggled. "You see I'm on the phone."

Cyd switched off her alarm. "Good morning to you too, Steph." She swung her legs out from under the warm bedding and shivered as they hit the air. The days were warm and muggy still, but the nights were increasingly cooler.

From a hook inside the closet, she grabbed her plum terry robe, which at Cyd's five-nine hit her above the knee, and slipped it over her cotton pajama shorts and tank. Her ponytail caught under the robe and she lifted it out, let it flop back down. It was a good ways down her back, thick with ringlets from air drying, a naturally deep reddish brown. Her face had the same richness, a beautiful honey brown, smooth and flawless.

Stephanie was giggling still as she and her fiancé, Lindell, whispered in the background.

I can't believe she woke me up for this. Cyd pushed her feet into her slippers and padded downstairs with a yawn to let out the puppy. "Do you do this when you're talking to Momma?"

Stephanie fumbled with the phone. "Do what?"

"Make it obvious that you and Lindell spent the night together?"

"Cyd, we are grown and will be married to*morrow*. Who gives a flip if we spent the night together?"

"Stephanie . . ." Cyd closed her eyes at the bottom of the stairs as all manner of responses swirled in her mind. Sometimes she wondered if she and Stephanie had really grown up in the same family with the same two parents who loved God and made His ways abundantly clear. Much of it had sailed right over Stephanie's head. Cyd had attempted to nail it down for her over the years, particularly in the area of relationships, but Stephanie never warmed to any notion of chastity, or even monogamy. In fact, when she'd called to announce her engagement six months ago, Cyd thought the husband-to-be was Warren, the man Stephanie had been bringing lately when she stopped by.

But Cyd had vowed moons ago to stop lecturing her sister and pray instead. She took a deep breath and expelled it loudly enough for Stephanie to know she was moving on, but only with effort.

"So, you forgot to tell me something?" She headed to the kitchen, where Reese was barking with attitude, indignant that Cyd was taking too long to get there.

"Girl, listen to this," Stephanie said. "LaShaun called Momma yesterday, upset 'cause we didn't include a guest on her invitation, talking about she wants to bring Jo-Jo. That's why I *didn't* put 'and guest' on her invitation. I'm not paying for that loser to come up in there, eat our food, drink, and act a fool. And why is she calling now anyway? Hello? The deadline for RSVPs was last month. Can you believe her?"

"Stephanie, was there a need to call so early to tell me this?" Cyd clicked on the kitchen light.

"Don't you think it's a trip?"

"Okay, yeah."

"I know! And you know Momma. She said, 'That's your cousin. Just keep the peace and let her bring him.' I'm tempted to call LaShaun right now and tell her both of them can jump in a lake."

Cyd headed to the crate under the desk portion of the kitchen counter. Tired though she was, Reese's drama tickled her inside. She was whimpering and pawing at the gated opening, and when Cyd unlocked it, the energetic twelve-week-old shot out. A mix of cocker spaniel and who knew what else, with dark chocolate wavy hair and tan patches on the neck, underbelly, and paws, she'd reminded Cyd of a peanut butter cup the moment she nabbed her heart at the shelter.

Reese jumped on Cyd, then rolled over for a tummy rub. Three seconds later she dashed toward the back door. At her age she could barely make it through the night without an accident. If Cyd delayed now, she'd be cleaning up a mess. She attached the leash and led her out.

"Well, what do you think?" Stephanie asked.

"About telling LaShaun to jump in the lake?" Cyd turned on the lights in the backyard and stepped outside with Reese, tightening her robe.

Stephanie sucked her teeth. "I mean about the whole thing."

"Well, Momma and Daddy are paying," Cyd said, since it seemed her sister had forgotten, "so if Momma doesn't mind Jo-Jo coming, why worry about it? You'll be so busy you probably won't see much of them anyway. No point getting your cousin *and* Aunt Gladys mad over something like this."

"Whatever," Stephanie said. "I should've known you'd say the same thing as Momma. I still might call LaShaun, just to let her know she should've called me directly, not tried to go through Momma."

"All right, go ahead and ponder that. I've got to get ready for class and—"

"I wasn't finished," Stephanie whined. "Did you talk to Dana?"

"I talked to her last night. Why?"

"So she told you about the shoes?"

"Mm-hmm." Cyd moved to different spots in the yard, tugging on the leash to get Reese to stop digging and do her business. A light popped on in the house next door and she saw Ted, a professor in the chemistry department, moving around in his kitchen. Many of her colleagues from Wash U lived in her Clayton neighborhood—six on her block alone.

"I wasn't trying to be difficult," Stephanie said, "but something told me to stop by her house yesterday to see for myself what kind of shoes she bought. You said they were cute, but those things were dreadful."

"Stephanie, they're flower-girl shoes. All flower-girl shoes are cute. Mackenzie tried them on with the dress when I was over there last week, and she looked adorable."

"The *dress* is adorable—because I picked it out—but those tired Mary Janes with the plain strap across the top have got to go. Is that what they wear at white weddings or something?"

"I don't know. Google it—'official flower-girl shoe at white weddings.'"

"Ha, ha, very funny. I'm just sayin' . . ."

Cyd led Reese back into the house, half listening as Stephanie droned on about some snazzier shoes with rhinestones Dana could've gotten and why she shouldn't have trusted Dana to make the choice in the first place.

She'd get over it. Stephanie did a lot of complaining about a lot of people, but there was no doubt—she loved Dana. Dana had been like family ever since she and Cyd met on the volleyball team in junior high, when Stephanie was just a baby. Stephanie had always looked up to her like a second big sister, and when Dana got married and had Mackenzie and Mark, Stephanie actually volunteered to babysit regularly. Those kids adored "Aunt Stephanie," and when it came time to plan her wedding, Stephanie didn't hesitate to include them . . . even though a couple of great-aunts questioned her appointing white kids as flower girl and ring bearer.

". . . so, long story short, I asked Dana to take 'em back and find some shoes with some pizzazz.'"

"She told me she's not hunting for shoes today. She doesn't have time." Cyd stopped in the office, awakened her computer screen with a shake of the mouse, and started skimming an e-mail from a student.

"She told me that too," Stephanie said. "So I'm hoping you can do it."

"Do what?"

"Find some cute shoes."

"I have to work." And even if she didn't, she wouldn't get roped into this one. She'd gone above and beyond for Stephanie already. This week alone, she'd taken care of several items Stephanie was supposed to handle. If her sister wanted to sweat the flower girl's shoes the day before the wedding, she'd have to do it alone.

"But your class is at eight o'clock. You've got the whole day after that."

Cyd donned a tight-lipped smile to beat back her annoyance. "Stephanie, you know that teaching is only part of what I do. I have a paper due for a conference coming up, and I'm already behind."

She unhooked Reese's leash and watched her run around in circles, delighted with her freedom. But when Cyd headed for the stairs, Reese fell quickly in step. No way would she be left behind.

"How can you even focus on work today?" Stephanie sounded perplexed. "Aren't you just too excited about the big event? Girl, you know this is your wedding too."

Cyd paused on a stair. "How is this my wedding too?"

"Since it looks like you won't be getting married yourself"— Stephanie had a shrug in her voice—"you've at least gotten a chance to plan one through me. You know, living vicariously. Hasn't it been fun?"

Cyd held the phone aloft and stared at it. Did Stephanie really think these last few months had been *fun*? She had involved Cyd in every decision from her dress to her colors to the style, thickness, and font of the invitations to the type of headpiece Mackenzie should wear—all of which *could* have been fun if Stephanie had really wanted her sister's opinions.

What Stephanie wanted was for Cyd to accompany her about town to every wedding-related appointment, listen with interest as she debated with herself about gowns, floral arrangements, and what to include on the wedding registry, and affirm her ultimate picks. She also wanted Cyd to handle whatever she deemed drudgery. And Cyd didn't mind; as the maid of honor, she thought it her duty to address invitations, order favors, and the like. What bugged her was Stephanie's ingratitude, which wasn't new but had taken on a high-gloss sheen. It was Stephanie's world, and everyone else revolved around it, especially Cyd, since in Stephanie's opinion she didn't have a life anyway.

Now she was telling Cyd—matter-of-factly—that it looked like her sister wouldn't ever be getting married. Cyd wished she could dismiss it as she did Stephanie's other flippant remarks. But how could she, when her own inner voice was shouting the same?

Tears crowded Cyd's eyes, and she was startled, and grateful, when the phone beeped to announce another call. She didn't bother to look at the caller's identity.

"Steph, that's my other line. I've gotta go."

"Who would be calling you this early? Besides me, that is." Stephanie chuckled at herself. "Probably Momma. Tell her I'll call her in a few minutes. By the way, what did you decide to wear to the rehearsal tonight?"

"Steph, really, I've got to go. Talk to you later."

Cyd clicked Off, threw the phone on the bed, and headed to the bathroom. She couldn't bear more wedding talk at the moment, and if it was her mother, that's all she would hear.

She peeled off her clothes, turned on the shower, and stepped under the warm spray of water. Now that she was smack up against it—the wedding, the birthday—everything seemed to rush at her. She wouldn't mind being forty, unmarried, and childless if she'd expected it. But from a young age she'd prayed repeatedly for a husband—and not just a "Christian" but someone on fire for the Lord. And she'd believed deep in her heart that God would answer.

Cyd looked upward, past the dingy housing of the lightbulb, as tears mingled with water, questions with accusation.

I trusted in Your promises, Lord. You said if I delighted myself in You, You would give me the desires of my heart.

The tears flowed harder.

You said if I abide in You and Your words abide in me, I could ask whatever I wish and it would be done. Haven't I delighted myself in You? Haven't I abided in You?

Her eyes moved to the tiny square tiles as she considered her mind-set over the years, always believing, holding out faith, weighing every major decision on a scale that counted marriage a given. Her house was Exhibit A.

To buy made financial sense. A capital investment would benefit her singly and the marriage later. But the details took some sifting. She'd thought about buying in the city and found great list prices, but what about resale? What if the promised revitalization didn't make it to her block? What if she—*they*—got stuck with two bedrooms and one bath in a declining neighborhood where they feared for the safety of their children and where their children—three, maybe four of them—were sleeping on top of one another because Cyd didn't think to buy bigger?

That was the other thing—how much house to buy? Would she buy comfortable-for-her small or a size that would attract a larger pool of potential buyers? Assuming she would sell when the time came to marry. Her fiancé might like the home, the neighborhood, the driving distance to work. *If* he worked in the area. What if they met as he passed through town on business? What if he lived in Atlanta, D.C., or Chicago? He probably wouldn't want to relocate.

Only one conclusion satisfied the scale: buy what she could easily sell. So she bought in Clayton, a suburb just west of St. Louis, known for its award-winning public school system and stately old homes. Hers she wouldn't call stately, but definitely old. And starter-home size, just right for the young family who would buy from Cyd one day and walk their firstborn to kindergarten a couple of blocks away. Or the professor who, like her, would enjoy a five-minute commute to Wash U. Through the repair work that was sorely needed, she could see its inherent charm. It was her investment.

Their investment. That was how she thought of it. That was how she thought of everything. That was how strongly she believed.

Cyd soaped her body, praying all the while. _Lord, I just don't understand. All things are possible with You. You could've sent a husband my way long ago. Someone I could share life with, love and laugh with. Why would You give me such a strong desire to marry and have children, only to leave me empty?_ She released an aggravated sigh. _And then for Stephanie to get married on my birthday . . ._

She stewed over that last bit as she washed and conditioned her hair. The last thing she wanted to do on her fortieth birthday was to be reminded all the day long that such blessings as love and wedding vows still existed—for others. One thing was sure—the weekend would be insufferable. She shut the water off and grabbed her towel, careful to dart back from the hot rain of the shower-head. She'd had it fixed twice, but like an old habit those drops reappeared.

The sound of the phone cut into her thoughts, but Cyd didn't move. She lathered on lotion, put on her robe, and combed a leave-in conditioning cream through her locks, stepping around the ever-present Reese, whose little brown body was stretched out on the small floor space. She put a glob of gel in her hands, rubbed them together, and scrunched it in her hair to give it a wavy curl as it dried. Before leaving for class, she'd pull it into a ponytail, her low-maintenance style of choice.

The ringing blared again as she put on a pair of beige slacks and a long silk button-down shirt. She groaned. If she didn't answer, it would ring until she walked out the door. Had to be Stephanie. Her mother would've called once and left a message. She grabbed the handset and glanced at it. "Oh." She pushed Talk. "Dana?"

"Finally . . . I knew you had to be home. I've been calling for the last half hour."

"Sorry, thought you were Stephanie." Cyd slipped on her mules. "I'm sure she's gonna call you. I told her I wasn't shopping for those shoes." She moved to straighten the lavender sheets on her bed.

Dana sighed. "Shoes are the last thing on my mind right now."

Cyd quirked her brow. Something in Dana's voice. "What's going on?"

"I need you to go somewhere with me around noon. Please tell me you're available."

"Why didn't you say anything last night when we talked?" Cyd smoothed the comforter over the top of the sheets.

"I wasn't sure about it then, but I couldn't sleep and I just . . . I don't know . . . it's something I need to do."

"Dana, what are you talking about?" Cyd tossed the decorative pillows atop the upper middle of the bed. "Where are we going?"

"I'd rather explain it to you and Phyllis in person. I'm hoping she can come, too, if someone can watch the baby."

"Phyllis is headed out of town today—and I completely forgot that we're supposed to be praying for her this morning." Cyd could've kicked herself. When the three friends got together on Sunday, Phyllis's stomach was in knots. They prayed for her then, and Phyllis asked specifically that they pray early Friday morning. Cyd had been too consumed with her own problems to remember.

"I forgot she was leaving today," Dana said. "I feel like I'm in a fog." There was a pause. "If Phyllis can't make it, then I definitely need you to come. Can you?"

Cyd didn't have much choice. She needed to work on this paper, but Dana had roused not only her curiosity but her concern. "Sure. Where should I meet you?"

"I'll pick you up," Dana said. "Will you be on campus?"

"No, I'm working from home after class so I can let Reese out. Just meet me here."

"Thanks, Cyd." Relief coated Dana's voice. "I'll see you at noon."

Reese nuzzled her nose to Cyd's leg, and Cyd slumped to the floor beneath the weight of all the cares. Her mind teetered between Dana's issue—whatever it was—Phyllis's, and her own. As she stroked Reese's back, a prayer ambled its way up through her thoughts, the only one she could muster right then.

Lord, just . . . help us.

Two

PHYLLIS OWENS CLOSED her eyes as her husband's hands moved between her shoulder blades and down her spine. They were big hands, powered by weight-lifting muscle, but even as she felt the deep pressure of the massage, she could feel his gentleness, the warmth of his love.

His palms fanned outward, kneading the sides of her back. She put her focus there, each press of the flesh, every touch of his fingertips. These were the moments she adored, when she and Hayes were truly in sync, enjoying one another, when everything was right in their world.

Hayes placed his thumbs at her lower back and with a circular motion worked his way upward. Phyllis wrapped her arms around the pillow she faced, trying to stay in the moment, but her thoughts were ebbing already. Hayes would be done shortly, and the mood would shift—as soon as she asked her question. She had waited days upon days, but time had run out.

Sighing softly into her pillow, Phyllis opened her eyes, staring at nothing. It was a simple question, really. *Are you taking the children to church on Sunday?* But the thought of asking it made her insides a wreck. She knew her husband. And as simple as the question was to her, to Hayes it could be contentious.

She'd tried to avoid the conversation altogether, telling her boys it would be best if they didn't pressure him, wouldn't hurt to miss one Sunday. But at twelve, ten, and eight, they had their own perspective. They had been praying for him for years. This, they thought, would be the perfect way for God to answer. With their mom away for the weekend, their dad would feel obligated to take them to church.

Phyllis didn't have the heart to tell the boys it wasn't that easy. Hayes wouldn't feel obligated. When he made up his mind, he stuck to it, and on this his mind was firm.

She knew.

When Phyllis became a believer almost six years ago, she returned from the church service ecstatic, the good news spilling out of her. She came quickly through the door looking for Hayes, her adrenaline assuring her that everything had changed. She was different, the world was different, even the house was different.

Before she'd left that morning, she'd been scanning the Sunday real estate section in the *Post-Dispatch*, drooling over newer homes with open floor plans, spectacular kitchens, and master baths with enough space for two people to walk past each other. She told Hayes she was tired of their eighty-year-old house with all of its creaks and warts. She had acquiesced to moving to Clayton because they were new to the area and a couple of Hayes's coworkers had touted the school district. But older homes had never been her preference, and each year of the three they'd been there, she'd grown more annoyed with it.

Instead of updating the place, a carrot Hayes had dangled, their money had gone into fixing a myriad of things apparently timed to break down the minute they left closing. Her favorite was the treads on the main staircase, which were so worn, the stair repair person informed them, that some unfortunate soul would've soon stepped down and sailed clear to the basement. No matter how good the school district was, she was ready to move to a suburb farther west where she could enjoy a modernized lifestyle and little amenities like three-pronged outlets in every room of the house.

But it wasn't the same house when she returned from church. Oh, the kitchen was in the same spot, on the far side of the first floor, accessible through one doorway and hemmed in by four stifling walls. But now she saw the ampleness of the space and three large windows on those walls that allowed natural light to pour through. Outside she glimpsed big beautiful trees swaying with gorgeous clothes of spring. Why hadn't she noticed the fuchsia flowers in the bush beneath the window where she ate her breakfast every morning? She beheld their beauty, but only for a moment. She had to find Hayes.

Phyllis moved through the living room, passed under another archway, and found him in the family room watching football. She kissed him hello and stood with a grin, waiting anxiously for the next commercial.

"What?" His eyes moved between Phyllis and the flat panel on the wall.

"I can wait," she said, despite her excitement. She knew Hayes had to focus on every second of every down, lest he miss a sack, strip, fumble, interception, or long bomb into the end zone. He even cared about the little things, little to Phyllis anyway, things like line formations and quarterback snaps.

He looked as if he could have played football himself at one time. At six foot three and thick, he filled an entire cushion on the sofa. He was glued to his favorite spot, the far left end, arm hanging over the side within easy reach of the brew on the end table. He wore a simple tank and nylon athletic shorts, his medium dark legs propped on a leather cushion.

"No, go ahead." He glanced up at her. "You look . . ." He shrugged. "I don't know. Strange. What's up?"

Phyllis eased next to him on the sofa, her black skirt grazing his legs. "Hayes, I can't believe it. I grew up in church, but I guess I never really 'got it.' You know, not in my heart." She took a breath, still processing it all. "Today the message just shook me. I was in tears at the end and went up for the altar call. They took me to this counseling room, and Cyd went with me. She knows the pastor, and she got him to come in personally and talk to me. He told me how I could be born again." Phyllis paused and sighed with a smile. "Hayes, I gave my life to Jesus."

He lifted his brow. "You're kidding, right?"

Phyllis's smile disappeared. "What do you mean?"

"Come on, Phyl." He was almost chuckling, looking back now at the game. "You didn't believe all of that, did you?" He grabbed his beer.

"All of what?" Phyllis's heart dropped. Had she only imagined the wonder of the morning? Had she been carried away by the beautiful music and melodic voices at the end of the message? Was that why she walked down that aisle? Had she been somehow seduced into believing?

"Man, the ball was right there! They pay you all that money to _catch_ the ball. Come on!" Hayes's legs hit the floor as he scooted to the edge of his seat.

Phyllis pushed his shoulder. "Did I believe all of what?"

"All that stuff about judgment and hell." His eyes were on the next play. "I know he went there. Scared you, didn't he?"

Phyllis's eyes fell, wondering now if maybe she hadn't been seduced, but scared into believing. She mulled over the pastor's words. He'd been so clear and kind. And Cyd had been sitting with her as he spoke, streaming tears right along with Phyllis. Cyd had been the one who invited her to church; they'd gotten acquainted through

Phyllis's walks around the neighborhood. The doubt vanished as she shook her head.

"He told me about hell, but I wasn't afraid, Hayes. He mainly spoke of the good news, not the bad. He focused on Christ. And yes, I did believe all of it."

Hayes grunted.

Phyllis took a breath. "Hayes, Cyd said this man is nationally known and well respected. With a congregation of thousands, I'm sure he's busy. Yet he said he'd be willing to meet with you as well. He said I could call his assistant and—"

"Phyllis." Hayes's tone was dry. "He can't tell me anything I haven't already heard. I grew up in church just like you, and unlike you, apparently, I 'got it.' I knew exactly what they were saying. I just didn't buy it. That pastor may be willing to meet, but I'm not. Not for that." He took a swig and hunched forward to catch the next play, shaking his head. "Whatever."

Tears sprang up and danced around Phyllis's lower lashes. She followed Hayes's eyes to the television to gather herself. This was the most meaningful day of her life, one she couldn't wait to share with her husband. She wanted him to rejoice with her. More than that, she wanted him to experience the same joy. She didn't think he would fall on his knees and give his life to Jesus the moment he heard, but she didn't think he would react this way either. *Whatever?*

At the next commercial, Phyllis doubled up her nerve. "Okay, Hayes, forget the meeting. I just want you to see this church. There's such a sweet spirit there, and this man really teaches. Why don't you go with me next Sunday and see what you think?"

She groaned inside when the crowd roared before he could respond. She'd never seen a commercial break zip by that fast.

"Phyllis, I told you when you asked two days ago, last night, and this morning that I wasn't going," he said, his eyes at half-attention. "And I'm not changing my mind just because you had some kind of religious experience." He tipped the bottle to his mouth and drained it. "In fact, let me make this real plain. I don't want to hear about that church or God. Period." He shrugged as if they had just disagreed on whether to take up horticulture. "It's just something we're not going to share."

Phyllis never talked to the boys about where Hayes stood. But as they rose for church every Sunday morning and left without him, they began to ask questions. Phyllis told them simply to pray that their father would join them one day, and that's apparently what they'd been doing. She was surprised when they announced with glee that this weekend could be the answer.

She felt guilty too. The boys were so full of hope, and it was clear hers had dwindled. She was the one who dealt with the tension firsthand, having to watch what she said and how she said it, feeling irrepressible joy at growing closer to God yet forced to keep it contained.

It was especially hard during her surprise pregnancy with their fourth child, Ella. Phyllis was awed that God was shaping a life in her very own womb. He'd done it three times before, but she'd never recognized it as such, so to her, this may as well have been her first. She would rub her tummy, muttering, "Thank You, God." She would serenade the little one with praise songs while washing dishes or making the bed, always softly if Hayes was home, never if he was in the room. Though they were both excited about the baby, she had to guard her joy, express it with the right words. She prayed harder than ever for a change in Hayes, but it didn't come. Lately she'd been wondering if it ever would. It was hard to keep the faith when Hayes hadn't moved an inch in six years.

She sighed. Maybe the boys were right, and this would be God's way of answering. Maybe, just maybe, Hayes's heart had softened a little. Maybe it was ripe for this very request. Phyllis told her sons that she'd ask on Friday morning, and she'd implored Cyd and Dana to pray.

Lord, let this be the right time.

Phyllis felt Hayes's breath on her neck as he whispered, "You'd better get in the shower, baby. You don't want to be late for your flight."

Despite his words, Hayes continued working his fingers across her neck, causing Phyllis to hug her pillow tighter and insert herself back in the moment. "This is too relaxing," she mumbled. "I don't want to get up."

"Oh, in that case . . ." Hayes pulled the burgundy and gold comforter over their heads.

Phyllis poked her head out, chuckling. Popping up on an elbow, she looked at him. "Are you sure you're going to be able to handle the kids by yourself?"

Hayes pecked her on the lips. "For the twentieth time, yes."

"But, Hayes, I don't think you've ever taken care of all four of them for longer than a few hours. It's a lot of work. And now that Ella's eighteen months, she's into everything. You really have to watch her because—"

He put a finger to her lips. "I've got it under control."

Phyllis smiled at him. "I really appreciate your taking the day off so I can leave early this morning."

"Had to," he said, pushing a curl out of her face. "I thought you would die if you missed any part of the festivities."

Phyllis smiled. She was headed to a reunion. She couldn't believe it, but it had been twenty years since she had pledged Alpha Kappa Alpha Sorority with fourteen line sisters as an undergraduate at the University of Maryland, College Park. The women planned the reunion celebration to coincide with Maryland's homecoming weekend to encourage a bigger turnout. As for arriving early on Friday, Phyllis had a confession.

"Well," she said slowly, "there's actually nothing on the official agenda until this evening, but, you know, we wanted to get together at Stacy's house beforehand to—"

"Gossip."

Phyllis lifted her head, swiped her pillow out from under, and hit him with it. "To catch up on each other's lives."

"Mm-hmm." Hayes sat up to guard himself against a second hit. "A bunch of women spending the weekend together equals gossip. And you're going to miss some of it if you don't get moving."

Phyllis turned to look at the clock. "Ooh, you're right," she said, scooting out of bed, "but only the part about needing to get moving." At the doorway to the bathroom, she paused. "I forgot to tell you, the boys want burgers on the grill tonight. I bought the meat yesterday."

"Okay."

"And I rented the movies you all wanted. And let's see . . . oh, Ella's church clothes are in her closet, facing outward. The boys can dress themselves." She avoided his gaze. "Let me see if there's anything else . . ."

Hayes leaned casually on an elbow. "We're not going to church, Phyl."

Phyllis looked at him. "But we go every week, Hayes. And the boys love their Sunday school classes and kids' church. They don't want to miss it."

"It won't kill them to miss one Sunday. It's no big deal. I'll think of something fun for us to do instead."

"But, Hayes . . . I was thinking it would be good for you too. You know, to go."

"I'm not going, Phyllis."

"But, Hayes—"

"Phyllis, don't start. We've had a great morning. Don't ruin it."

Phyllis turned into the bathroom and closed the door, tears welling. Hayes was as resolute as ever. Couldn't even bend for the sake of the kids.

Lord, I'm tired of trying to keep the faith.

"Sweetheart, you're going to miss your plane."

Phyllis heard Hayes's voice booming up the stairs as she stooped beside her overstuffed luggage, fighting to pull the zipper closed.

"The security lines are crazy this time of morning."

She walked to the dresser, her heart heavy still. She'd taken extra time in the shower, trying to dredge up some joy, but it hadn't worked. She didn't even feel like speaking to Hayes.

Her husband breezed into the room in shorts and a T-shirt, having hopped into the hall shower . . . and let out a low whistle. "Wow! Look at you."

"Trying to say I don't normally look like this?" Phyllis fished through her jewelry box and lifted thin hoops from the mix as her emotions played tug-of-war in her heart. She wanted to lighten up, leave with a right spirit, but sadness had the upper hand.

Hayes wrapped his arms around her waist. "You're always beautiful, don't get me wrong. But no, you don't always look like *this*."

He was right, of course. Her usual attire this time of morning—and often all day—was sweatpants, a T-shirt, and slippers. Her hair would be pulled back and her face free of makeup, often until Sunday. Now she stood a couple of inches taller in skinny-heeled black boots, with comfortable but stylish jean gauchos and a black shawl-neck sweater. Her hair, past her shoulders, had loose curls from the wet set she'd given it the night before, and her makeup, unlike Sundays, even included mascara and eyeliner. She'd be seeing people she hadn't seen in years, some not since she graduated. A decent look was definitely in order.

Phyllis slipped on the earrings and a bracelet as Hayes watched her in the mirror.

He kissed her cheek. "You know I love you. Let's let that other stuff go."

Easy for you to say. She sighed. "I love you too."

Hayes gave a slight chuckle. "You don't have to sound so excited about it." His eyes caught hers in their reflection. "Seriously, Phyl, please let it go. I want you to have a good time." An eyebrow lifted. "But not _too_ good a time. One of your old college buddies might take a liking to the new you."

The compliment lured a half smile out of her. Her weight—a steady two fifty—had kept romantic relationships at bay during college, though several guys adopted her as a "sister" while they chased her girlfriends. But she'd lost close to ninety-five pounds since she'd last seen any of them, a feat that began slowly but steadily five years ago— interrupted, though not derailed, by the surprise pregnancy with Ella. Her college friends would truly be surprised, but the notion that an old buddy might "take a liking" to her was nothing but Hayes trying to pry her out of her funk. It was enough at least to prompt a reply.

"Yeah, I'd better watch out. Might have to beat 'em all back with a stick."

Hayes chuckled and headed to her luggage. "I should've gotten a plane ticket and come with you. Then _I_ could beat 'em back. Ready?" He had the suitcase in hand. "I forgot you've got to find parking too. Wish you'd let me take you."

She waved him off. "Then we'd have to wake the baby and bring her. I'm fine. Plus, it's no easy task prodding those boys along before school. You'll see." She stopped as Hayes took the stairs. "Be right down after I kiss the kids."

"I'll load this in the car," Hayes said over his shoulder. "And, Phyllis—"

"I know. I'm hurrying."

Phyllis scurried into the profusion of pink that was Ella's room— soft pink walls, two plush pink area rugs with a border of pink roses in full bloom. Pink in the window valance, side table scarf, the painting on the side of the toy box, the bunny and teddy bear perched atop the toy box, and bold pinks in two framed wall prints. After three boys, she couldn't resist diving headlong into the world of cute and totally girly.

Ella was curled in a ball, her bottom in the air, chest rising and falling gently as she slept. Phyllis's heart melted. This would be her first extended time away from her baby girl. Ella stirred, flopping her head to one side then the other as Phyllis stared from above the crib. The rails were too high for her to reach Ella's face, so she blew a kiss, rubbed her back, and eased out, heading next to Drew and Sean's room. She heard their bodies shifting as the hardwood floor beneath her creaked in the usual places. A faint light seeped through the wide wooden blinds, casting a soft glow on the deep-sea animals painted in motion around the room.

Drew and Sean had grown fascinated with these creatures after a family trip to Sea World, and Phyllis got Hayes to paint the ceiling and upper half of the wall sky blue and the bottom half dark blue for the ocean. Then she traced a variety of fish and other ocean creatures on the dark blue background and badgered Cyd and Dana into helping her bring them to life, despite their insistence that they had no skills with a brush. Dana got so into it that she free-handed some green seaweed in strategic places up the wall. And when Cyd discovered they had sponges, she braved the ladder, which Phyllis wouldn't do, and made clouds on the sky above.

Eight-year-old Sean popped his head up as Phyllis's footsteps neared. "I'm up, Mommy," he said, struggling to keep his head raised.

He still had a baby face, round with big eyes and long lashes. His little body shivered in his space pajamas, his latest fascination. Phyllis was already pondering how she might get Hayes to paint the planets overhead.

She knelt beside him and caressed his head until it lowered to the pillow again. "It's not time to get up yet, sweetie," she whispered. "You have a few more minutes till you have to get ready for school." His eyes were closing as she spoke. "Mommy's leaving for her trip. I'll call you this evening, okay?"

"Mm-hmm," Sean said.

Phyllis leaned over and kissed his forehead. "I love you."

She stood and looked at ten-year-old Drew in the top bunk. Since his entire body was buried under the covers, Phyllis assumed he was in a deep sleep until she spied a tiny shaft of light.

"What are you doing?" She climbed a few steps of the wooden ladder and pulled back the twin navy blue blanket.

Drew scrambled to keep his page, closing his book with a finger inside, and turned off his flashlight. With big brown eyes that matched his brothers', he said, "Mom, I woke up early and couldn't get back to sleep, and I'm at the part where the Rohirrim arrive at Pelennor Fields."

"And you were dying to know what would happen?"

Drew had seen *The Lord of the Rings* more times than she thought humanly desirable, and this was his second pass through the books.

He made no apology. "It's just *good*, Mom."

Phyllis heard Hayes's footsteps downstairs. "Lean over here, my boy." She kissed him. "I've gotta go, but I love you and I'll call and don't forget your homework on the kitchen table." She backed down the ladder. "And I'm going to tell Daddy to take that book from you at bedtime tonight."

"*Mom.*"

Phyllis chuckled as she stepped quickly into the room next door, negotiating an obstacle course of yesterday's clothes, a few CDs, a basketball, a football, and K'nex pieces used to build a roller coaster. LeBron James greeted her as she came near, his body poised for a slam dunk over Cole's head.

She sighed as she looked at her son, legs long like his dad's, dark and handsome like him too. He was the one who had pressed her the most about asking Hayes to take them to church. Thankfully, he was still asleep. She couldn't bear his disappointment right now, not when she was trying hard herself to keep positive. She'd tell him this evening. Bending, she kissed Cole on the forehead and turned to leave.

"Mom?"

Her shoulders slumped. "Good morning, Cole. I just came to kiss you good-bye." She tried to tiptoe out.

"Did you ask him?"

Phyllis turned and looked at him with what she hoped was a smile. "Yes, I did. He said you all will do something fun on Sunday."

Cole frowned and came up on an elbow. "Church *is* fun." His voice was scratchy. "We have a good time, and my friends are there." He shook his head. "I don't *get* it. Why won't he take us this *one* Sunday?" He paused. "Does Dad hate God or something?"

"Sweetheart." Phyllis stooped at his bedside. "Your dad just—"

"Phyllis, *what* are you *doing*?" Hayes called from the bottom of the stairs.

She jumped up, regretting the lack of time to deal with this, yet also relieved. "Cole, this is just one Sunday. Don't lose hope. Maybe God wants to answer your prayers when you least expect it."

Cole lay silent.

"Sweetheart, I've got to run. I'll talk to you later today, okay?"

She heard nothing as she dashed out of the room and down the stairs. Checking her watch, her eyes widened—7:30. Her flight was scheduled for 8:45. It would take fifteen minutes to drive to the airport, if traffic wasn't bad. She grabbed her purse and tote bag from the credenza in the foyer, and Hayes walked her to the front door.

"Love you, babe." He gave her a quick kiss and opened the door.

"Love you too." She headed to Hayes's SUV at the curb, leaving the minivan for him and the kids. "I'll call you this evening."

Phyllis opened the door, threw her things onto the passenger seat, and started the car. As she drove off, a long sigh filled the air. She'd been under so much stress just to get up the courage to ask Hayes one little question, all for nothing. She should've told the boys no. Now she had to contend with their disappointment as well as hers.

Cole's words reverberated in her mind. *"Does Dad hate God . . . ?"*

Phyllis had a sudden realization that twisted her gut. She'd always prayed for faith and patience, looking to the day when Hayes would have a change of heart . . . but what if she needed faith of a different sort? What if she needed faith to endure because his heart would never change?

She sighed again and put her focus on the trip ahead. Only two days, but she needed them. Two days to laugh and reminisce. Two days to recharge and refresh.

At least, she hoped to return refreshed. Until this morning, she didn't realize just how weary she'd become.

Three

CYD DASHED DOWN her front steps to the curb, opened the passenger door, and jumped in. By the way Dana had zoomed down the street in her car, causing the tree trimmers to look about anxiously from their perch, she figured time must be of the essence.

It was nothing new. Dana had an effervescent way about her, not only bubbly but brimming over—big smile, warm hello, full of purpose, ever moving from one thing to the next, sometimes already at the next thing before she needed to be . . . which was usually where Cyd came in. They balanced one another, often joking that Cyd's favorite word was *wait* and Dana's was *go*.

Cyd reached for her seat belt. "Okay, Dana. Where are we going? And I hope a quick lunch figures in somewhere because I haven't eaten yet."

Dana stared straight ahead, her profile still new and amazing to Cyd. In all the years Cyd had known her, Dana had had umpteen hairstyles, all varying degrees of long and, since college, lightened to a honey blonde. But on a whim two months ago, she got several inches whacked off and decided she'd feel even freer if she returned to her natural color. Her curly hair now sported a short blunt cut that left her neck feeling the breeze. She looked great.

"Dana?" Cyd looked into her friend's face.

"We're going to my house." Dana's voice was flat, her eyes on the road.

"Really?" Cyd wondered why Dana would pick her up and drive back out to Creve Coeur, twenty minutes away, rather than ask Cyd to meet her there. "Is that where we're *going*, or did you forget something?"

Dana moved a trembling hand through her dark brown locks, then rested it again on the console.

"Dana, why don't you pull over somewhere so we can talk?"

Dana gave a quick shake of the head. "No time." She sped through a light Cyd was sure had turned red. "But we do need to talk. I, um . . ."

Cyd's heart skipped with the faltering of Dana's voice. Her eyes remained glued on her friend.

"I signed up to volunteer at the school library on Fridays for the month of October."

Cyd nodded. She already knew that. Half the time, Cyd was the one who reminded Dana what she had scheduled herself to do and when.

Dana took a big breath and let it out. "So that's the only day of the week that I've been out of the house regularly. On the other days, Scott likes to meet me at home for lunch when he can."

"Oh, I know," Cyd said, unable to resist this one. "Wasn't Mark conceived over the lunch hour?" She chuckled.

Dana didn't respond in kind.

"Cyd, I think Scott's having an affair."

Her eyes met Cyd's for the first time, brown, intense eyes that returned quickly to the road.

Cyd frowned. Scott? Not the man who grabbed his wife's hand and drew her close every chance he got. Not the man who looked into his wife's eyes as if the whole world could fall off a cliff as long as she alone remained. Not the man who talked to every young man who would listen about the blessings of finding an excellent wife.

Not the coleader of Living Word's marriage ministry.

"Dana, why would you think such a thing?"

"For one thing, he never comes home for lunch when he knows I won't be there. But when I got home the last two Fridays, I knew he'd been there, 'cause a load of laundry was sitting in the washing machine. Scott chips in around the house, but he does *not* do laundry. When I asked about it, he said he just wanted to help out."

"Okay," Cyd said, listening.

Dana stopped at a red light and turned to Cyd. "Both times, our sheets were in the washer, and towels."

Cyd's stomach tightened. "Okay." Her mind searched for reasons. "Well, had the two of you, maybe the night before . . . ?"

The light changed, and Dana gunned the engine. "No." She turned into her subdivision. "That's the other thing. These last couple of weeks he hasn't come to bed when I do, and when I *am* home for lunch, he doesn't show up."

Cyd frowned again, bereft of a response.

Dana parked around the corner from her house and popped loose her seat belt. "I'm finding out *right now* what's going on." She flew out of the car.

It suddenly hit Cyd what they were doing. She flew out, too, to coax Dana back in. "Dana! Wait!"

When Dana didn't stop or look back, Cyd sighed and pushed her door to a close, rushing to catch her. She grabbed her friend's arm, pulling her to a stop. "Are you trying to catch him in the act?"

Dana looked aside.

"Oh, Dana! Have you *thought* about this? Have you even prayed? I don't know why you got me into this, I don't know why *you're* getting into this, but I don't have a good feeling about it *at all.*"

Dana took a frustrated step back. "I *knew* you would say this. That's exactly why I didn't tell you in advance. You want to think everything through, pray on it for months, wait for an angel to bring the decree. Sometimes you've just got to move." She put a hand to Cyd's shoulder. "I need you to come with me. If Scott has someone in there—"

"Exactly. What if he does? Then what? Do you want that image in your mind? Is this the best way to handle it, Dana?"

Dana glanced in the direction of her house. "What am I supposed to do? *Ask* him if he's having an affair?" Her legs fired up again. "There *is* no 'best way.' I just need to handle it." Over her shoulder she pleaded, "Cyd, please come with me. I really don't want to do this alone, but I will if I have to."

Cyd started after her and began to huff as Dana cut between two houses and upped her power walk to a light jog along a walking trail. She had to be moving on sheer adrenaline, because Dana, who had kept a little weight after each pregnancy, never jogged, and didn't walk either if it looked too much like exercise. Cyd was the one who got a regular cardio workout, but it seemed her heart had forgotten, palpitating the way it was, and mules and slacks were not her exercise gear of choice.

Dana left the trail and dashed across a grassy knoll, her attire much more suited to the mission—loose-fitting capris, a short-sleeved button-down shirt, nice and airy-looking flat sandals. When Cyd caught up to her, wet and dehydrated, Dana was poised at the door to the lower level, key in the lock, hand trembling.

Cyd covered it. "You don't have to do it, Dana. I just don't think—"

A finger flew to Dana's lips. "Shh."

She turned the key and pushed the door open, plunging them both inside a nightmare. Cyd could feel it. Though her mind still couldn't fathom catching Scott in an indiscretion, chill bumps rose on her arms, despite the beads produced by the heat. Her eyes darted here and there, as if in a haunted house, waiting for something to pop out and spook them.

She didn't know what she'd expected, but when things looked normal, she gathered herself. She saw the sectional sofa and chairs, the foosball and ice hockey tables. Nothing spooky at all. Cyd was sure they would comb every inch of the house and find it clear. Dana would feel silly, but she'd be satisfied.

Dana took off her shoes and motioned for Cyd to do the same. After peeping into the guest bedroom on the carpeted lower level, they moved to the stairs. Heads angled to the side, they took each step gingerly, coming at last to the top stair, which led to a spacious hallway off the foyer. Cyd's heart lurched and she put a hand to her chest when she saw a light in the kitchen. But she chastised herself. It was *just* a light. Goodness. Could have been left on this morning.

Dana elbowed Cyd as they approached the kitchen, pointing to the granite counter. From where they stood they could see a take-out bag. Stepping into the kitchen, they found two clear containers side by side on the kitchen table, one with remnants of a salad, the other of a sandwich. Dana gestured at the evidence and put a hand to her hip.

Cyd shrugged, whispering, "What? Scott can't handle a salad and a sandwich by himself?"

As Dana moved over to the door that led to the garage, Cyd grabbed a glass from the cabinet and tilted it under the spout on the refrigerator door, anticipating the cold water that sloshed the sides. Dana whirled toward her, putting a severe finger to her lips again, eyes wild as if Cyd had blown the mission.

Cyd stared back at her, unfazed. The mission would've been

blown anyway had she collapsed on the floor from heat exhaustion. Dana should've been happy she didn't use the ice dispenser.

She let the glass fill and gulped water as she joined Dana at the opened garage door. No car inside. They peered over the kitchen sink and out of the window. No car in front or in the driveway.

Cyd was relieved, but when Dana tiptoed out of the kitchen and headed upstairs, Cyd could feel her heart pounding. She placed her empty glass in the sink and followed. _Lord, if he's in there with some woman, please make them disappear. Can't You do that, Lord? Just, poof?_

They passed the children's rooms, sun streaming toward them through the open doors, offering lightness of heart—which Cyd would have gladly taken if it were streaming from Dana and Scott's room as well. Why was the door closed? Did they typically close their bedroom door during the day?

And even if Scott was in there with someone, why close the door? He wouldn't be expecting anyone. And if someone came—_like his wife_—what would he expect her to do, knock? Maybe he wanted a chance to jump out the window if he heard the knob turn.

Lord, that's it. If he's in there doing . . . you know . . . make him jump out the window. And break his leg.

Dana gazed back at Cyd, her hand to the knob. Cyd closed her eyes.

When Dana turned the knob, Scott's voice sounded first, an expletive, something Cyd had never heard from his mouth. Cyd stood against the wall outside the door, paralyzed, not wanting Dana to enter, certainly not wanting to enter herself. She couldn't tell which woman screamed. Her body began to shake. _Oh, God._ Should she run in and pull Dana out? Stand beside her in a show of support? She wasn't crazy about the idea of seeing Scott _naked_.

"Dana, what are you doing here?"

Oh, God.

"Dana, take your hands off of her!"

Oh, God.

Cyd couldn't see straight for her tears. She pushed up off the wall and entered the scene, Scott standing to one side of the bed, a sheet his shield. And on the other—

"Heather?"

The woman ran hurriedly into the bathroom with her clothes slung over her arm, but Cyd caught a quick glimpse of the face and the long blonde hair . . . Had to be her. Heather was part of the twenty-something crowd that Stephanie hung around at church. Cyd had exchanged hellos with her on several occasions.

Cyd was so shocked she followed Heather into the bathroom and stared at her in disbelief. "Heather, what are you *doing* here?"

"Save it, Cyd. You wouldn't understand." Heather buttoned her olive-colored business skirt.

Cyd wiped her eyes, emotions spinning quickly from sadness to anger. The nervy edge in Heather's voice was as bad as the sight of her. *She's got attitude?*

Getting caught should have yanked her back to her senses. She should've been offering up a sob story about how temptation came so strong she couldn't find the way out that God promised but, hallelujah, they showed up and saved her in the midst of her giant free fall into darkness. But Cyd wasn't hearing any of that. What she was hearing, amazingly, was the tune of gum popping.

"I wouldn't understand?" Cyd said this calmly, and it took every ounce of strength she had. "Let's see, you're in another woman's house, in another woman's bed, with another woman's husband. Am I missing something?"

Heather rolled her eyes and sauntered to the mirror, fixed a few strands of her bed-tousled mane.

It was the calm that went *poof.* Cyd flung her arm around and pointed to the door. "Heather, you need to leave."

A smirk rose on Heather's face as she folded her arms. "I don't think so. I was invited."

"Invited? Heather, you've got to be—"

A crash sent them both to the outer room. A photograph surrounded by broken glass lay on the floor near Scott, and a lamp was set to sail his way.

"Dana, no!" Cyd yanked the object from her hand and set it on the nightstand.

Scott raised his palms as if in surrender, his bottom half now covered in suit pants. "Look, I just need to talk to Heather. I just need a moment to—"

"You need to talk to _Heather_?" Dana whipped a shoe past Cyd and conked Scott on the nose. "Get out! _Go_. Talk to your whore! Get a room for all I care!"

Dana looked wildly about her, and Cyd didn't know what she might throw next. She went to Dana and held her tight, pinning her arms to her sides, and watched from the corner of her eye as Scott grabbed his shirt from the floor and his other shoe. He swiped a couple of items from the dresser, grabbed Heather's hand, and they were gone.

Dana's legs gave way, and she crumpled to the floor. "Why, Cyd?" she wailed, sobbing for the first time. "Why?"

Cyd sank down beside her and tucked Dana's head into her bosom, asking herself the same question.

Four

PHYLLIS STEPPED FROM the Jetway into the sights and sounds of the terminal of Washington Dulles International Airport and felt a pleasant surge of the familiar. She was home.

Well, northern Virginia actually, about forty-five minutes from her hometown in Maryland, but whether she flew into Reagan National, Baltimore-Washington, or Dulles, it was all the same to her. Home.

It had been almost two years since she'd been here, a family visit that time. Her younger cousin had gotten married. As often happened, a weekend didn't afford enough time to see everyone she would like. That trip had been confined to family, and only her mother's side. This one would be college friends. She'd already warned her parents not to expect her. One day, she always said, she would plan two weeks at home and spend quality time with everybody from long-lost junior high friends to second cousins once removed.

A swell of excitement rose as Phyllis checked the arrival boards for flights from Dallas and Atlanta. On a three-way call, Phyllis and sorority sisters Natalie and Gretta, sitting in front of their computers, found flights that would arrive within minutes of one another, making it easier on Stacy, who would be picking them up and housing them for the weekend.

Although most of the women who pledged with Phyllis had formed a closeness in the process, these four had had a bond from the beginning of freshman year. They lived in the same dorm on the same floor, ate dinner together in the dining hall, and in the fall of sophomore year decided together to attend the AKA rush. Phyllis thought it a wonderful blessing that each of them had come to know the Lord since leaving Maryland. They were more than her sorority sisters now; they were her sisters in Christ.

Phyllis groaned when she saw that Gretta's flight from Atlanta would be delayed forty minutes, but when she found Natalie's her face lit up. Not only had it landed at the same time as hers, but they were on the same concourse. Noting the gate, she set off in that direction, scanning the faces in the crowd that came toward her. Phyllis hadn't seen her friend in ten years, but she recognized her instantly from several yards away, and she chuckled. Some things never changed.

There was Natalie, just off the plane, in line for a Dunkin Donut. Natalie had been her doughnut buddy at Maryland, but unlike Phyllis, she never gained a pound. Phyllis could see that that much hadn't changed either. Though Natalie had had two children, she seemed to have the same petite waistline she'd had at twenty. She looked cute in stonewashed denim jeans and a white, short-sleeved button-down shirt with a sweater tied around her waist.

Phyllis waved her arms when Natalie turned in her direction, and Natalie cocked her head and then dropped her jaw. Smiling, Phyllis quickened her pace down the corridor and moved into Natalie's waiting arms. After hugs and squeals of joy, Natalie pushed her back.

"I saw some woman waving at me, and I couldn't believe that

was you! You look fabulous! You didn't tell me you'd lost so much weight."

Phyllis smiled. "I didn't tell any of you. It was a long process, and I didn't know if I could stick with it." She gave her a sideways look. "You know how many times I tried to lose weight. I wanted to be sure *this* time would last. When we started planning the reunion, I thought I'd surprise you all."

"Well, honey, you succeeded."

They moved up in line.

"So how did you do it? Low-carb diet, Mediterranean—"

"Noooo." Phyllis shifted her big tote bag to the other shoulder. "Been there, done that. Old-fashioned exercise and healthy foods. And staying out of lines like this." She laughed.

"Girl, I know." Natalie moved to the counter and placed her order, then turned back to Phyllis. "You know doughnuts are my weakness, but I rarely eat them now."

"And you only ordered one," Phyllis said, looking impressed.

"I can't eat like I used to."

Phyllis looked her over. "Mm-hmm. I can tell you're struggling."

"I'm serious!" Natalie handed payment to the woman and took hold of her treat, straightening her wheeled carry-on.

"Whatever you're doing, it's working, because you look fabulous too."

"Thanks, Phyl!"

Phyllis's phone chirped as they followed the signs to the shuttle that would take them to the main terminal and baggage claim. She showed the caller screen to Natalie and flipped it open.

"We're here!" they both declared into the mouthpiece.

Stacy's voice boomed through the phone. "Yeahhhh! I can't believe y'all are really here!"

"It's just Natalie and me so far," Phyllis said. "Gretta gets here in the next thirty minutes or so."

"Oh, that's perfect," Stacy said.

"Why?" Phyllis gave Natalie the eye. "Where are you?"

"Um, in the car, finally. It's been a crazy morning, so I'm running a little late."

Phyllis shook her head and spoke over the top of the phone. "Can you believe she's just leaving the house?"

Natalie shook hers too. "Some things never change."

Stacy laughed. "I hear you two talking about me! I'll be there in fifteen minutes, tops. Right outside baggage claim."

Phyllis and Natalie talked from the time they boarded the shuttle until they'd retrieved their luggage. Distance and the busyness of life had kept all of them from calling as often as they would have liked.

They found a couple of seats and parked, one-upping each other with tales of their boys, relieved to hear that the antics they dealt with might actually be normal. Before they knew it, Miss Gretta, as they liked to call her, strolled into their midst.

Phyllis and Natalie jumped up to hug her, but before anyone could say anything, Gretta had her hands to her hips, exclaiming, "Oh no, you didn't."

Phyllis looked back with a puzzled expression—and a grin, because Gretta still had a commanding aura about her. At five foot ten with a curvaceous figure and hair that flowed full with carefree spirals from the twists she usually wore, she drew a double take from many a passerby.

"What?" Phyllis said.

"We were in this thing together." Gretta pointed between the two of them. "Now you gonna leave me and join the skinny girls?"

Phyllis was suddenly transported back to the playground at recess when the boys would run past her on the blacktop, chanting, "Phyl, Phyl, the big fat wheel." The girls would call out choice words after them, demanding that they leave her alone. They thought they were helping. But by the time the girls yelled for the boys to stop, and the boys, further inspired, insisted they couldn't help it because Phyllis *did* look like a wheel, she'd feel infinitely worse. She'd thought often of what it would be like to be one of the skinny girls, and now here was Gretta saying she *was* one of them. She was exaggerating, of course. Phyllis was nowhere near skinny. But she was nowhere near where she used to be either. Gretta had dredged up a memory that, surprisingly, no longer pained her.

"Gretta, give me a hug, girl." Phyllis wiped a surprise tear from her eye. "No need to worry about me leaving you. You were already in a class by yourself, Miss Diva."

"You know I was kidding." Gretta hugged her tight. "I just couldn't believe that was you. You look fantastic!"

"And you look marvelous yourself, dahling." Natalie reached for a hug. "It's so good to see you!"

"It's good to see you too!" Gretta fixed Natalie in full view. "If you're not still the cutest little thing . . . The guys sure used to fawn over Natalie."

"And Stacy," Phyllis added. "And you too, Gretta. They just couldn't say anything because of Vance."

Gretta rolled her eyes. "Vance was a trip, wasn't he, acting like he owned me?"

Natalie put a hand to her hip. "He might've been protective, but at least he backed it up with a ring."

Gretta flashed her hand and laughed. "Can't argue with you there."

The women gabbed nonstop during the fairly short ride along the Dulles Greenway, and as they piled out at the top of Stacy's drive, they marveled aloud at the natural beauty of living among rolling hills, adjacent to the Potomac River and Goose Creek.

Phyllis took a deep breath and let it out. "It's so peaceful and beautiful. And this house is gorgeous."

"Where are we exactly?" Natalie pulled on her sweater. "Y'all are _out_ here."

Stacy nodded as a cool breeze whipped her hair off her shoulders. Slim like Natalie, she had light skin, light eyes, and a lighthearted personality. "Yeah, you'd be surprised at how far people are willing to commute in the Metro Area these days, trying to get more for their money. But this isn't _too_ far out. We're in Leesburg, about thirty-five miles from D.C."

Gretta gave her a dubious look as she lifted her luggage out of the trunk. "And that thirty-five miles will take you two hours in rush hour."

"Yep." Stacy pulled another bag out. "And _that's_ why Wesley works out of the Reston office."

A swirl of red, orange, and russet-colored leaves tumbled past the women as they moved to the door with their luggage. Their eyes widened as they walked through the double doors, at once taking in a winding double staircase and beyond that, a wooded preserve that seemed to stretch forever.

Gretta was the first to move beyond the marble to the hardwood. "You know what, Stacy?" She looked this way and that. "You missed your calling. As stunning as this home is, it wouldn't have near the impact without your design know-how. And I know you did this yourself 'cause I saw your last house, and it was just as elegant."

"Look at the walls." Phyllis was staring upward. "The colors are so dramatic. I would've been afraid to paint that one over there so dark, but it's striking."

"Thank you!" Stacy was beaming. "I do enjoy decorating. It's kind of a hobby. Wes has to remind me that we don't have an unlimited budget, and that patience is a virtue."

Natalie moved into the sitting room, and Stacy and Gretta followed, but Phyllis was drawn to a wall of artwork. Three ornate frames of antique gold showcased different verses of Scripture in gold lettering on what looked like handmade papyrus. Phyllis couldn't take her eyes off of them, struck by their beauty but even more by the prominence they'd been given in the home. Once she'd bought a small plaque with the names of the fruit of the Spirit painted whimsically around a bowl of grapes, oranges, berries, and bananas. She perched it on the kitchen windowsill above the sink as a personal reminder to keep a right attitude, but Hayes accused her of trying to preach at him. It was gone by night.

"Stacy, where did you get these?" Phyllis called.

Stacy and the others joined her. "Oh, a local woman makes them. Each one custom. You give her the verses, select the frames and the matting, and she goes to work."

"You picked great verses." Phyllis eyed the middle one: *Choose for yourselves today whom you will serve; as for me and my house, we will serve the Lord—Joshua 24:15.*

"Wes picked them, actually. He said he had dibs on this one wall, and told me what he wanted to do. Of course I was all for it."

Phyllis lowered her eyes.

"These are awesome." Natalie surveyed each one. "Does she ship out of state? I know Michael would love it—Oh!" She turned to them excitedly. "I don't think I told you all that he started taking classes part-time at the local seminary. He loves it!"

"No way!" Gretta hit her arm. "Wait till I tell Vance. That's his dream, to go to seminary. Just doesn't know how he'd carve out the time."

Phyllis listened to the three of them trade husband stories as Stacy led the way into the kitchen. The guests settled on barstools and watched Stacy, the gourmet among them, toss a salad to go with the shrimp and broccoli frittata she had made.

At a break in the chatter, Natalie turned and said, "Phyllis, how's Hayes doing?"

Phyllis opened her mouth to give a quick answer—an easy

answer—but her emotions wouldn't let her. The well had been filling and began to overflow.

"Oh, Phyllis." Natalie hurried to her side. "What's wrong?"

Phyllis lifted a tissue from the box Gretta put before her. "Just something that happened this morning." She dabbed her eyes.

"What happened this morning, Phyl?" Gretta stood with an arm around her.

Phyllis tried to compose herself. "The short version is Hayes refuses to take the kids to church on Sunday, and the boys and I had really been praying." Phyllis hadn't talked to her friends regularly, but they knew Hayes didn't share her faith. She'd asked them to pray long ago.

Gretta nodded. "Remember I was praying those same prayers for Vance? Looked like he'd never turn around. But God did it, Phyllis." She squeezed her. "I know He'll do the same for Hayes. I'm believing with you."

"So am I," Natalie said. "I'm still praying for him. That's why I asked."

"I pray for him too," Stacy said.

Phyllis acknowledged them with grateful eyes. "Thank you." She almost said more, how her life was an exercise in walking on eggshells, how she couldn't play the music she wanted to play because he didn't want to hear it or give the opinion she wanted to give because it was too "spiritual." But talking about it would only make her more depressed.

She balled up the tissue in her hand. "You know what? I told myself to focus on the weekend, and that's exactly what I plan to do—have fun."

"Amen." Stacy set their salad plates before them. "We're going to have a great time. We get to have a pajama party here, plus a reunion, plus homecoming festivities."

"Absolutely!" Natalie said. "I can't wait to see everyone at Jasper's tonight."

Phyllis started into her salad as the ladies bandied about names of people who'd be there tonight and people they weren't sure about, sparking outbursts of "Remember when . . ." Phyllis was fine there. The past she could laugh about.

It was the present that had her crying on the inside.

Five

"So, I'm still not hearing what I was waiting to hear. What did Scott have to say for himself?" Dana's sister, Trish, stood with arms crossed, staring down at Dana and Cyd as they sat at Dana's kitchen table.

Three years older, Trish had the same dark brown hair—hers shoulder length and stick straight—and the same pear-shaped body that directed excess to the hips and thighs. But where Dana was usually sunny and animated, Trish could be moody and gruff, especially since her divorce five years ago. She wasn't the best person to call at a time like this, when well-chosen, comforting words were key, but Cyd didn't have much choice. The wedding rehearsal started in one hour, and she didn't want to leave Dana alone.

Trish stepped closer to her sister. "And, Dana, you've got to eat. You don't need to get sick on top of everything else. Cyd said you haven't eaten all day."

Dana looked down at the food Trish had brought—Dana's favorite, Chinese—and picked at it some more. She had yet to take a bite. "He said he needed to talk to *her*."

Trish grunted. "But what did he say *after* that? Didn't he call or come back home at some point?"

Dana continued picking at her food.

Trish threw up her arms. "Okay, really. What is up with Scott? You haven't heard from him *yet*? It's six o'clock! He should be home by now . . . begging. What on earth is he doing?"

Cyd sneaked a look up at Trish from the other side of the table. *Hello? You are* not *helping.*

Cyd had been thinking the same, though, biting her tongue, watching the minutes and hours tick by, willing Scott to walk through that door. She was sure every second of his absence multiplied the hurt. He was with Heather, that's all her mind could conjure. What was the man thinking?

Cyd had been with Dana since the incident, easing from her side only long enough to call Hayes to ask if she could pay the boys to walk and feed Reese. They had keys to each other's homes in case of emergency.

Dana stayed in the same spot on her bedroom floor for hours, crying intermittently until she grew silent. When the bus brought Mackenzie and Mark home, Cyd helped provide a happy welcome and a snack for them. Trish had since dropped them off at her home where her teenaged kids could look after their cousins, leaving the women to deal with the situation in private.

"Did you see how thin she is?" Dana's voice was a shell of itself.

"Don't even go there." Cyd's heart ached. "You were thin when you were twenty-five too."

Trish plopped down in the seat next to Dana and opened her own to-go entrée. "Twenty-five? Hmph. Sounds just like Frank." Trish didn't find out about her husband's affair with his administrative assistant until he announced that he was marrying her. She looked at Cyd. "I can't believe you know this woman, and I really can't believe she goes to our church. I wish I knew who she was."

"You do." Living Word packed in thousands of people every week, of all ages and multiple ethnicities, yet Heather stood out. Cyd shook her plastic fork at Trish. "Two weeks ago she sang one of the solos. Remember? Long blonde hair, petite—" Cyd cringed and sneaked a peek at Dana.

Trish almost choked on her noodles. "*That's* her? She looks like Barbie!"

Dana nodded her head slowly. "So that's the connection. I thought she looked familiar."

"Oh yeah, it's all clear now." Trish nodded as well. "Scott in choir practice, supposed to be worshiping the Lord—"

"Trish, *please*." Cyd gave her the eye outright this time.

"What?" Trish's voice took on a high pitch. "I'm just—"

The three of them jumped when the garage door groaned as it rose from its slumber. Cyd stood, looking at Dana. "We can leave out the front door."

"No." Dana's back was to the garage door, and she turned to look at it. "Stay. He might have that girl with him still, for all I know."

Cyd took her seat, and Trish, water in hand, lowered herself into the chair next to Cyd. A second later the key went into the lock and the door swung open.

Scott crossed the threshold. He was alone, dressed in the same suit pants and long-sleeved white shirt. About six-one, he had boyish good looks with dark hair and a handsome twinkle in his eye.

Could've been a typical entrance after a day's work, except there was no greeting. No hugs. Whenever Cyd was at the house when Scott walked in, he would hug his wife and then he would hug Cyd.

She had known him since he and Dana were dating, more than fifteen years ago, and they had always gotten along famously. He was easygoing and fun. Next to her father, she'd always thought of Scott as a model of the kind of man she wanted, a man who loved his woman fiercely and loved God even more. Part of her wanted to snatch him into the next room and jerk him back to his former self.

Scott held his keys and met the gaze of each of them except Dana, who eyed the table. "Where are Mackenzie and Mark?"

"At my house. They're staying there tonight." Trish's tone indicated she'd been waiting for the chance to say something to him.

He tossed his keys to the counter. "I need to talk to my wife." His voice held the same emptiness as Dana's.

Cyd jumped up, but Trish stayed put, leaned back in her chair, and crossed her arms.

"I'm not going anywhere. Whatever you've got to say to my sister can be said in my presence. There've been way too many stories over the years about men killing their wives over an affair. Everybody *thought* they knew the guy and found out after the fact that he was crazy."

Scott put his hand to his forehead and ran it back across his head. He looked exhausted. "Trish, I can't right now. Really. I need to talk to my wife. Now. Alone."

Cyd grabbed her purse from the countertop. "Actually, Trish, I need you to run me home so I can change for the rehearsal. And can you bring Mackenzie and Mark to church? Then I won't have to come back out this way to pick them up."

Trish pursed her lips, her eyes boring a hole into Scott.

"Go ahead, Trish." Dana's voice was a whisper. "I'm all right."

"Don't tell me you're all right," Trish said, still focused on Scott. "I know how it feels when your husband—"

"Trish!" Dana covered her face with her hands.

"Okay, fine," Trish said, rising. "But I've got my mobile. If he even looks at you funny, don't hesitate to call me."

Cyd started toward the front entry, with a slow-moving Trish behind her. When they stepped outside, both women took a deep breath and stared back at the door.

Cyd repeated her prayer from earlier that morning. *Lord, help her.*

DANA HADN'T MOVED from her initial position. She had yet to see Scott's face, and as the sound of his shoes clicked closer toward her, she felt her arms begin to tremble. She held herself, and as hard as she tried to prevent them, tears slid down her face.

She didn't mind crying in front of Scott when the reason for her sadness lay elsewhere, when he could hold her and comfort her and tell her everything would be all right. But she didn't want him to see her cry now. With the betrayal he had switched sides. He was no longer her comfort and protection, the soother of what hurt. He was responsible for the hurt—and his leaving with Heather spoke more to her heart than the actual affair. If he could do that, if he could treat her so coldly, she didn't want him to see her sobbing, pitiful and broken. She couldn't lay bare her heart like that. She couldn't trust what he would do with it.

Scott put an arm to her shoulder, and Dana flinched, shrugged it off.

"Baby, I . . ." He stopped and sighed, walked a few feet away.

He stayed there so long Dana almost turned to see what he was doing, but she couldn't look at him. Not yet. From the corner of her eye, she saw him undo two top buttons before he returned, pulled out the seat next to her, and sat with his legs spread apart, forearms on his thighs.

Dana smelled the faint scent of his cologne, and her heart pounded. It was her favorite. She had tested it at the mall and taken a chance he'd like it. On Christmas morning he opened it and dabbed it on right then. It had become his favorite as well.

Wonder if it's Heather's favorite too.

Dana closed her eyes and turned her head farther away from Scott, reliving the afternoon. She couldn't get Heather's face—and body—out of her mind. The woman was beautiful, shapely. Scott obviously thought so. Dana had never felt fatter or uglier. Why hadn't she kept her longer hair? Why hadn't she kept coloring it? Did he prefer blonde? And was it really so hard to establish a workout regimen? How many times had Cyd and Phyllis encouraged her to do so?

All day Dana had had these thoughts and tried to push them out. She knew she shouldn't blame herself for Scott's affair, and she didn't, but what if she had done some things differently? If only she hadn't _seen_ the other woman. Cyd was right. The images were seared on her brain. They were relentless.

Scott blew out a gust of a sigh and sat back in his chair, touching Dana's arm to turn her toward him. When she flinched again, he lifted his hand. "Okay. Okay. Um, I'll just talk, and if you want to face that way . . . okay." Another gust of wind. "Dana, I'm sorry. If you only knew how badly . . ."

Dana saw a hand rise to his face and rolled her eyes. _Aww. Tears, Scott? You're upset?_

"Sweetheart, I want you to know it had nothing to do with you. It just . . . happened. I didn't go looking for anything. She and I were friends, that was it. She would ask for advice"—Scott grunted at the irony—"about men. And that's all it was, and then she started doing little things like asking about my day, and—"

Dana whirled her head toward him. "Are you saying I never asked you about your day?"

"No, I'm not saying that. But, I mean, you would ask, but most of the time you weren't really listening."

The softness of his tone, the deep brown of his pupils wouldn't let Dana take her eyes off of him.

"You know? If I said I had an all right day, you didn't ask any follow-up questions, you just moved on. And I understand that. You've got a lot on your plate, the kids need attention. But I guess . . ." Scott dropped his head and pinched the bridge of his nose. He sighed for the twentieth time. "I guess when she would say, 'What happened at the meeting?' or 'How did that make you feel?' it just . . . I don't know."

"So you're blaming me, because I wasn't attentive?"

"No. Never." He stood and walked partway around the table. "I think I'm trying to understand what happened myself, what took me to that place."

"So where *did* all this take place, all this 'friendly' conversation? To have started off so innocently, I never heard you mention her."

He lifted his hands. "That's 'cause it was no big deal. Remember the time I sang that duet? That was with Heather—"

Dana's stomach cramped, hearing him say her name. She hadn't remembered that duet. And as she thought about it, that was *months* ago.

"—and we practiced it a few times at church without the choir. That's how we got to talking, and it would be dark when we finished, so I'd walk her to her car. That was it. She'd call me from time to time on the cell for advice, like I said. It only moved to, you know . . . that was a recent thing."

Dana ran her eyes along each slat of the mini blinds. She wanted to know exactly when and how it moved from the phone to the bedroom, and yet she didn't want to know. No matter what he said, it wouldn't make sense.

She thought back to the Scott she'd first met at church. It was his first Sunday there, and Dana was serving in the hospitality room after the service. The church was small enough still that the pastor himself met interested visitors and answered their questions. Dana had noticed Scott before he came into the room, the moment he entered the building actually, handsome as he was. They struck up an easy conversation, and she learned he'd just moved to town. They found one another every Sunday after that and dated for a year, deciding early on to honor

God in their relationship, waiting until marriage to be sexually intimate. How could she reconcile that Scott with this one?

Several minutes passed as they sat silent. Dana guessed he was giving her the next word, but she hadn't much else to say. She already had enough to wade through. Well. She cocked her head a bit, still facing the blinds. "Why did you leave with her, and where did you go?"

"Sweetheart, I didn't know *what* to do. I was shocked, ashamed. I was *caught*. I wasn't thinking straight. I knew I couldn't tell her to leave because she didn't have a way home—"

How thoughtful of you.

"—and to be honest, I couldn't face you right then . . ."

She turned now, glaring at him. "And where did you hide your car?"

He mumbled, "A few houses down."

Dana was mad she'd missed it, entering the back way. "So you went to her place and took a shower."

He affirmed almost imperceptibly.

She stared back at the blinds. "And you left your wife here for hours . . . *drowning*"—she gulped to keep control, but the sobs came strong—"while you played house with *her*."

"No," Scott said, pulling her to him.

Dana stood, and the chair scraped the floor. "Get off of me!"

Scott looked up at her. "Sweetheart, that's not what happened. I left her apartment as soon as I got dressed. I've been driving around, sitting in my car, walking around Forest Park, thinking about how badly I messed up, how we're going to move on from here . . ."

Crying still, she crossed her arms. "I don't know whether we *can* move on from here." She swiped her cheek with the back of her hand.

Scott peered down at the table. "I wondered too."

Dana's insides took a dive. "Wondered what?"

"Whether we can move on from here."

She closed her eyes, his words nearly knocking her flat. The trembling began anew. Wasn't this her decision? Didn't she hold the cards? Her entire world had been rocked off its foundation, but up until this very second, there was a comfort—slim but real—that the power lay in her hands as to whether they would rebuild. Her family didn't _have_ to fall apart, the kids didn't _have_ to lose one parent in the home, she didn't _have_ to lose the one man who'd been a walking illustration of God's abundant love toward her . . . till now. This one transgression didn't _have_ to cancel out fifteen years of blessing, did it? She didn't have the answer, but she'd assumed she'd be the one to give it. What was Scott saying?

"What . . ." She cleared her throat, unsure of what to ask. "Why were you asking yourself that question?" She watched the back of Scott's head hang lower and waited . . . until she couldn't stand it. "Scott, answer!"

He stood and faced her, stroked her cheek with a finger, and because of the rapid beating of her heart and the tension that hung in the moment, she let him.

"It's complicated. I have these feelings—_No_." He locked his arms around her, tucking her head in his chest. "Don't move. Please," he whispered. "Hear me out. I've hurt you so much that the only way I can begin turning this thing around is to be honest."

Dana could only think that her world hadn't been rocked from its foundations; it had been ripped from its base and hurled into outer darkness, spinning, spinning . . . If Scott hadn't held her, her legs would have given way.

"I can't explain it. I'm not saying I love her . . . but it wasn't simply physical either. I care about her and—"

Dana tried to tear herself away again. She couldn't bear it. Was he just afraid to tell her he loved Heather? Was he about to say he needed to move out to sort his feelings for the two women? Was that why he wondered whether they could move on?

Scott tightened his grip around her waist. "Let me finish, Dana."

He tipped her head up with a finger and slowly wiped her tears with it. His own tears eased down his face. "I know these feelings I have for her aren't right. None of it is right, and I know you won't believe me, but I'm glad I was caught." He sighed and flicked a tear from his cheek. "When you're in a place like that, you can only stay in it if you distance yourself from God. I hadn't felt that far from God in my whole life, and I've asked Him at least a hundred times today to forgive me."

His cheek brushed hers as he lowered his head. "Dana, I said I didn't know if we could move on from here because I know it'll be hard. I need to get rid of the feelings I have for this woman, but how do I do that overnight? I need to earn my wife's trust back—how do I do that? There's so much that needs to be made right, and none of it will be easy."

He took both of her hands, and their eyes—red with tears—met one another. "But all things are possible with God, and if you're willing, we can lean on Him and make it happen. I love you, Dana. I want my marriage."

She couldn't deny the relief that swept over her. He didn't need to make up his mind. He'd already chosen—and he'd chosen his marriage. But relief didn't bring healing to her heart. She let go of his hands and walked a few feet away.

Dana wanted the marriage, too, the marriage they'd had before the affair, the untainted one in which his love was one hundred percent undivided. What kind of marriage would it be now, with him trying to get over feelings for someone else and her trying to get over what he'd done? Theirs had always been a fairy-tale story. Their courtship, their love and respect for one another even in disagreement, the way they held hands still while walking in the mall.

It could never be the same. She would never view Scott the same. How could she ever trust him again?

Six

CYD RACED DOWN I-270 East with the moon roof open and every window down in her Volvo, the breeze whipping cool and strong. She thought maybe it would help. Maybe she would get lost in the rush of the wind and the stars of the night and forget the nightmare of today, for a little while. But the scene played again and again in her head, and with each remembrance her heart ached for Dana.

Her iPhone played its tune, startling her out of her thoughts. She grabbed it from the center console, hoping it was Dana so she could find out how she was doing.

"Everybody's lined up and about to walk in," Stephanie said. "I can't believe you're not here yet."

"I know. I'm sorry. I'm getting ready to exit now." Cyd talked loudly over the wind and noise of the highway. "You got my message, right?"

"Yeah, but I still don't understand what's going on. Were you with Dana? Why isn't she here either?"

"Are Mackenzie and Mark there?"

"They got here fifteen minutes ago, but Trish brought them. Aren't Dana and Scott coming to the rehearsal dinner?"

"No. Wish I could explain, Steph, but I can't. Anyway, sounds like I haven't missed too much. Good thing I'm in the back of the line."

Stephanie clucked her tongue. "You haven't missed a thing. Cassandra's gettin' on my nerves, acting like she's running the show, telling me the bride's not supposed to participate, just sit up front and watch. I know I'm not participating *directly*, but she can't stop me from standing in the back and making sure things are the way I want. What's up with her?"

Cyd and Cassandra had known each other from the time Cassandra joined the church as a single eight years ago. She'd since gotten married, and after the birth of her first child left the event-planning business she worked for. Now she volunteered part-time at the church, helping to organize the weddings held there.

Because Stephanie didn't have a coordinator, Cassandra had been involved from the beginning, guiding her as to what she needed to do and when, as a favor to Cyd. After a couple weeks' involvement, Cassandra confessed she was glad Stephanie preferred to handle most of the planning details herself. "She's a piece of work," Cassandra had said. "I don't know if the baby or I could handle the stress if this were a full-time assignment."

Cassandra was two weeks from her due date. Cyd hoped the stress from the rehearsal wouldn't send her into an early labor.

"Steph, Cassandra has a lot of experience with weddings. Relax and trust her direction."

"Hmph."

Cyd could hear her mother telling Stephanie the pastor was ready to get started.

"Tell Cassandra to go ahead," Stephanie told her, "but if it doesn't look right, we're starting over."

"Everything will work out fine, Steph." Cyd moved a few wind-blown hairs out of her face. "I'll be there in about ten minutes."

"All right," Stephanie sighed.

Cyd ended the call and held the phone, struck by how small the drama with Stephanie and the wedding had become. She remembered her mind-set in the shower, the dread she'd felt about the weekend. Her eyebrows furrowed. _Was that this morning?_ It seemed so far removed from where she sat now. She felt no dread at all about the rehearsal, was glad to have something to occupy her time. If she had had nothing to do tonight, she would have worried herself to death about Dana.

She exited at New Florissant Road and a couple minutes later veered into the parking lot of Living Word Community Church. She'd been a member of the church since its early days. Her family moved to St. Louis when she was in seventh grade and Stephanie was just a baby, because her father had taken a position on the faculty at Wash U. As they acclimated to the area, Bruce and Claudia Sanders had sought a Bible-teaching church and found young Dr. Mason Lyles, a black man three years out of seminary with a passion for preaching the unadulterated Word of God. And when they met Dana and her family—also new to St. Louis—and learned they were Christians, they got them excited about the church too.

The ministry was small at the time, about forty members meeting in a high school, yet it was diverse from the beginning. Pastor Lyles's prayer was that Living Word would be a true picture of the body of Christ, welcoming people from all nations. His personality certainly helped. He had a winsome delivery, naturally lively and hip, but earnest and forceful, always challenging, always zealous in his love for truth and seeing it at work in the lives of others. That zeal drew folk, who would often testify later that they didn't understand the whole counsel of the Bible until they came to Living Word.

The church had outgrown three structures since its inception, and five years ago built a complex of three buildings: one for the main sanctuary, adult education, and administrative offices; one for children's and youth ministry; and the third dedicated to the pastor's burgeoning national ministry of written Bible studies with accompanying DVDs.

Cyd pulled into a spot near the main entrance, raised her windows, closed the moon roof, and hopped out. She loved the view of this building at night. The two-story glassed entrance that flooded the space with natural light during the day had the opposite effect at night, as the lighting inside shone like a beacon to the outside world.

Stepping quickly up a cascade of steps, past a courtyard that connected the main building to the youth building, she slid lip gloss across her lips, unclipped a wide, crystal-adorned barrette, smoothed her hair with her fingers, and clipped it back on. She wore a two-piece shimmering metallic brocade suit with a portrait-collar jacket and sequined tie belt. The slim skirt hit her at the knee, and the soft metallic sling backs had a much higher heel than she was used to. It had been a long while since she'd had a reason to dress up like this.

Inside, she walked through the spacious common area where people milled about between services and after church. There wasn't a soul in sight now, but when she made her way around the bend of the wide hallway, she saw Stephanie and Cassandra conferencing outside the sanctuary doors.

Cyd fixed immediately on what Stephanie was wearing, a platinum baby-doll dress with a rhinestone empire waist, shoulder straps that crisscrossed on a bare back, and a plunging V in the back and front. It had been the subject of much discussion in the store dressing room.

Stephanie and Cyd were both tall and shapely like their mother. Claudia had always extolled modesty, but she could only make Stephanie toe the line while her daughter lived at home. When she went out on her own, her tops got tighter, necklines dipped lower, and skirts, shorts, and dresses climbed higher.

Talking did no good, so Cyd relegated the clothing issue to the same sphere she'd sent Stephanie's romantic entanglements—prayer. But with the wedding, she knew she'd have to deal with it head-on, especially since Stephanie would be choosing what _she_ would wear as well. To her surprise, though, they didn't clash at all over the bridesmaids' attire. In one day, Stephanie, Cyd, and three of the attendants visited two boutiques and tried on several dresses. One was a clear favorite of Cyd's, in style and color, and she was shocked when Stephanie and the others declared it their favorite as well.

The wedding gown was an altogether different story, starting with the odyssey that took them from St. Louis to Chicago and back to St. Louis. Cyd had a headache from the first boutique as Stephanie tried on anything and everything that showed more skin than average, asking repeatedly, "Isn't this _gorgeous_?" Cyd treated the question as rhetorical and got away with a noncommittal smile the first couple of times, until Stephanie began asking, "What do you think?"

She tried to be positive, pointing out the beauty and intricacy of the embroidery on one, the luxuriousness of the fabric on another, hoping Stephanie wouldn't press for her _actual_ opinion until she had narrowed down her choices, at which time, hopefully, she would have gotten these out of her system and graduated to a spectrum of styles that wouldn't give the pastor apoplexy. But by the time she had done the two-city circuit of boutiques and indulged Cyd by trying on a few "traditional" gowns, the one she'd zeroed in on was still up there in apoplectic range.

Playfully labeled "slightly sinful" by the bridal consultant, it was a sultry silk-charmeuse halter gown that skimmed the sides of her breasts and plunged low in the back, so low that the woman advised Stephanie as to the type of undergarment she would have to purchase, sold in the boutique, of course, and the magic the alterations person would perform to keep it hidden.

"I _love_ this one." Stephanie had admired herself on the raised platform with mirrors all around.

"It's daring, that's for sure," the bridal consultant said, "but you seem to have the personality to pull it off. You've certainly got the body."

"Don't you think it's me, Cyd?" Stephanie asked, eyes glued to the mirror.

Cyd had tried more than once to exchange places with their mother, but Momma graciously bowed out from the beginning, citing a history of clothing battles and assuring them she could be much more supportive from afar.

Cyd knew patience would be key. "It's definitely you," she said.

Stephanie posed and turned and tossed her head over her shoulder, viewing herself from different angles. "I think it's perfect."

Cyd waited.

The consultant beamed. "You'll look *fabulous*."

"What do you think, Cyd?" Stephanie asked. "Is this the one?"

Cyd sat up in her chair, crossed her legs, and tossed her head aside, as if considering. "Well, you'll be in Living Word, at the front of the sanctuary, in front of the pastor, your back to Momma and Daddy, Ma Marge, aunts, and other family, not to mention our church family." She paused and added, "And you'll be standing before God, of course—"

The consultant smoothed her dress and tried to smile.

Cyd continued, "Do *you* think this is the one?"

Stephanie blew out a sigh and looked at herself in the mirror again. "We should have planned to get married on an island, just the two of us and some rent-a-preacher, away from all y'all *folk*." She sighed again. "Let me try on the other one I liked over there."

The consultant helped her out of the dress as Cyd sat back, relieved. Her mother would have killed her if Stephanie had purchased it, and with their mother's credit card, no less.

But now here she was, in another dress with "issues." They had had a similar conversation in the dressing room over this one, and Stephanie admitted it "probably" wasn't suited to a wedding rehearsal and dinner, but she loved it so much she'd get it for the honeymoon. Cyd couldn't believe she had actually put this thing on tonight. She was glad she was late. She could only imagine the buzz when Stephanie strolled in.

"How's the rehearsal going?" Cyd asked, determined not to give her sister the "momma look," as Stephanie called it.

Cassandra looked wearily at her. "It's _not_ going," she said. "Half of the bridesmaids and groomsmen got down the aisle, and Stephanie called them back."

"Why?"

"Because the way she had them walking in was just dumb," Stephanie said. "The groomsman would walk halfway down the aisle, stop, and hold out his arm, waiting for the bridesmaid to walk down the aisle and take it." Stephanie took a few steps to act it out as she explained, then stuck out her arm. "It looked silly. Just let them walk down the aisle together."

"And I said that was fine," Cassandra said.

"Okay . . ." Cyd said, waiting to hear why action hadn't resumed.

"Then Stephanie wanted to talk about how you and the best man would walk in."

"I thought the best man stood up front with the groom," Cyd said.

Cassandra rested a hand on her butterball tummy and sighed with a smile. "Traditionally. But Stephanie wants to mix things up. She's even talking about walking down the aisle with Lindell instead of your dad."

Now Cyd couldn't help giving Stephanie the momma look. "If you wanted to be unconventional, you should have thought it through long before now," she said. "You've got people waiting."

Stephanie tossed her hand. "They'll be fine. And anyway, I just decided. I do want Daddy to give me away, even though it's old-fashioned and ridiculous since Lindell and I are already . . . you know.

But I like the idea of you and the best man walking down the aisle together. Let's do *something* different."

"Sounds fine." Cyd moved toward the sanctuary doors, but her mother pushed one of them open before Cyd could pull it.

Claudia looked stunning in a cornflower blue long silk skirt with a matching beaded crocheted sweater. "Cyd, good, you're here," she said. "I was just coming to see what the holdup was about."

Cyd hugged her mother. "It's been resolved. We were just coming in."

Claudia leaned back to get a good look at her. "And everything's okay with you? Stephanie said there was an emergency."

"I'm fine."

Stephanie and Cassandra walked past them and through the door, marshaling the wedding party back into place.

Claudia followed Stephanie with her eyes, then grabbed Cyd's arm and stepped farther out, letting the door close. "Did you see that dress your sister's wearing?"

"Mm-hmm."

"I thought she was wearing the knee-length black number. It looked beautiful on her."

"Thought so too."

Claudia looked exasperated. "I can hardly face the pastor or anyone else. What must Lindell's mother think of her? Why would she *do* this?"

Cyd shrugged. "Same reason she does everything else. All she cares about is herself."

The door opened, and Cassandra peeped her head out. "We need the mothers in line."

Claudia and Cyd walked through the door. "I really want this to be a memorable weekend for Stephanie and Lindell," Claudia whispered, "and not because she caused a stir with her cleavage."

Cyd didn't respond. She was following the pastor as he strode with purpose through the bridal party, toward Stephanie in the very back, holding something folded in his hand.

Dr. Lyles was in his late fifties now, but he hadn't lost any fervor for his ministry of teaching and preaching. The church was so large that he rarely conducted wedding ceremonies anymore, delegating the task to his associate pastors. But he'd agreed at once when Cyd's father, Bruce, approached him. Dr. Lyles said he would have it no other way.

Cyd watched as he reached Stephanie, spoke into her ear, gave her a hug, and unfolded a gorgeous silver stole, draping it around her shoulders. He headed back to the front.

Cyd and Claudia made a beeline for her. "What happened?" Claudia asked.

Stephanie looked as if she was still trying to understand it. "Pastor said after I walked in, he called Sister Gloria to see if she had anything for me to cover up with. He said he'd known me all my life and loved me like a daughter, and I was too precious to God to wear something like this." Stephanie fingered the ends of the stole, which fell well below her chest.

Gloria, Pastor Lyles's wife, had the perfect answer.

"When Sister Gloria heard what color I was wearing, she said God must have meant for me to have this. She said I could keep it."

Claudia sneaked a glance at Cyd, and Cyd knew they were thinking the same thing. She and her mother had often emphasized Stephanie's worth to God when discussing her choices, but never with this effect. Stephanie was visibly overcome.

"This is beautiful." Claudia's hand skimmed the material. "Wait till I see Gloria. She's always blessing somebody."

"Mrs. Sanders," Cassandra called, "we need you at the front of the line."

Claudia scurried away, and Cyd moved down the line, hugging seven bridesmaids—two cousins, two college friends of Stephanie's, two high school buddies, and—

"Hi—you must be Kelli. I'm Stephanie's sister, Cyd." Cyd smiled and reached for a hug.

Lindell's younger sister, a grad student at the University of Texas at Austin, had flown in just today. Tall enough to claim the last bridesmaid's spot before Cyd and attractive, she had at least two groomsmen vying for her attention.

Kelli returned the hug and greeting, and Cyd turned to find her place in line—when a body bear-hugged her from behind, causing her to stumble. She pivoted and looked down at a semi-toothless grin.

"Hi, Aunt Cyd!"

"Hi, Mark!"

Mackenzie was with him, grinning just as big, and Cyd gave them both a big hug. Mackenzie wore a pretty floral-patterned dress, and Mark had on dress pants and a long-sleeved collared shirt.

"You two look so cute!"

Mark made a face. "*Cute?*"

"Oh." Cyd tried not to laugh. "*Handsome* to you, sir."

"He's not a sir." Mackenzie nudged him. "And Mom told you to stop being so touchy about people calling you cute."

"All right, all right." Cyd settled them in their places directly behind her just as her father made his way toward her. Just seeing him stabilized her heart somewhat. He always had that effect on her—a strong, calming, everything-will-be-okay effect.

"Hi, Daddy," she said, hugging him close.

"Hey, sweetheart." Tall and trim, Bruce Sanders fixed her with a stare. "I heard something about an emergency. What happened?"

"Oh, nothing you need to worry about," Cyd answered in a sing-songy voice. And she knew he would worry. He loved Scott and Dana.

Bruce looked skeptical, but Cyd eased to her place in line before he could ask more questions.

Cyd noticed Cassandra speaking with a guy up front, who began walking toward the back using a side aisle. Had to be Lindell's brother.

She'd never met him, and her eyes kept skittering in his direction because she'd had no idea how utterly good-looking he was. Lindell was handsome enough, if you caught him at the right angle—hair thinning already at the top, _maybe_ taller than Stephanie in bare feet, and chubby. But his brother had to be at least six foot two with a strong, athletic physique, obvious even in his blue pinstripe tailored suit.

He walked right up to Cyd. "I don't believe we've met," he said, "but given the resemblance, you must be Stephanie's sister. You are a family of good-looking women."

"Thank you." She held out her hand. "I'm Cyd Sanders."

"Cedric London," he said, "and since we're about to be family, I think we can forgo the handshake."

He pulled Cyd into a hug, and the faintness of his cologne mingled with his handsome looks caused her skin to tingle.

Stephanie headed their way the moment she saw. "I see you met my sister," she said. Angling her thumb at Cedric, she continued, "I love him, but you'd better watch out, Cyd. He's a real ladies' man."

Cyd turned arched eyebrows on him.

Cedric pleaded with his accuser. "Aww, Steph, I can't believe you said that."

"Uh, yeah, I did." Stephanie looked at Cyd. "You know I know the deal, right? He's forty-two and a big-time bachelor. Just letting you know, 'cause he _will_ try to run some game." She graced Cedric with a smile. "Gotta look out for my big sister. Not that she'd fall for it anyway. She's too smart for that."

With the mothers seated, the piano struck up the bridal party song and Stephanie took a seat in a middle pew to observe the rest of the procession.

Cyd and Cedric moved into line formation as the bridesmaids and groomsmen began the slow march up the aisle.

Cedric leaned over to Cyd and whispered, "So you're smart, huh? What do you do?"

Their eyes met briefly. "I'm a professor at Washington University."

"For real? *Dr.* Sanders?"

Cyd nodded, staring ahead.

He nodded, too, in approval. "Smart, sexy, and single." He lowered his head to hers. "You *are* single, right?" He looked around at the smattering of people in the pews who had accompanied bridal party members to the rehearsal. "No fiancé out there? Boyfriend?"

She took his arm as they waited for his sister to finish her walk down the aisle. When they got the nod from Cassandra, they started down.

Cyd spoke under her breath. "I don't have anyone out there," she said, "but looks like you do." She tipped her head toward a woman sitting on the end of an aisle, arms crossed, eyes leveled on the two of them. Amused, Cyd gazed ahead, keeping a steady pace. "Fiancée? Girlfriend?"

Before he could answer, if he even intended to answer, Cyd moved left and took her position in front of the first bridesmaid. She couldn't help but look at the woman, who was looking at Cedric . . . who was looking at Cyd. When their eyes connected, her stomach dipped . . . and she bounced her eyes away from him.

The bridal party practiced the recessional and, with a collective groan, ambled to their original places when Stephanie announced she needed one more run-through to be sure she liked it.

Cedric stopped and said a few words to Kelli, and Cyd checked on the kids. "How are you two holding up?"

"Fine," Mark and Mackenzie chorused, and got back to the riddle game they'd been playing with one of the bridesmaids. There'd been no shortage of people looking after them, but Cyd hung beside them anyway, for cover. They didn't flirt. Or give her goose bumps.

The line inched up and Cedric sidled up to her, causing the two to pair off again. "You don't go to this church, do you?"

Cyd glanced at him. "Ever since I was a teenager."

"Really?" Cedric's head drew back in surprise. His eyes bored into her more intently. "Why haven't I seen you? I go to the eleven thirty service."

"That's why. I go to the nine o'clock."

"Huh." He nodded to himself. "I may have to get out of bed a little earlier." His hand brushed hers as he pointed between them. "Being paired up like this . . . kind of crazy, isn't it? Both of us single, the older siblings—mind if I ask how old you are?"

Cyd never minded sharing her age. "Thirty-nine."

His eyes grew big. "No way. And single? Good as you look? Are you divorced?"

"Never married."

"Kids?"

"No."

"Wow."

The line moved steadily forward, and she was thankful for the distraction. It was becoming apparent that she couldn't, by sheer will, force her insides to quit the stupid dips and twirls when he looked at her. Or talked to her. Or stood too close.

"So when's the big day?" he was saying. "When do you turn forty?"

"Tomorrow."

His eyes grew big again. "Seriously? What are you doing to celebrate? I hope you have something planned besides this wedding."

Cyd shrugged. "Not really."

With Phyllis leaving town, the three friends had made plans to celebrate the following weekend. But after today, she doubted Dana would be in the mood anytime soon.

"Oh, that's crazy." A glimmer entered his gaze. "I can fix that. Let me take you out after the reception. I'll plan a special evening in celebration of you."

Dip. As they began their walk down the aisle, she leaned her head over. "I'm thinking someone might have a problem with that, and I don't think it was ever established—fiancée or girlfriend?"

"I knew I shouldn't have brought her," he muttered under his breath. "She kept hassling me about it, and now she thinks she's coming to the wedding. If I had known you'd be here . . ."

Focusing on the woman helped Cyd to steel herself on the inside. "Oh, it's no problem. My little sister warned me, remember? And if *she* says I need to stay away from some man, I'd better listen." Cyd let her arm drop from his as she moved away and into position at the front.

She was glad Cedric was occupied at the dinner, which was hosted by both families in a private room at a downtown restaurant. As he mingled, took trips to the bar, and seated himself for the meal, his woman—pretty, tall, and slender in a short, revealing dress—was pasted at his side, grabbing his hand or arm if Cyd came near.

Cyd ignored them both and enjoyed family from out of town and the after-dinner presentations, proud of the way Stephanie and Lindell honored their parents and showed appreciation for bridal party members. She did cringe, though, when Lindell shared the story of how they met.

"I had only recently returned to St. Louis," he said, "after my residency in Ohio. I'd been going to Living Word for six months and kept noticing Stephanie. It's hard to miss her, beautiful as she is, but she never noticed me, which was kind of good, I guess. She was there to worship, not to pick up men." He looked with admiration at his fiancée.

"Then the church held a wellness clinic one Saturday and asked doctors and nurses to volunteer their services, and there was Stephanie, giving her time, signing people in and directing them to the help they needed. By the end of the clinic, I had a date. The rest, as they say, is history. I'm thankful she agreed to marry me."

They kissed, and the crowd roared with applause, but Cyd knew the history a little differently. Stephanie had declared from a young age that she was going to be well off, and she was going to marry a doctor or lawyer to make it happen. When the church advertised that clinic, Stephanie, who never volunteered for anything, told Cyd she'd find herself a doctor there. Late that evening, she called with her report.

"I told you I'd meet somebody," she said. "And we've already gone out. Can you believe he's been going to the eleven thirty service? Not surprised I never noticed him. He's not really my type, a little overweight and kind of nerdy. But he's a doctor, and, girl, he's head over heels already, from a good-bye kiss. I decided to play hard-to-get and make him wait."

"And what about Warren, Stephanie?" Cyd asked. "You've been seeing him for two years, and he loves you. You're playing with people's lives."

"Warren is sweet, but he doesn't make enough money."

"Then cut him loose so he can find somebody who appreciates him," Cyd said.

"Why would I do that? Lindell might not work out, so I've got to keep my options open. And anyway, Warren's talking about getting his MBA. That could make all the difference."

After Lindell proposed, Stephanie said she ended things with Warren. Cyd could only hope.

People were slow to leave when dinner ended, finishing last bits of conversation, double-checking the schedule for tomorrow. Cyd said her good-byes and headed for the exit, Dana on her mind.

The groomsmen had gathered near the door to the private room, and Cyd watched as Cedric's girlfriend headed out from among them and made her way toward the restroom. Cyd threaded her way through the guys, dispensing another round of good-byes . . . and felt fingers tugging her to a stop. She turned, her hand in Cedric's, as he pulled her toward him, enfolding her in a hug. She left her arms at her side as he whispered in her ear, "See you tomorrow."

She backed out of his embrace. "Good night, Cedric."

Cyd fumed all the way out of the restaurant. He had a lot of nerve, flirting the minute his girlfriend left his side. She hated men like that, always looking for the next conquest, plotting and scheming, leaving a trail of broken hearts. A male version of Stephanie, but ten times worse.

Her mental rant persisted all the way to her car and halfway home . . . until somewhere along Highway 40 that voice pushed through.

"See you tomorrow."

Her stomach dipped again. Suddenly, the wedding day/birthday had taken on a whole new dimension.

Seven

THE *CLICK-CLACK* OF heels was swift and rhythmic as Phyllis, Stacy, Natalie, and Gretta hurried to get inside Jasper's. With Friday evening traffic, it had taken close to an hour and a half to drive from Leesburg to Greenbelt, and they were running late to start. Luncheon talk had extended well into late afternoon, and by the time the four women freshened up and declared themselves ready to go, their cell phones had each amassed several missed calls from others wondering where they were. The local women who organized the reunion had designated an arrival time of six o'clock to ensure they'd get enough tables before the place swelled with people. It was already eight when Stacy pulled into a parking space in an extended lot.

Gretta opened the restaurant door, and heat, laughter, music, and conversation came pouring out. The women could barely walk through the entry area. The crowd was thick with people waiting to be seated and others milling about. With a bar in the middle, booths and tables all around, and bodies in every available space in between, the atmosphere was tight and hot and filled with energy.

Gretta led them past the hostess—who was telling folk the wait would be three hours—and into the main area of the restaurant. "I haven't seen anybody I recognize yet," Gretta yelled back to the others. "Where is everybody?"

Natalie cocked her head and looked at her.

"I mean everybody *we* know," Gretta said.

Phyllis stood on her tiptoes and craned her neck to see over the sea of heads. "I see some pink and green balloons way over there." She pointed to the far right corner of the restaurant and motioned for them to follow.

As they made their way over, Phyllis marveled, too, at the change. Ten years ago at this event, she was bumping into people she knew from the moment she hit the door. Now every face was foreign and young, as if a new age had been ushered in and hers had left the scene. But when she passed the last group of young men and women toward the end of the bar and moved into an area of seating in the corner, she gasped in delight.

Two long tables were pushed together and decorated end to end with the sorority's pink and green colors, from the balloons that adorned the backs of the chairs to the beautiful apple green cloth gift bags at each place setting, to the cake prominently displayed in the middle of the table, to the sparkly pink confetti sprinkled about. And gathered around those tables were the familiar faces of her era. Her contemporaries hadn't left the scene at all. They had just carved out their own private party.

"It's about time y'all got here," Sonya called from beside the table. She left her conversation and headed toward them, then stopped in her tracks. "Uh-uh," she said, shaking her head. "I know that's not Phyllis."

In short order there was a flurry of greetings for all four women, but the buzz centered chiefly around Phyllis.

"Look at you!"

"You look *gorgeous!*"

"Girl, turn around."

Phyllis hugged people she hadn't expected to see, people she'd forgotten about, and—a big surprise—two of her favorite "big brothers" on campus—Randy and Vic. Vic used his large frame to cut through the circle, exclaiming, "Phyl! What's up, woman!"

"Hey, Vic!" Phyllis's voice was muffled as he bent her backward with a consuming hug.

Vic stood her straight again. "Where you been hiding? I ask about you from time to time and all I hear is, 'She's out in the Midwest somewhere.'" Before she could answer, he stepped back with a smile. "And check you out. Me and Randy put on all this weight, and you've been taking it off."

Phyllis chuckled, noting his face and midsection.

"Man, step aside." Randy nudged Vic out of the way. "Phyl liked me better anyway." He nearly lifted her off the ground with a hug.

"I guess we're chopped liver." Natalie folded her arms as she looked to Stacy and Gretta for agreement. "They haven't said boo to us."

Vic turned. "Oh, *now* you want attention." He shook his head at the shame of it. He and Randy had had a crush on Stacy and Natalie. "All those times I tried to give you my undying devotion."

"And that's the truth!" Gretta said, bursting with laughter.

Natalie laughed, too, and the guys rushed to make up for their oversight, giving each of them a big hug.

Over an hour later, after spending a few moments with each person she knew, Phyllis settled herself at the table. Her sorority sisters were chatting up a storm, finishing what looked to have been tasty entrées.

Phyllis stared at their plates. "Did anybody order me anything?"

"We kept calling you to come sit down." Gretta munched the last of her buffalo wings. "And you kept putting up a finger, telling us to wait. Girl, I was starving."

"I didn't know y'all were ordering," Phyllis said, looking pitiful on purpose.

"We told the server you'd be ordering when you joined us, and he said he'd put a rush on it." Sabrina edged her appetizer plate over to Phyllis. "Meanwhile, I saved you a couple stuffed potato skins."

The next couple of hours passed quickly. More alumni from their era had trickled in steadily, making for fresh waves of laughter, conversation, and picture taking.

Phyllis and Daphne, another sorority sister, were returning from the restroom when Daphne elbowed her. "There's Rod Clarke. And he's still *fine*."

Phyllis looked to her right. Rod had lost his wife in a tragic shooting last year. Michelle was a real estate agent and went one evening to a home she had listed for sale. The owners had moved out, but the three-million-dollar estate was staged with expensive furniture. When she walked inside, she happened upon a burglary and was shot on the spot. Stacy had forwarded her the online coverage in the *Washington Post*, and Phyllis had shed tears as she read accounts of the shooting and thought of its effect on Rod and their children. She'd been acquainted enough with Rod to exchange pleasantries, but she didn't know him well.

Rod and Michelle had been college sweethearts. He was one of the most sought-after guys on campus, and not just because of his looks—all the ladies agreed he was a special kind of fine with his buttery brown skin and eyes that seemed light brown one minute, hazel the next—and not just because he was genuinely nice, but because they couldn't have him. He was something of an enigma. But he only had eyes for Michelle, and word was, he had the nerve to be faithful.

Phyllis and Daphne could tell he was looking for familiar faces, and they stood in place as he neared them. Above average height and medium build, he wore a simple navy blue cable knit sweater and jeans. The only evidence that a couple of decades had passed was the few threads of silver near his temples. When his eyes met theirs, he smiled immediately.

"Hey," he said with recognition. Then, pointing at them, "Don't tell me. Daphne and . . ." He searched his memory. "I know you look familiar, but it's not clicking."

"Phyllis."

He looked at her quizzically, as if still trying to verify it in his mind. Phyllis knew it was her weight loss that was throwing him. She also knew why he remembered Daphne so readily. She was one of the ones who tried to woo him from Michelle.

"It's good to see you both," Rod said. "You look great."

"It's good to see you too, Rod. Where's my hug?" Daphne moved forward and embraced him.

Phyllis remained where she was. "I hope you don't mind, but I want to offer my condolences. What an awful, awful tragedy you've been through. Please know that many of us were praying for you."

Daphne took a small step back. "I wasn't able to make the funeral, but I'm sorry."

Rod nodded slowly with a sigh. "I really appreciate your support, and I felt your prayers," he said. "I really did. I can't begin to explain the supernatural peace God has given me. Even before they caught and convicted the perpetrators, I had a peace." He glanced aside. "Helps to know she's with the Lord. That's one thing I'm so thankful we shared— our love for Jesus." He paused. "God is good."

Phyllis was almost moved to tears. These were the most words she'd ever heard from Rod, and they were beautiful words, spiritual words. She hadn't expected that.

"You're both still in the area?" Rod asked.

"I've been gone for a while," Phyllis said. "I'm in the St. Louis area now."

"I'm here." Daphne perked up as if her answer would lead somewhere. She was still eyeing him when he turned to survey the crowd.

"Have you seen Leo or Temple or any of those guys?" he asked.

"They're over by us." Daphne hooked her arm through his. "We'll show you."

Rod was surrounded in no time, the crowd clearly surprised to see him. Back at her table, Phyllis asked Stacy, "Did you know Rod's a Christian?"

Stacy nodded over the top of her glass of water. "He gave an awesome testimony at the funeral." She looked over at Rod. "He's truly allowed God to use him through this. The tragedy gave him a platform, because people are amazed he's been able to go on the way he has."

Phyllis looked over at him too. "I didn't know he spoke at the funeral."

"I didn't tell you?"

"I remember you told me about the sermon—"

"Gretta! Sonya!"

Startled, Phyllis turned and saw Ria standing at the side of the table, signaling with her digital camera for them to come.

"Daphne! Natalie!"

Stacy chuckled. "Ria, you're a shutterbug from way back, when you had that little Instamatic."

"I know." Ria chuckled too. "You should see how many scrapbooks I have from college days." She called the ladies again who hadn't budged from their conversations. "We've got to get a picture of everybody before people start leaving," she said. "What if someone doesn't show up tomorrow? We need to capture the moment."

When everyone had assembled, Ria passed her camera to one of the guys. The women posed in front of the table, smiling broadly.

When the crowd returned to mingling, Rod walked up to their table. "Guess I missed the celebration." He peeped at the crumbs inside the cake box.

No one heard but Phyllis, who was nearest him. She pointed to her place at the table. "You can have my piece."

He lifted the coveted slice playfully, giving her an opportunity to change her mind.

She dismissed it. "Help yourself."

He grabbed a fork from the pile. Savoring a bite, he said, "Thank you. This is good. You don't like chocolate cake?"

"Just the opposite." She sighed mournfully. "Chocolate is my weakness, so I have to refuse it on occasion, let it know who's the master." She laughed.

Rod swallowed a bite, nodding. "I hear you. It's lawful but not profitable, huh?"

"Exactly," Phyllis said with a touch of surprise. "That's actually the verse that helped me."

Rod gave a puzzled look and waited for more.

Phyllis felt embarrassed, tucked her hair behind her ear. "It just . . . helped me to be disciplined about losing weight."

"I knew it was *something*," he said, pointing his fork, "but I couldn't put my finger on it. You were . . . a little heavier back in college, right?"

Phyllis smiled softly. "You're being kind. I was a lot heavier."

"And that verse helped you lose weight?"

"I wish it were that simple," Phyllis said. "It was that verse and many others, prayer, and basically, the power of God in my life. It wasn't until after I became a Christian that I was able to have some control over eating and discipline regarding exercise."

"That's an awesome praise." Rod put the empty paper plate on the table. "So what led to your becoming a Christian?"

Daphne walked up next to him, but when she heard the topic, she kept moving.

"A neighbor invited me to church a few years ago," Phyllis said, "and the pastor's message just spoke to me. I met with him afterward, and by the time I left the building, I knew I was a changed woman. How about you?"

Rod smiled as he thought about it. "Believe it or not, it was on the playground, fifth grade, Waylan Thompson. A few of us boys were talking about what we were going to have when we went to heaven. It's wild that we were even thinking about heaven, but we were naming mountain bikes and televisions and lizards, all that kind of stuff." He chuckled. "And I was a bad kid. I was the one who got the other boys in trouble."

Phyllis exaggerated a look of shock.

Rod nodded with wide eyes. "Oh yeah, big time. So when I was going on about what I would have in heaven, Waylan, who couldn't stand me 'cause I teased him all the time, said, 'Rodney, you won't even *be* in heaven. You don't even know how to *get* to heaven.'" Rod cracked up at the memory.

"I told him I would go to heaven when I died just like everybody else, and oh man, he started clowning me, saying, 'Rodney is stupid; he doesn't even know how to get to heaven.' The other boys started laughing, too, though I doubt they knew either, and for days this thing just bothered me. Finally, one day I pulled Waylan aside and said, 'All right, Waylan, how do *you* think a person goes to heaven?' He looked at me to see if I really wanted to know or was I trying to tease him. When I convinced him I was serious, he started talking. Can you believe that boy shared the Gospel?"

"No way . . . and let me guess. You and Waylan became best friends."

Rod rubbed his chin as if trying to remember. "Um, no. Wish I could say God did a mighty work and turned a troublemaking boy into an angel overnight, but . . . nope." He smiled mischievously. "I didn't tease him as much, though."

She put a hand to her hip and scolded him with a finger. "See, you were one of the ones I would have pulled aside and given a talking-to. I had a thing about teasing with my students. It was not allowed."

Rod laughed. "So you're a teacher?"

"Only for two years. Then I got married, we moved away, and I had a baby. I've been home with the kids ever since. But I taught sixth-grade history at a middle school in P.G. County."

"Really?" Rod said. "I'm a middle school teacher in Baltimore. Science."

"I didn't know that," Phyllis said. "How long have you been there?"

Rod was smiling. "Eleven years," he said. "I'll probably never leave. I love those kids. The phys ed teacher and I started this awesome mentor program—"

Stacy tapped her on the shoulder, her purse and gift bag in hand.

"Phyl, we need to get going," she said. "It's almost twelve thirty, and it'll take us at least forty-five minutes to get home."

Phyllis looked around and saw a thinned-out crowd. "Okay. Let me get my things." She turned back to Rod. "I want to hear about this mentor program," she said. "Will you be at the tailgate tomorrow?"

"I hadn't planned to," he said. "Actually, I hadn't planned to come tonight. Some of the guys had been encouraging me to come, and I said I wasn't up for it. But then my mom and dad wanted the girls for the weekend and I was home doing nothing, so—here I am." He glanced around briefly. "I'm glad I came. It was good to see everybody, and I haven't laughed like this in a long time. So I'm thinking—"

This time Daphne walked up and hugged Phyllis, then reached for a hug from Rod. Others mixed in as well with their hugs and good-byes.

Phyllis hung there a moment, waiting to wrap up their exchange. But those others kept coming. Seemed everybody was leaving at once, and the path to the door went past Rod. She watched him smiling, hugging, and felt a longing to hug him, too, just a customary quick one like everybody else. She had enjoyed their conversation—best she'd felt all day.

On the ride to Jasper's she'd called home and gotten an earful of attitude from Hayes. Cole had told him, "Dad, I don't see why you can't take us to church. You must hate God." Hayes had never been challenged like that by the kids, and he blamed Phyllis for putting the idea in Cole's head.

"That's not what happened," was all she could say with the women in the car. They'd discuss it later, and the thought of it weighed like lead on her mind. Tonight, at least, she'd felt free.

She looked at Rod again and felt something else—a connection. And it scared her. She grabbed her purse and the gift bag with its assorted goodies and followed Stacy out the door. She didn't know whether Rod would be there tomorrow or not, but given the flutters of her heart, she needed to steer clear of him.

Eight

DANA WOKE WITH a start and sat straight up in bed, heart thumping. She'd had fitful nightmares in which she'd been running—no, fleeing—though she could never see from what or whom. Just running, stumbling, falling, running again in pitch darkness, no end in sight, her life a hairbreadth from certain extinction.

The phone must have awakened her, because she could hear it now in the distance. Breathing in and out slowly, she tried to get her bearings in the real world, but when she looked about her in the pale morning light, things only got worse.

She was in unfamiliar surroundings, unfamiliar anyway for first thing in the morning. The bright yellow walls, light honey dresser drawers, dolls, dishes, and a plastic kitchen brought the real-life nightmare of yesterday into sharp focus. She slid back under the covers. Her chest heaved, and she grabbed a crumpled tissue from the pillow and held it, knowing the tears would come.

When she finally went to bed last night, she lay there forever it seemed, weeping until her eyes burned and her nose chafed from blowing. It was the first time she'd been entirely alone since it happened. There was nothing to distract her from the images. They just played and played. Her husband kept lying in their bed with that woman, kept taking her hand and leaving with her, leaving Dana behind. It all moved in slow motion. She could see their fingers intertwine as he led her out. One, two, three fingers, until their hands were one.

She would never sleep in that bed again. She wished she didn't have to enter the room at all. She wanted it cordoned off like a crime scene with yellow tape stretched across the door. She wanted someone to declare it off-limits and chuck everything in there from her clothes to the furniture to her toothbrush. Last night she'd kept their bedroom door shut and slept in Mackenzie's room as is—clothes, teeth, and all, which felt foul because she had a thing about brushing and flossing three times a day ever since her dentist warned her she was on her way to periodontal disease. She kept thinking—and it made her cry all the more—that there wasn't one thing Scott's affair hadn't touched, right down to her gums.

She blew her nose as Scott's voice played in her mind. *"I want my marriage."* The relief she felt when she first heard those words turned to anger overnight. *"I want my marriage."* Why didn't he think about that when he was walking Heather to her car late at night after choir rehearsal? Why didn't it come to mind when their conversations veered into forbidden territory? There had to be numerous times his conscience told him to cut off contact, yet he kept traipsing willingly over the line. The first time he kissed her, the second, the third . . . Weren't there warning bells? And how could he throw caution to the wind and invite her into their home, their *home*?

How could you, Scott?

She grabbed a Beanie baby from the bed and hurled it across the room. So *now* he wanted to pick back up with his marriage, after he'd enjoyed his romp with Heather? Wasn't there a price to pay? Was she supposed to forgive him just like that? "Okay, honey, I understand. Now that you've had your fun and come to your senses, we can carry on."

If he's even come to his senses.

Dana pondered that a moment. He didn't exactly come to her and confess. He got caught. And Dana was to believe he was glad about it? That he could turn now from the desires and feelings he had for this woman?

Her arms began to tremble as the scene flashed through her mind, when she first walked in, and Scott had his hand behind Heather's head and—

She hopped out of bed and stood on Mackenzie's sunflower area rug. Sleep wasn't working. Lying in bed awake wasn't working. No. It was consciousness that wasn't working, and the ability to think, feel, and remember. Everything was painful. Every place was painful within the home and, she could already imagine, outside. She knew for sure she wasn't going to church this Sunday, or the next. Might never return. She'd been a member of that church for more than twenty years, but Scott had ruined that too. How was she supposed to enjoy a worshipful experience with Heather in the midst? And how would they deal with the fallout from Scott's affair?

There was no way they could continue as leaders of Marriages for Christ. She loved that ministry. They had helped organize classes and social events for married and soon-to-be-married individuals. Her favorite was the program they'd started in which couples married a minimum of five years would mentor younger married or engaged couples. Dana loved talking to younger women, encouraging them in their roles as wives. She had met with many women in troubled marriages. Always she exhorted them to trust God in their circumstances. "He's the God of the impossible," she liked to say, "and He's faithful. He'll never put more on you than you can bear."

Dana unfolded a tissue in her hand, close to shreds, and wiped her nose. Her own words rang hollow now. She believed them, but they hung in the outer reaches of her mind, too far to touch the trembling and the tears. Too far to lift the weight of betrayal that was crushing her heart. She understood now why those women would tell her to come down from the clouds and get real. Those verses she had lived by for so long sounded like mere platitudes. Why couldn't she bring them closer?

Why did God feel so far away?

The second the question came, the answer followed, and she fell to her knees, her head hitting Mackenzie's sheets.

She hadn't prayed.

From the moment of that awful encounter yesterday till now, she hadn't once lifted her heart up to God. Her heart raced with self-examination.

Why wasn't prayer natural and automatic, as it used to be? She used to pray about everything, especially in the season following Mackenzie's birth, when she left her position in marketing to care for the baby full-time. It had been a step of faith. Without her salary, they had to cut way back and hope for enough to cover expenses month to month. But Dana and Scott had prayed about the decision together and knew it was what they wanted to do.

Daily Dana prayed for God's provision, for help with unexpected bills and managing the household budget. She'd prayed as she made her grocery lists, asking God for economical meal ideas. She'd held adorable pink sweaters and tops and cute frilly dresses in the clothes store, praying, *Okay, God, does Mackenzie really need all of these, since she'll grow out of them in a couple of months?* Prayers for protection, prayers that their baby would know and love God, prayers for wisdom and guidance in raising her. Always prayers.

By the time Mark was born, Scott had been blessed with a couple of promotions, improving their financial situation. Dana wasn't praying as much for provision, but as she held the new baby in her arms, her prayers poured forth for his physical and spiritual well-being, as they had for Mackenzie.

Surely she'd been praying in the years since then. But when did the spontaneous fellowship with God slacken? How could she have gotten to this point—turning inward instead of upward in her time of greatest need?

The house phone pierced her thoughts as it rang for the third or fourth time. She looked at the clock—7:15. Probably Mackenzie wondering when Dana would pick her up from Trish's.

And realization dawned.

Mackenzie had an eight o'clock hair appointment . . . for Stephanie's wedding. She'd been worrying about church on Sunday, but she needed to be at church *today*. Sighing, Dana stood and paced the room. There was no way she could be around people. No way could she smile and act happy with Scott at her side. And they'd *have* to show up together. How would it look if they didn't? Their son and daughter were both in the wedding. And Mark and Mackenzie would never understand if their parents weren't there, together.

Now the doorbell was ringing, as if someone were leaning on it. *What in the world?* Dana ran her fingers through her hair and descended the stairs as Scott came bounding up from the lower level. He'd slept in the guest room. In sweatpants and a T-shirt, he stopped at the top of the stairs and allowed her to pass. She avoided his eyes and opened the door.

Mackenzie, Mark, and Trish bustled inside with the cool morning air.

"Daddy!" Mackenzie said, hugging his waist. "I didn't see you before we left last night."

"I know. I missed you guys," Scott said, pulling Mark into the embrace.

"Mom, we've been calling for forever," Mackenzie said, reaching to pull Dana into the group hug as they often did.

Dana took her hand and squeezed it, hoping it would be enough.

"Why didn't you answer?" Mackenzie continued. "We even called from the car a few minutes ago." She looked fresh as the morning sun, bright and, Dana could tell, brimming with excitement about the day. Her chestnut hair hung high in a ponytail, and she wore jeans, a long-sleeved lilac top, and a light jacket.

"I'm sorry," Dana said. "Mom and Dad were still in bed."

Separate beds.

"We decided to just come on over," Trish said. "Mackenzie said they needed to get home to get ready for the wedding." Trish gave Scott the eye as she added in a low voice, "And I needed to check on you anyway. Not answering the phone got me nervous."

Mark dropped his overnight backpack on the floor. Two years younger than Mackenzie, he was thicker and already weighed more than she. He had dark hair like the rest, with his own brand of zest. Where Mackenzie's showed on the social side, his showed in a need for constant movement. "Dad, do we have time to throw the ball out back?"

"We have all the time in the world . . . later this afternoon. Right now we've got to go get haircuts."

"But I don't have to be there until eleven thirty."

Scott put a hand to Mark's shoulder. "By the time we get to the barbershop and get back, it'll be time to get you dressed and over to the church."

"We have to be at Grandma Claudia's by ten o'clock, Mommy," Mackenzie announced. "All the ladies are dressing there."

"Okay." Dana was thankful she and Scott were on different tracks. She wouldn't have to deal with him until she got to the church.

Mackenzie stepped closer. "What's wrong with your eyes, Mommy? They're all red."

"Oh. It's just . . . maybe allergies."

She thought a moment. "I thought you get that in the spring."

"Can I have some orange juice, Mommy?" Mark was already heading to the kitchen. "I'm thirsty."

Dana exhaled. "Sure, honey."

"Me too." Mackenzie ran after him.

Opening the door, Trish said, "I've got to get back home, but I'll see you at the church."

"Thanks for taking care of the kids, Trish," Dana said.

"You're welcome," she said.

Scott nodded. "I appreciate it."

Trish rolled her eyes at him and closed the door.

Dana turned to go in the kitchen.

"Dana."

She kept walking.

"Dana," he said louder, and she stopped so Mark and Mackenzie wouldn't think something was wrong. "May I talk to you a moment, please?" He moved into her peripheral vision. "A quick moment?"

She crossed the foyer and walked well into the living room, outside of the kids' hearing. They rarely used this room, a space decorated with creamy white walls, a taupe sectional, and an oversized square, wooden coffee table.

The phone was ringing again as Scott tried to stare into her eyes. Dana refused to cooperate.

"I wanted to tell you that I spent most of the night praying and reading the Bible," he said. "It was unbelievable. God is showing me some amazing things."

Whoop-de-do.

"I really feel like I'm plugged in again, like He's guiding me." He paused. "He's with us, Dana. And He's *for* us. I know God will see us through this."

Dana pierced him with cold eyes. "Because of you, I couldn't pray at all last night." In that instant, she'd decided Scott was the reason she hadn't prayed. She was too distraught. He had messed that up too. "I feel *dis*connected from God. I feel alone."

She hated to cry again, but it started up anyway. "I feel like

He left me on a dirt road in the dark, in the middle of nowhere, and I've fallen into a pit. Because of *you*, I can't see hope anywhere in sight."

Scott tried to brush a tear from her face, but she swatted his hand.

"Dana, I'm so sorry. Please, let me—"

"Mom, we've got to get ready." Mackenzie breezed back from the kitchen and took to the stairs. "I'm going to get my dress."

Scott lowered his voice further. "Are you going to be all right, going to this wedding?"

"No," Dana said. Then, "*No!* Mackenzie, wait!" She hated the thought of her daughter entering that room.

She dashed up the stairs, but it was too late. Mackenzie was in the master bedroom, halted in the middle of the floor. "What happened to the bed?"

Dana frowned. The bedding and the mattress were gone. Only the headboard, footboard, bed frame, and box spring remained. Scott stood behind them, silent.

Mackenzie shrugged and dashed into Dana's closet, grabbed the garment bag that housed her dress, and left.

Dana stared at the crime scene. "So when did you do this?"

"In the middle of the night. I'm buying a new mattress today."

"Why?"

"Dana."

"Really. Why? You slept with her those other times in our bed and didn't get rid of it." The anger surged afresh. "I can't *believe* you had that whore in my bed." She felt the trembling again as she glared at him. "Did you use protection?"

"Dana, can we please—?" He folded his eyes to a close.

"Did you use protection, or do I need to get tested?" She brought her voice down. "No telling who else she's been with."

Scott looked pained. "I used protection, Dana, but she's not like that. She's not—"

She got in his face. "Oh, you don't like me talking about your little whore, Scott?"

He sighed again. "Dana, I know you're hurting. I just don't want to talk about her. I want to talk about *us*."

"You ruined *us*. What, you want to talk about the fragments, the little pieces of us?"

"Yes, let's do that, then. Let's talk about the fragments and how we can put them back together. I know they can be put back together, Dana." His hand grazed the side of her head. "I love you so much."

The image flashed, Scott's hand to Heather's head.

She flinched and ducked under his hand. "Don't touch me. Just leave me alone."

The anger was so palpable she could barely see, barely think. She braved the master bathroom—positive she could smell Heather's perfume—slung her robe over her arm, gathered a few toiletries, and stormed past Scott to the kids' bath down the hall. In the shower, she hadn't the strength to stand, so she sat and held herself as her body heaved with sobs.

All she could think was how much she loved him.

She wanted to hate him. Parts of her wanted to hurt him. But the predominant feeling was love, a love he had stomped on and trashed. She could feel the pain shooting through her fingers, cramping her stomach, throbbing in her head, crushing her heart. She could feel the pain standing guard over her mind, tossing any hope that tried to enter.

Don't believe him. He didn't turn to God. He's still got feelings for that woman, probably called her last night.

He probably did. He couldn't cut himself off from her that easily. If he had feelings for her, that meant they'd done more than have sex. They'd been intimate in conversation—sharing, laughing, whispering. Picturing him taking those steps, building those moments, taking what belonged to Dana and giving it to another woman—that's what hurt most. That a piece of him, a piece of *them*, had gone to her.

Nine

"You look stunning." Cyd gently guided the zipper up the back of Stephanie's wedding gown. "Turn around so we can see you."

The gown rustled as Stephanie turned toward Cyd and Claudia, beaming ear to ear. It was a dusty gold silk-organza strapless gown with an embroidered bodice and a lace-accented dropped waist. Cyd was surprised when Stephanie first selected it. She was far from traditional in style, of course, but every dress she'd considered had been white to off-white. This one she pointed to on a whim, "just to see," but when she tried it on, she was quite taken with it.

To Cyd, after all the slopes and plunges of the white gowns, an unconventional color seemed a tame proposition. And looking at her now, Cyd couldn't imagine white or ivory having near the impact as this against Stephanie's bronze-colored skin. She was glowing.

Claudia held forth her arms as she walked toward Stephanie and hugged her tight. "You couldn't be more beautiful." Her eyes held

Stephanie's. "This is so you. I _love_ this dress on you." Her head bowed. "I said I wasn't going to cry." She pulled a tissue from a box on the nightstand and dabbed an eye. "At least not yet. But seeing you dressed as a bride, in this room . . ."

They were in Stephanie's old room, in the house their parents bought when they first moved to St. Louis twenty-seven years ago. Only a few blocks from Wash U—and minutes from Cyd—their University City home had been remodeled extensively over the years. But "the girls' rooms" had remained largely untouched—white furniture, twin beds, and Nancy Drew on the shelves.

"We want to see," several voices called on the other side of the door.

Stephanie had shooed her bridesmaids out before slipping into her gown. Now she faced the door and smiled broadly. "Ready!"

The door flung open, and six bridesmaids in various stages of dress gasped from where they stood.

"You didn't say it was gold!" Wendy said.

Tina had her hand to her mouth. "Oh my goodness! It's beautiful!"

As they filed in, the photographer with them, Cyd eased out, pulling her robe tighter. Some things never changed—her father had a thing about waiting until November to turn the heat on. She went down the hall to her own room, picked up her cell phone, and dialed Dana. Her brow furrowed when no one answered the home phone or cell phone, again. Was Dana okay? Was she even coming? Cyd couldn't imagine Dana missing Mackenzie and Mark in the wedding, but she was twenty minutes late and hadn't checked in.

Cyd sighed and sat on the cushioned stool of her pink floral and white vanity table. She needed to get dressed, but mind and body craved a short break. Stephanie had awakened her at 5:20 a.m.—the earliest yet—asking her to drive a bridesmaid to the airport to pick up her boyfriend. From there she'd put out one wedding-related fire after another, including a run to the nail salon for gold polish after

Stephanie chipped her ring finger. It was only midmorning and she felt drained already . . . and a teensy bit sorry for herself because no one, not even her mother or father, had yet acknowledged her birthday.

She didn't *blame* anyone. They were busy. Things were hectic. But still . . . Cyd fingered a mood ring from among the cheap treasures stored in the vanity, slid it onto her pinky to see if it would change color, and threw it back down. Sighing, she rose and walked to the closet, tucking her hair behind both ears. She wasn't used to her hair falling about her face like this. The stylist had washed and blow-dried it this morning, working lots of loose curls throughout that cascaded down her shoulders and back. It looked beautiful, but as soon as the reception ended, she'd pull it back into her ponytail.

She eased her maid-of-honor dress from the hanger and laid it across the twin bed. The bridesmaids were wearing chocolate tissue taffeta gowns with shoulder straps and a camel-colored sash that reached almost to the floor. Cyd's was the opposite, a camel-colored gown with a chocolate sash.

Lord, I didn't want the wedding on my birthday, but it is, and it would be nice if somebody remembered. She stared across the room. *But if the entire day passes without a single "Happy Birthday," help me to be okay with that. Help me to focus on Stephanie and Lindell and celebrate with them from the heart.*

The doorbell snapped Cyd from her reflective posture. She hastened out of her bedroom and down the stairs to the front door and yanked it open. Dana's face brought relief, her eyes a renewed sorrow. Cyd held her gaze for a second, then smiled big.

"Mackenzie!" She wrapped her arms around the little girl. "Your hair is so pretty!"

The front half of Mackenzie's hair was gathered to the top of her head, with a fall of curls on the side and behind. Her natural blonde highlights seemed to shine. "Thank you, Aunt Cyd." She stepped inside with a wide smile. "You wouldn't believe how long it took. I thought we'd *never* get out of there."

"Honey," Cyd confided in her ear, "I know what you mean. I thought the same thing this morning."

When Dana crossed the threshold behind her, Cyd grabbed her hand and pulled her close. "I've been trying to call you all morning."

Dana's face was drained of color. "My cell was turned off, and I wasn't answering the home phone."

"Is that Miss Mackenzie who just arrived?" Claudia came from the kitchen and stopped a few feet away with her hands on her hips. "You couldn't look any cuter."

Mackenzie grinned again and went to hug her. "Hi, Grandma Claudia."

Claudia tossed a few of the curls. "I can't wait to see you in your dress. You might be the prettiest one in the church." She raised her eyes to Dana. "We missed you last night, sweetie. Everything all right?"

"I wish I could've been there," Dana replied. "I had sort of an emergency." Dana moved to hug her like normal, attempting a smile.

Cyd knew she was hoping to smooth Claudia's concerns. Claudia could read Dana as well as she read her own daughters.

Dana stood back. "I'm thinking *you'll* be the prettiest one in the church. That dress is gorgeous, Ma Claudia."

Claudia tugged on her lace bolero jacket. "Cyd helped me pick it out. But I can't get used to the jacket. I keep wanting to pull it down." Claudia looked classy as always in a floor-length gown with thin shoulder straps. The long-sleeved jacket was white lace.

Dana nodded her approval. "It's sharp. I love it."

Claudia took a closer look at Dana. "You didn't answer my question. Are you all right? You look pale and sick or something."

Dana glanced at Mackenzie. "Um . . . I'm okay."

Claudia's expression showed doubt.

"Any bagels and fruit left, Mrs. Sanders?" Three bridesmaids were on their way to the kitchen in their dresses, pantyhose, and slippers.

Claudia nodded. "Plenty."

Mackenzie perked up. "*French toast* bagels?"

"Yes, Papa Bruce made sure you had some French toast bagels." Claudia picked up the small garment bag Dana had laid on the floor and took Mackenzie's hand. "Come with me. We'll get a quick bite, and I'll help you get dressed." Claudia winked at Dana and Cyd over her shoulder. "I think your mom and Aunt Cyd need to talk."

"They don't have time to talk." Stephanie stood on the top stair with a hand on her hip. "I can't believe how late y'all are, Dana—and, Cyd, I can't believe you're not dressed. The photographer's ready to take pictures."

Cyd and Dana mounted the hardwood and carpet-lined stairs, with Cyd giving Stephanie "the look." She could ignore her sister, but Dana didn't need this right now.

"And, Dana, since you didn't make it last night, I'm thinking you must have had time on your hands to get some new flower girl shoes."

Cyd sighed. "Steph, you have no idea—"

Dana raised her hand to Cyd. "Stephanie, trust me. I was in no position to buy shoes. And I would've been there if I could." She hugged Stephanie when she got to the top of the staircase. "And you look too good to be stressing. This dress is ten times prettier than I remember it. You look gorgeous."

Stephanie softened. "Thanks. Besides Momma and Cyd, you're the only one who saw it beforehand, you know."

Dana smiled through her pain. "I know you love me." She continued down the hall to the room she'd visited hundreds of times.

"Don't go in there and start talking," Stephanie called after them. "Y'all need to dress in separate rooms so you can hurry up. The makeup artist is waiting for you, Cyd."

Cyd had barely closed the door when she asked, "So what happened?"

Dana dropped her garment bag on the bed and flopped down beside it. "I don't even know where to start."

Cyd picked up the package of pantyhose she'd left on top of the dresser and sat next to Dana. "Where was he coming from? What was his attitude?"

Dana stared vaguely at the floral pattern on the old bedspread. "He said he was sorry. He had tears, the whole bit."

"Well . . . did he sound like he was really sorry, or are you thinking he was just sorry he got caught?"

Dana gave a shrug. Tears began to trickle down her cheeks. "He claims he's glad he got caught. He _claims_"—her voice broke, and she took a breath—"that it moved him back into close fellowship with God. He said he was up praying half the night and believes God will see us through this."

She looked up finally, only because she rolled her eyes.

Cyd cocked her head. "Wow. Definitely wasn't expecting to hear all that." She mulled it over a second. Actually, she would have expected that from the old Scott. It was just that the old Scott wouldn't have had the affair, so it was hard to know what to expect at this point. "So . . . you sound like you don't believe he's sincere."

"After what he did?" Dana shook her head slowly, wiping the tears. "I just don't see how he could do this, Cyd. I don't see how he could let it get that far. He's always been so . . ." Dana searched for the word.

Cyd gave it to her. "Perfect."

A knock sounded at the door. "Cyd, they sent me with a message. The makeup person needs to see you in five minutes."

"Okay, Daddy." Cyd pulled the pantyhose from the package, gathered one side, and stretched out her leg.

Dana stood and took off her sweat jacket and pants. "I never thought he was _perfect_."

Cyd gave her a look as she pulled the hose over the other leg. "I did." She stood and pulled them to her waist.

"You did not. You've always been cynical about men." Dana unzipped her garment bag.

Cyd held up a finger of correction. "Most men. But I've always said there were a few Calebs and Joshuas out there. Scott's definitely in that category." Her voice trailed off. There had been another man she'd once thought perfect . . .

"You mean *was* in that category." Dana pulled out her dress.

"I think he still is, Dana." Cyd looked at her before lifting her gown from the other bed. Stepping into it, she continued, "What do we love so much about Caleb and Joshua?"

"They were faithful." She pulled the dress over her head. "Scott wasn't."

"Is it really that simple?" Cyd turned for Dana to zip her up. "Yes, they were faithful to God. They believed Him when He said the Promised Land was theirs, and they were the only ones of their generation who got to see it." She faced Dana again. "But, Dana, even *they* weren't perfect. No man on earth has ever been perfect except Jesus. Even David, a man after God's own heart, committed adultery. Scott's not perfect, but he follows after God. I think that's worth holding on to."

Dana sat back down with a sigh. "Easy for you to say. You don't have to put your trust in Scott . . . and your heart hasn't been shattered into a million pieces."

Cyd lifted her sash from the bed and draped it around her waist. "True. I'm not saying it'll be easy. Your heart's been broken, but don't give up. God is able to heal. He's the One you put your trust in."

Dana walked to the window and looked out at the treetops.

"Cyd," her father called, "the makeup artist needs you *now*. The photographer wants to take some shots in five minutes. The limo will be here in twenty."

"Coming, Daddy."

Cyd put her arm around Dana, her head to Dana's head. She spoke softly. "Lord, I pray that You will heal Dana's broken heart and her marriage. Help her to take one step at a time, trusting in You."

Cyd opened a balcony door to the sanctuary, walked in, and looked down. Tulle bows with white lilies adorned the ends of the pews down the middle aisle, and beautiful bouquets and a candelabra were prominently displayed up front. Twenty minutes before the start of the wedding and a sizable crowd was present already.

Close to three hundred had been invited. Stephanie and Lindell had large extended families; Bruce and Claudia had several friends they felt obliged to invite, as did Lindell's mother; and Stephanie included every friend she'd ever known, it seemed. It was a big celebration, she said. Not every day someone gets to marry a doctor.

Cyd scanned the faces below until finally she spotted them. Scott and Dana sat a few rows from the front, on the aisle, probably to get a good view and great pictures of the kids. Dana's face was cast downward. Even from here, Cyd wanted to cry just looking at her. She said another prayer.

The door opened behind her, and Cassandra gestured for her to come. "The guys are finally here—can you believe they're thirty minutes late?" She sighed her annoyance. "I need to talk to the bridesmaids and groomsmen about some last-minute details before we start."

Cyd and Cassandra hustled to the room where the bridal party was gathered, and the first person her eyes snagged was Cedric, smiling in animated conversation with a groomsman, more handsome than yesterday in his black tuxedo. She scooted her gaze past him before their eyes could meet—but not before her heart skipped—and grabbed a spot next to Mark and Mackenzie. They stood with her parents, looking like a miniature bride and groom with Mark in his tux and Mackenzie in her white dress. Cyd couldn't even see the shoes.

Cassandra quieted the people and gave a series of instructions about what to do and where to go after the ceremony. When the bridal party was free to mingle again, Cyd headed to the bride's room to check on Stephanie and saw Cedric from the corner of her eye, making his way over to her.

He came up from behind, leaned his head down, and spoke into her ear. "You ought to wear your hair like this all the time. It's very sexy."

His breath sent a chill through her, not to mention his words. She looked sideways at him. "And how are you doing today, Cedric?"

He lowered his head again. "May I speak with you a moment?" He motioned with his head. "Out there."

Cyd gave him a puzzled look as he made for the door. She followed behind, down the hall and around a bend. He stopped and faced her, reaching into his jacket pocket.

"I know the color's a little off, but I'm hoping you can sneak this inside your bouquet somewhere." He produced a lavender rose. "Happy fortieth birthday."

Cyd accepted it, one eyebrow raised. Her cynical side knew he was angling. She had just seen his girlfriend from the balcony, sitting at the end of the pew again, and here he was up here trying to curry favor with her. Even managed to get a lavender rose from somewhere in the limited time he had this morning. He was definitely skilled at his game.

But no one else had acknowledged her birthday. Not even Dana, which was understandable, but the birthday Cyd once thought would be the most special, the most celebrated, had so far been the most uneventful. Cedric, a complete stranger before yesterday, had added some color. Game or not, she had to admit it was nice to be remembered. And she had to admit something else. Being this close to him again was making her heart flutter.

She brought the flower to her nose to smell its fragrance—and to gather herself. "Thank you. It's beautiful." She looked askance at him. "I'm guessing the color has some significance?"

A slow smile spread across his face, and for the first time she noticed his teeth were perfect. "I thought you might ask," he said. "Red roses are for love and yellow for friendship. But lavender, that's unique." His dreamy eyes bored into hers. "Lavender symbolizes enchantment." He entwined his fingers with hers. "I'm enchanted with you."

Her heart hammered inside her chest. Warning bells blared. She backed up and slid her hand from his. "You are something else."

"What?"

"You know my sister told me what type of man you are. You know that I know you're here with your girlfriend. And you think you can just give me a rose, talk a little sweet talk, and . . . what?" She folded her arms, careful not to mar the rose. "What exactly were you hoping to accomplish?"

Cedric stayed calm, his eyes twinkling. "I'll tell you exactly what I was trying to accomplish. It's your birthday, your _fortieth_ birthday, yet you have no plans to celebrate. The reception will be over by late afternoon. I want to take you to dinner, help you celebrate, get to know you a little. Is that a crime?" He didn't wait for an answer. "By the way, where do you live?"

Cyd was still processing his words, poised to reject them. "In Clayton."

"Seriously?"

"What?"

"I'm not far from you. I'm in the Central West End."

She was curious. "Where?"

"In those high-rise condos, the new ones that went up a couple of years ago."

Cyd knew exactly what he was talking about. She'd read articles about them in the paper, in particular how expensive they were. She wanted to know what he did for a living, but she didn't ask. "I hear they're really nice."

He smiled. "You'll have to come see for yourself."

She could hear Cassandra's voice in the distance, telling the bridal party it was time to go downstairs and line up.

Cyd started down the hall, Cedric beside her. "There's a new Italian restaurant near my building," he said. "Excellent food. I can call after the ceremony and make a reservation for seven o'clock. What do you say?"

Cyd's heels clicked, her eyes kept ahead. "So what's the plan? You'll drop your girlfriend home after the reception, get changed, and then pick me up?"

He didn't hesitate. "Exactly."

She smirked at him. "And how do you think she'll feel about that?"

"Why do you care?"

Cyd flashed him a look as they melded into the group that was headed for the stairs. She dashed into the waiting room, picked up her bouquet, and surveyed it. There were pink astilbe flowers that stood tall, plumelike, flanking creamy white roses and white freesia. Gingerly she tucked the lavender rose behind the pink plume nearest her chest. No one else would see it, but already, as she walked, it was becoming her focus.

Downstairs things were moving quickly. The music changed, cueing the mothers to begin their walk down the aisle, and seconds later the first bridesmaid and groomsman were disappearing through the double doors that led into the sanctuary. Before taking her place in line, Cyd walked to the end to see about Stephanie.

"Where were you?" Stephanie asked. "I had a couple of people looking for you upstairs."

"Oh no. Did you need something?"

"Not really. I just thought you were going to be there in case I did."

Cyd fluffed the bottom of Stephanie's gown. "I'm sorry. I was talking to Cedric."

"_Cedric?_"

They moved forward.

"Shh." Cyd turned to see if he'd heard.

Stephanie leaned her head toward Cyd. "I knew it. I knew he was going to try to get with you. Cyd, I'm telling you—"

"Steph, this is not the time." Cyd smiled, mostly for the benefit of their dad, who was looking at them and up the line at Cedric with a curious eye. "So, little sis, you ready? Lindell's in there waiting."

Stephanie took a deep breath. "Definitely."

Bruce looked down at his daughter. "You sure? It's not too late to turn this ship around." He chuckled.

"We're not turning anything around." Stephanie threw her head back. "We will be Dr. and Mrs. Lindell London within the hour."

Cyd gave Stephanie's hand a squeeze, pinched the cheeks of Mackenzie and Mark, and took her place next to Cedric. He peeked into her bouquet and smiled. She pretended not to notice.

The faces in the pews were turned to the back when Cyd and Cedric entered. She slipped her hand through his arm and smiled, following the rhythm of his medium-slow gait. The entire walk up the aisle was a battle. She was drawn to him. She was sure of it. His voice reverberated in her head. His aura made her skin tingle. The man was good-looking and smooth, and the way he looked at her with those eyes . . .

Those mischievous eyes.

Reality jerked her back when they passed his girlfriend. The woman had probably been dating him for years, enduring all kinds of hurt and betrayal.

Get your mind off of him, Cyd.

Why would she dwell even a second on that man? She'd seen betrayal up close and personal just yesterday. She didn't need to invite obvious trouble into her life.

She dropped her arm from his and took her place in front of the bridesmaids. Mark was coming up the aisle with Mackenzie behind him, both at a rapid clip that made the guests giggle. Scott stood to snap pictures as Dana looked on. She appeared to be smiling, but when the kids passed their pew and got closer to the front, Dana lowered her head and dabbed her eye with a tissue.

Cyd kept her eyes in Dana's direction as the guests stood for Stephanie's march down the aisle. She looked dazzling, her smile wide as she and Bruce took their time in the spotlight.

Seconds later Cyd noticed another guest three rows back from Dana and Scott. Of course. Her own hand had written *Heather Anderson* on the white envelope two months ago. One of the twentysomething crowd from the eleven thirty service that Stephanie invited.

Cyd grew hot as she watched her. How dare she come to the wedding.

"Who gives this woman to be married to this man?" Pastor Lyles peered over his reading glasses with a hint of a smile.

"Her mother and I do." Bruce guided Stephanie to Lindell and took his seat.

Stephanie and Lindell locked hands, and Pastor Lyles began the exchange of vows, which had to be fodder for reflection for Scott. But Cyd could hardly focus. With the drama with Dana, Scott, and Heather; Cedric eyeing her across the way; and the lavender rose peeping up at her, her thoughts were shooting this way and that. A soloist sang, someone read the love verses from First Corinthians, Stephanie and Lindell lit the unity candle.

Before Cyd knew it, Pastor Lyles was saying, "I now pronounce you husband and wife," and Lindell was kissing his bride.

The recessional went quickly, and as the bridal party waited to reenter the sanctuary for pictures, Cyd sneaked through a side door and hunted for Dana. She was sitting in a pew, jaw raised, staring straight ahead. Trish sat beside her. Scott and Heather stood a few feet away engaged in a discussion that ended abruptly, prompting Heather to leave the sanctuary. Scott whispered to Dana, then walked toward the pastor at the front.

Cyd slid next to Dana and took her hand. "Are you okay? I can't believe she showed up here."

Dana had a fire in her eyes. "That woman's got a lot of nerve. Before the ceremony started, she sauntered past our pew just so we would see her."

"What did Scott do?" Cyd asked.

"He ignored her," Dana said, "and after the ceremony, she pranced over here and told him, 'We need to talk.'"

Trish looked at Cyd. "Can you believe her?"

"I don't even know what they said yet," Dana said. "Scott told me he wanted to catch the pastor and set up a time to meet with him."

Cyd watched the pastor lean his head toward Scott. "Do you think he's going to tell the pastor what he did?"

"Given his leadership position, I think so."

Trish grunted. "Pastor's probably wondering what's going on around here."

"What do you mean?" Cyd asked.

"Noah York stepped down last month from overseeing the men's ministry because of an affair."

"Oh, that's right," Cyd said. "And there's Jessica Handy."

Jessica had gotten pregnant while serving as director of the kids' choir—and she was single.

"Remember when all that strife was going on in different ministries," Cyd said, "and folk were leaving left and right?"

Trish crossed her legs. "I remember. Pastor started that series on walking in love."

Dana looked at them both. "Can you imagine if he did a series on all of this?"

THE SOUND OF glasses tinkling echoed all around the ballroom. Lindell put down his fork, leaned left, and kissed the new Mrs. London for the umpteenth time.

Cedric had started it. When it was time to give the toast, he carried his butter knife and water glass to the podium and, before he said a word, lifted the glass and started the chorus. This one was the longest thus far, and the crowd was cheering now as Lindell and Stephanie hung with them.

Cedric lowered his glass, and the others followed. He leaned to the microphone. "I have the privilege as the best man to toast the groom, my little brother." He looked at Lindell and smiled. "Those of you who know Lindell and me are not surprised that he's getting married first, though he's several years younger. I'm the confirmed bachelor, right?" He looked out at the elegantly decorated tables with pale gold-and-white place settings. "Where are my aunts? That's what they like to call me."

Three aunts waved their hands and nodded vigorously. "That's right," one said.

Cedric turned his torso toward his brother. "Lindell is different. I think he came out of the womb looking for someone to settle down with."

Lindell hid his face behind his hand.

"I had to caution him at fifteen, eighteen, twenty-one—'Don't be so quick to give your heart to one girl. Play the field, for goodness' sake.'"

The young men in the room roared in agreement. The young women booed. From her seat on the riser up front, Cyd could see

Cedric's girlfriend at a table with people she likely didn't know, eyeing Cedric with a bothered expression.

Cedric adjusted his tuxedo jacket and smiled at the bride and groom. "But while he was hitting the books in college and med school and slaving away in his residency, he was still looking for the woman of his dreams. And finally now, in Stephanie, he's found her." Cedric paused and held the sides of the podium. "I remember when he called and told me, 'Ced, this is the one, man.' I had to test him, find out why he thought she was so special. He said she was thoughtful and caring, she listened to him, made him feel he was the most important person in her world."

He leaned back to get a good look at Stephanie, then added, "I'm sure the fact that she's beautiful didn't hurt."

The guests chuckled. Cyd glanced at her sister. Either Lindell brought out the best in her, or she was good at her game too. Given Stephanie's history, Cyd was prone to think the latter. She looked over in Dana's direction as she'd done all afternoon. She seemed okay, considering, sitting with Scott, the kids, and Trish. Heather hadn't shown up at the reception.

"I have to tell this one story, and I'm done. My brother has a big heart, but he's not exactly the most romantic. He told me he was going to propose and that he planned to take Stephanie out to dinner and pop the question during dessert. I said, 'And? What about flowers, a string quartet? I know it's old, but at least hide the ring in the dessert or something.'" Cedric looked at Lindell with brotherly love. "And I'll never forget this. He said he didn't want any extras, because they couldn't come close to conveying what was in his heart. He just wanted her to focus on what he had to say about his love for her. And I'm guessing he conveyed it well."

Cedric raised his champagne glass. "To Lindell and Stephanie: may the gift of true love bind your hearts together for the rest of your days."

He led the guests in taking a sip, and someone started tinkling a glass. It caught on quickly again, and Lindell and Stephanie happily obliged with another long kiss.

Cyd noticed Dana, Scott, and the kids leaving.

"I hate to cut into the merriment." The disc jockey's deep voice penetrated the action. Mike was a friend of Lindell and Cedric's and a real on-air personality. "But I'm sure the bride and groom won't mind. I'm told it's time for the first dance."

Lindell scooted his chair back, placed his napkin on the table, and guided Stephanie to the middle of the floor as someone cut the main lights. A circular swath of blue light glowed above the dance floor, creating a romantic mood. When "Someone to Love" began, Lindell swayed with his wife, arms tight around her waist.

Stephanie had said he loved Mint Condition and couldn't decide which song to feature, so he told Mike he wanted a Mint concert, as if the band were playing all their love songs just for them.

Cyd didn't listen to music much since she spent most of her time reading or writing, and when she did listen, it was almost always praise music. But she knew about Mint Condition. The one guy she'd been serious about had been a fan as well and played one of their old CDs to death. It included this very song, and she'd fallen in love with it.

Cedric bent over Cyd's shoulder. "Wanna dance?"

She gave him a look. "This is their dance."

"Okay." He sat down. If she wasn't mistaken, he had a gleam in his eye.

Mike's mellow voice cut in as the song faded. "We need the best man and the maid of honor to join the bride and groom on the floor."

Cyd's stomach took a dive. Cedric was already out of his seat, hand extended to help Cyd out of hers. They'd been sitting side by side throughout the meal, and she couldn't help but enjoy his company. He had a way of hanging on every word, looking deep into her eyes, making her feel like nothing else mattered. She had tried to keep her distance by casting her eyes about the crowd and talking to the bridesmaid on her left. But now . . .

With the guests waiting, she rose and took his hand. It wrapped tightly around hers. As he led her to the floor, "U Send Me Swingin'" floated from the speakers. The midtempo was good, she thought. They wouldn't have to get too close. But what happened next was almost worse.

Cedric took both of her hands and goaded her into an old-style bop, pulling her in and back out, stepping side to side. Every few seconds, he would come close, grab her waist and sway with her, then step back again, twirling her around. She followed his movements and added some of her own, lost in the melody.

Before she knew it, Stephanie and Lindell had stopped to watch, and there was a crowd growing at the edge of the dance floor, egging them on. Embarrassed, Cyd slowed and her steps faltered, but Cedric pulled her close again and locked eyes with her, rocking her back into rhythm. When he twirled her back out, she caught a glimpse of his girlfriend in the watching crowd and felt bad for her. She let his hands go as the song ended and took a step toward her seat, but DJ Mike had his eye on her.

"Not so fast, Ms. Sanders." He said it with a low voice, as if she alone could hear. "All bridesmaids and groomsmen to the floor," he called. "All bridesmaids and groomsmen wanted on the floor." With a low voice again, he said, "Ms. Sanders, you're stuck with your partner for one more song."

When she heard the intro to the song, she looked at Mike, then Cedric. They had to be in cahoots.

The bridal party members, paired up according to the way they had walked down the aisle, fell into place on the dance floor to the sultry sound of "So Fine." The attendants all struck a distant posture, but Cedric took Cyd's hand again and pulled her close. This time he wrapped his arms around her waist and kept them there.

Cyd leaned her head back. "Cedric, I don't feel right. Your girl-friend's just standing there watching us."

He didn't turn to look. "She's not my girlfriend. I've always been straight with Tamia. She knew from the beginning that I wasn't look-ing for a commitment." He nudged her head close to his chest. "She just thought she could change my mind."

Cedric moved his hand slowly up her back, in time with the vibe of the music. He reached his other hand toward his chest, unbutton-ing his tuxedo jacket, and brought her closer.

Cyd thought she would melt.

He whispered in her ear, "Don't you think we need to spend some time getting to know each other better this evening?"

She closed her eyes against his chest. His voice, the lead singer Stokley's voice, Cedric's wandering hands, the pulsating guitar, all mingled together to send her beyond any place she'd ever inhabited. How long had it been since she'd been held? She wanted more than anything to see him again.

She needed this song to end.

"I don't know, Cedric."

Walk in the Spirit, not in the flesh.

Cyd shuddered, needing to tear herself away this very second—this was crazy!—but her body and emotions were on a ride all their own.

He played with the hair down her back. "How about I pick you up at six forty-five? We'll go to dinner, have a nice celebration, and take it from there."

Take it from there?

No reverberated in her head, but it careened with her other thoughts and feelings. It was just dinner. Why shouldn't she do some-thing special for her birthday? What was her alternative? Go home and celebrate with Reese over soup and kibble?

She took a deep breath. "I guess six forty-five is okay."

Ten

Phyllis spotted a Toyota Camry pulling out of a metered parking spot near the student union. She tapped Stacy's arm. "Stacy, right here."

Stacy parallel parked, and Phyllis quickly swung the passenger side door open. In a flash she was out, fluffing her hair, waiting on the curb. "What is taking you all so long? I can't believe we're late again."

Gretta poked her head out from the back. "I'm trying to get my shoes on. What is the deal with you today?"

Phyllis looked around at the growing horde of fans in Terrapin red heading to the parking lots. "Is the game over?" she asked one passerby.

He gave a thumbs-up. "Yep. Terps pulled it out, 13–6."

Phyllis gaped at the women. "We're so late we missed the game!"

Natalie got out and stretched. "We weren't going to the game."

"I know. But we missed all the tailgating that happens *during* the game. I'll bet people are leaving the tailgate too."

Stacy's head popped up from the driver's side. "They won't be going anywhere for at least a couple of hours." She closed the door and went to the trunk to grab her purse.

"I don't see what the rush was," Gretta said, emerging finally. "We were having a good time talking at the house. We could have skipped the tailgate and hooked up with everybody at dinner."

Phyllis gave Gretta a look. "The whole point of scheduling the reunion on this weekend was so we could enjoy our twentieth anniversary *and* homecoming, and so far today we've done neither."

She started walking the minute the other three hit the curb. "We missed breakfast with our line sisters because you all didn't want to get up early enough to drive out here. We missed Maurette and the Maryland Gospel Choir concert—same reason. And now we've missed most of the tailgate."

"But the four of us are kind of a mini-reunion." Natalie was trying to keep up. "I'm glad we got to stay in our pj's half the day and talk. You just can't do stuff like this at home. And you all helped me sort through the issue with my mother."

"I know. That's true." Phyllis did appreciate their time together. "I guess the weekend is too short. I wanted to spend quality time with you all *and* make it to the events." She turned to Stacy, keeping her stride. "I hope you're right. I hope people are still here."

They passed the front of the student union and saw right away that a sizable crowd was still milling about on the terrace where alumni gathered.

"Happy?"

Phyllis rolled her eyes at Gretta.

They made their way onto the scene—music pumping, little ones playing and eating hot dogs, their parents enjoying the alumni tradition. They stood in place, scanning the crowd.

"There they are," Stacy said, pointing left.

The women made their way toward the congregation of sorority sisters, but Phyllis was stopped every few feet by people who hadn't been at Jasper's—and she got the same chorus: "Look at you! Turn around! Wow!"

Stacy, Natalie, and Gretta walked on, and when Phyllis finally caught up with everybody, she couldn't believe they were ready to go.

"We just got here!"

Sonya put a hand to her hip. "Uh . . . no. Most of us have been here for three hours. We need to get changed and ready for dinner."

Phyllis had one eye on Sonya, the other on the faces in the crowd. "Why do we need to change? We're not going anywhere fancy."

Daphne nodded. "I'm not changing. But I'm still ready to go. We've seen about all there is to see here today."

Crestfallen, Phyllis glanced around again and saw him sitting away from the throng on a grassy area with two other guys. Her pulse raced and she looked away. It would be way too obvious if she—

Phyllis sucked in a breath. He was walking her way. She felt silly pretending not to notice—worse for wanting to see him in the first place. She tracked him from the corner of her eye, thinking he could be headed someplace else. But in a matter of moments, he was beside her.

"Hey." He smiled that smile, wearing a simple Maryland Terrapin long-sleeved shirt, jeans, and a jacket. "I was thinking you might not be coming," he said.

Was he looking for me too?

"It took us a long while to get moving today, and then we had to drive from Leesburg." She hadn't noticed how thick his eyebrows were. "How long have you been here?"

"A couple of hours." The cluster of pink and green moved past them en masse. "Looks like your crew is leaving."

"Yeah, we have a dinner to go to, and most of them have been here for hours."

"Don't let me hold you," he said. "Just wanted to say hi."

"Glad you did." She let her gaze fall on the people around her. Neither of them moved.

Rod shoved his hands in his jacket. "When are you headed back home?"

She chanced a look into his eyes. "Tomorrow morning."

"Okay," he said. "Guess I'll say good-bye, then . . . unless you're going to the homecoming party tonight."

Phyllis felt a surge. "Are you going?"

"Yeah. My buddy over there just talked me into it."

The wheels started turning. Earlier the four women had discussed the party and vetoed it. They weren't into parties anymore, and no one was up for hanging out late and making the long drive home, especially Stacy. But at Jasper's, some of the others had talked of going. Maybe Phyllis could go with them. She turned to see where they all were. Natalie was waving for her to come on.

She turned to Rod. "I might be there."

"Okay," he said again. "And in case you don't make it . . ." He gave her the hug she'd wanted last night. "Glad I got to talk to you a little. It's nice to meet people from college days who are brothers and sisters in Christ now."

Phyllis said good-bye and made her way to the car, trying to get a read on her heart and mind. There was something about him. She'd thought about Rod off and on all day, how refreshing it was to talk to him. She liked him, liked being around him, much as she liked being around other believers such as Cyd, Dana, Stacy, Gretta, and Natalie.

Was it wrong to enjoy the fellowship of a Christian brother?

Admittedly, her heart didn't dance around her female friends the way it did around him, but she could ignore that. She would only see him once more anyway.

She hoped.

PHYLLIS'S PHONE VIBRATED amid the hoots and cackles that had dominated their time at dinner. With all the memories and exaggerated stories flying across the table, she hadn't laughed this much in years. She flipped open her phone and her mood fell. Home.

"Excuse me a minute," she told them. "It's my husband." Phyllis answered as she walked to the lobby. "Hi, babe."

She heard a giggle. "It's not Daddy. It's me, Mommy."

"Hi, sweetie!" Sean's voice cheered her again instantly. "How's my honeydew?"

"Fine. Guess what, Mommy? We've had Reese all day today."

"You have?"

"Yeah. At first we were just gonna walk her for Miss Cyd, but Daddy asked if we could bring her over here, and she let us. And guess what else?"

"What?"

"She's *paying* us to play with the puppy."

Phyllis chuckled. She was sure Cyd was giving them way too much.

"I wanna talk to Mom," she heard Drew say. Then, "Mom, guess what Daddy let me do?"

"Hi, pumpkin."

"Hi, Mom. Now guess."

"I'm afraid to, Drew."

"He let me stay up and read *Lord of the Rings* until eleven o'clock."

Phyllis gasped. "You're kidding."

"He did! And he let me watch the movie today too—the extended version."

Phyllis laughed. "I'm glad you're having a good time. Where's Ella?"

"Taking a nap."

"This late?"

"Daddy said she's off schedule, but you'd get her back on when you come home."

"Oh really?" That wouldn't be fun. "Where's Cole?"

"Joe's house."

Phyllis took a breath. "Where's your dad?"

"Right here. Bye, Mommy."

"Sounds like the kids are having a good time," she said when Hayes took the phone. She hoped they could keep it light. "You were right about being able to handle things. I can't believe you even took on a puppy."

"Me either." Hayes laughed a little. "And of course they're asking for their own dog now."

Good. He seemed to be in a decent mood. Phyllis went with it, a smile in her voice. "Of course . . . but Mom's not up for that one. Guess we'll borrow Cyd's every now and then."

Silence hung between them a few seconds.

"Cole's still acting funny today. Didn't want to be around me much at all."

The joy she'd been trying to hang on to was slipping away. Phyllis moved into a more secluded corner. "I think he'll get over it, Hayes. He has a good heart."

"I've never seen him like this." Hayes's voice took on an agitated tone. "He's upset because you told him I hate God."

She leaned into the phone. "I didn't tell him that. He's old enough to draw his own conclusions. If you'd only agreed to take the kids to church . . ."

"Here we go," Hayes huffed. "You know what, Phyllis? We'd be fine if you hadn't started going to that church. It's already come between you and me, and now it's coming between me and my son."

Phyllis sighed. "Hayes, I'm in a restaurant, and I'm not going to argue with you. I'll talk to Cole when I get back. He'll be fine."

"Well, I'm not so sure," Hayes said. "But I'm tired of talking about it right now anyway." He paused. "I'll see you when you get back."

Phyllis tried to shake off the conversation as she walked back to the table. The women were divvying up the bill, talking about the homecoming party. She looked over Allison's shoulder to see what she owed and took out her wallet, listening.

"Maybe if I didn't live so far out," Stacy was saying. "But I don't know . . . I'm just not into parties anymore."

Gretta laid her money on the table. "I don't have a problem admitting it. I'm too old to stay up that late. Y'all had me up late at Jasper's last night, and I had to sleep till ten to recover." She laughed. "I can't do that tomorrow. My flight's at 7:45 a.m."

Daphne pouted. "But it won't be as much fun without all of us there, like the old days."

Phyllis added her money to the pile. "So who's going?"

"All of us," Daphne said, "except you four."

Phyllis surveyed Daphne and the rest. "I'll join you all, if somebody'll give me a ride back to Stacy's afterward."

"Way out there?" Daphne exclaimed. She lifted her eyes as if thinking about it, then smiled. "I guess we can arrange it."

Natalie looked surprised. "What made you change your mind?"

Phyllis shrugged. "Might as well make the most of my time here."

ABOUT TEN THIRTY, Phyllis and six of her sorority sisters walked into the closeout homecoming event on campus, and it really did feel like the old days. The theme was Old School, and the song playing—"Set It Off"—was the one that got everyone on the dance floor twenty years before. The place was packed, and with dim lighting it was hard to tell who was who. But their pink and green served as a magnet in the semi-dark, and right away they were in the thick of a good time.

Vic pulled Phyllis onto the floor, Randy grabbed Sonya, and the four of them mimicked one another with old dance moves from college, then pre-college when Vic and Randy broke out the Bump. That got everyone going in their corner of the floor, which moved the DJ to switch from the eighties to the seventies with George Clinton and Parliament Funkadelic, which got *everyone* going.

After four songs Phyllis left the floor and stood on the side talking to a couple of friends. A few feet away she spotted Rod with the same guys he'd been with earlier.

The heart dance began. "I'll be right back," she told her girlfriends.

He saw her coming and met her halfway. "You were having fun out there."

Her eyes widened. "You saw me? Why didn't you come over?"

"You were having a good time with your friends. Didn't want to interrupt."

His demeanor was easy, nonchalant, but his eyes were mesmerizing. Her gaze drifted to the dance floor for a moment to keep steady.

"So," she said, locking eyes again, "I never got to hear about your mentor program."

"Oh, I could talk about that all day. Those are my kids." Rod told her about the program he and the PE teacher founded, pairing kids at the middle school with students from Morgan State University, also in Baltimore.

The PE teacher had recently graduated from Morgan and played football for the school, so he used his influence to get over a hundred students to sign up. Mentors had the permission of the principal to visit mentees at school, have lunch, and sit in on certain classes. Once a month they planned an outing for all of the mentors and mentees.

"Basically, we want to give these kids vision," he said, "show them they can succeed in school and in life by making the right choices. And of course, I take every opportunity I can to shine the light of Jesus."

Phyllis was floored. "You'll probably never know this side of heaven how much you've impacted those kids," she said. "That sounds like a big-time commitment on your part."

"It is, but it's worth it. Actually, it's good to keep busy."

Phyllis nodded with understanding. "I'm sure your girls keep you busy too. How old are they?"

Rod smiled. "They're ten and eight, running the house." He laughed. "They keep me going."

"Do you think you'll ever marry again?" The question escaped before Phyllis could lasso it.

He looked away for a moment. "The whole thing is still so fresh that it's hard to even consider right now. I guess if I found the right person . . ." He looked at her again. "But there's so much superficiality out here. I know this sounds strange, but what's appealing to me is a love for the Lord. That's what drew me to Michelle."

"Doesn't sound strange to me."

Not at all.

"So tell me about your family. You said you had kids."

She nodded. "Four—twelve, ten, eight, and eighteen months."

"Whoa." He smiled with surprise. "You're a busy momma. And your husband, what does he do?"

"He works with investments."

"Sounds like you've got a blessed life."

Phyllis smiled faintly and watched the dance floor. Seconds later she felt a tap on her shoulder.

Daphne spoke into her ear. "I was wondering where you'd gone. You gonna stay with Rod all night or hang out with us?"

Phyllis cringed inside. It figured that Daphne had been keeping tabs on them. She probably wished _she_ could hang with Rod all night.

Rod touched her arm. "I'd better let you get back to your friends."

Phyllis spent the rest of the night wondering if they would have a chance to say good-bye.

When the lights came on at one thirty, the crowd moved slowly toward the door. Phyllis knew exactly where Rod was, but with Daphne near—and probably watching—she let slide her opportunity to say good-bye.

The women had driven to the party in two cars and parked in the nearest lot. As they walked out, Phyllis noticed Rod walking ahead of them, alone, in the same direction. Turned out his car was a few spaces from theirs, and as the women were hugging one another, he called out, "Which one of you lives in Leesburg?"

The women showed confusion, so he came over. Looking at Phyllis, he said, "I thought you said you all had driven from Leesburg."

"Oh, that was earlier," Phyllis said. "Stacy lives there, but she didn't feel like going to the party, so she drove back after dinner."

"So they're about to take you way out there?"

Daphne came closer. "Can you believe it? We won't get home till three thirty. We're such good friends, aren't we?"

He turned to Phyllis. "My parents live ten minutes from Leesburg, in Ashburn, and I'm headed there now so I can bring the kids back in the morning. It doesn't make sense for them to ride out there. I'll just take you."

A reaction rippled through her instantly—surprise . . . and a tentative thrill. But she sobered quickly. How would it look if she got in the car with this man at one thirty in the morning? Then again, he was driving to Virginia anyway. Didn't it make sense for him to take her? And it wasn't just any man. They all knew him, and knew him to be a good person.

Daphne looked sick.

Ria yawned. "I don't see what there is to think about. I could be in my bed in fifteen minutes . . . or two hours. Let's see." She made her hands a balance and weighed the two. "Let me get my hug, girl."

They all exchanged another round of good-byes, and Rod led Phyllis to the passenger side of his SUV. "You know how to get to her house?" he asked.

Phyllis reached into her purse and gave him a piece of paper. "Stacy wrote it down."

He studied it, then backed out of the space and navigated his way off campus, then up Route 1 toward 495 North. They were both silent, and she thought she might need to stay that way for the length of the ride. And keep staring straight ahead. Being this close to him in a closed space was raising a commotion inside.

When they reached 495, he glanced over at her. "So how do you like St. Louis?"

She just decided—conversation was better. Her mind had been floating with the scent of his cologne, the way his arm held the steering wheel, the angle of his leg. This would keep her mind in one spot.

"I like it fine," she said, casting a glance. She continued, facing forward. "The kids have good schools, and I love my church."

"What church do you go to?"

"It's a nondenominational church called Living Word."

He shot her a look. "Dr. Mason Lyles?"

Phyllis turned in surprise. "Yeah. How do you know?"

Rod chuckled. "This is so wild. I love Dr. Lyles. I do his Bible studies and listen to his CDs. I always said I would love to go to his church."

Huh. Can't drag my husband into the place.

"I forget people know him from his Bible studies. His teaching is awesome."

"Definitely," Rod agreed. "I love my own pastor too—Pastor Collier. Every Sunday and Wednesday night, I'm right there. Between him and Pastor Lyles, I'm tight." Rod laughed.

They fell into silence, eventually hitting the Dulles Toll Road. Rod slowed to toss some coins into the bin. So many thoughts vied for Phyllis's attention, so many places beckoned, like the one that wished she and Rod were both single, able to have these conversations for days on end, getting to know one another, going deeper. He was it—her dream, the man she'd been praying for Hayes to be, a man in love with the Lord.

Why was life so unfair? She was dealing with pain and disappointment at home because she couldn't have these kinds of conversations, this kind of bond. And now there was someone with whom she could—but she couldn't.

Rod pulled into Stacy's neighborhood and found her house, letting the engine run out front. Phyllis looked up at the windows. All was dark.

She couldn't bring herself to say good-bye.

She noticed he was silent, too, that they both were sitting there, unhurried. Finally she said, "I'm glad I got to know you a little better this weekend, Rod." It came out: "Maybe we could keep in touch."

He surprised her with a humorless chuckle as he examined the steering wheel. "I don't think so."

She stared at him, hiding her disappointment, waiting.

He met her gaze. "I like you," he said simply, and she thought her insides might never find calm again. "You're the first person I've met since Michelle who I could actually see myself getting to know better. But I can't, not that way. So I had just been asking myself as we drove up, 'Okay, could we be friends? Should we keep in touch?' And I'm thinking no, not when temptation could just sneak in. You know?" He let his gaze fall back to the steering wheel.

Phyllis was a few sentences back. Did he say he *liked* her? That he would want to get to know her? The evening was instantly more surreal. To hear that it wasn't one-sided, that he felt something, too, was more than she could fathom, especially when this was Rod, the enigmatic wonder.

She tried to focus on the rest of what he said, after the part about liking her. She spoke carefully. "I don't see how temptation could be a problem—I'm clear across the country. Picking up the phone or shooting an e-mail every blue moon . . . not a big deal, is it?"

Rod thought a moment, rested his arm on the door. She wished she could read his mind.

"You're probably right." He reached into the glove compartment and pulled out a small pad and pen. "Kind of silly to be extreme about it," he said, writing.

He shot her a smile, and goose bumps rode her arms. "You can't be too dangerous way out there in St. Louis." He tore out the paper and handed it to her.

She folded it and tucked it in her purse. Her hand on the door handle, she brought her eyes to his one last time. "Thanks for bringing me out here, Rod. I really appreciate it."

"Glad I could help." He was leaning back in the seat, his head against the headrest, eyes holding hers.

She kept up the gaze, wanting suddenly to go to those deeper places, wanting him to lean over, hug her good-bye. And if he kissed her . . .

But he broke the stare and looked ahead.

Phyllis opened the door and stepped out. Even as she closed it, she hoped he would get out, too, come around to her side, hold her.

But he stayed in the car as she walked to the front door and waited until Phyllis let herself in with the key. As she walked inside, she heard him drive off.

Eleven

CYD STEPPED OUT of the shower and wrapped herself in a luxurious peach bath towel, ambivalent still about the evening ahead. She hadn't been able to bring herself to pray about it in there. Prayer would have opened wide the issue, reminding her of all she'd felt at the reception, the desires that had flitted through her mind. Prayer would have forced her to face the truth that she had no business going out with this man tonight, and that the only reason she'd agreed was the passion in the moment.

She knew she couldn't go there tonight. But she couldn't deny the buildup of anticipation inside. She would see him again in fifteen minutes.

Every move raised a question. Why was she putting on perfumed body spray? She never wore that. Why the black jersey skirt and boots, when pants were always her preference? Why was she leaving her hair down when it was getting on her nerves—because Cedric thought it was sexy?

Cyd hurried down the stairs with a purse, almost tripping over the puppy bounding between her legs. In the kitchen, she threw a few items from a tote into the smaller purse and glanced at her watch— six forty-five. The doorbell rang seconds later, and Reese ran to it, barking at the intruder. Cyd herded her to her crate and returned to answer the door.

She pushed open the screen door. "Hi."

Cedric smiled. "Hi yourself." He wore a brown sweater and beige slacks. As he came inside, he brought a bouquet of roses from behind his back, all lavender.

"Oh, Cedric." She told herself he'd done this for every woman he'd ever gone out with, same color and all. But the thrill shot through her nonetheless. "Thank you." She took the roses and inhaled their fragrance. "They're gorgeous."

Cedric surveyed the living area to the left of the foyer. It wasn't very big, but it was cozy, with hardwood floors, a cream-colored over-stuffed sofa and chair, a glass-top table, framed art, and lots of plants. He was nodding his head. "I'm impressed. You know how to give life to a place."

"Thank you," she said. "I have a long list of things to do in this house, and plants are cheaper than gutting the kitchen." She smelled the roses again. "I'd better put these in water."

Cedric followed her toward the kitchen, chuckling. "What have you done to that little dog you were telling me about? She sounds awful upset."

"She's in her crate. That's why she's making all that noise. That and the fact that there's an unfamiliar voice in her midst."

"You didn't have to lock her up on my account. I grew up with two dogs."

"I didn't want her to jump on you," Cyd said. "She doesn't have good manners."

Cedric walked into the kitchen and unlocked the crate. "Hey, pup-pup. Reese, right?" Kneeling, he stroked the puppy until she turned over on her back with her paws bent in complete comfort and submission. "You're a cutie. You do look like a peanut butter cup."

Cyd retrieved a vase from an upper cabinet. Felt weird to have a man in the house. Well, this kind of man. Scott had been over with Dana, and Hayes came by with Phyllis from time to time when she needed handyman help, but in the seven years she'd lived here, no one had been by for a . . . What exactly *was* this?

She filled the vase with water. It wasn't a date, because she would never date a man like Cedric. She never went for the slick, handsome, player type. She had one real requirement—that the man be truly committed to God—which is why she never got far with most men. She could tell from the get-go where their head was. Just like she could tell where Cedric's head was within a nanosecond of interaction. Without an intervening circumstance like the wedding, her world never would have collided with his. Now here he was in her kitchen.

The roses arranged beautifully in the vase, Cyd turned to him. "She would be in dog heaven if you rubbed her tummy like that all day."

He gave the dog a couple more strokes. "I wish I could, pup. I'll have to see you when I get back." Cedric went to the kitchen sink to wash his hands.

He'd be in for a surprise. Cyd had no intention of entertaining him in her home after dinner.

Cedric turned from the sink and took a good look around. "Why did you say you needed to gut this? I was expecting something horrible. This must've been updated recently."

Cyd looked around herself. "The previous owner did update it, about twenty-five years ago. It's not too bad . . . if you like hospital gray." The cabinets and drawers were white with gray pulls, and the floor was linoleum with a white and gray design.

He inspected a cabinet, pulled on the door, and looked behind it. "What would you do if you could change it?"

"I'd get a warmer color, maybe a light cherry," she said. "Why? You do remodeling on the side?"

"Just trying to see if we had similar taste," he said. "I would've said light cherry myself." He winked at her and headed to the door.

Cyd smirked and followed him out.

They walked down her walkway to the BMW convertible parked at the front curb. Cedric opened the door, and Cyd lowered herself inside, moved the seat back. Tamia was a tad shorter than she.

It took less than ten minutes to ride to the restaurant. The host greeted Cedric by name.

Cedric shook his hand. "Good evening, George. Is Francesca working tonight?"

"Reserved your table in her section, Mr. London."

They were taken to a semicircular booth in a secluded alcove. Cyd slid in toward the middle, and Cedric sat close beside her. George handed them the dinner and wine menus and filled their glasses with ice water. He tipped his head. "Enjoy your dinner."

Cyd noted the chic décor, the soft recessed lighting, and the smooth jazz playing in the background. "This is nice."

"Wait till you taste the food."

A server greeted them with a basket of assorted bread. "Mr. London, it's good to see you this evening." She placed it on the table. "I brought a fresh batch from the oven."

"Thank you, Francesca. It's good to see you as well." He gestured to Cyd. "This is my guest this evening, Cyd Sanders."

"How do you do, ma'am?"

Cyd smiled. "Fine, thank you."

Wonder how many women he's brought here this week alone.

"Will you be starting with an appetizer this evening, Mr. London?"

Cedric fingered his menu. "Absolutely. I have a taste for calamari tonight." He looked at Cyd. "You'll share it with me, won't you?"

"I love calamari," Cyd said.

Francesca made a note. "Your usual bottle of wine?"

"Yes, please."

"Very good. I'll return shortly to take your order."

Cedric passed the basket to Cyd.

She chose a wheat roll and set it on her bread plate. "So how long have you lived in the Central West End?"

He chose the bruschetta. "Almost two years. I had a condo farther west, but I like this location a lot better. It's much closer to the office."

"What do you do?" She pinched a piece of bread and popped it into her mouth as her mind flashed to this afternoon. She'd shared an intimate dance with this man and barely knew anything about him.

He drizzled olive oil on his plate and dragged the bread in it. "In layman's terms, I'm a head hunter." He took a bite.

"And in your terms?"

He donned a look of importance. "I'm a vice president with an executive search firm." He chuckled. "I like to call myself a match-maker. When one of our corporate clients needs a new chief executive, for example, I try to find the perfect qualified candidate to fill the position. I'm very much in the people business."

No doubt about that.

"Do you work with universities? I get calls sometimes from head hunters—or whatever I should call them—asking if I'm interested in certain faculty positions."

"There are people in our office who handle education, yes. Not as lucrative, though." He shrugged. "Universities don't pay their presidents what Fortune 500 companies pay theirs. And since we get paid a percentage . . ." He saturated his bread again and took another bite.

Francesca returned with a bottle of wine and popped it open. She poured a small amount into Cedric's wine glass and allowed him to taste it. When he nodded, she poured more, then held it over Cyd's glass.

She raised her hand slightly. "No, thank you."

The woman questioned with her eyes. "No?"

Cyd smiled and shook her head.

A different server came from behind and set the calamari and two plates before them.

When they both had left, Cedric reached for her hand and bowed his head. "Thank You, Lord, for this food. And thank You for the company of this beautiful woman. Amen."

Cyd said, "Amen," brow raised. She decided to seize the opportunity. "I'm impressed. Didn't know you were a praying man."

He thought a second. "I wouldn't exactly say I'm a praying man. My mother prayed over the food when I was young, so I guess it became a habit." He speared a piece of calamari and dipped it into the sauce. "You've got to try this."

Cyd had no idea he would feed it to her. He passed the fork slowly to her lips, teasing up a slow gaze . . . and a pull she had to fight to resist. She looked away as she tasted it. "That's really good." She transferred some to her plate. "So how long have you been going to Living Word?"

"About ten months."

"What made you start coming?" She dipped a piece of calamari and ate it.

"I'd been courting this client, and he told me about Living Word. Said I should check it out." He stabbed several calamari. "Then I realized it was the same church Lindell went to, *and* it had a late service so it wouldn't be too painful. I figured I could score some points with the guy if I started coming." He ate them all at once.

Cyd took a sip of water. "So now that you've been there almost a year, what do you think?"

"Worked out real well. I'm doing a search for him right now for a CFO."

"Oh. I meant, what do you think about the church?"

Cedric nodded, waiting to swallow. "I don't make it every week, but I do enjoy the service. Music is awesome, people are friendly. It's a nice vibe."

"What about Pastor Lyles?"

"He's cool. I like his style. I respect a man who doesn't pull any punches. He knows what he believes, and he doesn't change it up to make folk feel good. I can respect that."

Cyd nodded. "That's definitely Pastor Lyles."

He sipped his wine. "At the same time, it's a little extreme now and then. All the talk about holy living—it's unrealistic to expect people to actually live like that."

Cyd sighed inside, thankful that Francesca had returned to take their order. She hadn't looked at the menu, so she turned to Cedric. "Why don't you order for me since you know what's good."

He readily took up the request. "Let's order her the pan-roasted grouper with lobster ravioli and oven-dried tomatoes. I'll have the grilled beef tenderloin with lobster. I want to substitute the gnocchi for the mashed potatoes—you have to try the gnocchi," he said to Cyd. He handed Francesca their menus. "I think that's good for now."

Throughout the rest of dinner Cedric talked more about his job, Cyd acquainted him with hers, and there was lots of small talk about favorite things to do and see in the area. No doubt about it—she enjoyed him immensely. But as much as she'd prayed over the years to find the right man, she knew this definitely wasn't him.

CEDRIC PULLED THE car up to her curb again, cut the engine, and turned off the headlights.

"Dinner was wonderful, Cedric." She looped her purse over her shoulder. "You made my birthday very special. Thank you for taking the time to celebrate with me."

"It's not over yet." He hopped out of the car.

What is he doing?

She opened her car door and got out.

Cedric opened the trunk and lifted a round box from inside. "The celebration's not complete without cake."

Cyd closed the passenger door. "Cedric, I appreciate it, but I had planned to just go inside and rest, get ready for church tomorrow. It's been a really long day."

He looked at his watch. "It's only nine o'clock. Come on. Thirty minutes?"

She gazed toward the house. The butterflies danced. What could she say? _I'm afraid to let you in?_

He held up the cake with a grin. "It's chocolate with whipped cream frosting. Your favorite."

No wonder he asked me at the reception.

She breathed in and out. "All right. Thirty minutes."

Cyd took Reese out back to potty, and when they returned, the cake was on the kitchen table in the breakfast nook. Big 4 and 0 candles were lit on top, and _Happy Birthday, Cyd_ was written in red letters atop the white icing. She was speechless.

He walked up beside her. "Make a wish and blow out the candles."

She leaned over the cake and closed her eyes.

Lord, give me strength.

She blew them out.

"Where are your dessert plates?" Cedric was searching the cabinets.

"That one," Cyd said, pointing.

He found a knife, brought everything to the table, and cut two pieces. Cyd gave Reese a special bone to chew to keep her busy.

She had barely finished half her hunk when a yawn escaped. "I'm so sorry. Lack of sleep has caught up with me."

"I hear you. I'm starting to feel it myself." He rose from the table, looking at his watch. "Thirty minutes, as promised."

Reese was pooped, too, probably from running around earlier

with Phyllis's kids. Done with only half the bone, she lay stretched out on her side.

Cedric extended his hand to help her up and held it as they walked down the hall and into the foyer. Her body tingled when he stopped to look at her.

"I'm glad it was your birthday today. I had a good time."

"So did I. Thank you again, for everything."

He leaned over and kissed her cheek, then tugged her hand to bring her closer and kissed the side of her mouth, then her lips. She took a step back, but his arm came around her waist, fingers explored her hair. The kiss grew deeper . . . and more passionate.

Half of Cyd was upset that he'd be so presumptuous. The other half was completely intoxicated by him.

"You smell so good," he said. He kissed her ear and moved her toward the sofa. Seconds later he had sunk down and pulled her with him, leaning into a reclining position.

Cyd was lost in the moment, caught up in passion she hadn't felt in years—passion she shouldn't be feeling now. If she didn't stop—"I can't." She got up.

He grabbed her hand. "Why?"

She pulled it back. "It's wrong."

"Wrong?" His brows knit. "I thought you weren't married." He glanced in the direction of the stairs as if she might be hiding a husband up there.

"I'm not. It's just . . ." Her eyes searched the floor, her heart trying to find its rhythm.

He tipped her chin. "If we're moving too fast, I understand. I won't lie. I want to make love to you, but I would never make that kind of move unless you're ready."

She closed her eyes. "You don't understand." She looked at him again. "That's not something I would ever be ready for. I'm not into casual sex."

"Oh." He sat straighter. "I . . . I can understand that. You want to be in a committed relationship first?"

She gave an empty chuckle. "Yeah. The very thing you avoid."

"It's not that I _avoid_ it—"

"Cedric, let me be real plain with you. I'm not interested in sex at all, not outside of marriage."

He stared deep into her eyes. "Are you serious? You're not a virgin, are you?"

She wished she could say yes. "No. But it's only been once, a long time ago."

He lowered his head and rubbed the back of his neck. "Wow."

The phone rang and froze them in place, Cedric gazing down, Cyd watching him, her emotions frazzled. After five rings, it stopped.

"I'm sorry." She stepped around him and to the door. "I know you feel like you wasted your time with the roses and dinner and the cake and everything."

"Not at all." He followed her. "I don't want you to think I did all that to get you in bed."

Her eyes questioned. "Didn't you?"

His mouth turned up in thought. "Okay, it may have crossed my mind. But really, I'm glad I did it." He paused, staring at her again. "So . . . I'm curious. What if you never get married? Why are you waiting to have sex?"

She looked at him. "Because I'm a Christian."

He lifted his hands in a shrug. "So am I."

She didn't know what to say. Slowly pulling the door open behind her, she gave a thin smile.

He walked beyond her and stopped, brushed the back of a finger against her cheek. Held her gaze so long she prayed for more strength.

And he was gone.

She closed the door and leaned against it, exhaling. When she'd gathered herself a little, she went to check the message. If it was Dana, she would call her right back.

"This is a recorded message from Living Word Community Church."

Cyd frowned. The church rarely did these.

"Pastor Mason Lyles is announcing an important sermon series to begin tomorrow morning, October 19. The life and health of our church and its individuals are the impetus for this series, which will deal openly with the issue of sexual sin. All members of Living Word are strongly encouraged to attend. We will be kicking off a new initiative afterward, and as a result, there will be one service only, at 9:00 a.m., utilizing all sections of the balcony and overflow areas.

"Finally, we realize this is highly unusual, but at the request of Scott Elliott, we want to inform you that he will come before his church family tomorrow with a public confession."

Twelve

SCOTT TIGHTENED THE knot on his necktie and drew it up to the collar, the floor mirror his guide. He did it more slowly and carefully than normal, it seemed, and it looked fine, but he grunted, untied it, and started over.

Dana caught herself watching as she strode from the closet. She averted her eyes and continued into the bathroom.

"Dana?"

"Mm-hmm." She opened a cabinet and pulled out her makeup bag.

"I'm glad you changed your mind about going today." His voice traveled from his spot at the mirror. "It'll make a world of difference to have you there with me."

Dana dabbed foundation on her forehead. Surely he didn't think she was going as a favor to him. If Pastor Lyles hadn't spoken to her personally, she'd be steering clear of Living Word today.

"I know you don't like the idea." He was in the bathroom doorway now. "I'm not crazy about it myself." He hung his head a moment. "You don't know how badly I wish none of this had ever happened. I wouldn't be doing this if I didn't feel strongly that it's what God wants me to do."

Dana tossed her eyes, nicking an eyelid with the mascara brush. *Now* he feels strongly about what God wants, when it'll publicly humiliate her? Since when did the Bible require a confession of this magnitude? The last thing she wanted was the entire congregation knowing their business.

"So you're still not talking to me?"

Not if I don't have to.

"I thought it helped to pray with the pastor yesterday."

Dana whisked a brush across her cheeks.

You have no idea.

Were it not for the pastor, she might not even be there still. Trish had been telling Dana she needed to bring the kids and stay at her house for a while to think things through.

"After what he did," Trish said, "he doesn't deserve you. You need to at least leave and make him sweat a little."

Dana had been giving it serious thought, until the pastor showed up.

Pastor Lyles had shepherded her through many seasons, conducting their premarital counseling as well as their wedding ceremony. But she hadn't realized what a father figure he'd become until he walked through the door yesterday. He'd come to talk to Scott, and when Dana let him in, he hugged her and with a voice of assurance said that God would see them through this. She'd wept openly on his shoulder.

After he spoke privately with Scott, he met with the two of them together, recommended one of his assistant pastors for counseling, and prayed with them. On his way out, he'd pulled Dana aside.

"None of this will be easy," he said, "but Scott loves you. Give him a chance. Don't throw away your marriage." His voice was soft and caring. "I want you to do two things for me." He had a father's gleam in his eye. "Don't move out . . ." The words wafted in midair, penetrating her soul. "And I want you to come to church tomorrow."

Dana had cast her eyes aside.

"The service will be unlike any we've had," he continued. "I think it'll bless people, and it might even bless you."

She dismissed that last bit—it would _bless_ her?—but she couldn't easily dismiss his requests. Maybe it was his prayer and words of support, or simply that she loved and trusted him. But she slept at home last night, and when she woke up, she felt an inner push to get ready and go to church.

Dana turned around now and saw that Scott was gone.

She exhaled and stared at herself as she applied lip gloss, Heather's face floating in her mind. It was always there. Without a doubt the girl was beautiful, and try as she might, Dana couldn't stop the mental comparisons between them. Heather had everything to do with her wardrobe this morning. Instead of the low heels and pants she usually wore—Living Word had a dressy casual culture—she wanted to look spiffier. She put on pumps and a long black skirt for the slimming effect, and instead of the black jacket that went with it, she added a mulberry long-sleeved top and jacket to at least look like she wasn't in mourning.

The makeup she took up a notch too—even found a blemish eraser thing she'd bought months ago. But the hair . . .

She took in her blunt cut, the one she'd felt such freedom about. She wished again that she'd kept her longer locks—and kept them blonde. Did Scott enjoy running his fingers through Heather's hair? Was the color enticing to him?

He said he told Heather after the wedding that their affair was wrong, that he was sorry it had happened. Told her not to call or approach him again in person. Even if he was telling the truth, it didn't mean Heather was behind them. If Dana was having a hard time getting Heather out of her head, what about Scott? He'd been intimate with her. He had feelings for her. Was Heather floating constantly in his mind too? Would she haunt them forever?

PHYLLIS UNHOOKED HER seat belt before the plane came to a full stop at the gate. When the bell sounded, she stood, grabbed her purse, and took to the aisle, dialing home. She'd arrived earlier than planned.

When she'd first made travel plans, she thought she'd want to linger longer at Stacy's, making the most of their weekend together. But she couldn't sleep last night, and lingering would have only invited questions about the party and possibly the ride home. Before the sun came up, she called the airline and asked about earlier flights and her chances of going standby. A departure time near Gretta's looked promising, and Stacy was able to take them to the airport together. Phyllis exhaled when they'd all hugged and gone their separate ways, thankful that most of the car talk focused on Gretta's stress with her part-time job and never once touched on the previous night.

She spent the entire plane ride trying to process her interaction with Rod, bringing his every word to mind, the thickness of his voice as he uttered them, the tentative gestures, those eyes. She turned them over and over until the pilot announced their descent, jarring her back to reality. She was home now, and whatever that was last night, there it would remain. She felt safe in that, knowing she didn't have to worry about crossing a dangerous line. Rod was hundreds of miles away, and she'd probably never see him again.

Now she could surprise her boys and let them know she'd made it home in time to take them to church. She checked her watch as the phone rang and rang—it was eight thirty. She shouldn't have been surprised that they were sleeping in, but she wanted them to be dressed by the time she got there so they could speed out the door. The passengers moved slowly toward the front and off the plane. Phyllis hung up, dialed again, and got voice mail once more. Looked like they'd be going to the second service.

She headed to baggage claim, a knot tightening in her stomach at the thought of Hayes. Would they clash again over Cole? The thought made her head hurt. She had hoped to return rejuvenated, her perspective brighter. And as she watched the first pieces of luggage circle around, she guessed she did indeed feel a spark of rejuvenation.

But only when she thought of Rod.

CYD AND DANA worked their way up the aisle left of center to the fourth pew from the front, the spot where they always sat with Scott and Phyllis. They thought they'd arrived early, but bodies mingled in the aisles and leaned over the backs of pews, engaged in livelier conversation than Cyd had ever seen this time of morning . . . except when Dana passed.

Those who knew her greeted her tentatively, like they weren't sure if they should. Others hushed and stared, and around the sanctuary Cyd saw heads turning their way and a couple of fingers pointing. She put her hand to Dana's shoulder and squeezed it.

Dana led the way straight to their pew and plunked down with a sigh, leaving just enough room to allow Cyd the aisle seat. But before Cyd could sit, she felt a hand on her shoulder—and the butterflies took flight. Cedric.

"Cyd, I saw you come in." He looked down the pew with a worried expression. "Can I join you?"

There were more people in their pew than normal but there was still plenty of room, since the middle to back rows were filling first. Cyd nudged Dana to move down, and she and Cedric sat. He had the semicasual look of most of the guys, a pair of slacks and a polo-type shirt. She leaned over so she could hear him.

His voice was almost a whisper. "What did you tell the pastor?"

Her brows knit. "What are you talking about?"

He brought his head closer. "When I got home after, you know, I heard this message about a sermon on sex, and it blew my mind. I know you're close to Pastor Lyles. Did you say something?"

"I would never tell the pastor something like that. This sermon series has nothing to do with you." Then she raised a brow at him. "Well, maybe it does. Just wasn't premeditated."

Cedric narrowed his eyes at her. "Very funny." He leaned across, extending his hand. "I don't think we met formally. I'm Cedric London. Weren't your kids in the wedding?"

Dana shook his hand. "Yes, they were. Nice to meet you. I'm Dana Elliott."

"I remember seeing your husband yesterday. Is he here?"

Dana nodded, eyes downcast. "He's in the prayer room with the pastor and the elders."

Cyd could tell this sounded curious to Cedric, and she hoped he wouldn't press it. He'd put it together soon enough.

"Mind if I stay here beside you?" The mischief in his eyes from yesterday had returned.

Cyd shrugged. "I don't mind."

She said a silent thank-you that the butterflies had died down. This morning had been the sweetest prayer time she'd had in weeks. Dana and Scott were her focus, but as her prayers got going, it didn't take long for God to shine the light on last night. She asked for forgiveness for ignoring the warnings in her heart and crossing boundaries with a man whose intentions she knew from the beginning. She also asked God to take away the desire she felt for Cedric, to purify her heart.

"Can you believe how many people are pouring in?" Cedric craned his neck toward the back. "This is crazy."

Cyd turned to see . . . and was stunned. "Dana," she said, tapping her shoulder. "Look."

Standing in the back of the sanctuary as people moved around him was Hayes.

"You should go talk to him," Dana said.

Cyd nodded and stood. "Excuse me, Cedric."

He moved his knees aside, and Cyd slid out and down the aisle. She couldn't believe it. This was what they'd been praying for. In the midst of the heaviness of the service, this was a glowing bright spot.

Cyd saw him leave the sanctuary. She followed through the doors. "Hayes?"

He turned. "Cyd. Hi." He straightened his tie, one of only a few men under fifty wearing a suit. He held a coat over his arm.

She gave him a light hug. She liked Hayes. Always friendly and helpful, and they could get going on some rather esoteric discussions of ancient cultures. When Cyd found out he had minored in classics—and when Hayes found out she was a classics professor—an odd bond formed immediately between them.

"Excuse me," Cyd said to a woman passing by, though she was the one who'd been bumped. She moved away from the doors. "It's kind of crazy here today because we're only having one service."

"I know." Hayes cleared his throat. "I answered the phone last night and heard the message." He looked around and lowered his voice. "Isn't Scott Elliott Dana's husband?"

Cyd lowered her eyes slightly, nodding.

"I thought so."

Hayes seemed to have more on his mind but kept it inside. Through the speakers in the lobby, Cyd could hear the first notes from the band and the singing of the praise and worship team. She gestured toward the door. "I think there's still room near us."

"Oh . . . okay." He followed Cyd back through the doors.

Cyd had never seen Hayes so reserved and unsure of himself, but

Phyllis had said he hadn't been to a Sunday church service since his youth.

Lord, draw him to Yourself. Open his eyes to the truth.

More than a dozen people stood at the top of the aisle Cyd and Hayes needed to go down, an usher blocking their way. As Cyd came near, she saw the back of a blonde head, then the woman's profile, and a tight blouse with a good amount of cleavage—Heather. Big as the church was, was it mere coincidence she was trying to get down the very aisle where Scott and Dana usually sat? The last thing Dana needed was Heather drama this morning.

But looked like no need to worry. The usher wasn't budging. "I don't know how else to say it," he told the mini assembly. "This section is closed. There are plenty of seats still in the overflow area." He motioned with his hands. "Out the door to the main lobby, take the staircase or the elevator to the lower level, to your right. You'll see everything these people will see, on a large screen."

A woman looked upward. "Is the balcony full? I want to *really* see what these people will see."

The usher followed her eyes to the balcony. "It's almost full. If you're by yourself, you'll probably be able to find a seat."

Cyd watched the people begin clearing away, and Heather was forced to leave with them.

Thank You, Lord. She went forward. "Hey, Michael."

"Hey, Cyd." The usher stood aside. "I know you already had your seat. You've got room for him?"

Cyd nodded, and when she and Hayes passed, Michael blocked the way again.

Voices rang throughout the sanctuary as they walked down the aisle. Everyone was standing, singing the lyrics that flashed on the big screens up front. When Cyd came to the pew, Cedric leaned back to allow her to scoot past. Then he noticed Hayes behind her, and his body filled the space again, giving Hayes the aisle seat.

He looked at Cyd as if she'd explain who Hayes was. She stared up front, joining in the chorus.

PHYLLIS HUSTLED ACROSS the courtyard to the main building with several other parents who'd dropped their kids off in the children's ministry building. She had gone there first, after stopping at home and finding no one, to see if it was true. Had her family gone to church? At first she'd thought they were out "having fun" as Hayes had said, but she doubted he'd get them up and out so early for that—and the little dress Phyllis had faced outward in the closet for Ella was gone.

She'd poked her head into Cole's sixth-grade class and couldn't believe he was there. When she got his attention, he was all smiles, and before she could even ask, he told her that Hayes had awakened them this morning and informed them that they were going to church.

"I couldn't believe it, Mom," he said. "God answered our prayers after all."

Speechless, Phyllis left his room, but before she could ponder the news, she had another question. She stopped Barbara, a Sunday school leader, in the hall and asked, "Is it my imagination, or is the church super crowded today?" That was when she heard the second piece of news.

Now she had two reasons to hurry to the sanctuary.

She scanned faces as she moved through several pockets of people inside. She didn't see Hayes or anyone else she recognized.

Probably eleven thirty folk.

She cast a glance at the stairs she could take to the balcony or down to overflow. No telling where Hayes was, and given the traffic jam in the parking lot and the number of people hanging in the fellowship area, the sanctuary had to be filled to capacity.

She headed to her usual doors anyway. If Cyd and Dana were in the normal spot, maybe they could make room for her.

Michael stopped her. "Phyllis. I know, I know, I know. But I can't."

Her eyes implored him. "Michael, come on."

"That's what all the nine o'clock regulars been sayin': 'Michael, come on.' Like I'm supposed to make space appear out of nowhere. Can't do it. Should've gotten here earlier."

Phyllis spoke over a woman giving the announcements. "But I just got back in town." She peered out over the congregation. "And my husband's here somewhere."

She didn't know why she added the last part. This was the extent of her acquaintance with Michael the usher. He had no cause to know her history, that in all of her years attending Living Word, she'd come with her children alone.

Michael looked curious. "Your husband? The one with Cyd?"

With Cyd?

"Dark skin brother, kind of thick?" He hulked his shoulders.

"Yes." She nodded. "That's him."

"Yeah. He was standing here by himself, looking like he wasn't sure if he was staying or going, till Cyd walked back and got him." He paused. "He doesn't usually . . . I mean . . . never mind, it's none of my business."

Phyllis's expression was warm. "No. He doesn't usually come. It's his first Sunday, in fact."

Michael took a single step aside, and Phyllis mouthed a thank-you.

Several thoughts strung together and flew through her head as she started down the aisle. What was Hayes *doing* here? He'd been so adamant that he wasn't coming. What changed his mind? And what was this about a sex series and a public confession by Scott?

She couldn't believe it when she saw Hayes with her own eyes.

There he was, in one of his best suits, looking down at the program. The men's choir sang a beautiful song of praise, a favorite, one that always lifted her heart to the throne and overwhelmed her with the majesty of God.

Lord, forgive me for my lack of faith. And for allowing my heart to stray. Thank You for bringing Hayes here.

She touched his shoulder, and he looked up with obvious surprise. A chain reaction started as the women moved purses to the floor and tightened up the spaces between them. As Phyllis took the aisle seat, she gave a tiny wave to Cyd and Dana and wished she could speak to Dana privately. Something awful must have happened over the weekend. But she'd have to hear it along with everyone else.

Her eyes met Hayes's.

"What are you doing here?" they whispered simultaneously.

Phyllis went first. "I decided to take an earlier flight. What are _you_ doing here?"

He shrugged and looked down, rolled the program into a slender furl. "The church called with this message last night—"

"I heard."

"And I wanted to hear what Scott and the pastor had to say."

Phyllis frowned. "Really?"

One of the elders began to pray. She tried to focus on the words, but there was too much swirling in her mind. Hayes wanted to hear what Scott and the pastor had to say? How many times had she attempted to share with him something the pastor said and he stopped her cold? And Hayes could barely stand Scott, much as she'd hoped otherwise, given her friendship with Dana and Cyd.

The three women had formed a close bond ever since Phyllis started coming to the church. They sat together every Sunday and gathered at Cyd's for dinners once or twice a month. Dana suggested they include the husbands in their circle from time to time, but Phyllis had mixed emotions. She knew a Christian man like Scott might rub

Hayes the wrong way. But if they hit it off, Scott could also be a great influence.

Eventually Phyllis had agreed and they set it up, but Hayes came home from the dinner with an attitude. Scott was too high and mighty, he said.

Phyllis was shocked. "Scott's one of the nicest people I know," she had said. "How was he high and mighty?"

Hayes gave her a look over the top of his eyes. "What about the story about the football game?"

"All he said was he and Mark prayed before the game that day that Mark would catch a pass because he had dropped two the week before."

"Yeah, and a miracle happened. Mark caught the pass."

Phyllis put a hand to her hip. "He didn't call it a miracle. He said God answered their prayer and Mark caught three passes. How does that make Scott high and mighty?"

"He just has that air like he does everything right." Hayes lifted his head in a mocking gesture. "'I even pray with my son before football games.'" He grunted. "All I asked him was how the season was going. He could've kept the other stuff to himself."

How strange that Scott was partly the impetus for his coming.

Oh well, Lord. I guess I shouldn't try to make sense of it. You got him here, and that's all that matters.

As the elder finished his prayer, Scott rose in the front row and made his way up the steps to the podium. Everyone in the church—including Hayes—seemed to lean forward in anticipation.

Thirteen

"GOOD MORNING, EVERYONE." Scott cleared his throat. "For those who don't know me, my name is Scott Elliott."

Dana felt the whole church closing in on her as Scott began to speak, as if the crowd had one eye on Scott and the other bearing down on her to see if she would break down during his "confession." The heat from their stares made her feel like she might hyperventilate.

Scott looked down to the front row. "I want to thank Pastor Lyles for allowing me this time. He said I didn't have to do it, and I understand. In fact, I wanted to take his word and run with it . . . but I knew I . . ." He lost his voice and cleared his throat again. "I knew I had to do this."

He paused. Then he nodded slightly and set his jaw. "I had an affair. I was unfaithful to my wife."

Dana sucked in a breath and closed her eyes. Hearing him say it—in front of everybody—slammed her heart against their new reality. How many times had she heard the words *affair* and *unfaithful* in reference to other marriages and felt a dim horror at the very prospect? Now the horror was hers. It was real.

"You might be thinking, *I would never*, and I don't blame you. I thought the same thing. Thought I'd never do something like this to my wife, my marriage. But temptation comes." A single humorless chuckle eased from his mouth. "And it can come stronger than anything you've experienced, in ways you hadn't anticipated. If you're not constantly praying, constantly clinging to God, constantly avoiding improper situations, you just might fall."

Scott allowed his words to settle over the sanctuary as he surveyed the pews. The church was unnervingly quiet.

"When I came to the podium," Scott continued, "I was thinking about all the times I've stood up here on behalf of Marriages for Christ, always with Dana by my side. We'd be announcing some event—a weekend conference or a movie night. Or some might remember that bowling night when the men bragged and then threw all those gutter balls, while the women showed us up."

A few seemed relieved to break the tension with a chuckle.

"Or we'd remind you of the mentoring program for younger couples and nudge the seasoned couples to volunteer some time. Some of the guys I mentored are out there right now . . ." Scott seemed overcome by the realization and bowed his head to collect himself.

Dana hadn't considered what would happen to Scott's mentoring relationships. Those guys really looked up to him.

"So after working to support marriages," Scott continued, his voice emotion-filled, "here I stand confessing the damage I've done to my own." He paused. "But I guess one thing hasn't changed. I'm still up here in support of marriages. I'm up here because I do hope you 'never.' I hope you never stand in my shoes." He stopped to gather himself again. "My sin is ever before me. Even though I've repented, it haunts me."

He released a sigh and gripped the sides of the podium, glancing toward the section of seating on his right. His eyes fell squarely on Dana. "I love my wife more than life itself, yet I've dealt her enormous pain. I don't know how she'll ever forgive me. I don't deserve it." His voice broke, and he swiped a tear from his face. "But I'm begging God for a second chance, and I'm begging you—" His eyes swept the congregation. "Please. Cling to God. Cling to your spouses. And . . . if you have a mind to, I'm asking you to please pray for my wife and me."

Scott left the podium and returned to his seat in the front row as Pastor Lyles made his way up the steps.

PHYLLIS STARED DOWN at the Bible in her lap, tears pooling in her eyes. She'd heard it from Scott's own mouth and still couldn't believe it. A heavy sadness had come over her as he spoke. She hurt for Dana, thinking what it must have been like when she found out, what she must have been going through since. Phyllis lifted her eyes a little and glanced at her friend. Dana was holding herself, her head lowered, hand clutching a tissue. Phyllis had begun praying for her before Scott even asked.

Phyllis hurt for Scott too. His pain and remorse were palpable. He'd probably never forgive himself completely. She felt compassion for him, knowing his character . . . and knowing that he was right. Temptation comes, and it can come strong.

His confession had propelled her back to last night, to her time in the car with Rod, and the overwhelming desire she had for him to hold her and kiss her. Even this morning on the plane she'd taken pleasure in the memory, in imagining what it might have been like.

She fished a tissue from her purse. The tears that watered her cheeks were for Dana and Scott, but also for her own shame—she'd been capable of the very sin Scott had committed.

146

She leaned closer to her husband, thankful to God for guarding her in that car from making a mistake for which she, too, might never have forgiven herself.

IN ALL OF her years at Living Word, Cyd had never felt such anticipation for the pastor's sermon as she did right now. What would he say about Scott's confession? How exactly did he plan to tackle this "sex series"? And what was this new initiative mentioned in the recorded message?

Pastor Lyles stared out at them with a sober expression. He was normally charged, a light twinkling in his eyes, brimming with eagerness to get going with the message God had laid on his heart. But now he stood away from the podium, silently taking in the congregation. He'd always worn conservative colors, but today the black suit seemed chosen specifically for the occasion. Even his tie had mournful hues.

Cyd was hanging on his words before he even began.

Pastor Lyles sighed and lingered in silence a couple seconds more. "As you all know," he began finally, "we were in the second chapter of First Peter, but I felt strongly that an interruption of that series was in order so that we might address an alarming reality that is pervading our church."

The pastor talked more slowly than normal, emphasizing each word. He walked now to the podium. "You heard from brother Scott Elliott, and while his situation grieves me deeply and served to jump-start this sermon, it grieves me more to report that his is an encouraging circumstance. He has acknowledged the wrong and desires to turn from it."

He let his words settle among the crowd.

"Unfortunately, too many situations come to my attention in

which there has been a wrong committed and that wrong is defended, even dressed up and justified, and our families are being torn apart. It's time to address this problem openly, examine it in the light of God's Word."

Pastor Lyles left the podium and walked across the platform, pointing his reading glasses at the congregation. "I know what you singles are saying. 'Why did we need a joint service? Why couldn't they have started a special evening study for married couples to deal with this?'" He stopped in his tracks. "Let me tell you why. Because adultery in the church is not our biggest problem; our biggest problem is fornication. Yes, that old-fashioned word for singles who engage in sex outside of marriage."

Cyd's eyes widened. She couldn't recall ever hearing the pastor hit this subject so hard.

Cedric shifted, crossed a leg over a knee, then planted both feet on the floor again. He leaned toward Cyd. "You're *sure* you didn't talk to him?"

Pastor Lyles continued a slow walk to the opposite side of the platform. "Adultery and fornication come under a single umbrella—sexual sin. And because they are *sins*"—he spoke the word in a low, deep tone—"they dwell together under another larger umbrella—unfaithfulness."

He turned now, that spark he was known for quickening his steps to the other side. "See, you call yourselves people of God, and then you get with a certain someone and that someone looks good to you and you start taking an inch, then another inch, and the breathing gets a little heavier—"

Faint chuckles sounded around the sanctuary, and he looked out at the congregation.

"Oh, don't act embarrassed now. You know exactly what I'm talking about. Some of you were there last night—"

Cyd's heart was beating so fast she had to fold her arms to calm it down.

"—and you ended up going the mile when you shouldn't have taken the inch, and guess what all that passion bought? An unfaithful heart." He nodded slowly, sober again. "That's where I want our focus to be during this short series, even more so than the sexual sins themselves. Where are our hearts before God? What does it mean to be true to God?" Pastor Lyles returned to the podium.

"Before I begin today's specific message, I want to explain something new we're doing in conjunction with this series. To encourage accountability and interaction with the Scripture verses we'll be covering, we're forming 'Intimacy Groups' after the service. That was the main reason for the joint service, so we could get everyone established in a group at one time.

"These I-Groups will meet in private homes once a week for two weeks to discuss the sermon from the previous Sunday. And every person who signs up will receive a copy of the sermon on CD and a list of questions and discussion points to serve as a guide. To make scheduling easy, we'll forgo Wednesday night Bible study here at the church this week and next, so those who normally attend can use that time for group meetings. Groups should consist of no more than eight to ten people, so your discussions can be open and meaningful."

Cedric leaned over again. "I want to be in your group."

Cyd wouldn't even look at him.

He just doesn't get it.

"After these two weeks, you will know what God has to say about sex." He took a single step to the side of the podium and paused. "The goal is that you give your hearts fully to God . . . that you commit to be faithful."

Fourteen

THE SOLOIST SANG softly with the backing of the choir. The lights in the sanctuary were dimmed. Dana felt herself begin to tremble.

Pastor Lyles, finished now with his sermon, spoke with a voice of compassion. "We've touched on some hard truths today. We've dug into some areas that I'm sure hit home with many of you, one way or another, and you've been challenged. But I want you to understand that God doesn't expect you to meet the challenge alone. He gives grace. All you have to do is surrender." He extended his hand. "We're offering a special time right now for you to come forward and pray with one of our volunteers."

The music had to be mingling with Dana's emotions. She couldn't figure out why this sudden surge. The tears had held during Scott's confession and during the sermon, which at points struck right at the heart of her pain, but now those tears wanted out, and not in a light, dignified way. They came from someplace deep, causing her chest to heave as she struggled to rein it all in. The very thing she didn't want to happen was happening—she was breaking down in public.

Hunched over with Cyd's arm around her, Dana wanted to remain there, but something within was urging her to get up. She shut her eyes tight.

God, no. I can't walk up there like this. And anyway, the pastor already prayed for me last night.

Dana lifted her head a tad and took a peek.

Okay, definitely not, Lord. There's no one up there! Everyone would be looking at me.

She hoped the music would fade and the pastor would say the benediction, but the soft melody continued to play and the soloist continued to sing, lyrics that reached deep into Dana's soul.

The urge came stronger, and she took a couple of breaths, pushed off of her elbows, and sat up straight. She came to her feet. Everyone in the pew stared, and those in her way slanted their knees as she walked past, head bent, a tissue poised beneath her nose.

In the aisle she held herself, thankful she didn't have far to walk. There were several volunteers standing along the front, and as she searched their faces, she was relieved to see Ma Claudia. The tears fell harder. She walked straight into Claudia's open arms and immediately felt another pair of arms behind her. She tilted her head. It was Scott. And something in the moment caused her to turn and allow her husband to hold her for the first time since he'd broken her heart.

She laid her head on his chest and wept as his arms tightened around her and he whispered over and over, "I'm so sorry, sweetheart. I'm so sorry." His cheek brushed her forehead, and she felt the wetness of his own tears. Slowly her arms rose behind his back and she embraced him. She only remembered they were standing in front of thousands of people when an applause rose and rippled like a wave across the sanctuary and up into the balcony. When she looked up, people were standing on their feet, some wiping their eyes.

As she took in the response, her eyes overflowed all the more. She tucked her head back to Scott's chest, overwhelmed. She had thought people would be critical, that they would hate Scott, that the consensus would be she should leave him. That the congregation seemed to be pulling for them, cheering even, was beyond anything she could have imagined.

It confirmed something in her heart—that it really was okay to want her marriage.

As the applause waned, Dana and Scott turned back to Ma Claudia and saw Bruce there as well. The four of them bowed their heads as Bruce and Claudia took turns praying for God to heal and restore their marriage.

Scott led Dana by hand to the front row where he'd been sitting. Others had come forward for prayer, and Dana was surprised to see Phyllis among them. When the last people had returned to their seats, Pastor Lyles gave the closing prayer and benediction, then gave instructions as to where to go and how to sign up for the Intimacy Groups.

"I can't require you to join one," he said, "but I strongly encourage it. It's only two weeks, and I believe those who make the commitment will be blessed."

PHYLLIS CAME OUT of the pew and stood to the side, waiting for Dana to come up the aisle. She wanted to see her up close, hug her, let her know she was there for her. Dana and Scott were headed her way, hand in hand, but were stopped every few feet by someone else wanting to hug them.

Phyllis glanced over at Cyd, still sitting and talking with the gentleman beside her. Who was that? In the six years she'd known Cyd, she'd never seen her this engaged with a man. The two of them had whispered back and forth throughout the service, and the way his leg grazed hers a few times, there was no mistaking—a familiarity existed between them.

"You ready?" Hayes slipped on his overcoat, his body turned toward the exit.

Phyllis gave him a tentative look. She'd been trying to find a way to ask if he would join an Intimacy Group with her, but hadn't come up with the words or the courage. She'd been so hopeful when she'd first seen him, thinking his heart might be bending, if only slightly, toward God. But his demeanor throughout the service had been stiff. He hadn't uttered a single word, and the couple of times she commented on the sermon, he only pursed his lips. But he really showed himself during the applause for Dana and Scott. He only stood when most everyone else had, and even then he didn't clap. All the joy she'd felt about him being there dissipated. He was the same old Hayes.

Still, she didn't want to give up. She'd made her way to the front and briefly explained their situation to a volunteer. "Please pray for God to touch his heart," she said. "Pray that he'll continue to come . . . and that he'll join an Intimacy Group."

She was hanging on to the volunteer's prayer now as she answered Hayes. "Oh, I was waiting to talk to Dana and Cyd." She waited a beat, the stress eating her up inside. "And I figured we would all sign up for a group together." She was purposely vague as to who she hoped the "all" would include.

"All right." He stuffed his hands in his coat pockets. "I'll get the kids and meet you at home."

What do I say now? She moved closer to him, playing with the strap of her purse. "So . . . you didn't tell me what you thought about what Scott and Pastor Lyles had to say."

Hayes shrugged. "It was what I figured—Scott cheated on his wife. I'm not surprised. It's the so-called holy ones with all the skeletons in the closet. And then we had to see the big contrition act." He smirked. "Bet he got caught. He would've never owned up otherwise."

Phyllis looked at her husband, wishing she could see into his soul. Why was he so cynical? "Hayes, it was obvious Scott was sorry for what he did, whether he got caught or not. I don't believe it was an act."

Hayes looked down the aisle to where Dana and Scott were talking to an older couple. "I'm not surprised about that either. We don't believe the same way about things."

"What did you think of the pastor?"

He allowed a slight nod. "He hit the issues straight on. Who knows if he actually lives what he preaches. Probably not." He looked around at the crowd. "These churches are all about the money the people bring in."

Her tentativeness was waning, in favor of anger. "Hayes, how can you stand here and judge that man? You don't even know him. Pastor Lyles is—"

From the corner of her eye, Phyllis saw Dana walking up. She was by herself, and when Phyllis looked down the aisle, she saw that Scott was talking to a younger guy whom Phyllis knew was one of his mentees.

Phyllis walked a few feet from Hayes and met her friend. Hugging her close, she said, "Dana, I was bawling when you and Scott were up there. I can't believe what you've been through." She pulled back and looked her in the eyes. "I didn't know. I'm sorry I wasn't here."

Dana shook her head. "No need to be sorry. I'm glad you're back, though." She gave her a knowing look. "I could use a Daughters' Fellowship about now."

Phyllis nodded. That's what the three of them called their potluck dinners. They liked to chat, but they wanted to make sure they spent the bulk of their time on the deep things happening in their lives. What was God doing? How were they responding? What prayer needs did they have? Calling it a "daughters' fellowship" kept them focused on whose they were—daughters of the King. "When do you want to meet?"

"This evening, if we could."

Phyllis thought a moment. She could spend the afternoon with the kids and then be back to tuck them into bed. "Sounds good. We just have to check . . . with Cyd." Phyllis was distracted as Scott walked past her to Hayes.

She saw Scott extend his hand. "Hey, man, it's good to see you."

Hayes shook it and gave him a nod. "You too, man."

Two seconds of silence felt like sixty to Phyllis. She took a step in their direction.

"Hi, Scott." When he turned, she gave him a hug. "I know it was hard for you to do what you did today. But God used you." His eyes held such sadness that Phyllis thought she might cry again. "I'll be praying for you both."

"I appreciate that, Phyllis." He tried to smile. "You're a good friend."

Cyd had come out of the pew and said a few words to Dana as she hugged her, then went to hug Scott. When she turned to Phyllis, she leaned in close as she embraced her. "I was so excited to see Hayes here. We've got to talk."

Phyllis sighed inside. She could never share the way Hayes had behaved during the service. "Dana said she wants to do a Daughters' Fellowship this evening. Are you available?"

Cyd didn't hesitate. "Definitely."

"Good. 'Cause it looks like we have a *few* things to talk about." Phyllis cut her eyes to Cedric. "Apparently I missed a lot this weekend."

Cyd followed her gaze and frowned. "That's just Cedric."

Phyllis raised her eyebrows. "*Just*? Mm-hmm. Plan to introduce him?"

Cedric had already begun a conversation with Hayes. Cyd walked up beside them.

"Excuse me, Cedric. Someone has suggested that you haven't been properly introduced." She gave Phyllis the eye. "Dana and Scott you already know, but for Phyllis and Hayes, this is"—she thought a second—"Stephanie's husband's brother. How's that for a mouthful?" She chuckled. "Cedric London. He was the best man yesterday in the wedding."

Phyllis smiled and shook his hand. She couldn't wait to hear how they'd gone from sharing wedding duties to leg grazing in the pew. They certainly looked good together.

"Hey," Phyllis said, taking in the scene around them, "there's hardly anyone left in here."

Scott looked around. "Everyone must have moved to the sign-up tables. Do we have our group right here?"

Cedric looked at Cyd with a playfulness in his eyes. "If I can convince Ms. Sanders here. I already asked her, and she said I couldn't be in her group."

"Cedric!" Cyd swatted him on the arm with the back of her hand. "Why did you tell them that?"

The corners of Cedric's mouth turned up with a sly grin. "I need backup!"

Cyd stared at Cedric in disbelief. Phyllis and Dana stared at each other.

Scott, normally witty but obviously not in a witty mood, cleared his throat. "So, Cyd, were you thinking . . . What _were_ you thinking?"

Cyd gazed downward, shaking her head. "Never mind. Fine. We can be in the same group."

Cedric gave the others a satisfied smile.

Scott turned. "Hayes, you in, man?"

Hayes raised a hand partway. "Thanks, but no. I'm not signing up."

Phyllis's heart sank.

Scott stepped closer to him. "Can I talk to you for a second?" He gestured with his hand. "Over there?"

They walked a few feet up the aisle, and the others followed with their eyes. Phyllis was worried. Whatever Scott was saying, she was sure Hayes didn't want to hear it.

Moments later the men were back.

"We've got our group," Scott said.

Hayes put his hands back in his coat pockets. "I'm in."

Phyllis turned questioning eyes on Scott. *What in the world did you say?*

CYD STARTED UP the aisle. "I'm excited, Hayes. Maybe we can weave in a comparison of Greco-Roman views on marriage with biblical standards." She smiled at him, and Hayes gave her a small one in return.

As they neared the top of the aisle, the closest door burst open and Stephanie peered in. "Here they are, Lindell," she called behind her. She had attitude in her voice, but held the door for him nonetheless. "We were looking all over for you all."

Cyd was taken aback. "I thought you left for your honeymoon this morning."

Stephanie cut her eyes at Lindell as he came through the door. He went to talk to Cedric as Stephanie pulled Cyd aside.

"Can you believe he canceled our honeymoon? I was supposed to be on my way to the beach, and here I am in the tired Midwest. Girl, I am fit to be tied."

"What happened?"

Stephanie blew out a sigh. "Last night we were in the hotel and Lindell left the suite to get some ice and some snacks. When he came back, he saw me on the laptop and asked what I was doing." Stephanie's hand went to her hip. "I was like, 'Why are you questioning me? We're married, but I'm still my own person.' He looked on the screen and saw I was writing an e-mail. Do you know he had the audacity to ask to see it?"

Cyd couldn't believe her ears. "Stephanie, don't tell me you were e-mailing some guy."

"It was only Warren."

Cyd exhaled hard. "What did the e-mail say?"

Stephanie was hesitant. "Something like, 'I'll see you when I get back next week. I miss you.'"

"You didn't."

"It was nothing, Cyd. But Lindell got upset, said I must still be seeing Warren. We'd been arguing about him before, and Lindell had told me to stop communicating with him. When he saw that e-mail, he blew up. Said he wasn't going on a honeymoon with a woman who'd be thinking about how much she missed some other man the entire time." Stephanie looked over at Lindell. "Can you believe that?"

"Well, yeah. But what about airfare and hotel? Didn't he lose a lot of money?"

Stephanie sighed hard. "I think God had this whole thing set up against me. Lindell had treated us to first-class tickets—turns out we can use them for another trip. The hotel allowed us to cancel without penalty. And then he checked his voice mail and found out about this new series, said it was right on time."

Cyd shook her head at it all. "So why were you looking for us?"

"Lindell said he was really moved by Scott's confession—" Her demeanor changed in a snap. "Could you believe Scott would do something like that? I was shocked!"

"Okay, so Lindell was really moved . . ."

"And I think he looked up to Scott before that anyway. He said he wanted to be in his group. I told him we could probably arrange it 'cause you'd be in it, too, because of Dana, and then he said that meant Cedric would be in it, 'cause Lindell could tell he's got his sights set on you." Her eyes got big, and she grabbed Cyd's arm. "And I haven't had a chance to talk to you about that dance floor scene at the reception."

She gave Cyd the "momma look" that usually went the other direction. "Don't say I didn't warn you. I told Lindell you wouldn't date somebody like Cedric. But he said if Cedric thinks he can't have you, he'll try all the harder. The thrill is in the chase for him, and once he gets what he wants, he'll be done." She gave Cyd another look. "I'm just sayin'. Be careful."

"I think you have enough to worry about. I'll be fine." Cyd ignored the flutters inside at the reminder of the dance she shared with Cedric.

Stephanie gazed over at Cedric and Lindell. "Mm-hmm. That remains to be seen."

Fifteen

PHYLLIS SAT BACK in her chair, moving her eyes in disbelief from Cyd to Dana and back to Cyd. "You're telling me you actually *saw* Scott and this woman, I mean actually . . ."

Cyd lowered her fork and gave Phyllis a pointed look. "Yes. It was awful."

The women were gathered around Cyd's kitchen table. Potluck usually consisted of Phyllis and Dana bringing the side dishes and Cyd cooking the meat. But with the short notice, Phyllis just returning from her trip, and Dana living far short of normality, Cyd volunteered to prepare the entire meal. She said she'd keep it simple, so Phyllis and Dana were surprised to see that she'd made roast chicken, au gratin potatoes, and green beans, and even stopped to get the dinner rolls they all liked. On top of that, she'd set a table complete with flowers and candles.

Recovering from her initial shock, Phyllis took a sip of Pellegrini from a crystal water glass, another first for their dinners. "I can't imagine what happened next."

Cyd held a forkful of potatoes. "Well, I had my little encounter with Heather." She eased the food into her mouth.

"*What?*" Phyllis had lifted a piece of chicken to her mouth but put it back down. "What happened?"

Dana hadn't touched her food yet. She'd been listening as Cyd told the story, her gaze cast downward. She looked up now. "I don't think we ever talked about that part. I heard some of it, but I never got the whole story."

Cyd leaned in, visibly annoyed by it still. "I was so stunned to see her that I said, 'What are you doing here?'" She frowned and lifted her palms. "She had all this attitude, saying I wouldn't understand and rolling her eyes, then fixing her hair in the mirror like it was no big deal. Something inside me just snapped, and I told her she needed to leave."

"So, Cyd," Phyllis began tentatively, "don't you think the attitude was a cover? I'm sure deep down she knows she's wrong. Maybe she never intended for things to go that far, and once she was in over her head, she didn't know how to step out of it emotionally."

Phyllis was experiencing the same feelings she'd had after Scott's confession. She was able to put herself in Heather's shoes. Though Rod wasn't a married man, *she* was a married woman, and if she had acted on the impulses she felt, she would have been no better than Heather.

Cyd thought a moment. "I don't know if it was a cover, and I don't know what she's feeling deep down. And frankly, up until this moment I didn't care, because I had zero sympathy for her." She broke off a piece of roll and held it. "But I guess we should be praying for her too."

Awkward seconds passed as Dana stared off to the side. Cyd quickly picked up with the rest of what happened Friday, up until the point when Scott returned and she and Trish left. Dana took over from there, sharing the nature of her exchanges with Scott on Friday evening, Saturday, and this morning before church.

"But things were different this afternoon." Dana paused now, reflecting. "After everything that happened at church, we were able to have our first real conversation where I could actually look at him without feeling utter disgust." She gazed into the flame of the tall candle. "The pain and sadness were still there, but it felt like we were on the same side again, that we both wanted the same thing. I could almost believe that if we worked hard and prayed hard, we just might get back to what we had."

Cyd pushed her plate back. "Or maybe something even better."

Dana had a doubtful look. "It's hard enough trying to imagine things as they were." She stared downward and tears tickled the corners of her eyes. "I can't see us making love again, not after seeing . . ."

Phyllis reached across the table and grabbed Dana's hand. "All things are possible with God, Dana. Take it one step at a time, one day at a time. On Friday evening you could've never seen where you and Scott would be today."

Cyd jumped up and brought a box of tissues from the counter.

Dana pulled one out and held it. "That's true," she said. "I know." Her voice was a whisper. "It's just . . . it's going to be so hard. When I think about it, I get angry all over again."

Cyd stood behind her and laid a hand on her shoulder. "Father, we come before You now in the powerful name of Jesus . . ."

Phyllis got up as well and laid a hand on Dana's other shoulder, her head bowed. She loved the way Cyd launched into prayer when an issue arose. Phyllis was more apt to talk it to death.

". . . on behalf of Your daughter Dana. Lord, You see her situation and You know her pain. We thank You, Lord, for what You've already done, moving Scott to repentance, turning him back to You, using him in the service today, causing them to embrace one another. Lord, You're awesome." Cyd repeated it again in a whisper—"Lord, You're awesome."

She continued, "Lord, we're praying that You continue to walk Scott and Dana through this, that Your power would reign in their lives and in their marriage, that You cast down the images in Dana's mind from Friday and help her to heal. We know You're able, Father, and we give You the glory and praise right now. In Jesus' name. Amen."

"Amen." Phyllis pulled Dana to a stand and hugged her, rubbing her back. "God *is* awesome, Dana. I can't wait to see what He does with you and Scott. You ministered to couples in the past, but just think how He'll be able to use you once you come through this."

Cyd brought her arms around them, making it a group hug. "I hadn't even thought about that. I can definitely see God using you two that way."

Dana wiped the inside corners of her eyes. A weepy smile poked through the sadness. "I knew I needed this dinner tonight. I love you two."

"We love you too," Phyllis and Cyd chorused together. They began to rock with Dana in the middle, causing her to laugh.

"All right, you guys are getting silly, and I'm feeling better." She wiped a tear. "Let's move on. I want to rejoice with Phyllis about Hayes coming to church today."

Phyllis's spirits took a nosedive. *Hayes, church,* and *rejoice* had no business in the same sentence. She and Dana took their seats again as Cyd carried her plate and Phyllis's to the sink, then brought over the bottle of Pellegrini to refill their water glasses.

Cyd talked as she poured. "We couldn't believe our eyes when we saw him." She took her seat, telling how she went to get him and brought him to the pew. "So did it happen like you were hoping? You asked him to take the kids to church and he agreed?"

Phyllis gave a single laugh that held no humor. "Please. I asked, he said no." She shook her head. "You should've seen me when I left town. I was so disappointed."

Dana leaned in, her chin set on her hands. "So what made him change his mind?"

"That call from Living Word. He said he wanted to hear what Scott and the pastor had to say."

A look of surprise crossed Cyd's face. "Really?" She shrugged it off. "I guess when you mention sexual sin and a confession, it's bound to pique people's interest. What did he think of the service?"

Phyllis ran her finger along the rim of the glass. "I don't know." There was no way she'd say what he thought of Scott's confession. "It's hard to know what Hayes is thinking when it comes to church."

"Isn't it awesome that he agreed to be in the group?" Dana said.

"I know!" Cyd said. "What did Scott say to him?"

"Scott really humbled himself," Phyllis said. "He said the group needed a married couple who could share from a standpoint of longevity and strength and unwavering commitment to one another. He told Hayes that his input would be valuable because he was the only man among them in a marriage that fit that description."

Cyd sat back. "God is something. He knew just what Hayes needed to hear. Now he'll be at church for another week. Between the church and the group, who knows what'll happen?"

Disappointment clouded Phyllis's expression. "He won't be going to church, only to the group."

"Why?" Dana spoke softly.

Phyllis could hear herself asking Hayes the same question earlier that afternoon.

Why?

She'd been in a good mood after hanging out with him and the kids, and when they'd gotten a moment alone, she'd asked him what Scott had said . . . and dared to express enthusiasm that they'd be going to church together. He'd quickly disabused her of that notion.

She breathed a heavy sigh. "He said he didn't care about the sermons. He's only participating in the way Scott asked him to, to provide a certain viewpoint on marriage."

Cyd sat up, hearing her friend's frustration. "But this is such a blessing, Phyl. Think about it. He was in church today. He'll be in the group on Wednesday. That's more involvement than he's had in six years." She folded her arms on the table. "What did you just tell Dana? One day at a time, one step at a time? And I heard you say something else—with God all things are possible. I know it's hard because you're dealing with it firsthand, but from where I'm sitting, this is exciting. He may not want to hear the sermon, but he'll hear us talking about it." She tilted her head to coax her. "Come on, now. Don't you see God?"

The fact that she couldn't made Phyllis want to cry. "I can't count the number of times I *thought* I saw God working. And every time I end up disappointed." She stared downward but could see Dana's eyes fixed on her.

Dana laid a hand on top of Phyllis's. "You're weary."

Her observation caused the tears to roll. Phyllis's voice broke. "Very."

"I'll take a cue from Cyd," Dana said, rising and moving behind Phyllis.

She placed both hands on Phyllis's shoulders as Cyd came around and put a hand to her arm. They both bowed their heads.

"Lord God," Dana began, "You are loving and You are merciful, and, Lord, we've prayed around this table many times for Hayes. We lift him up again, praying that Your love and mercy would engulf him. Take away his heart of stone and give him a heart of flesh. Open his eyes to the truth, to the glorious truth that Jesus died for him, that he might live. Cause him to bow the knee and acknowledge Jesus as his Lord and Savior."

Dana squeezed Phyllis's shoulders. "And, Lord, as we wait on Hayes's deliverance, I pray that You fill Phyllis with strength and patience, joy and peace. Cause her to mount up with wings like an eagle and soar with great faith, knowing that You are sovereign and nothing is too hard for You. We thank You, Lord. We thank You, in Jesus' name."

Understanding dawned in Dana's eyes. "That's the bottom line, isn't it? Phyllis said it before, but it's just now taking hold in my heart. Nothing is too hard for God. Nothing."

Cyd walked back around the table to her seat. "Yes, ma'am. That's the bottom line."

Phyllis looked up with grateful eyes at Dana. "Thanks, Dana. I needed that. I need to keep my focus on God and not on the way things look with Hayes. In fact, I'm tired of talking about Hayes." She turned to Cyd. "I'm ready to find out the deal with Cyd and Cedric."

CYD TOSSED HER hand dismissively. "There is no _deal_ with me and Cedric."

Dana gave her the eye as she carried her plate to the microwave. "Yeah, I was wondering too. I might've been going through a tough time at the service, but don't think I didn't notice all the whispering you two were doing." She punched a couple of buttons and the microwave fan sounded. "How did you get to be so close so fast?"

"_Close_?" Cyd turned in her seat and looked at Dana. "Okay. I need to nip this because you two have a totally wrong impression. There is absolutely nothing between Cedric and me. He's nowhere near my type." She crossed her legs. "I'll tell you like Stephanie told me. He's a ladies' man."

Cyd pointed at Dana. "You weren't at the rehearsal, but he had a date with him and was flirting with me anyway. Then on Saturday—"

Cyd realized she was stuck. She didn't want to share everything that happened.

"Saturday . . ." Phyllis made a "continue on" gesture.

Cyd had no choice. "When I got there, he had this rose for me—"

Phyllis gasped, staring at the middle of the table. "*Lavender* roses?"

"Well . . . that was later in the evening, when he gave me those."

"What?" Dana carried her steaming hot plate back to the table. "I thought you bought these roses as a special touch for our dinner. *Cedric* gave you these? You saw him last night, after the reception?"

Cyd put her elbows on the table and gave Dana a look. "You're way ahead of me. I'm at the church, Saturday morning. Can I tell the story?" She had no desire to relate the evening's events any sooner than she had to.

"I'm all ears." Dana ate her first bite.

"So he gave me the rose, telling me . . ." She stopped again, realizing she had to mention her birthday, which neither of them had yet remembered. She didn't want them to feel bad, but it was integral to the story. "Telling me it was for my birthday."

Phyllis gasped again.

"Oh. My. Goodness." Dana fell back in her chair and put a hand over her eyes. "I cannot believe this." She peeked at Cyd through her hands. "I cannot believe I forgot your fortieth birthday."

"I think you might have had some other things on your mind." Cyd shook her head. "Don't give it another thought."

"But still," Dana said. "I haven't forgotten your birthday in all these years. And this was the big one."

Phyllis expelled a rueful sigh. "I'm so mad at myself. I knew you'd be busy with the wedding, so I had planned to call you last evening. I just plain forgot."

"You two weren't the only ones." Cyd gave a slight chuckle. "With all the wedding activity, my parents even forgot. But they called before church this morning, begging forgiveness."

Dana looked incredulous. "Oh, Cyd. I feel even worse now. You must have felt nobody cared."

"Except Cedric," Phyllis added, playfulness in her voice. "Did he say why he chose lavender?"

Cyd pursed her lips. "Girl, he's good. He said it symbolizes enchantment, and he was enchanted with me."

Phyllis and Dana stared at her, wide-eyed.

Dana spoke first. "He didn't."

"I told you," Cyd said.

"What happened after he gave you the rose?" Dana asked.

"He said he wanted to take me out that night to celebrate my birthday, and I tried to blow him off. But then there was the dance at the reception." A shiver came from nowhere, and Cyd held her arms.

Dana and Phyllis exchanged a glance.

"What dance?" Dana asked.

Reese woke up from her nap beside the table and lifted her head, as if she wanted to hear the story too.

Cyd took a sip of water as the butterflies danced in remembrance. She slowly lowered her glass. "You had already left. The DJ called the best man and maid of honor to the floor and they played 'U Send Me Swingin'.'"

Dana's eyes lifted. "Uh-oh. Your song."

"So . . . you know . . . we did this little step dance to it, and some people kind of gathered around."

"No way." Dana's mouth hung open.

"And when I was about to sit down, 'So Fine' came on—"

Phyllis cupped her face in her hands. "Oh boy."

"—and Cedric pulled me into a slow dance."

Phyllis sat back and crossed her arms. "All righty, then. And next thing you know, Mr. Ladies' Man is over here with a _bouquet_ of lavender roses."

Cyd sighed. "It was a mistake, and I knew it was a mistake, but he just . . ." Cyd hated to admit it. "He has this effect on me."

"So . . ." Dana looked as if she wasn't sure if she should finish. "What happened when he was over here?"

"Well, we went to dinner, came back inside for cake, then I walked him to the door . . ." Cyd knew she had to tell it all to keep herself accountable, but her tongue was thickening by the second. "And we kissed . . . sort of, I guess, passionately, and he said he wanted to, you know."

Cyd had never seen her friends' eyes wider.

"On the *first date*?" Dana said.

Cyd looked at her. "Dear, you've been in the married world so long I guess you're a little out of touch. That's how it is out there. I knew I had no business having that man in my house last night, especially when I knew what he was about. I had to tell him I'm not interested in sex outside of marriage."

"I guess he's fine with that," Phyllis said, "since he still wants to be around you, and even wants to be in the group with you."

"Um, Phyl," Cyd replied, patting Phyllis's hand with feigned sympathy, "sorry, but you're out of touch too, dear. He's not fine with it. This is part of his game." Cyd sat back and sighed at what she'd gotten herself into. "I should've stood firm about not being in the same group with him. I could tell by the way he kept brushing his knee against mine and whispering in my ear that his intentions were still the same."

"Well . . ." Phyllis had an amused expression. "Looks like we'll have one of the more interesting I-Groups. Hayes had to have his arm twisted, Cedric had to twist Cyd's—"

"And Lindell had to twist Stephanie's." Cyd half chuckled. "Yeah. I'd say it'll be more than interesting."

One thing was certain—it was going to take lots more prayer for strength if she wanted to feel nothing around him.

Sixteen

THE DOORBELL RANG Wednesday night as Cyd moved a second folding chair into position. Reese raced out of the family room toward the door, barking as if she had a fierceness to back it up. Cyd did a mental count, making sure there was enough seating for eight, and glanced at her watch. Six forty-five. The meeting was scheduled for seven.

Who's here so ear—?

The bell sounded again, and Cyd knew. She grabbed the furniture polish and dust rag from the coffee table and carried them into the kitchen, taking her sweet time. She should have known Cedric would come early. He had called last night offering to help set up, and she told him she could handle it. Then he'd asked if he could help clean up. She assured him there wouldn't be a need—they weren't having a party.

She didn't have to guess the motive behind his overtures. He wanted to be alone with her—the very thing *she* wanted to avoid. She couldn't trust that he would keep his distance. Even the look in his eyes dripped seduction. She needed to be vigilant about toeing the line . . . since she wasn't completely confident that she could trust even herself.

Reese darted back and forth between the door and Cyd, making sure Cyd understood they had a visitor. The third ring sounded as she tucked the cleaning supplies behind a cabinet door.

"Down, Reese!" The puppy had taken a running jump at her, impatient in her desire to know who was out there. Her paws moved with excitement beside Cyd as she made her way to the door and opened it. "Hi."

"I thought I had the wrong night for a minute." Cedric locked her in his gaze.

Cyd turned hers aside and stepped back for him to come in. "Right night, wrong time."

Cedric walked in and pushed the door closed. "It starts at seven, right?"

Reese leaped her little body clear off the ground and tagged him on the chest.

"Whoa! You've got serious vertical." He stooped down, and Reese lay on her side for a rub.

Cyd stared down at them. "Right. Seven. It's six forty-five."

Cedric looked up, the angle of his stare arresting. "I'm right on time, then. I wanted to talk to you before everybody got here."

Cyd's stomach did a little flip. "About?"

Cedric stood and took off his jacket, and her stomach did a bigger flip. It was the first time she'd seen him in a pair of jeans and short sleeves. She could tell he had a nicely built body in the slacks he'd worn. Now it was confirmed. He had well-appointed muscles, firm tone. He motioned toward the living room. "Can we sit down?"

She took his jacket and laid it over the arm of the living room chair but kept moving. "I don't have time, Cedric. I still have some things to do before everybody gets here."

"Can we talk afterward?"

"Now is fine," she was quick to say. "We'll just have to talk as I finish up." She led the way to the kitchen.

"I'm used to seeing you in skirts and dresses. You look good in those jeans."

She felt her face grow hot, self-conscious, as he followed behind. "Thanks."

They'd been thinking the same thing about each other. Leave it to Cedric to actually say it.

When they entered the kitchen, she noticed his hands. "You forgot your Bible?"

"Oh. I don't really have a Bible. I always use the one in the pew." He added, "I can look off of yours, right?"

"No need. I've got extra Bibles." She pulled a large jug of spring-water from the refrigerator. "What did you want to talk about?"

Cedric leaned against a counter a few feet away, and Reese flopped down at his feet. He sighed. "I wanted to apologize for Saturday night. I know things moved too fast, or . . . not like you wanted them to."

Cyd lifted a pitcher from the drying rack by the sink. "You don't have to apologize. I was in the moment just like you."

"But I tried to push it, and as a result, I can tell you've pulled back." He paused. "If I hadn't done that, maybe we would've gone out again by now."

Cyd stopped what she was doing and looked at him. "Cedric, that's actually not true. I was hesitant about going out with you from the beginning, because of your girlfriend. Remember?"

She watched his head tip to a nod. "And can I just be plain?" She didn't wait for an answer. "The girlfriend wasn't the main reason I was hesitant. I could tell we weren't compatible."

He looked at her more intently. "What do you mean?"

The clock on the microwave told her she had five minutes. She began pouring the springwater into the pitcher. "You're out here dating whoever and how-many-ever you can, even sleeping with them."

She stopped pouring, used a dishrag to wipe up water that sloshed over the side, and resumed. "I'm not trying to be rude"—she glanced over at him—"but you brought it up, and I want you to understand where I'm coming from. If I date someone, I have to know that we both love the Lord and desire to honor Him in our relationship."

Cedric came up beside her. "But I know you felt something when we were together."

His voice, low and nearing a whisper, stirred a flutter. Their eyes connected, and her mind flashed to swaying with him on the dance floor . . . and kissing him. There was no doubt she was drawn to him, and if he kept staring at her like this . . .

She moved around him, pulling a large wooden tray from a lower cabinet. "Of course I felt something. You're a handsome man, fun to be with. And you have a way on the dance floor." She gave him a slight smile as she placed eight glasses and some coasters on the tray. "But I can't follow feelings, Cedric. I have to let my mind lead, and my knowledge of what's right."

Cyd carried the pitcher and an ice bucket to the "family room," which had been a garage before the prior owner converted it. Cedric followed with the tray in silence. When they'd set the things down on the coffee table and she'd arranged the tray, she stood and looked at him.

"Can I ask you something?"

"Anything."

"Do you think you'd be here right now for a Bible study if we had slept together Saturday night? Or would that 'enchanted' feeling be gone and you would have moved on?"

He stared at her again for long seconds and looked away when the doorbell rang. Cyd let the question hang between them as she gated Reese in the kitchen and went to the door.

Cedric stood behind her as she opened it.

"Hey, you two." Cyd hugged Dana and Scott as they entered, and Cedric shook their hands.

Dana still wasn't herself—much more subdued than normal, without the high-wattage smile—but her eyes held a peace. Hayes and Phyllis were coming up the walk, so Cyd waited at the door to greet them too.

"Who'd you get to watch the kids?" Cyd asked, doling out hugs.

"One of your grad students." Phyllis looked relaxed and cute in a pair of jeans and a light jacket. "Lisa. Remember, you gave us her name a few months ago?"

"We really like her," Hayes added, shrugging off his jacket. "She's good with the kids."

"Oh, good," Cyd said, taking their jackets and draping them over a chair. "She's a good student too."

After a few moments of light conversation, Cyd ushered everybody toward the family room.

Hayes glanced in the direction of the kitchen, where Reese was jumping frantically, trying to clear the gate. "I've got to greet my little friend. We bonded on Saturday."

"I haven't even seen the puppy yet," Scott said.

Cyd got a kick out of watching the two men love on Reese, reaching over the gate and petting her wavy fur. As soon as they stopped and walked away, Reese was frantic again, yelping for them to return.

They settled into their seats just as the doorbell sounded again. Cyd was glad to see Stephanie and Lindell. Though her sister would've rather been on an island, in the long run this study could be good for her if she let it.

"Hey, it's my new brother." Cyd embraced him. "How are you?"

Lindell smiled. "I'm good, sis." He glanced at Stephanie. "And it's good to be here."

Cyd could tell Stephanie was still nursing an attitude. She noticed a wrapped gift in her hand. "What's that?" She hugged her before Stephanie could answer.

"Momma told me we'd forgotten your birthday, and I felt bad. Lindell too. We got you this." Stephanie handed it to her.

Cyd's eyes lit up. "Really? Let me open it real quick."

Cedric came up from behind and gave his brother and Stephanie hearty hugs.

Cyd tore the paper off and lifted the lid on a box. Inside was a gift certificate to one of her favorite restaurants. "Thank you! I love this place."

Stephanie added her coat to the pile. "I hope you make it a romantic dinner for two." She added, a thumb aimed at Cedric, "As long as it's not with him."

Cedric raised his eyes in mock offense. "Lindell, man, why are these sisters against me? I'm a nice guy."

Lindell headed to the family room. "I'm keeping my mouth shut."

When everyone was seated, Bibles in their laps—except for Hayes—Cyd passed out the discussion questions. They all looked at each other.

After a few moments, Cyd spoke up. "I'm hosting, but I didn't plan to facilitate. I guess we should've discussed this part in advance."

Cyd, Dana, and Phyllis exchanged quick glances, and Cyd knew they were thinking the same thing. This was the perfect venue for Scott to lead, but given all that had happened, he probably didn't feel right stepping into that role.

Seconds ticked by. Finally Lindell sat forward. "I don't know much about the Bible, but if all I have to do is read the questions and move the discussion forward, I guess I can handle that."

"Thanks, Lindell," Cyd said. "Can you start us off in prayer?"

Lindell, in a folding chair beside Stephanie's overstuffed chair, turned to Scott with a sheepish look. "You mind, man?"

"Sure, Lindell. I'll pray," Scott said. He bowed his head. "Father, You are holy; You are righteous; You are God. And we thank You for the awesome privilege of coming before Your throne. We ask, Lord, that You lead our discussion and renew our minds. If we've been operating in our own way, teach us Your way. If we've been forging our own path, show us Your path. Show Yourself strong in this room tonight. We ask it in Christ's name."

Lindell lifted his sheet of paper and looked around. "I guess we can get started." It was more a question than a statement. "Number one: 'Why is marriage such an important institution?'" Lindell sat back, waiting for someone to answer.

Phyllis, on the love seat with Hayes, crossed her legs. "Hmm . . . this isn't a quiz with one right answer, is it?" She chuckled. "I'll say because it's a covenant, a binding promise."

Lindell leaned forward, his elbows on his thighs, nodding. He looked at the others, waiting for follow-up.

"I love how Pastor Lyles put it." Cyd sat straighter. "About how God performed the first marriage ceremony between Adam and Eve. I had never thought about it like that." She added, "When you think about it, marriage is all over the Bible."

"Well . . ." Dana paused, as if second-guessing whether she should continue. Scott reached for her hand. They sat beside one another on the sofa, with Cyd on the other end. "I think it's interesting that God called Himself Israel's husband. And when Israel disobeyed, He used words like _unfaithful_ and _adultery_ to describe it. He was truly hurt, like . . . any spouse would be."

"I'll tell you what blew me away." Lindell skimmed his notes. "The part about husbands loving their wives the way Christ loves the church. I was like, 'Whoa!'" Lindell looked around as people nodded.

When no one spoke, he said, "Okay, next question." He sounded more assured now. "How do *you* view marriage?" He looked up. "Can I go first on that one?"

Everybody chuckled.

Lindell chuckled, too, but with an earnestness in his eyes. "I can definitely say that when I got married just four days ago, I didn't view marriage the way I do now. Now it seems like it's so . . . I don't know . . . a high calling. It's almost scary, like you don't want to mess up."

Lindell realized what he'd said and glanced over at Scott. Scott nodded in agreement to let him know it was okay.

No one spoke for a few seconds, then Hayes cleared his throat. "I want to comment on this question. I always viewed marriage as a high calling, but not because of anything biblical. To me, it's a high calling because it's bringing together two lives, and then children come into the fold, and I have a duty to make sure I treat those lives with the utmost respect and honor. As a man, there's no higher calling than for me to love and protect my wife." He looked at Phyllis, then shot a pointed glance over at Scott. "I couldn't imagine betraying her."

"Well . . ." Lindell raised his paper quickly. "Let's move on to the next question. 'What is the path to adultery? Where does it start and how does it build?'"

Silence reigned.

After a few long seconds, Scott quietly turned the pages of his Bible. When he looked up finally, he seemed surprised to see that they were all looking at him.

"I think this tells us where it starts," he said. He looked back at the page. "When the serpent tempted Eve, it says she *saw* that the forbidden tree was good for food and a delight to the eyes, that it was desirable. That was when she took it and ate." Scott paused. "As long as she kept clear of that forbidden fruit, she was fine. But when she looked too long at it . . ."

"That's an excellent point, Scott." Cyd was reading over the passage. "So true—keep away from whatever's forbidden."

"_As in_, we shouldn't be sending e-mails to members of the opposite sex, telling them we miss them?" Lindell directed the question to Scott, and Stephanie cut her eyes at him. "And we shouldn't be making plans to hook up with them?"

"From personal experience," Scott said, "no, we definitely shouldn't be doing those things. It doesn't lead anywhere good."

Hayes sat forward. "I don't see why we had to go to Genesis to understand that we have no business handling forbidden fruit. It's common sense. If the woman isn't your wife, you shouldn't be in her face. You don't need to be calling her, going to lunch, meeting here and there. I've always made it a policy not to even meet with a woman alone in my office with the door closed."

Hayes's words hung in the air, along with the feeling that no one knew what to say after that.

"O-kay," Lindell said, "sounds like we're already answering this next question, 'How can the sin of adultery be avoided?' We've gotten some practical advice—keep away from forbidden fruit, make sure we avoid situations where we're alone with someone of the opposite sex." He looked at no one in particular. "And no suggestive notes, e-mails, and the like. Anyone like to add anything more?"

"Ultimately," Scott began, "it takes the power of Christ in our lives to avoid sexual sin. That's why He came and died for—"

"Man, that's a bunch of bull."

Phyllis, who had looked downward the other times Hayes commented, now snapped her head his way, eyes full of shock.

Hayes focused like a laser beam on Scott. "You're going to sit here and tell me it takes the power of Christ to avoid sexual sin, when you call yourself a Christian and you slept with another woman?" His jaw was firm, his eyes hard. "And here I am, an 'unbeliever'"—he smirked as he curled his fingers into quotes—"and I've avoided sexual sin quite well. It doesn't take the power of Christ. It takes loving your wife enough to keep your pants up around other women."

"Hayes!" Phyllis stood, her Bible and paper falling to the floor. Stephanie, closest to her, tipped over and picked them up.

"I can't believe you!" Phyllis said.

Hayes came to his feet. "I can't believe *him*." He flipped his hand toward Scott. "He's got a lot of nerve peddling this Jesus talk after what he did."

Lindell was up now, taking a couple of steps toward Hayes. "With all due respect, Hayes, Scott was just sharing the truth about—"

"The truth." Hayes's voice was calmer now as he stared at Lindell, then glanced around the room. "You know what the truth is? The truth is that you're all in a cult. I thought I could come tonight and infuse some reality into the discussion, but you all can't get beyond Jesus and the Bible." He shook his head. "It might make you feel good to believe all that, but don't call it *truth*. There's nothing true about it." He looked around the room. "I'm out of here."

Cyd didn't know whether to run after Hayes or comfort Phyllis, who was in tears in the middle of the floor. When Cyd saw Dana and Stephanie gathered to her side, she rushed to the foyer, where Hayes was lifting his leather jacket from the chair.

"Hayes." When he turned, she didn't know what to say. "Can we talk? I just wish you wouldn't leave like this."

"I don't have anything else to say." He slipped his jacket on and reached for the door handle, then turned partway. "You and I have always gotten along, Cyd, and I'm sure I offended you. I'm sorry, but I had to say what I felt. I understand if you don't want anything to do with me."

Cyd stepped closer. "We're still friends as far as I'm concerned."

Hayes looked down and turned back to the door. "Tell Phyllis I'll see her at home."

Cyd watched Hayes take the walkway and turn right onto the

sidewalk, leaving Phyllis the car. She felt an incredible sadness . . . for Phyllis, because of the hope she'd had for the evening—hope Cyd had talked her into . . . for Scott, because of Hayes's biting comments . . . and for Hayes. Mostly for Hayes. She said a prayer for him as she closed the door.

Cyd returned to the family room, where Phyllis was sitting on the sofa between Dana and Stephanie, distraught, the three of them in whispered conversation. Lindell, Scott, and Cedric were huddled off to the side.

Cedric came to her when he saw her. "You need me to do anything?"

Cyd answered with a slight shake of the head. "How's Scott?"

"He's better than I would be." He looked over at him. "He wanted to pray for the guy. We just finished when you came in."

Cyd was about to comment when she saw Phyllis rise and grab her things. She went to her.

"Phyl, I was thinking we could talk for a while. Maybe the women could all stay, and I'll give Dana and Stephanie a ride home."

Dana and Stephanie were nodding, but Phyllis kept moving.

"I can't, Cyd." She wiped a tear as the women followed her to the foyer. "I just want to be alone. I need to think or . . . I don't know. I just need to be alone."

Cyd put an arm around her shoulder and hugged her. "Hayes said he would see you at home."

Phyllis took her jacket, opened the door, and shut it behind her.

Seventeen

PHYLLIS STARTED THE car and shifted it into gear. She didn't know where she was going as she wheeled down the street. All she knew was she wasn't going home. She kept straight at the stop sign rather than turn right toward her house and continued to Wydown Boulevard. There she made a right and drove about a mile, past the stately old homes and majestic trees she always admired along this stretch, especially this time of year when the leaves were brilliant with reds and oranges and yellows. She couldn't appreciate them in the dark, but even if it were light it wouldn't have mattered. She couldn't appreciate anything beautiful right now, not with this heavy cloud hovering over her world.

When Wydown ended at Skinker Boulevard, across from Forest Park, she paused on the quiet street, pulling a tissue from her purse and wiping her nose. She often walked to Forest Park for exercise, taking different trails, enjoying the scenery and the activity of golfers, bikers, and other walkers. She needed that wide-open space right now, a space bigger than her cares. She needed to gaze into a limitless sky, just to focus on something beyond her own corner of the world, to know that this wasn't all there was. Just to breathe.

It was too late to walk in the park by herself, but she turned left and headed inside anyway. She could do her gazing from the car. She drove slowly until she came to the water basin. Hardly anyone was around, only a few parked cars and a handful of couples walking their dogs. She parked where she could see the water and sat back in the seat, Hayes's voice engulfing her. _"That's a bunch of bull . . . You're all in a cult."_

She would've been upset if he'd said it in the privacy of their home. That he'd said it in the group—that and everything else that came out of his mouth—was more than she could bear. How could he have been so rude? Didn't he know these were her friends? All that talk about treating his wife with utmost respect. What about treating _people_ with basic respect? How about not rubbing Scott's nose in his affair every chance he got?

Through tears, she watched a blurred vision of a man jogging by with a big black dog. She closed her eyes and hung her head as emotion flowed at will. How could she have thought it would be a good thing to have Hayes come to the group? Why did she get her hopes up? She _knew_ better. Now things were worse than they'd ever been. His _words_ were worse than they'd ever been. Never mind that he had no respect for her friends. He had no respect for God. Where did he get the gumption to say that the Bible—and even Jesus—was basically nothing? Nothing but the makings of a cult.

She let the wave of tears pass and stared out at the darkened sky, a sad realization washing over her. It was true—Hayes might never believe. Might never know what it was to walk in sweet fellowship with God . . . which meant _they_ might never know the blessing of marriage as God intended, where they would be one with one another and one with Him. Their love and their lives would always be missing that vital element, that Spirit-connection that comes only from above. They would live at a level that was fine for Hayes but could never be enough for Phyllis. Not when she knew there was so much more.

She was meditating on it, facing it as a very real possibility, telling herself to stop building hope upon hope that Hayes would change—when Rod popped into her mind. Her heart rate accelerated, and everything tilted.

Rod.

Suddenly she was back in Jasper's again, at the tailgate, the old-school party. In the car. She knew she shouldn't go there, but her spirits took an upturn just thinking about going there. The images skirted the edges of her mind, shadows of the two of them talking, his profile, the way he held his head. She heard his voice now, that thickness, like a soft caress . . . and those eyes.

She took a breath and zapped herself out of the weekend . . . which only took her back to tonight and all the heartache associated with it, and thoughts of the future and all the heartache associated with that. Before she knew it, she was reaching for her purse, just to see. She swiped a tear and brought it into her lap, fumbled through it. There it was, wedged near the bottom. She opened the piece of paper and stared at his handwriting, the numbers he'd written. Then she looked at the clock on the dash. Close to nine thirty his time. Not too late. Her stomach tied in knots of warning and exhilaration as she contemplated dialing. He was that close, a few seconds away. What would he be doing? What was his evening routine? How would he receive her call?

She held the paper as a couple walked past her car. What would she even say? As she thought about it, she really didn't know him well, wouldn't know how to begin a conversation. The whole thing would be awkward. He probably thought she wouldn't actually call. She was married, after all.

A sigh released itself. Yes, she was married. She couldn't call Rod. *Shouldn't* call Rod.

And yet . . . what would it hurt? It was just a phone call. What was wrong with talking on the phone once in a while, seeing how the other was doing? That was it. She would say she was just calling to say hi, see how he was doing. Simple. No big deal.

She took her cell phone from her purse and looked at the paper again, deciding to try his landline first. With each push of a button, her finger twitched. She brought the phone to her ear and listened, her insides growing jumpier with each ring. Had she decided what she was going to say first?

"Hey, Phyl."

His voice, soft and welcoming, was soothing to her soul. Had he called her _Phyl_ before? She settled into her seat, glad caller ID had broken the ice. "Hey, Rod. Is this a bad time?"

"Not at all. What's going on? Must be a blue moon out." She could hear the smile in his voice.

"I'm, um . . ."

Sitting in my car, in a park, too upset to go home.

". . . on my way home from a friend's house. You crossed my mind, so I thought I'd give you a quick call. What are you up to?"

"We got home from church about an hour ago, got the baths going, did the bedtime routines. Now the girls are asleep and I was just sitting down catching a breath, about to grade some papers." He paused. "What about you? You said you were at a friend's house?"

Phyllis sat up, trying to still herself. How could this man's voice stir such a sensation inside? "Normally I would've gone to church tonight, too, but Pastor Lyles started a special series and wanted us to meet in discussion groups to talk about it."

"A special series? Must be deep if he's got you meeting like that to discuss it. What's it about?"

She felt awkward saying it. "This first sermon was on adultery."

"Hmm. Bet that discussion was interesting."

"Yeah, you could say that." Last thing Phyllis wanted to talk about was the meeting. "So what were you all studying?"

Rod chuckled. "My pastor's been giving the men a rough time. He's on a series called How to Be a Real Man, and he's hitting it hard on Sunday morning *and* Wednesday evening."

"So what's a real man?" Phyllis was smiling inside, enjoying his company.

"A real man is a man who knows and fears the Lord." Rod was having fun, trying to sound like his pastor. "A real man is the spiritual head of his home and leads his wife and children in the ways of the Lord." He laughed at himself. "Seriously, though, it's been good. Challenging."

Wonder what Hayes would say about that series.

"So what's been the most challenging for you?"

"Hmm," he said, turning thoughtful. "Probably the reminder of how much I need God. It's like, I know it, it's there, but in the day-to-day I can get caught up in everything I have to do, and I'm not praying like I should. I can get lax."

It was almost comical. She'd easily take one of Rod's lax days over one of Hayes's so-called best. "I know what you mean," she said. "Sometimes life can throw you off track."

"Everything okay, Phyllis?" Rod's tone took on a softness. "You sound kind of down."

"Oh, I'm fine. Listen . . ." Talking to him was making her sadder now, making her long for what she couldn't have. "I won't hold you. I know you've got work to do."

"Hey."

"What?"

"I'm glad you called."

If she weren't crying she might have smiled. "Me too. Take care, Rod."

"Bye, Phyl."

She held the phone to her chest, replaying the conversation, recording his voice, wishing she could transport herself eight hundred miles east. She would much rather go there than the one mile home to her husband.

Eighteen

LATE SATURDAY NIGHT Dana opened the garage door and entered the kitchen, amused by the sight. Scott stood before a sink full of bubbles, arms deep inside, working a dishcloth beneath. His sweatshirt sleeves were pushed all the way up, and he looked like he wanted to turn around to greet her but was afraid he might lose the rhythm of what he was doing. Reminded her of the carefree days when scenes like this would turn her silly with laughter. At least she was able to smile.

"Hey, babe," he called over his shoulder.

She pushed the door closed. "You didn't have to do the dishes."

"I wanted to." He peered back at her finally as he rinsed a plate and put it in the dish rack. "I was trying to have everything done and put away by the time you got home so we could relax."

Dana's stomach tightened. "Relax" had always been their code word for sexual intimacy. She dropped her purse on the kitchen table, next to a pizza box. "I see who won the dinner debate."

"Can you believe it?" he said, bubbles threatening to spill over as the water continued running. "You saw what I had on the menu—oven-fried chicken fingers, fried potato wedges, a salad. And they insist on pizza!" He threw his hands up and bubbles flew into the air.

"Hon." She pointed to the water trickling down the side.

"Oh. Thanks." He moved the spout to the second sink.

She slipped off her coat and laid it on the back of a chair, eyeing the back of her husband. He was as handsome to her now as when they first started dating, even in a simple Cardinals sweatshirt and athletic pants. In all their years together, her attraction to Scott—sexy dark hair, toned body—had never waned. And yet, because of his indiscretion, she couldn't view him the same. "Are they asleep?"

"I think so. We watched a movie, played hide-and-seek and a million games of UNO, and they still complained when I said they had to go to bed so they could be up for church tomorrow—you know the routine." He glanced back at her. "So did you all have a good time?"

Dana pulled out a chair at the table and took a seat. "We did. The Alvin Ailey Dancers were awesome, and I didn't think I'd like that fondue place Cyd wanted to try, but it was really good. We almost missed the start of the show because it takes so long to move through the courses."

Scott put the last plate in the rack and let the water drain from the sink. "Glad you all got a chance to celebrate Cyd's fortieth." He rinsed and wrung out the dishrag, placing it between the double sink. "I'll put the dishes away later."

Scott wiped his hands on his sweatshirt and pulled her up by the hand, flicking the lights off as he led her upstairs. As they passed the kids' rooms, Dana poked her head in and confirmed that they were asleep. She'd come back and tuck them in before she went to bed.

Scott went straight to his closet and kicked off his shoes. "How was Phyllis?"

Dana removed her heels and sat near the edge of the bed, one leg tucked underneath. "She put on a good face tonight, but she's hurting. When we asked about Hayes, she said she didn't want to talk about it. I've never seen her so down that she didn't want to talk."

Scott sighed, walking over to her. "I've been praying a lot for Hayes, but I guess I need to pray as much for Phyllis. It's got to be hard. Their whole situation is hard." He paused. "Just like ours."

Scott pulled Dana to her feet and slipped his arms around her waist. "But I'm so thankful it's not too hard for God. So thankful we're still together." He pecked her cheek, then her lips, then touched the sides of her face as he took the kiss deeper.

Dana's skin began to crawl. "I can't, Scott. Not yet." She turned her face and moved away.

Scott exhaled hard. "I'm sorry, Dana. I should've known you weren't ready." He plopped down on the bed and ran his fingers through his hair. "I *hate* what I did to us." Hunched over, he gazed off into the distance.

Dana joined him and they sat, silent, lost in thought. She hated what he'd done to them, too, but she could almost believe it hurt him more than it hurt her. He had to live with the guilt as well as the consequences, consequences like this one—she could barely stand for him to touch her.

Holding hands was fine, but she couldn't bear physical contact that hinted at more. Suddenly she'd see Heather in his arms— Heather's *taut, shapely body* in his arms. Surely Scott had compared them . . . marveled at Heather's, wondered why Dana had let hers go.

She glanced down at her black slacks, three sizes larger than when she was a bride. How could she undress in front of him now? How could she not feel the pain of knowing he'd size her up against Heather— subconsciously or not—and find her lacking? All of this *before* the actual lovemaking, which held its own painful images and emotions.

She looked at Scott from the corner of her eye. Right now, he

understood her hesitancy, but what if it took months for her to overcome this? Would he be strong enough to wait? What if Heather tried
to see him again? Given his feelings for her, would temptation pull
him back to her?

HAYES RAN HIS hand under Phyllis's nightshirt, kneading her back.
Her face away from him, she opened her eyes a peep and saw the light
of the rising sun through the blinds, felt Hayes nudging closer to her
under the covers.

She rolled her eyes closed again, feigning sleep.

He must be crazy.

She was hardly in the mood, not after last night.

When she'd come in from dinner and the Alvin Ailey show, all the
kids were asleep except Cole, who got out of bed and came downstairs
to say good night to her. On his way back up, he said, "Maybe we'll
finally get to church on time tomorrow, now that Dad's going."

The house joke was that Phyllis could never get anywhere on
time unless Hayes was going too. He hated to be late and would do
all he could to hurry her along.

Hayes called him back. "Cole," he said, pausing a moment, "I
won't be going tomorrow."

Cole's face fell. "Why?"

Hayes sighed, and his eyes darted briefly to Phyllis. "I only went
last week because it was a special service that I wanted to hear. I don't
plan to return."

"But *why*, Dad?" Cole's eyes filled with dismay. "It's what I said
before, isn't it? You hate God."

Hayes waited a moment. "You deserve to know where I stand,
Cole."

Phyllis had stepped closer. "Hayes—"

He held up a finger to Phyllis and turned back to Cole. "It's not that I hate God," he said. "I just don't believe in Him. I did when I was your age, but then I wised up."

Cole frowned as if he'd just learned his father was from another planet. He looked at Phyllis, and Phyllis stepped between them, ushering him upstairs with an arm around his shoulder. "Come on, sweetheart."

She walked him back to his room and talked with him at length. When she left his room, she headed straight to Hayes—who was in the bedroom, stretched across the bed watching a basketball game. She grabbed the remote and clicked it off, throwing it back on the bed. "You've gone way too far, Hayes, trying to poison Cole's mind against God."

Hayes bunched a couple of pillows under his neck to prop himself up. "If you ask me, you're the one who's been doing the poisoning. All these years they've been going to that church, they're brainwashed now."

Phyllis was so upset she began shaking. "Believe what you want to believe, but don't talk to the children about it. It's not right."

He brought a leg up and rested it atop his knee. "Maybe it wasn't right for me to let you take them to church. I thought it wouldn't hurt for them to learn some morals, how to treat people and all that, but Cole especially is taking it way too seriously. When it starts coming between our relationship as father and son, it's time to cut it off."

His statement hit her in the gut. "Cut what off?"

"They don't need to be at that church, at least not every week." He sounded calm and assured.

Phyllis worked to gather her own calm for the sake of the children, to plead their case. "Hayes, listen." She took a breath as she pondered what to say. Better to avoid anything spiritual. "The boys have been going to Living Word for six years. Their closest friends are there. You've said yourself that the one drawback to this neighborhood is that it isn't diverse. Church balances it out. They're surrounded by diversity there."

"That's true. I do like that part," he said. "But I don't like the effect it's having on Cole and me. Our relationship is more important than his little friendships at church." He reached over and picked up the remote, holding it in his hand. "They can go tomorrow. I'll see after that." He clicked the game back on.

The noise from the crowd and the buzzer and the announcers filled her ears.

Why is this happening?

Why was God letting things get increasingly worse?

She'd gone to bed without saying another word to him, and now here he was, thinking she could generate a desire to be with him. They hadn't been intimate since earlier in the week, before his Wednesday night tirade. Since that time they'd been agreeable in front of the children, but alone, they hadn't had much to say.

Well, Phyllis hadn't had much to say. Hayes tried to talk about work and the kids and whatever else, but Phyllis let him know she wouldn't pretend everything was fine. He needed to acknowledge he was wrong.

But he only defended himself. And the stunt he'd pulled last night with Cole only added fuel to the fire.

Phyllis got out of bed.

"Baby, what's wrong?"

She wouldn't look at him. "I have to go to the bathroom."

"You're coming back, right?"

"Mm-hmm."

Phyllis took her time. A strong urge to pray came over her, but when she hung her head, the only words that came were Hayes's words from last night and Wednesday night.

How am I supposed to make love to him?

She had a hard time *liking* him right now. She held herself, and the urge came again—*pray*.

A tear slid down her face as she realized where she was, a place of heartache and overwhelming discouragement, a place where hope didn't reign, only reality. A place where prayer only made things worse, only heightened an expectancy for change, only made the heartache deeper.

She was in a place distant from God.

She wiped the tears that dotted her face, a resolve she couldn't avoid coming over her. Fine. Though her heart wasn't in it, she would go in there and give herself to her husband. And then she would get ready to go to church and worship God.

Though her heart wasn't in that either.

= *Nineteen* =

LIVING WORD WAS back to normal with two services, but it was still more crowded than usual. The church had posted the Sunday morning program on its Web site midweek, and Cyd suspected word had gotten around that another member would be addressing the congregation.

This wouldn't be a surprise confession like Scott's. Everyone knew Jessica Handy's situation. The former kids' choir director was twenty-five, single, and about five months pregnant. But no one had seen her in weeks. Once she stepped down as director, she seemed to disappear. The surprise was simply seeing her name on the program. People were curious as to why she was back and what she had to say.

"Do you know her?" Cedric leaned over and whispered as Jessica made her way to the podium.

Cyd hadn't talked to Cedric since he left her house Wednesday night. When she arrived at church, she wondered whether he'd come to the nine o'clock service, and if so, whether he'd sit with them again.

While in the fellowship area talking to friends, she saw him enter but continued her conversation. He saw her, too, and came directly over, easing his arm around her waist for a side hug. She brushed off the feeling it gave her and introduced him, watching eyebrows rise among these people she'd known for years.

When they all moved into the sanctuary, each to his or her favorite section, Cedric fell in step with her and they joined Scott and Dana, who were already seated. Cyd told herself he was there because of the group. When Pastor Lyles returned to his series in First Peter next week, Cedric would return to his occasional attendance at the eleven thirty service.

Cyd answered him, tipping her head to the left. "I've known Jessica since she was a little thing. Her parents have been here a long time."

Stephanie hit her arm on the other side. "Did you see Marshall down there in front where Jessica was sitting?" She lowered her voice further. "People have been wondering who the father is. Must be him."

Cyd whispered back, "If she thinks it's any of our business, I'm sure she'll tell us."

Stephanie had surprised Cyd when she joined them in the pew. Other than last week's combined service, it had been years since she'd come to church this early. Stephanie wasn't thrilled about it, of course. It was Lindell's doing. After the Wednesday night meeting, he called Scott to ask if he would mentor him. Scott suggested they have coffee after the first service to talk about it.

Cyd looked up now and did a low wave as Phyllis took a seat at the end of the pew beside Lindell, causing them all to shift over. Phyllis was known for being late, but late usually meant breezing in during the first song. Today she'd missed all of praise and worship and the announcements.

Jessica took the microphone from its stand and walked out from behind the podium. "Good morning," she said, her voice naturally sweet sounding but tentative. She wore a long black knit skirt and a royal blue scoop-neck blouse that flowed over her belly.

"Good morning" sounded around the sanctuary.

She was about to speak but paused, bowed her head, then looked up again. "If you had told me last week that I'd be speaking to you all here at Living Word today, I would've said you were crazy." She took an audible breath. "After what happened, I couldn't bear to be around my church family. I grew up here, and I knew people had high expectations of me. Plus, directing the kids' choir made me sort of a leader. I couldn't face people's stares every week, reminding me how badly I had messed up."

She paused and lowered the microphone to her side. "You can do this," she said to herself. It came across as a whisper.

She looked out at the crowd and continued. "I had planned to find another church, but then I told myself that they'd stare at me, too, soon as they found out I didn't have a husband. And I didn't think I'd like anyone else's sermons anyway, not after growing up on Pastor Lyles's." She looked down at the front row and gave the pastor a shrug.

"So I've been staying home on Sundays, and my mother has brought me a CD of the service each week. When she brought last week's, she said I should listen right away, and I did. I was in tears."

Her head dropped even now, and she brought her hand under her eye. She stayed that way a moment, finally sweeping her hand to the side. "As I listened to Scott—and, Scott, I know you're out there, and I have to tell you how much you blessed me with your honesty—"

Cyd leaned forward and acknowledged Scott. Dana covered his hand with hers.

"—but as I listened, I knew God was telling me it was time to return to Living Word. Then when the pastor said he'd be talking about singles and sex this week, I knew why it was time to return. I knew I had to say something on the topic. When I called the pastor, he was totally supportive." She took another breath. "But it's still hard."

"It's all right," one of the older members told her. "Take your time."

Jessica did, waiting a few seconds to begin again. "I wanted to stand out here away from the podium so my pregnancy would be right here before you the entire time I was talking." She rubbed her belly with her free hand. "Sex is so enticing . . . until you get a good look at the consequences . . . I have no excuse. My parents told me the truth growing up, that God's perfect plan for me was to remain pure until marriage. I intended to wait, and I did wait . . . for a while. But this guy came along and I thought I was in love and, well, here I am." She held out her arms and looked down at the place where a baby was growing inside of her.

Stephanie bopped her head over. "All she had to do was use protection."

Cyd cut her eyes at her and shook her head. She was too consumed in her own thoughts to deal with Stephanie. She knew exactly what Jessica was saying. She, too, had waited until that one guy came along . . . and her ideals went out the window. But for God's grace, she could have ended up pregnant too.

"Saving sex for marriage is so outdated," Jessica was saying. "Right? I mean, who does that? Do you actually know anyone who's doing that?"

Cedric sneaked a look at Cyd.

"I'm standing here today with the message that *I'm* doing that. I'm saving sex for marriage."

The congregation responded with applause.

Jessica began a slow walk across the riser, more comfortable now about what she came to do. "I know somebody's saying, 'It's too late. You're not a virgin anymore, so what's the point?' But there *does* come a point when you have to just make the decision to obey God."

She pointed at her stomach. "This is not the only consequence of sex before marriage. The worst is having to live with the fact that you sinned against God. When you _know_ it's wrong and you do it anyway, you have to live with that. And it's the worst feeling in the world."

She stopped pacing and reflected a moment. "I was listening to the part of Pastor's sermon last week where he talked about a marriage ceremony between God and Israel in the Old Testament where they exchanged vows. God said, 'If you obey Me and keep My covenant, you will be Mine,' and the people responded, 'We will.'" Jessica paused, overcome.

"That's all He wants," she said, her voice broken. "Obedience. And He gives us _so_ much more in return. Pastor Lyles included marriage vows on the last page of the handout, and at first I couldn't figure out why. But then I got it—they were vows between us and Jesus, our bridegroom." She took a breath. "He had one line in bold, and when I read it, I got on my knees in the middle of my bedroom floor and made it a prayer: 'I pledge to be true.'" She said it again in an almost whisper. "I pledge to be true."

A woman to Cyd's left stood up. She was holding herself, tears streaming down her face.

Jessica started pacing again, her voice stronger. "If you've never had sex, if you decided to wait until marriage, please keep your vows of obedience to God. But if you've failed like me, God will give you strength in that too. Dust yourself off and make up your mind today to obey God. Say to the Lord, 'I pledge to be true.'"

She took a few steps in the opposite direction. "You heard Scott's confession. Maybe you've had an affair. Maybe you're on your way to having an affair. Turn from it and say, 'I pledge to be true.'" Jessica raised her hand as high as she could, given her belly. "Who's willing to stand with me and say, 'I pledge to be true?'"

Cyd came to her feet, weeping from the sorrow she felt still from her own bad choices, and at the same time overcome with joy that God was using Jessica in a powerful way. She waved her hand in agreement.

Others were up, too, young women in their late teens and women in their twenties and thirties, all with hands raised. Scott was up and Dana with him. Lindell grabbed Stephanie's hand and brought her up. A minute later most of the congregation were on their feet, some waving hands, some holding the pew in front of them, heads bowed, many in tears. Phyllis and Cedric were among the last to stand in their row. They were both looking on.

Jessica took in the response, smiling. "Glory to God. He's worthy! Can we pray?" She bowed her head. "Lord, You've done this, causing us to rise to our feet and pledge to be true to You. Strengthen us all. In Jesus' name. Amen."

Pastor Lyles walked up the steps and hugged Jessica on her way back down. He said something to her, his hands on her shoulders, then hugged her again. "Guess we don't need a sermon today," he announced. "What an awesome, awesome testimony. What an awesome move of God."

Applause sounded again, and the pastor waited for it to die down. He walked to the podium. "Y'all know I was playing about not needing a sermon, right?"

"You didn't fool us," that same older woman said.

"After we hear from the choir, we'll dig into the Word of God and see for ourselves what He has to say about sex." He smiled. "Should be some interesting conversation in your I-Groups this week, huh?"

People chuckled.

"I'm hoping," he continued, "that your discussion will center around what God thinks about sex—and ultimately, that your *lives* will center around what God thinks. Amen?"

Cyd said, "Amen," along with a few other voices in the congregation.

Pastor Lyles cupped his ear. "I didn't hear you."

Cyd poked Cedric and Stephanie in the sides with her elbows. A weak "Amen" sounded from their mouths.

SMALL TALK MADE its way around the room as the group waited for its last member to arrive. Cyd was about to call, but just as the thought crossed her mind, the phone rang. She left the family room and picked it up in the kitchen.

"Phyllis, where are you?" Cyd knelt to rub Reese's fur. "It's quarter after seven."

"I won't be able to make it tonight, Cyd. Sorry for the late notice."

"What happened?"

"Nothing really." Phyllis didn't sound like herself. "I was getting ready, but then I realized it just didn't make sense to go. The subject is premarital sex. Not exactly relevant to the season I'm in."

Cyd stood. "But did you look at the discussion questions? They deal with obedience generally, having a faithful heart. I think it could be a really good discussion."

"I know, but . . . I went back and forth about it, and I think I'll just stay home."

Cyd frowned. "It's about last week, isn't it? Phyllis, you don't have to stay away because of what happened with Hayes."

"No, I know. That's not it." Phyllis paused. "Hey, Cyd, I've got to run. I can hear Ella crying."

"Okay. Let's talk tomorrow, okay?"

There was a moment's silence, then she answered, "All right."

Cyd joined the others and let them know Phyllis couldn't make it. Dana quizzed her with her eyes, and Cyd gave her a faint nod. They both knew it was strange. Phyllis was always excited about Bible study and fellowship. She was the one who'd urged them to form the Daughters' Fellowship so they could meet regularly. Cyd made a mental note to call her later.

Stephanie and Lindell had the sofa, Dana and Scott the love seat. Cyd took the overstuffed chair beside Cedric's folding chair. Lindell asked Scott to pray again, and when Scott was done, everyone waited for Lindell to begin.

Lindell looked down at the discussion questions. "Before we start," he said, "I have to admit that this lesson put me through some changes this week, and I want to apologize openly to my wife."

Stephanie dropped her jaw and shifted her weight to face him, exaggerating her surprise. "I can't wait to hear this one."

Lindell sat up straighter and spoke to the group. "I was excited about this new sermon series because I wanted *Stephanie* to hear that she was out of line trying to hook up with her old boyfriend."

Stephanie hit his arm. "I thought you said this was an apology. So far you're just making me look bad."

He put a hand on her leg. "I'm sorry, babe. I wouldn't be this open if we weren't among family." He looked at Scott and Dana. "I do consider you two family now." He cleared his throat.

"Anyway, I didn't know I would find out that *I* was out of line in my relationship with Stephanie before we got married . . . you know . . . the sex and all that. I never gave it much thought." He looked into Stephanie's eyes. "So I wanted to apologize for being so hard on you when I needed to be looking at myself."

Stephanie shifted away from him. "You're still making me look bad. Now you put it out there that we were sexually active before we got married."

Cyd and Cedric arched their eyebrows.

Dana spoke up. "Uh, Steph, that wasn't a secret. I thought you two were basically living together."

Stephanie crossed her legs. "I didn't know it was that obvious."

"Moving right along . . ." Lindell lifted his paper. "The first question says, 'What did you learn from this week's sermon that you didn't already know?'" He looked up. "I guess I started us off on that one. Who wants to go next?"

Cedric leaned over and anchored his forearms to his thighs, staring downward.

After a few seconds, Lindell chuckled. "Oh, I was the only one who learned something?"

"Not at all," Cyd began. "I definitely learned something." She wasn't thrilled about divulging her thoughts with Cedric near, but she continued. "I always looked at those verses on sex as 'meanwhile' verses—something I had to abide by while waiting to get married. This time they spoke to me in an entirely different way, especially coming after Jessica. Now that I've turned forty, I'm realizing those verses might govern the rest of my life. I had to really consider that. I had to confirm in my heart, 'I pledge to be true' even if I never get married."

Stephanie made a face. "Can we be real here?"

"I was about to say the same thing." Cedric spoke under his breath, but everybody heard him.

Stephanie turned her head to Cyd. "You're telling me if you never get married, you plan to abstain from sex for the rest of your days?"

Cyd rolled her eyes over to her sister. "Steph, were you tuned in on Sunday? The pastor laid it all out—the purpose of sex, the holiness of God, our bodies as holy temples . . ."

"Yeah, I heard him, just like I heard Jessica—who, by the way, wouldn't have been saying all that if she hadn't gotten pregnant. I just don't see how the writings of some white men halfway around the world, two thousand some-odd years ago, should influence how I'm living today."

Lindell looked confused. "I thought they were Jewish."

"Whatever."

Dana's voice drifted in. "So, Stephanie . . . just askin' . . . Are you saying you don't see how the Bible applies to your life?"

Stephanie smoothed her jeans. "Pretty much."

"And you're serious?" Cyd stared at her sister.

Dana tossed Cyd a look. "Steph, we should talk. This is so much bigger than the sex issue." Dana paused. "I know you've been around the Bible your whole life, but it's so awesome when you actually connect with it."

Stephanie gazed aside.

Scott leaned forward. "What about a mentor situation, like the one Lindell and I are starting? Maybe you and Dana could meet once a week as well." He caught Stephanie's dubious expression. "You don't have to make a lengthy commitment," he added.

Stephanie's eyes bounced from Dana to Cyd. "I don't know. I wouldn't be able to sneeze without Dana telling Cyd about it."

"Everything would be held in strictest confidence," Dana said. "You've always been like a little sister to me anyway." She smiled. "Except I think we've always gotten along a little better than you and Cyd."

Stephanie glanced at Cyd. "True."

Cyd rolled her eyes. "Don't get me started. Dana can have you."

The laughter from the ladies lightened the moment.

Lindell patted Stephanie's knee. "Try it, babe. One time. If you think it's a waste of time, you can just quit."

She half frowned at him. "That's a given."

Lindell tried again. "Okay. Consider it a wedding gift to me. I don't know why, but I'm really pumped about this. I think it's just what we need."

"All right," Stephanie said, though it was mostly a sigh. "I'll meet once and see what happens."

"Cool!" Dana came over and hugged her. "I'm excited. We get to hang out together."

Scott hugged her, too, then Lindell stood and he and Scott clasped hands and pulled one another into a hug.

"Well," Lindell said, grabbing his paper, "we've discussed one question off the entire list."

"And yet I think we accomplished a lot," Scott said. He took a look at the rest of the questions. "I think we'll address these in a different way, through the mentoring."

Lindell seemed satisfied. "Okay." He turned to Cedric. "You want to join us, Ced? I don't think Scott would mind."

"Absolutely not," Scott said. "I'd love to have you join us, Cedric. With our schedules we have to be flexible, but right now we're planning to meet Tuesdays for lunch."

Cedric stood and slipped his hands in his pockets. "That wouldn't really work for me—"

"Ced, don't you pretty much make your own schedule?" Lindell asked.

"Nah . . . I wish. It's hard for me to make a weekly commitment like that. Appreciate it, though."

Cyd took note of Cedric's response, not at all surprised.

The group proceeded slowly to the door and found their coats. Scott and Dana said their good-byes and filed out, with Lindell and Stephanie behind. When they were gone, Cyd turned to Cedric, who was hanging back. He hadn't put on his jacket yet.

"I was just thinking," he said, stepping toward her.

Cyd felt her heart skip. She'd been fine all evening. It helped that Cedric had arrived after Scott and Dana, and he'd been so quiet that it had been easy to focus her attention away from him. Had he left with the rest, the evening would've been a success. And this was their last group meeting, so she'd be free and clear of him after tonight.

She waited, but he was only staring at her with his arms folded. "Yes?" she said.

"I was thinking that a spiritual mentor might not be a bad idea." _Stop looking at me like that._

"But," he continued, "I'd like _you_ to be my mentor."

She closed the front door and started toward the kitchen. Reese had been quiet the entire meeting, probably asleep, but now she was barking at the gate, frantic to get out. Perfect distraction. She looked over her shoulder as she walked.

"Uh . . . no."

Cedric followed her. "Why not?"

She stepped over the gate and found Reese's leash. "Cedric, you're not interested in being mentored. If you were, you would've agreed to meet with Scott and Lindell."

"Lindell wants Scott to mentor him because he feels a connection to him. You're the one I feel a connection to."

Cyd flipped him a look as she led Reese to the back door. "I think you're talking about two different kinds of connections."

"I'll give you that," he said, following them out. "But the point is, I could get up for that—meeting with you, learning from you. Isn't that a good thing?"

The air was brisk, and Cyd hadn't stopped to put her jacket on. She shivered as she waited for Reese to take care of business. "Actually, no," she replied. "It's not a good thing, especially since you've already said you want to make love to me, and Stephanie already warned me you'll do whatever you can to get what you want. This must be new for you, though—working a spiritual angle."

He came closer. "You already made it clear you're not interested in me. I'd respect that." He leaned his head in until she looked at him. "Or maybe you're thinking you can't trust yourself around me."

His nearness sent a different kind of shiver through her. Why did he have that effect on her?

"That's not the problem."

"Then what's the problem? I'm saying I want to be mentored. There's a lot I don't know. I'm asking you to help me."

Reese was done, and Cyd brought her back into the house, shooting up a prayer.

Lord, I know he's playing games, and I'm thinking it wouldn't be wise for me to do this . . . and yet I want to acknowledge You. Could You have a plan in this? What should I do?

Cyd led Reese and Cedric to the front door, waiting for direction. When the words came, she held them a moment, surprised. Then she spoke them. "We can meet one time. Saturday morning, eight o'clock."

Cedric looked at her like she had flipped her lid. "Eight o'clock? I sleep in on Saturday mornings. I was thinking we could meet over dinner."

"That's when I can do it, Cedric."

He blew out a sigh. "I guess that'll have to be when we do it, then."

She opened the door for him. "I'll call you before Saturday to let you know the place."

"Aren't we meeting here?"

She smiled. "Nope. Someplace else. Someplace public."

"Oh. Okay." He lifted his jacket from the chair and slowly put it on.

As he made his exit, Cyd said, "And, Cedric?"

"Mm-hmm?"

"As a gift, I'll buy you a Bible for our meeting."

He went out the door. "Okay. That, uh, sounds good."

She closed the door and watched Cedric through the window as he walked to his car. One question consumed her. Would God really use her in his life?

Twenty

PHYLLIS STARED AT the computer screen. Dressed in capri pajama bottoms and a short-sleeved tee, she would normally be in bed right now, and in fact she had been. She and Hayes had turned out the lights at eleven, but as he drifted into a soft snore, she had lain there wide awake, depressed by her thoughts. It had been this way every night for a week.

Nights were definitely the worst.

Almost every other part of the day was filled with activity. In the mornings she hopped from cooking breakfast to a battle with at least one son about what he'd wear to school, to a battle with the youngest about lying, since he liked to say he'd washed his face when he hadn't, to last-minute searches for homework. Once the boys were off to school, she was busy with Ella, playing with the little girl as she toddled from one thing to the next, reading to her, taking her for walks in the stroller.

At Ella's naptime, Phyllis was still moving, exercising on the elliptical machine in the basement, cleaning the house, doing laundry, starting dinner. When the boys returned, there was nonstop action until they said good night, and even then Phyllis couldn't rest until the kitchen was in the order she liked. She ran a mop across the floor almost every evening.

That was life as usual and she loved it, but she also loved two other distinct times of day—her early morning quiet time and the nighttime climb into bed, when all the voices and commotion and responsibilities were suddenly silenced. That was when she could think on the day and lull herself to sleep with thank-yous to God for small victories and blessings.

But these last seven mornings and evenings had been different. Now when the alarm buzzed at five thirty, she wondered why she'd set it. The internal push to get up, the desire to snag precious moments with God, had waned. Instead she felt a sluggishness that asked why she was sacrificing sleep for the sake of a few prayers, prayers that for years had featured Hayes at the top of the list. Prayers that had yielded nothing but disappointment. Better to sleep than to drown in the quiet of the morning, pondering disappointment. Which is what the nights had also been about.

Tonight a single thought kept circling in her head: that the two relationships she valued most—God and Hayes—were the two causing her the greatest heartache. It was nothing new with Hayes. But in the past, the joy in her relationship with God would offset the pain with Hayes. Now she couldn't find her way to that joy with the Lord. What joy was there in knowing He could change Hayes's heart but had chosen instead to let it grow harder? Now she had no joy in either relationship, and the reality of it saddened her.

She thought about Cyd and Dana, too, how even her relationship with them was feeling strained. She knew why. They wanted to draw her out, see how she was feeling. But she didn't want to share her true thoughts. They wouldn't understand that she didn't want to be encouraged, that she was through with getting her hopes up. Had she gone to the meeting tonight, it would have been more of the same. She loved them like sisters, but on this one she would have to go it alone.

Well, almost alone. There was Rod. When her mind glimpsed him, a pinpoint of light shone through her thoughts. He was the one person in her life who could help, though not directly. She wouldn't discuss her marital problems with him. He could simply be an oasis, someone who could take her mind off her troubles, be a friend during one of the most difficult times of her life.

That was why she got out of bed, to travel to her oasis. She had gone down to the office, stopping first in the kitchen to get the note with Rod's e-mail address from her purse. She was in the office chair now, at the family's desktop computer.

Phyllis clicked open the e-mail window, clicked the New Message button, input Rod's e-mail address, and paused at the subject line. What to say? She typed *Hello*, then backspaced to delete it. She cocked her head. Maybe *Hi*. Or *Hey*. The message needed to come across just right, like it wasn't a big deal. Just a quick hello to let him know she was thinking about him—though she wouldn't *say* she was thinking about him. That would be too much, like she was up late at night with him on her mind—which she was—but she couldn't let him know that. They were friends. Nothing more.

She sighed at all her mental maneuverings and typed *hello* again, this time with a lowercase *h*. Somehow that made the difference.

She tabbed to the body of the e-mail and lingered there, too, trying lines, deleting them. Finally she was staring at these words:

Good evening, Rod,
Or maybe it's "Good morning," depending on when you get this.
I didn't have anything earth-shattering to say. Just hello. Hope all is well.
Sincerely,
Phyllis

It didn't say much, but it said a lot. He'd know she cared about staying in touch. She proofed it once more and clicked Send. It was on its way.

There was no way Phyllis could go to bed now, too much nervous energy. She opened Internet Explorer and watched her home page unfold the headlines of the day. She skimmed through a couple of stories, then followed the link to the fitness page and perused exercise and nutrition tips. By the time she'd finished an article on the healthiest fish to eat, it was past midnight and she knew the only reason she was up was to see a message pop in from Rod—and he'd probably been asleep for hours. She hung around cyberspace another few minutes, finally turning off the computer at twelve thirty.

The next morning she awoke with a start at six, but instead of heading to a comfy chair for quiet time, she headed straight for the office. Anticipation fluttered as she turned on the computer and waited for it to power up. When the screen allowed, she opened the e-mail program and watched as the new message indicator lit up: _Receiving 1 of 3 messages._

Message one appeared, an ad about pay-per-view movies from her cable company. She sighed and waited for message two.

Why is this computer so slow?

Stacy Summers with the subject line _Happy Thursday!_ Stacy often sent short messages like _Hope you're having a blessed week!_ or _Thinking about you. Hope all is well!_

Phyllis bypassed it and waited for the third. When it downloaded, she felt a thud of disappointment. Spam about Viagra.

Over the next two hours, she made breakfast and hustled the boys through their morning routine, taking a minute here and there to dip into the office and check the computer. Middle school started earlier than elementary, so when he could, Hayes would drop Cole off on his way to work. Phyllis and Hayes had been moving past one another all morning, and when she saw that he was about ready to leave, she called from the bottom of the stairs, "Cole, come on. Dad's ready to go."

Phyllis made sure Cole's coat was where he could find it and doubled back into the office again. Hayes was on the desktop computer.

Her heart rate sped up. "What are you doing?"

Hayes looked over his shoulder, hand on the mouse. "Checking e-mail."

"Why aren't you using your laptop?"

"My laptop is packed up. I just needed to find out if my meeting got rescheduled." He glanced at her again. "You need to use it? I'll only be a minute."

A minute was all it took for an e-mail from Rod to download. She could see it now. All this time waiting for him to reply, and it would come right this moment.

Phyllis heard Sean calling and left the office reluctantly to see what he needed. Ella was calling as well from her high chair. Five minutes later she heard Hayes open the front door and call Cole again—relief. She didn't know how Hayes would react if he saw a message for Phyllis from a man he'd never heard of. But she guessed he'd certainly ask about it. She preferred to keep her friendship with Rod to herself.

Phyllis grew more and more antsy as the day wore on. Why hadn't Rod responded? He'd probably seen the message last night and spent the day debating whether to respond. Maybe he thought she was contacting him too much. Maybe he decided they shouldn't be friends after all. Maybe he'd ignore her and hope she went away. The maybes were driving her crazy.

By bedtime, she was chastising herself for anticipating his reply all day, but as she lay tucked under the covers, she fought the urge to check one last time—and gave up. She had to see.

She tiptoed down the darkened staircase and into the office. She'd left the computer on, and when she jiggled the mouse, the glow from the screen brought a soft light into the office. She brought up the e-mail and saw *Receiving 1 message*. She'd been through this all day and told herself it was just another marketing ad. Still, she couldn't help moving forward in her chair.

She blinked when she saw it. *Rod Clarke* appeared on the screen. The subject line read *Re: hello*. A double click brought his words into view.

Hey Phyl,
Just got your message. Work was hectic today and after school I had to drive the girls to my parents' house because I'm leaving town in the morning for a science teachers' conference. (Good thing the girls had no school tomorrow anyway.) Maybe we can catch up after I get back in town.
Rod

P.S. I'll wave at you when my plane lands. You're not too far from Chicago, are you?

Phyllis read the message three times. Was he coming to the Midwest? Tomorrow? Her heart beat out a rhythm she'd never felt as thoughts flew through her head, all of them featuring her in Chicago this weekend. How could he come so close and she not see him? Well, it wasn't *close* close, but close enough, much closer than the East Coast. Even if they could only spend an hour together, it would be worth it. She could talk to her new friend, get her mind off her problems for a while, laugh a little. She felt better just thinking about it.

She tapped out a response in the adrenaline of the moment, hoping he was still near the computer.

You're going to Chicago tomorrow? Are you free for dinner Saturday night? I could meet you up there.

She sent it, and he must have been on the computer still, because to her delight she had a reply within minutes.

Phyllis, I was just kidding about it not being too far. That's a long drive, isn't it? And would your husband be down with that? Seems like a lot just to go to dinner. But if it works out, I guess it could be a nice break after hearing sessions on "Exploring the Electromagnetic Spectrum" and "Infectious Diseases and Bioterrorism." lol Call me Saturday if you're able to make it and we'll figure out where to meet. I'm staying at the Embassy Suites downtown.

Phyllis formulated a plan that minute. She didn't care if Hayes would be down with it or not. She'd tell him she needed some time to herself to think through this last week and a half and get her head together. That was actually the case. And a Chicago trip wouldn't seem extreme. Hayes knew she thought nothing of road trips, didn't mind driving even when they traveled as a family. As she thought about it, most of her time *would* be spent alone. She had a four-and-a-half-hour drive each way, plus she'd have time overnight to put this season of her life in perspective. It could be quite fruitful. In the middle of it all, she'd have dinner. With Rod.

Just so happened that that was the only part of the weekend that truly excited her.

Twenty-one

DANA TRIED HER best to stay focused on the task at hand. She was in the home office on the lower level, typing up the minutes from the PTO meeting. She'd finished the first section with the list of attendees and the treasurer's report, and was starting on the principal's report when her fingers left the keys and found the mouse, clicking open the Web browser.

A couple of clicks later, she was at the Web mail page for a pharmaceutical company—Scott's employer. Just looking at it made her anxious, so she switched back to the document, finished the principal's report, then typed the next heading, *Faculty Report*—and switched windows again to stare at the Web page.

She had told herself not to do this again. Two days ago she had figured out how to access Scott's e-mail account at work. It was fairly simple. All she needed was his password, and Scott was never big on creativity when it came to passwords. After a handful of tries, she found out he was using the same one he'd used on their old desk-top—*Markenzie*, a combination of the children's names.

Once inside the account, she'd run though the names in his in-box from the last couple of weeks, looking for Heather's, but she didn't see it. She was sure the girl hadn't gone away, and checking Scott's text messages wasn't easy since the phone stayed glued to his hip. This was the next best window into what was happening . . . other than asking him directly. But she didn't want to talk about it with Scott. It would only aggravate the wounds. This was a relatively pain-free way, she told herself, to keep tabs on them.

But it wasn't guilt-free, which was why she had decided not to do it again. She didn't feel right afterward, like she wasn't trusting God.

But today was Friday, the day Scott and Heather had rendez-voused for three weeks straight. She didn't think Scott would sleep with Heather again, but she didn't put it past Heather to try to see him. It wouldn't be hard to play on his feelings. They'd shared an intimate oneness, an act that had bonded them emotionally. It would take a lot of strength for Scott to walk away and never look back, strength he'd have to maintain constantly. If Heather said she needed to talk to him face-to-face one last time, he might agree in a weak moment. And who knew what she might try from there.

Dana had to stay on top of the situation. If Heather made a move, she wanted to know about it.

Despite the gnawing at her conscience, Dana typed in the pass-word and saw a series of e-mails from this morning alone about test batches, an upcoming FDA conference, questions about the expiration date for a drug. She kept scrolling down, moving into yesterday's messages, and saw one that stopped her cold. *Heather Anderson.*

Fear dropped its cloak over her, causing her arms to tremble and her mind to race. The e-mail was marked at seven thirty last evening. Had Scott checked his e-mail last night from home? Certainly he saw it when he arrived at work this morning. Why hadn't he told Dana about it? This was something he should have shared.

Dana opened the message, her stomach clenching as she read.

Hey Love,

It's been almost two weeks and you haven't returned my calls. Haven't we laid low long enough? I miss you. All of you. Let's at least meet tomorrow for lunch at our favorite spot. Twelve sharp.

Heather

Dana's eyes darted to the clock at the bottom right of the screen. 12:10. She snatched the handset from the base and punched the numbers for Scott's office. When she got voice mail, she pushed 0 for the receptionist.

"Hi, is Scott Elliott available?"

"I'm sorry, Scott left for lunch a few minutes ago. May I put you through to his voice mail?"

"No. Thanks."

Dana paced as she dialed Scott's cell number, suspicion and dread flooding her being. She didn't know what she would do if voice mail—

"Hello, you've reached Scott Elliott . . ."

Dana threw the phone across the room. The back flew off and the battery skittered into the wall.

"I _hate_ her!" She yelled it so loudly her throat hurt. Hey _Love_? Is that what she called him? Is that what he called her? She bent down and glared at the screen again. What was this about lying low? Did they have an agreement? Pretend it was over until Dana was lulled into believing it was so?

She paced the room again, so angry she couldn't cry, an anger that worsened by the second because she didn't know where they were. She couldn't be more sure that Scott was with Heather. Right in some restaurant, proving by his very presence that he cared, that she had a hold on him.

Dana picked up the phone and battery, pieced them together, and dialed his office again. She got the receptionist.

"Hi, this is Scott Elliott's wife, and I need to reach him. Did he happen to mention where he was going for lunch?"

"I'm sorry, Mrs. Elliott, he didn't. Should I tell him you called?"

"No. No, thank you."

She placed the phone on the desk this time and moved her deliberations upstairs, stopping in the foyer. What could she do? She stared at the wall and it came to her.

Stephanie. If she knew Heather well enough to invite her to the wedding, there was a good chance she had her number.

Dana grabbed the kitchen phone and dialed.

"You're trying to meet for mentoring today, aren't you?" Stephanie said.

"Stephanie, I need Heather Anderson's cell phone number. Do you have it?" She found a pencil on the counter and snatched a telephone bill to write on.

"Why?"

Dana sighed. "Steph, it's private, but I really need it."

"She's the one Scott had the affair with, isn't she?"

Why did I call Stephanie?

"How on earth did you jump to that conclusion?"

"There's something about her. I've never really liked her. I invited her to my wedding because she hangs out with some friends of mine, but I wouldn't be shocked if she bedded a married man. And if you're trying to get her number, that has to be it. Why else would you be calling her?"

Dana didn't have a quick response, so Stephanie spoke again. "I don't see what good it'll do to call her, Dana."

Dana wasn't in the mood for a lecture, least of all from Stephanie. "Will you give me the number or not, Steph?"

Stephanie paused. "Let me find it. Don't say I didn't warn you."

She gave Dana the number, and Dana stared at it as *Hey Love* looped through her mind, rekindling her anger. She stabbed the numbers with the pencil eraser and seconds later heard a "Hello" that sounded confused.

"Heather, this is Dana Elliott."

"Dana?"

"Dana. You know, Scott's wife."

"And you're calling me because . . ."

"I'm calling to tell you to stay away from my husband. Don't call, don't e-mail—"

"Oh, how about 'Don't go to lunch,' because he's sitting right here." The phone shifted. "It's for you, love."

Dana could tell she was smiling.

"It's your wife."

"Dana?" Scott sounded hurried and anxious, as she'd expect him to sound when he was caught. Again. "Dana!"

She let the phone fall, mostly because she couldn't help it. Her body was trembling so badly she dropped to the floor and pulled her knees to her chest, folding her arms tightly around them. The tears came now, a flood of them. How stupid she'd been to trust Scott! He must have missed Heather as much as Heather missed him. Dana was sobbing so hard she began coughing. He and Heather could have each other. She was through.

When the waves of tears passed, she came to her feet, walked calmly to the bedroom, and started tossing Scott's clothes from the closet onto the bedroom floor. She wanted him out by nightfall and she didn't care what they told the kids. Let *him* come up with a story.

She'd been thankful up to now that Mackenzie and Mark were

oblivious to his affair. They'd been in kids' church during his announcement, and though she'd braced herself for the church chatter to reach their ears, God must've had a shield around them, because it hadn't happened. But now they'd know—and maybe they needed to know the truth, that their father was a liar and a cheater. Dana took two shoes at a time from the shelf and threw them across the floor. The tears had started again, angry tears. She snatched a few silk ties from a hook and—

"Dana!"

Scott had entered the bedroom, greeted by the tornado of a mess she had made. When she saw his face at the closet door, she threw the ties at him, though they landed short of the target.

Scott rushed to her and held her tight. "Oh, baby, I can't believe this."

"Believe it." She wrestled to get free. "I want you out."

He lifted her chin with a finger. "Baby, it's not what you think." He held her again. "Oh, Dana. Sweetheart, you've got to hear me out."

Shaking again, Dana broke free and moved into the bedroom. She swiped some tears with the back of her hand and headed for the door.

Scott grabbed her hand and pulled her back. More forcefully this time, he said, "Dana, we have to talk."

He walked her to the bed and, practically numb, she followed. But she refused to sit as he did. She folded her arms and looked away.

"I have no idea how you got Heather's number or how you happened to call when I was with her, but let me tell you why I was there." He anchored his forearms on his thighs and clasped his hands. "For the last couple of weeks, Heather's been calling me every day, several times a day, leaving these long voice mails."

She glowered at him. "You never told me about that."

He threw up his hands. "I was trying to ignore her and move on. Why would I want to talk to you about her?"

Dana rolled her stare back to the distance.

"Then she started e-mailing me at work every day, and I wouldn't reply. I'd just delete them. Seemed like her messages were getting more and more insane, calling me 'love' and acting like we were going to pick back up where we left off. We never called each other names like that, and I made it clear it was over."

Dana stared downward now, listening more intently.

"I get to work this morning, and she's sent another e-mail asking me to meet her for lunch. I ignored that one, too, and had to run to a meeting. When I got back to my office, I found out she had come up to my job! She actually came into my building and said she needed to see me. They said I wasn't available, and she said to tell me she'd see me at lunch."

Scott shook his head. "I said, 'This is it. I've got to tell this woman I'm sorry things went where they did between us, but she has to stay away from me. Period.'"

Tears slid down Dana's cheeks again. She should've trusted God to handle it. God _was_ handling it.

"I was only there for five minutes, long enough to tell her what I had to tell her, when the phone rang. She was upset and accusing me of using her and throwing her aside. But her whole tone changed on the phone, and when she said it was you, I thought she was playing games—especially when she gave it to me and I didn't hear anything. I tried to call and you didn't answer, so I came home. As soon as I walked in here"—he looked at the shambles she'd made of the room—"I knew it really was you."

He took her hand and pulled her down beside him. "What happened? What made you call her?"

Dana bit the inside of her lip. "I . . . I read her e-mail about lunch today."

Scott showed his surprise. "How did you get into my account?"

Dana gave him a look.

"Okay, it was easy to figure out. Wow. How did you get her number?"

"Stephanie."

"You weren't messing around, were you?" Scott's tone was free of accusation. He wove his fingers with hers. "If I hadn't violated your trust, you wouldn't have felt you had to do all of that." He sighed. "I should've told you she was contacting me, but I just didn't want to talk about her. I was kind of working it out between me and God."

"I guess . . ." Dana stared at their fingers. With all she'd done, she might as well bare her soul. "I guess part of the problem is I was jealous of her. I thought it would be easy for her to step back into your life because she's so pretty. And she's got the body . . . and the hair."

"Baby, are you kidding?" Scott stood and brought her up with him. "Come here," he said softly.

He led her into the bathroom and stood behind her as they faced the mirror. "I'm glad you cut your hair, because it showcased this."

She turned and looked up at him. "What?"

"Your face. With short hair, the shape of your big, beautiful eyes stands out, your smooth complexion, everything. And the cut gives you a carefree look, like you're confident in who you are. I love that." He brought his arms around her waist and grazed her cheek with his.

"And I love every inch of your body. Every curve was made for me. And what I love especially is how it changes with the seasons, from young woman to mother, and eventually to middle age and older, because it's a reflection of God's goodness and grace in holding us together through those seasons."

He turned her around. "You and me, Dana. That's it. That's all I want." Scott kissed her, softly at first, more passionately by the second.

Dana brought her arms around his back and savored the moment. They hadn't been this close—she hadn't been this aroused—since before the affair. Most of her wanted to make love to her husband, but one part cried out still that it wasn't ready. It couldn't yet erase that image of Scott and Heather lost in one another's arms. It made her sick still to think about it, and at their first counseling session yesterday, the assistant pastor had told her to take as much time as she needed. She felt torn as Scott slowed the kiss and groaned, an eye on his watch.

"I've got to get back for a meeting, sweetheart. I hate to leave you like this."

Her heart settled down.

Thank You, God.

"It's okay. I'm so glad you came home." She kissed him again. "I love you."

He traced a finger across her brow. "I love you too." He took her hand and together they walked out of the bathroom. "What are you doing this afternoon?"

"I've got a little time before the kids get out of school." She scooped up one of Scott's shoes from the floor and gave him a sheepish smile. "Guess I need to do some picking up."

He headed toward the bedroom door. "You mean I don't have to move out?"

"Not unless I'm moving with you."

Scott blew her a kiss and bounded down the stairs.

Dana got on her knees and bowed, face to the ground, thanking God. Because in the midst of the most painful trial of her life—even when she hadn't sought Him and even when her prayer life hadn't been what it should—He had been faithful. And because, though she wouldn't have thought it possible, never had she felt as much love and appreciation for her husband as she did in that very moment.

Twenty-two

CEDRIC PULLED INTO the parking lot of the Missouri Botanical Garden at seven fifty, a grande latte sprinkled with chocolate, nutmeg, and cinnamon at his lips. He needed the jolt. When his alarm sounded at seven, he remembered why he'd set it and his mind kicked into gear, but his tired body lagged behind.

It didn't help that Tamia had tried her best to get him to stay in bed. She knew where he was going and whom he was meeting, and she had no grounds to be upset. But it didn't stop her from trying to change his mind. It almost worked, but when Cedric weighed what he'd be giving up against the immediate pleasure of Tamia, the two didn't compare. There was nowhere else he'd rather be this morning.

But that was what bugged him. He didn't know why he had such a desire to be here. He had asked to be mentored only as a way to be alone with Cyd, something he'd wanted to do since the night they celebrated her birthday. With some quality time, he was sure he could persuade her that what they felt was worth pursuing. He wasn't used to being turned down.

But this setting and the hour—not to mention talk of buying a Bible—had killed his vision of their time together. So why was he looking forward to it still? What _was_ it about this woman? She had laid down the terms of their meeting, terms unfavorable to him, and here he was, couldn't wait to get here. He felt drawn to her in a way he couldn't explain, like he truly wanted to get to know her—something else he wasn't used to.

He saw Cyd's car on the left side of the lot and drove over, parking beside her. He was surprised by the number of cars here already. He'd heard the Garden was a popular place for morning walks, but he couldn't remember when he'd been here last. Had to have been years, back when a buddy got him to go on a double date to one of the summer evening jazz concerts.

Cedric hopped out and left his jacket in the convertible. With the sun shining and the temperature mild this first Saturday in November, his jogging suit was all he needed. He strode to the glass doors, chucked his empty coffee cup into the wastebasket, and once inside, paid the fee of a couple of dollars. The woman handed him a ticket and a map of the Garden, and he headed upstairs to the café.

He saw Cyd right away at a table for two, next to the floor-to-ceiling window that overlooked the gardens. She had her back to him, her head buried in a book.

He got that weird feeling again, the one he'd gotten since the first time he met her, the feeling that he couldn't wait to be near her. She had her hair pulled back, and he almost chuckled to himself. He'd told her she looked sexy with her hair down. When he told Tamia the same, she'd made a point of wearing her hair down whenever he saw her. Not Cyd. If she cared at all what Cedric thought, there was no way to know it. He was starting to love that ponytail, though. It was one more thing that made Cyd uniquely Cyd.

He came up behind her and saw that the book she was reading was the Bible. He leaned down to her ear. "Good morning."

She looked up and smiled as he took the seat across from her. "Good morning. How are you?"

He held her gaze. She wore a jogging suit as well, navy blue with lime green stripes down the sides. Far as he could tell, she wore no makeup, and she still looked beautiful. "I'm good. How about you?"

"Real good," she said. Her gaze didn't falter, but her smile took a playful turn. "I'm proud of you for getting up and out so early this morning."

He shifted to a more comfortable position. "Did you doubt I'd make it?"

She shrugged slightly, mostly with her head, and lifted her coffee mug. Peering over the top, she said, "Nothing would surprise me with you, Cedric." She took a sip.

He decided he didn't need to know what she meant by that. He leaned back in his seat. "So what'd you do last night?"

"Nothing special." She took another sip. "I did some reading for my Greek lit class. How about you?"

"Not much. I was home." He felt strangely secretive. He didn't mind Tamia knowing he was here with Cyd, but he didn't want Cyd to know he'd spent the night with Tamia.

Cyd pushed a small plate over to him. "I took a chance you might like a banana muffin. I got orange juice, too, but you'll have to get your own coffee. I didn't want it to get cold."

"I love banana muffins." He was taken by her thoughtfulness. "Thank you. And orange juice is perfect. I just had a latte on the way over."

"Well, shall we get started?"

Cedric wondered what would come next. "I'm ready if you are."

"Why don't we pray first."

Cyd extended her hands and Cedric took hold, closing his eyes. He couldn't resist running a finger across the back of her hand.

"Lord God," Cyd began, "bless our time together this morning. I'm praying that You mentor us both. Lead us where You want to lead us and teach us what You want to teach us. Give us hearts that are willing to listen and follow. In Jesus' name. Amen."

Cyd eased her hands from Cedric's and reached into a messenger bag beside her chair. "I had a hard time deciding which Bible to get you," she said, "but I ended up getting one like mine." She smiled before she produced it. "And no, mine isn't a women's devotional Bible."

She handed him a big leather Bible. When he took it, he flipped through the pages out of courtesy, to look interested, but was surprised when his insides fluttered with anticipation. He'd never had his own personal Bible.

"Turn to the front. I wrote a little note."

Cedric did and saw handwriting on the first page. It read, _To Cedric, This book changed my life. I pray it does the same for you. Cyd._

He stared down at the page, her words drawing him in. His life needed to change. That's what she was saying. Was she talking about the sex, or was this deeper? His gut said it was deeper, and the meeting took a mysterious turn. It seemed suddenly that she knew more than he did about his own life, at least about where it stood. He wanted to know what she knew.

"Cedric, I'm not sure where to start. When you said you wanted to be mentored, you said there was a lot you didn't know. Did you have something specific in mind that you wanted to talk about?"

Cedric looked at the Bible again, at Cyd's words. He cleared his throat. "When I said I wanted to be mentored . . ." He looked up now. "I did have something specific in mind—spending time with you, just like you thought."

Cyd arched her brows, but her eyes were smiling.

"But it's true. I'm starting to see there's a lot I don't really know."

Cyd allowed Cedric to hold her gaze. "There's a lot I don't know either, Cedric." She sounded sincere.

He gave a slight chuckle. "I think I've got you beat. I'm looking at this Bible and realizing I barely know anything about it, just a few stories I've heard on Sunday."

"Okay, well . . . tell me this." Cyd looked deep into his eyes. "What do you know about Jesus?"

Cedric felt as if the answer should be obvious, but he was drawing a blank. "Jesus. I mean . . . He's Jesus. I'm not sure what you want me to say."

"I'm honestly not trying to make it difficult, Cedric. This just helps me to know where we should start."

Cedric reflected on the question. "This is basically what I know about Jesus. He was a great man, a prophet. Had a lot of wisdom, did a lot of miracles. Died on a cross."

"Okay," Cyd said, nodding. "That's all true. There's just a lot more *really* good stuff, but that's why we're here."

Cyd smiled and her tone was light, and it struck Cedric that he wasn't used to this kind of vibe between them. She was normally guarded or short with him, admittedly because she wasn't trying to go where he was leading her. Now she was relaxed. She seemed to care.

"Let's turn to the Gospel of John," she was saying, already flipping there.

Cedric followed suit and turned toward the back as she was doing. When he saw *John* at the top of the page, he slowed down.

"Cedric, what do you think about love?"

The question surprised him. "Um, it's nice, I guess."

"Have you ever been in love?"

He thought about it. "Not really, no. I mean, I had times when I was younger and thought I was in love, but it was probably more . . . well, lust, if I'm being honest."

She leaned in. "Why do you think you've never been in love?"

Cedric felt her questions at his core. She was tapping into areas he never thought about, never acknowledged were there. The scary part was he was willing to let her explore.

"I don't know why. I guess I've never met anyone I felt I could truly trust, someone I could commit to. Maybe I never met someone who I felt would love me unconditionally—for me, you know, not because of what I could give them."

"I can understand that," Cyd said. She sat back. "We're about to get to know Someone you can trust and commit your life to, Someone who has loved you unconditionally since the beginning of time."

Cedric couldn't say a word. Everything in him said to sit tight and listen.

"He's the Word, the *logos*—" Cyd chuckled. "I'll try to contain myself from getting too much into the Greek—guess it's the professor in me. Anyway, John really breaks down who Jesus is. It's an awesome place to start."

Cyd's enthusiasm was infectious, but more than that, every word seemed to unlock a secret treasure. He wanted her to keep talking so he could behold it in full.

And she did—for almost an hour and a half. Cedric was trying to process everything he had taken in as Cyd reached a hand across the table.

"Would you mind if I pray, Cedric?"

Cedric nodded and took her hand.

"Lord, thank You for being faithful in leading us this morning. I pray You give Cedric understanding of everything we discussed. Give him faith to believe that Jesus is the Christ, the Son of God, as the book of John tells us. Amen."

Cedric looked up at Cyd, emotions he'd never felt swirling inside of him.

Cyd stared out the window. "It's so beautiful out there. You want to walk the gardens?"

"That sounds perfect," he said.

They cleared the trash from their table, walked their things to their cars, and used their tickets to reenter, going upstairs and out the doors this time. As they stepped outside, Cedric was taken by the spectacular water fountain, high and full. He walked into the plaza where it was located, surrounded by oak trees and flower beds, and listened, the sound of the water rushing his senses. He was captivated.

Something about it brought to life one of the passages Cyd had highlighted, Jesus saying He would give living water that would spring up to eternal life. The more he listened the more he was sure of it—this fountain was speaking to him, beckoning him. He closed his eyes and meditated on "living water."

He realized Cyd was beside him and opened his eyes again, glancing at her. She was in her own contemplation, and when their eyes met, it was as if they both knew. Now was not the time for words. Something deeper was happening.

They strolled from the plaza and took a path that led them to the Rose Garden, which they sauntered through, past the Bell Tree, which Cedric absentmindedly touched, to the sound of tinkling as they passed. They gazed into the reflecting pools and admired the water lilies and the bronze sculptures poised within, taking the pathway around the huge domed Climatron.

A cacophony of birds sounded nonstop in the trees surrounding them, transporting him to his boyhood, when he'd pore over field guides and test how many birds he could identify outside by sight and sound. How long had it been since he'd taken real notice of them? They were abundant here, and he recognized the symphony still—the American robin, the common grackle, and his favorite, the mourning dove. Everything was alive and seemed to be calling to him, calling him to awaken.

They walked through the Chinese Garden and came to the lake in the Japanese Garden, and Cedric was sure when he saw it that this day, this moment was meant for him. A large white great egret swooped over the lake and perched on a tree branch, causing everyone who saw to gasp and watch. Cedric had never seen one, only admired them in pictures, yet here it was. Beautiful, lingering. He could see its penetrating eyes taking in the scene, and in his own eyes, tears rushed to the surface, though he tried hard to blink them back.

He turned to Cyd, who'd been quiet the entire time, and said the words that were burning in his heart. "How do I do it, Cyd? How do I believe?"

Cyd's gaze went straight to his soul, a place no other woman had ever been. "You don't have to work to figure it out, Cedric. Just believe."

"Don't I have to pray or something?"

Her eyes sparkled. "God would love to hear from you. He loves you."

It was all he could do to keep the tears from falling. "Will you help me? Pray with me?"

"I'd love to."

Cyd turned to see where they should go and followed a cobblestone path that led to a wooden bench nestled in a secluded area of trees. They sat next to one another, and when she held out her hand, he shuddered inside, knowing where she was leading him. This had to be the moment she wrote about in the Bible. The moment his life would change.

Cyd couldn't believe she'd just led Cedric in a prayer to receive Jesus as his Lord and Savior. He'd been so quiet during the Bible study and then during the walk that she didn't know what he was thinking. Was this for real?

Still holding hands, Cedric shifted toward her. "So does this mean we can go out now?"

Confused, Cyd looked up at him. "What do you mean?"

"Well, before, you said we weren't compatible; but that's changed now, hasn't it?"

Cyd was dumbfounded. Was this really the first thing on his mind after everything they'd covered? Was that prayer just another avenue for him to get what he wanted? She stood, releasing his hand. "You don't give up, do you?"

"It's not what you think." Cedric came to his feet as well. "I know. Your birthday, the Intimacy Group, the mentor thing—I used those things to get next to you. But this is different." He sighed, walked a few feet away, and threw his head back, looking to the heavens. When he turned back, he was shaking his head.

"I can't even explain what I'm feeling right now. It's like, right now my life is beginning or starting over or whatever you want to call it. I see this path in front of me"—he was gesturing with his hands—"and I have no idea where it leads. But based on what you told me, God will be with me. And I know who else I want with me, walking the path." He came closer. "I want you with me, Cyd."

"Cedric, you're being way too impulsive, and I don't even think you know what you're talking about. What do you mean you want me with you? Do you even *know* what you mean?"

Cedric sighed again and stared at a sparrow flitting around a magnolia tree. "Maybe I am being impulsive." His eyes were on the bird still. "This is all new to me. I've never felt this way in my life. I guess it does sound crazy, but for once I wanted to be real." He turned to Cyd. "You know? I wanted to say what was really in my heart."

They were silent until Cedric knocked his hand against hers. "Hey," he said. "Let's go out to lunch and celebrate."

"Celebrate what?"

Cedric gave her a mock look of hurt. "Didn't my life change a few minutes ago? Isn't that cause for celebration?"

She could only hope it was real. With a sideways glance, she gave an affirmative nod. "Definitely cause for celebration."

"I know the perfect place," he said. "We can go just as we are."

Cyd pulled out of her parking space to follow Cedric to the restaurant, but after a few feet, he slowed and waved her forward. When Cyd lowered her window, he said, "I forgot my phone at home, and a client is supposed to be calling me this afternoon. Do you mind if we run by my place so I can get it? It's right down the road."

"Sure," Cyd said.

They exited the Garden and took the street to the main road, following along Kings Highway about two miles, past the Washington University Hospital and the St. Louis Children's Hospital, turning onto Forest Park Avenue. Cyd didn't spend a great deal of time in the Central West End, but she always thought it was vibrant and eclectic in its restaurants and shops, not to mention its diversity of people. It seemed a perfect fit for a guy like Cedric. She could see him hanging out in bars, walking the neighborhood, a fixture in every hot spot . . . he and whatever woman he happened to be with.

They turned onto the street of Cedric's high-rise, and instead of parking in the garage, he pulled along the curb in front, which offered fifteen-minute parking. Cyd pulled behind him and rolled down her window.

"I'll wait for you out here," she called.

He walked to her side of the car. "Why don't you come on up? I want to show you where I live. It'll only take a minute."

She cut the engine, and together they entered an upscale lobby with several seating areas. Cedric greeted the guy at the security desk and headed to the elevator, riding to the eighteenth floor. Cyd loved the décor. The walls in the hallway were a soothing dark beige and the doorways were spaced out, tucked into their own enclaves.

Cedric approached his and unlocked the door.

"Wow," Cyd said when he opened it. "This is fabulous."

The kitchen, to their immediate right, had an oversized brown and beige marble counter that jutted out over two leather barstools. The cabinets were Euro style, flat wooden slabs with a dark stain that matched the leather, and the appliances had a gleam hers had never seen. Farther in and to her left were a dark brown leather sofa and two matching armless chairs.

Cyd stepped farther into the living room. "Cedric, these art sculptures are—"

Tamia sauntered toward them from the back of the condo in a revealing piece of lingerie.

Cedric let loose an expletive. "I thought you said you were leaving." He pushed the door to a close, looking as if he was still registering what was happening.

Tamia strolled up to him, taking his hand. "I wanted to surprise you, baby."

Cyd backed to the door, ready to leave.

Cedric lifted his hand from Tamia's. His voice was low, but Cyd could hear.

"I want you to put your clothes on, get your things, and go." He walked over to the counter area by the sink, unplugged his phone from the charger, and opened the door, holding it for Cyd.

She could tell he was seething, trying to keep it under control.

"You know what?" Cyd said when they were on the other side of the door. "I'm just going to go home."

Cedric looked devastated. "Cyd, if I had known she would be here—"

"You would've let me wait in the car. But she still would've been here." Cyd flashed her palms. "Which is cool. It's your life."

She started toward the elevator, and Cedric grabbed her gently and turned her around. "That's not fair. I'm a different person now than I was when I left this morning. Tamia is part of the before."

Sighing, Cyd turned more fully toward him. "I understand, but

233

the reality is, you might've been changed on the inside, but your life won't change overnight. You've got a lot to work out, Cedric. I'm thankful God used me in your life today, but I think the part I had to play is over."

She could feel his eyes pleading with her, but she needed to make a break—a clean one.

"Bye, Cedric."

All the way to the elevator, and as she waited for the doors to open, she knew Cedric's eyes were on her. Once she was safely inside, she closed hers. And the tears fell.

Twenty-three

NO MATTER HOW much Phyllis tried to downplay it, no matter how often she squashed the wave of anticipation, no matter how many times she told herself to tread carefully, there was no denying it.

She could not wait to see Rod.

She slid her card key in the lock and at the green light, pushed the door open. She was thrilled she got a room. An online search yesterday had yielded nothing. With the National Science Teachers Conference and at least two other big events, downtown Chicago was booked. Phyllis had to reserve a room farther out, but on the drive to the city she called the Embassy Suites on State Street, where Rod was staying, to see if there had been any cancellations. Sure enough, one room had opened up. It was one more thing about the day that excited her.

Phyllis dropped her overnight bag on the floor of the living area and flicked on a couple of lights, mentally ticking off things she needed to do—shower, dress, makeup . . . call home. She'd get that last one over with first. She dug the phone out of her purse and speed-dialed home.

Hayes had been surprisingly supportive of the trip. Her mood had been sullen of late, and he knew he was the reason. If an overnight getaway could provide a pick-me-up, he was all for it. It was Cole who had a problem, wondering again whether Hayes would take them to church. Probably not, she told him, and no, she wouldn't ask. Her thoughts mirrored Hayes's this time around—wouldn't hurt to miss one Sunday.

Phyllis heard her voice playing on the recorded message, and she looked at her watch—5:10. They rarely ate this early. Must be playing a board game or watching a movie. She left a message saying she'd arrived safely and would try them again later.

A rush started building inside. She and Rod would be meeting in the lobby at five forty-five. She'd spoken to him on the road and told him she'd secured a room in the same hotel. They would walk together to a restaurant on Michigan Avenue. Reservations for six o'clock.

Phyllis unzipped her overnight bag and retrieved a smaller zipped bag of toiletries. On her way to the bathroom, she took out the bottle of lavender vanilla shower gel Dana had given her last Christmas and inhaled the fragrance. _Sweet._ Tonight she'd use it for the first time. Just a way to pamper herself on her getaway weekend.

After a shower, she put on black pants, a black jersey tank, and a quilted multicolor-print silk jacket. Ten minutes later she'd applied her makeup and fluffed her curls with her fingers. Checking herself in the mirror, she got that rush again. She felt fabulous.

Phyllis slipped into her boots and leather jacket, tucked the card key inside her purse, and took a breath as she held the door handle. Her gut tightened, and instead of a rush of excitement, she felt a rush of caution. As if she shouldn't go. Shouldn't take the elevator down to the lobby to meet Rod, who was waiting for her. But she couldn't just leave him there.

This is ridiculous.

She pulled the door handle. A friendly dinner, that's all it was.

Phyllis stepped off the elevator and into a throng of people milling about, their conversations lively and in some pockets boisterous. They were all wearing badges, many holding beers and other drinks, ready for an evening away from sessions and workshops. She walked a few feet, scanning faces, and suddenly he was in her line of sight, standing by a coffee bar. It seemed so weird. Every time she had ever run into Rod, it was on campus or at Jasper's, which may as well have been an extension of campus. To see him in a different city, a different setting, brought that sensation she'd had before she left the room, like something wasn't quite right. What was she doing here?

Rod moved from his position when he saw her. He had a cool dressy casual look—sports coat and slacks with a white collared pullover shirt. They smiled as they came together easily in a hug.

"Hey, lady." His words grazed her ear. "I see you made it safely."

"Mm-hmm." His scent, his voice, his total nearness assaulted her being, even with all the people crowding them. She took a slight step back. "How are you?"

"I'm good." He was nodding, taking her in, his voice raised above the noise. "And you? You certainly look colorful and cheery."

Phyllis gave a bashful smile, glancing at her jacket. "I guess I do feel cheery."

For the first time this week.

He leaned over. "Ready to get out of here so we can hear ourselves?"

Phyllis nodded and they headed to the exit. When they were out on State Street, Rod remembered his badge and took it off, tucking it inside his coat pocket.

"Why did yours have a special ribbon?" Phyllis asked. They turned left onto Ohio, and the air, much cooler than in St. Louis, made her quicken her step. She wore the leather to look cute, but she would have been much warmer in a wool coat.

"They give these to presenters," Rod said. "My session was yesterday."

Phyllis looked at him. "Really? At the national conference? That's quite an honor."

He shrugged. "It wasn't a headline event or anything, just one of the hundreds of sessions offered. But I was pretty pumped when they accepted my proposal. It was on engaging at-risk learners, and I got to talk about how we can get students excited about science inquiry, in particular by using robotics. We've been doing that in my classes, and those kids love it."

"Sounds like you love it too."

"Definitely."

They turned onto Michigan Avenue, where the number of people diminished the sidewalk space considerably, causing them to walk single file for a time. A couple of blocks later they arrived at Grand Lux Cafe, located on the large second floor, with glass windows all around that overlooked Michigan Avenue. They took the elevator up to the hostess stand, waited in line, and Phyllis gave her name. There was a sizable crowd, as she and Rod had expected, and despite the reservation they had a twenty-minute wait.

They moved off to the side and Phyllis looked at the waiting patrons, experiencing that weird feeling again. What if one of them knew her? What if a friend or colleague of Hayes's was here? How did it look, her being here with another man? _She_ knew it was harmless, but it might not seem so.

She felt the same when they were led to their table. She'd hoped for one in a corner, preferably in one of the secluded dining areas, so she wouldn't feel paranoid about who might be there that she and Hayes knew. But the hostess led them instead to a table with a great view, smack in the middle of the main dining room.

"How's this?" the hostess asked, feeling she'd done them a favor.

Rod looked to her, but Phyllis wasn't willing to object openly. "It's fine."

When they were seated, gazing at their menus, Rod asked, "How's the family?"

Phyllis didn't look up. "They're doing well."

He chuckled a little. "You and your husband must have a real solid relationship. Michelle would've said, 'You're driving where? To meet who? I don't think so.'"

She paused, her eyes cast vaguely on the description of the miso-glazed salmon. Then she looked up. "Well, this is more of a personal getaway for me than anything else, so that's how I styled it."

Rod turned a page in the menu book, his brow lifted. "Oh." He stroked his chin and met her gaze. "Guess that's nice too, then, that he would give you an opportunity to have a personal getaway." He kept looking at her, as if he suspected there was more. "Everything all right?"

"With what?"

"Obviously you must have *needed* a getaway. I'm just wondering how things are really going."

Phyllis didn't want the cloud that had hung lately over her home life to follow her here as well.

"Things aren't perfect, to be honest with you, but they never are, right?" She shrugged. "It's nothing I want to dwell on."

She could feel Rod staring at her as she went back to the menu. After a beat, he returned to his again, and their server returned to take their order. When they'd handed him the menus, Phyllis took a sip of water, hoping they'd move to a different subject.

Rod gazed out the window. "This is my first visit to Chicago, believe it or not."

"Really?"

Phyllis tried to stay away from bread in restaurants—too many calories—but tonight she splurged and took a piece from the basket.

"How do you like it?"

Rod was spreading whipped butter on his. "I love it from what I've been able to see, which isn't much. I've been in the hotel mostly."

"You'd love the Museum of Science and Industry." She wished they could spend the day tomorrow exploring.

"I know. I'll have to schedule another visit and bring the girls."

Phyllis smiled at him. "You enjoy being a dad, don't you?"

He nodded, finishing his bite. "The hardest and most wonderful job I'll ever have." He rolled his eyes upward. "All the emotions girls go through, drama at school with friends, already talking about boys . . . So many nights I'm at their bedside wishing they had their mother to talk to about all this stuff."

Phyllis's heart went out to him. "But, wow, you're at their bedside listening to them."

"Got to," he said. "That's Daddy time for each, one at a time. First they share what's on their heart, and they've always got something. Then we do the Bible verses we're memorizing, they give me prayer requests, and we pray. And we have this thing where they have to tell me at least one thing about the day that they're thankful for."

"That's awesome, Rod. I'm impressed."

Why couldn't I have a man like this?

The thought shot clean into her mind and stuck. Just looking at him made her heart spin, but his handsome features were nothing compared to his spirit.

Her thoughts were interrupted when their entrées arrived. Rod had gotten the slow-roasted beef short ribs, and Phyllis the Mahi Mediterranean.

"Let's pray," he said when the woman had left. Phyllis looked to see if he would take her hand, but he didn't. She kept hers in her lap and lowered her head.

"Lord, thank You for the food before us," he said, head bowed. "We ask that You bless it." He paused and she peeked, but his head was still down. "And we ask that You be with us this evening, that You may be glorified in all things. In Jesus' name. Amen."

"Amen." Phyllis's eyes went first to her plate, which looked delicious, then to Rod. Still thinking about his bedtime routine, she decided to say what was on her mind. "It would be a shame if you didn't get married again someday. So many women would love to have a strong Christian man." She took a small bite of her crusted fish.

Rod sliced a piece of beef. "Unfortunately, all the strong Christian women are taken." He gazed up with a hint of a smile, then tasted his beef.

She tried not to blush. "That's not true. One of my closest friends is a strong Christian woman. Forty years old and still single, 'cause she hasn't found a man like you."

Rod chuckled. "Maybe you should introduce us."

"Hmm. I'm thinking distance would be a factor." She speared one of her roasted tomatoes. No way would she connect the two of them.

He scooped some mashed potatoes and a small carrot onto his fork. "You must feel blessed not having to worry about all the things singles tend to worry about. You've got your strong Christian man."

"Wrong." Phyllis half sang the word. She tried to stave off the emotion charging at her with a quick stab of an artichoke.

Rod leaned in. "What do you mean, Phyllis?"

She dabbed her mouth with the cloth napkin. "I mean, Hayes isn't a strong Christian man. He's not even a Christian." She tried to sound matter-of-fact, keep the cloud away.

Rod sat back, lowered his eyes. "I didn't know. That . . . that must be hard."

Emotion came unbidden again, and she moved her head into something of a nod. She lifted her glass, but her hand had begun shaking so she set it back down. The cloud was hovering.

"So, I remember you said you were saved a few years ago, after you got married." Rod had stopped eating. "Your husband just hasn't—"

She gave him a pointed look. "*Refuses* to listen to anything concerning Christianity."

"Oh, it's like that?"

"It's like that."

Rod blew out a sigh. "I can't imagine . . . But I know—and you know—that God can do anything. I'm sure you've been praying, and it's just a matter of waiting for Him to answer."

She tried not to toss her eyes. "Yeah."

"Really, Phyllis."

"I know."

They let the subject lapse as they resumed eating, their remaining time spent on more talk about the conference and the city. On the slow walk back to the hotel, Phyllis's mind traveled to the night in the car with Rod. Once again they were about to say good-bye. Once again she didn't want to.

What if she weren't married to Hayes? The question permeated her being. What if Hayes got fed up with the tension surrounding her faith and left? Would she care? Right now she wasn't too sure. Hands in her pockets, she stared at her feet as she and Rod strolled in silence. Maybe she'd been going about things the wrong way. She should've been expressing her faith around the house without reservation, singing and praising God at will. Maybe Hayes would have already been gone . . . and she could get to know Rod in a deeper way. Like she wanted to.

Truth was, she could see herself with Rod. Could see them building a relationship, a home, their kids together under one roof being raised to know the Lord, all of them in harmony. The thought of returning to the marriage she had was choking the life out of her.

Phyllis entered first through the revolving door of the hotel. It was close to eight o'clock and the lobby was much quieter now, though by no means empty. She and Rod took slow steps toward the elevator, stopping short of it near a section of lounge chairs.

Phyllis, still chilled from the walk, kept her hands in her coat pockets. "You've got an early start tomorrow morning?"

"First session's at eight. Not too bad." His eyes drifted to the passersby, then back to her. "What time are you pulling out?"

"No special time," she said. "Whenever I get up and get ready."

He nodded, taking in the scene again, and Phyllis wished she could read his mind. Was he as reluctant to say good-bye as she?

Did they even have to say good-bye right now? They'd never get another evening like this to hang out and talk. She checked her watch. "It's kind of early yet," she said. "What do you plan to do the rest of the night?"

Rod thought a moment. "Maybe catch a movie. I hadn't realized how long it's been since I've seen one, and the hotel's got a good selection."

Longing coursed through her veins. "I like that idea. How about we watch it together?"

Rod looked skeptical. "Phyllis, I don't think it's wise for us to be in a hotel room together."

"Well, true . . . if this were a normal hotel. But it's a suite, so we can watch it in the living area." Phyllis knew she was reaching. "It'll be over by ten, and we can call it a night."

Their eyes locked. She didn't know what he meant by his gaze, but it set her on fire. She felt herself being drawn all the more, saw herself in his embrace. She wanted him. She couldn't deny it. And more than that, she wanted to fall in love with him.

He led her farther out of the way, to a more private spot in the lobby, and seemed to search for words. "Phyllis, I need to apologize."

Her heart beat still with the possibilities before them. "For what?"

"I should've never agreed to your driving up here and meeting me for dinner." He shook his head, clearly upset with himself. "When you brought it up, something told me to say no, but I enjoyed your company in Maryland. And to be honest, I liked the thought of seeing you again." He paused. "But it wasn't right. And hearing that things aren't going well for you at home only made me feel worse."

Phyllis's gaze fell on a couple side by side in club chairs, lost in conversation. She felt like crying.

Rod shifted away from her briefly and sighed. That this wasn't easy for him was small consolation.

"Phyllis, you awaken things in me," he said suddenly. "Things I can't allow myself to feel." He stared at his shoes and glanced back at her. "I care for you. And because I care, I know we can't go to my room to watch a movie. We shouldn't call or e-mail either. I want what's best for your marriage."

She cut her eyes away. *She* wanted what was best for her marriage, too, but what had that mattered all these years?

Long seconds erected a gulf between them. Phyllis took a deep breath and put on the best face she could. "Guess it's good-bye, then, Rod."

She walked away before he could respond and cried for nearly an hour. Her whole world had come crashing down, the last glimmer snuffed out. She missed Rod already, just the thought of him and the friendship she'd hoped they could have. He was her one refuge—and now that was gone too. Why did he have to end things that way? She'd only suggested a movie, not a romp in the sack. He didn't have to push her away for good, as if they'd had some illicit affair. But then . . .

If her thoughts had had their way, perhaps it would have been an affair . . . and those thoughts suddenly scared her. *Oh, God.* Her heart beat a panic rhythm. Did she really imagine herself in a passionate embrace with Rod?

How did she *get* here? Why was she curled up on a strange hotel bed? As if awakening from a dream, she looked around herself. Fresh tears spilled when she saw her baggage. She'd actually driven four and a half hours to see another man. If Rod hadn't held firm in that lobby, she'd be in his room right now. Maybe in his bed.

She wished she could check out of the hotel and blink herself back home. She needed to be there to get her head and heart right—this room was only accusing her. But she was too tired to drive home, so she took the next best escape—the shower. She stood under the water almost afraid to pray—it had been so long. But a verse emblazoned itself in her heart.

"Come to Me, all who are weary and heavy-laden, and I will give you rest."

Sobs gathered again in her chest. How could God speak that to her? How could He offer her rest after the days and weeks she'd ignored Him? After the desires she'd had of sleeping with Rod?

She went to her knees, the water cascading her face, skimming her shower cap, likely seeping into her hair, but she didn't care.

Father, I come before You heavy with shame. She took a breath and let it stutter out. *How often I've prayed for You to change Hayes's heart, and my own heart is impure. Please forgive me, Lord.* Her shoulders bowed with grief. *Lord, I've been unfaithful. I haven't honored You and I haven't honored my marriage. Change my heart, oh God. Renew my love for Hayes. Renew my love for You.*

Phyllis shifted and sat with her head lowered, arms around her knees, the warm water pummeling her shoulders, remembering the words Jessica Handy had spoken last Sunday: *"I pledge to be true."* She had stood when it became apparent that the whole church would, though it wasn't in her heart. But after tonight, that had changed.

Whether Hayes came to know the Lord or not, whether he continued to be hostile toward her faith or not, she would stay committed to him mind, body, and spirit. Because in the end, it wasn't about her marriage to Hayes so much as her marriage to Christ. She needed to be faithful to *Him.* She needed to be true.

Twenty-four

DANA HADN'T LAUGHED this much in weeks. It was Tuesday, and she was supposed to be here helping Stephanie at their first mentor meeting, but she was the one being helped, feeling like her old self. Laughter really was good medicine.

The two women had already covered the spiritual ground Dana had planned. They'd met early at The Bread Company at the St. Louis Galleria, after Dana's kids had gotten off to school. Dana and Scott prayed together in their quiet time this morning—a new habit they'd started—asking God to touch Stephanie's heart. And He had. Not that Stephanie had made a dramatic about-face, but she'd come with her Bible, though Dana had forgotten to tell her, and she seemed to be sincerely listening. She asked thoughtful questions and even took notes.

But somehow near the end, as Dana talked about living by the power of the Holy Spirit, the discussion fell apart.

Stephanie pointed and said, "Let's talk about that right there. I want to know how to make love by the power of the Holy Spirit, 'cause the thrill is gone already."

Dana had looked concerned. "After three weeks, Stephanie?"

Stephanie smirked, head cocked.

"Okay, it's been longer than that, but how could the thrill be gone so soon?"

"Girl, maybe it's payback, God telling me, 'See, you shouldn't have been dipping and dabbling beforehand, then it could've been fresh and new.' Or maybe it's because before, I was eager for him to be my husband, and now that he is, the anticipation's gone. But I'm really thinking it's because Lindell started trippin'."

"What did he do?" Dana had finished the last of her orange juice, intrigued.

Stephanie rolled her eyes up as if she still couldn't believe it. "The night of the wedding." She stopped for effect. "My man calls himself being sexy and busts out with some briefs under his tuxedo—he normally wears boxers—and, Dana, I don't mean any harm, but his flab rolled over the top of the briefs."

Dana kept a serious expression, trying her best to contain herself. "Okay."

"It was not sexy, Dana. Then . . ." Stephanie looked off in the distance, shaking her head. "Mr. Sexy Man decides he's going to dance for me. Dana, you know Lindell can't dance. You saw him at the reception, right?"

Dana's insides were bubbling. "No, we had left."

"Okay." Stephanie shifted in her seat. "Let me see how I can explain this. His rhythm is a little off. You know how folk think all black people can dance?" Stephanie gave her the eye. "All black people can't dance. So here he is in the hotel suite, making this grand entrance into the bedroom—in the briefs with the flab—doing some kind of gyration thing—"

Dana tried hard not to laugh, but it started in her belly, rose, and forced its way out.

"—with a serious look on his face like he was really trying to concentrate and do his thing. I'm sorry, but it was so _not_ a turn-on."

Dana was bent over now, trying to collect herself, but the dam had broken and she couldn't stop.

"And on top of all of that, Dana, I kid you not . . ." Stephanie held her same even expression. "I found out he had gotten a whole set of these briefs—from who knows where—all different colors, some with sayings we don't need to get into. And he had the nerve to get this increased sex drive after the wedding, so I've been treated to this same performance every night." She sat back and folded her hands. "Every night."

People at nearby tables were casting an eye in their direction.

Dana held forth her hand. "Stop. Just stop, Stephanie." She had to be turning beet red.

"Can I say one more thing?"

"No!"

Stephanie leaned in anyway. "After I leave here, I'm putting an end to this madness. I'm going right to the department store"—she pointed out the door—"and I'm buying him some more boxers. I'll tell him these are special, picked just for him, and he can dance to his heart's content to 'When a Man Loves a Woman.'"

"'When a Man Loves a Woman?'" Dana was getting control of herself, but not totally. "That's a slow song. I was picturing him doing some upbeat dance."

Stephanie raised a brow. "He was. Didn't I tell you his rhythm was off?"

Stephanie got Dana, who was still chuckling, to go with her to Dillard's, where she found some boxers she liked right away. When she'd made the purchase, Dana was hit with an idea that made her pause.

"Hey, Steph," she said, "let's stop in women's lingerie."

"Ooh, gonna get a little something for Scott?"

Dana giggled. "I think Lindell just inspired me."

DANA COULDN'T WAIT for Mark and Mackenzie to go to bed. She had enjoyed the family time they'd had after dinner playing foosball, but now that they'd bathed, done their evening routines with Scott and Dana, and settled under the covers, her anticipation was growing.

Scott was down in the office, and Dana waited until she was sure the kids were asleep before retrieving her shopping bag from a corner of the bedroom closet. Opening it, she pulled out the beautiful black silk nightgown just to look at it, then tucked it back in the bag while she took a shower, luxuriating in the body gel that made her feel special.

She couldn't believe she was doing this, and not just because of her hesitancy since the affair. Even before the affair, it had been a long time since she'd made a big deal of their intimate moments. She knew it was God giving her the desire and even the strength to put all else aside and feel that oneness with her husband again.

Dressed in her nightgown, Dana lit votive candles around the room, picked up her cell, and dialed the home phone.

"Dana?"

"Hey, babe. Busy?"

Scott paused. "I'm doing a little work . . ." He sounded puzzled. "Did you need something?"

"Mm-hmm. You."

Another pause. "You need me? To come up there?"

"Mm-hmm." Dana ended the call.

Seconds later Scott was trying the door.

"One second," Dana called.

She pressed the Play button on the remote. As smooth jazz filtered through the room, she opened the door.

She took Scott's hand and led him inside, to the middle of the floor, into a slow sway to the music.

His arms tightened around her, and he whispered in her ear, "Baby, I can't believe this." He leaned back to meet her gaze. "Are you sure?"

She pressed her face against his chest. "Very."

They swayed, unhurried, enjoying the closeness, the feel of their bodies against one another. Tears started in Dana's eyes. She had thought this moment would be painful and forced, a pure act of faith on her part, but it was nothing of the kind. Her desire was growing with every passing minute.

Scott looked into her eyes again, long seconds it seemed, and brought his lips to hers. He took his time, touching her lips lightly, caressing her face with his hand. "I love you," he said. "I love you so much."

Dana lost herself in the kiss as her tears fell. She'd never needed Scott more than this very moment. As she led him to their bed, an image darted through her mind, a vague one of Scott and Heather, but before it could register, it was gone. Her mind filled with the two of them alone, a joyful filling that encouraged her all the more to take back what had been stolen, territory that should have been hers alone, territory she'd been forced to yield out of pain. When they came together, she felt the pleasure, the renewal, the healing power of stepping back in, into her rightful place.

Heaven, she was certain, was rejoicing.

Twenty-five

CYD WAS TRYING to be as patient as she could.

"Try that again, Jonathan." She sat back to show a relaxed demeanor and stared across the room at her student. "Remember, the *thing* by which or with which an action is performed takes a noun in the dative case without a preposition, but if there's an *agent* by which an action is performed, it takes *hupo* with the genitive." She smiled faintly. She'd only said it five times. "And the verb was supposed to be in passive voice, not middle voice."

"Oh." Jonathan looked down at his notes. "I don't think I totally understand all the distinctions yet between passive and middle voice."

He flipped his notes and studied them as Cyd decided, once again, that high school English was totally inadequate. These were among the best and brightest in the nation, yet Cyd spent more days than she could count not advancing her students in Greek grammar but shoring up the English.

The class of twelve undergraduates waited. They were seated at tables that formed a U-shape with Cyd at the top left corner so she could rise if need be and write on the board. She never tired of her Greek 101 class, but she did tire of lack of preparation on the part of the students, and she tired of the result: wasted time. A couple of students whispered with one another, one swigged a bottle of water, and one's head was starting to bob every few seconds. She motioned to the guy next to the head-bobber, and he poked his neighbor with a pencil, startling him awake.

"Okay, I've got it." Jonathan looked up. "ἡ μήτηρ τοὺς παῖ·δες ἔλουεν."

"Jonathan, have you been doing the homework exercises?"

He cleared his throat. "Professor Sanders, I've been really bogged down with papers for other classes."

Cyd nodded, coming forward in her chair. "And you thought you could cram and catch up whenever you needed to, right?" She looked around at the other students. "I stressed at the beginning of the semester that it's imperative that you stay on top of the work. You need to regularly drill your vocabulary, noun declensions, and verb forms—in English and Greek. You need to do the readings, the assigned exercises, both Greek-to-English translations _and_ English-to-Greek, and if it would help, you should do the online reinforcement exercises that you've been given links to."

Cyd turned back to Jonathan. "That was active voice you gave me. You said, 'The mother was washing her children,' when the sentence should have said, 'The children were being washed by their mother.'" She looked around again. "Can anyone give me the correct translation?"

Audrey raised her hand, and Cyd was thrilled. She'd been struggling in the class, not because she hadn't been doing the work but because she simply found it difficult.

"Audrey?"

"οἱ παῖδες ὑπὸ τῆς μητρὸς ἐλούοντο."

"That's correct."

Audrey smiled to herself.

Cyd looked at the clock and rose to her feet. "It's time to go, but I have an announcement first. As you know, papers are due Friday, but some of you have let me know that you have real conflicts because of work in other classes. Just to prove that I'm merciful, I'll extend the deadline to Monday."

One guy pumped his fist at his side.

"But if I don't have your paper in my inbox by midnight, I'm deducting points."

Worry lined Judith's face. "Now *I've* got a conflict."

Cyd showed her confusion. "But you didn't have a conflict with the Friday deadline?"

"Not as much."

Goodness. Sometimes she felt these *were* high school students, given the simple problem solving she had to do for some of them. "Judith, pretend the deadline is still Friday, and get it done and out of the way."

Her head tilted. "I could, couldn't I?"

The students made their way toward the door, two stopping to schedule an appointment during Cyd's office hours. Cyd tucked her books and papers into her bag, and when the room was quiet and she knew she was headed home, her thoughts drifted to a familiar subject of late—Cedric.

It was Wednesday, and they hadn't spoken since she'd left his condo on Saturday. He didn't even come to the nine o'clock service on Sunday. She'd thought he might call, say something to challenge her decision to move on. Nothing. Not that she intended to change her mind, but part of her wanted to know he was serious at the Botanical

Garden when he said he saw them together, that he wasn't just playing with her head. He'd been persistent when it came to pursuing her for the wrong reasons. Interesting how he'd given up so easily now, when it supposedly meant more.

Cyd shook the thoughts from her head. Her inclination on Saturday had been right. She needed to move on. Cedric had a lot of baggage to sort through, some of it dressed in lingerie. Besides, she wasn't convinced he'd really been changed. The whole morning at the Garden seemed like a distant dream.

She shrugged into her jacket and walked into the hallway—and her whole world skidded to a halt as she wondered whether _this_ was a dream.

Cedric was on campus, in January Hall, leaning against the wall near the door to her Greek 101 class, holding an armful of white roses. He held her gaze a few seconds, then pushed off the wall and came toward her.

"How did you . . . ?" She tried again. "How did you know where I'd be?"

He gave a slow smile. "Class locations and schedules aren't confidential information."

Her heart was beating fast. He was here. And he looked handsome as ever in a tailored blue suit. She stumbled for words. "Shouldn't you be at work?"

"I've had meetings all morning, got another one in a couple of hours. But I had to do this first." He came closer.

"Do what?" Her heart was pounding.

"Let's walk. It's a gorgeous day, and you're done with classes."

Her eyes widened. "How do you know?"

"The administrative assistant in your department is very helpful."

"I bet, especially when you show up with roses."

They walked out of the building and onto the artfully manicured grounds, with more than a few glances from students at the roses he was carrying.

When they came upon an out-of-the-way wrought-iron bench, Cedric gestured toward it. "Is this okay?"

Cyd nodded, her heart out of rhythm still as she sat, hands in her lap. What was he going to say?

Cedric lowered his head a moment and looked away. When he looked up again, he stared into her eyes, and she was almost certain she could see a depth in those brown eyes that she'd never seen there before.

"First," he began, "I want to say that I have a new mentor."

Cyd wasn't expecting that these would be his first words. "Okay. Who is it?"

"Scott."

She frowned, surprised. "Really? How did that come about?"

He laid the roses between them on the bench. "I called him Monday night. I did a lot of thinking Saturday and Sunday." He sighed at the remembrance. "A lot of thinking," he said again. "And I was reading a little in the Bible you gave me. I had so many more questions, and I remembered Scott and Lindell were meeting for lunch on Tuesdays, so I asked if I could come."

"I'm glad, Cedric." She truly was. "I think it's awesome that you want to find answers to your questions."

"Believe me, I had a lot of them," he said. "One thing I wanted to know was how Scott went about dating his wife before they got married."

She frowned again. "You asked him that?"

He gave her a slow nod, his eyes boring into hers. "And I told him why I was asking. I told him and Lindell about Saturday morning—even the part at the condo—and I said I needed to make a lot of changes, but I didn't know how to go about it."

"I'm not following you. What do you mean, 'make a lot of changes'?"

He gazed into her eyes so long she thought she would float on the feeling it gave her. "I said I wanted to make you my wife."

Cyd watched the students and faculty and birds and squirrels move in slow motion as his words played over and over in her head. By the sixth time, she could almost be sure she'd heard him right, but she was just as sure that he was crazy.

"Cedric, we barely know one another. I think you have good feelings toward me because God used me in your life, but that doesn't mean we're meant to be together."

His expression didn't change—except the gleam that entered his earnest eyes. "I told them you'd say that. That's why I wanted to know how Scott dated his wife. I want to show you that I'm serious, and I want to do things the right way, however long it takes. Because I do believe we're meant to be together."

His words alighted on her heart, someplace deep within, and in that unguarded space she could almost believe it too—that they were meant to be together. But her head commandeered deliberations. The whole thing was crazy. Cedric? Talking commitment? Sounded like he meant well, especially given his meeting with Scott and Lindell, but how long would those good intentions last? He was four days into a new mind-set. He'd had decades of living the other way. The pull to return to it would be strong.

But she was feeling an undeniable pull herself . . . to get to know him. Her mind couldn't grasp the wife part—too far-fetched. But she no longer wanted to walk away.

Maybe she never had.

"For your birthday," he was saying, "I gave you lavender roses—and by the way, I'm still enchanted with you, but in a different way. Anyway, now I'm giving you these." He lifted the white roses. "I know it sounds corny, but God must have seared these words on my brain, because I hear them in my sleep: I pledge to be true. These roses are a symbol that I want to do things God's way, the pure way. If you agree to let me see you, that's what our relationship will be about—purity. I don't even want to kiss."

Cyd's expression made clear she found that hard to believe.

"Okay, let me clarify." His smile melted her heart. "It's not that I won't want to kiss you. I'm not *going* to kiss you. I'm that committed to showing you that I'm all about getting to know you for you. The rest will come, after you become Mrs. London." He placed the bouquet into her arms.

Cyd didn't know what the next hour, day, or month would bring for her and Cedric. But she knew that right then in her heart, scary as it was, she had stepped onto a new path.

CEDRIC CALLED THAT evening after she'd eaten dinner. He seemed unusually shy at first, at a loss for what to say. After an awkward silence, he said, "Just tell me about you. All about you, from childhood on."

They talked for more than three hours, and Cyd learned much about him as well, like the kinds of rocks he collected as a boy, his knowledge of bird species, and his experience on the basketball team in high school. They shared favorite movies, laughed at favorite scenes, counted the number of states each had visited, then countries, marveled that neither had been to an island, and agreed there was no point in eating ice cream if you couldn't have chocolate.

They only hung up after Cedric made sure they would talk the following night—which they did, for *four* hours. This time they made dinner plans for the following night, and all day Friday Cyd had a giddiness about seeing him again. They chose a casual restaurant— jeans and a sweater for both—and hunched over in a booth like two schoolkids who couldn't get enough of one another, deep in conversation and laughter. Already they had an unspoken rule: they could delve into anything. Nothing was off-limits.

Still, Cyd was taken aback when Cedric said, "So who was the guy?"

Cyd's brow furrowed. "What guy?"

Cedric took a sip of cappuccino. They'd long been finished with their meal.

"You told me that first night we went out that you had been with a guy once, a long time ago. I know he had to be special. Who was he?"

"Gary." Cyd's mouth went dry, and she took a gulp of water. "There's not a whole lot to tell really."

Cedric raised a brow. "I doubt that, not if you let him get that close."

"True." She looked sheepishly at him. "To be honest, I just don't feel like talking about him." She traced a finger along the condensation on the outside of her water glass. She'd never talked to anyone about Gary but Dana and Phyllis.

"You don't have to tell me," Cedric said. "I understand." He sounded sincere.

Cyd bit her lip, considering. "No, we've basically made our lives an open book. I want to tell you."

"Yeah, I've shared things with you I've never shared with anybody. Even _feelings_ and stuff like that." He shook his head in mock disgust.

Cyd gave him a brief smile, then sighed. "I was twenty-nine, and I thought I had found my future husband. Gary and I dated for more than a year, saw each other constantly, held hands at church. We were in love. Or so I thought. He got a promotion that required a move to Philadelphia, and interestingly enough, Bryn Mawr had been trying to recruit me to their faculty, and they're right outside Philly. We decided he would go, get settled, and then I would follow up with Bryn Mawr. So before he left . . ."

Cyd took a steadying breath. "We had a special dinner, and he came back to my apartment and stayed later than normal. Said he wanted us to spend as much time together as possible. Things just got out of hand. He said if I loved him . . ." Cyd looked down, her emotions rising.

Cedric finished for her. "If you loved him, you would make love to him."

Cyd barely nodded. She still remembered how she felt the next morning, waking to him in her bed, feeling stripped of all that was sacred. But she did have one thing to hold on to—their relationship.

"After he moved," she continued, "we kept in touch almost every day for the first couple of months, but the calls lessened on his end, and then he was slow to return mine. It took him weeks to admit that he'd found someone else."

She met Cedric's gaze with a sigh. No tears had fallen, but they were pooled there for him to see.

He reached a hand across the table and locked his fingers with hers. "I'll bet he really did care for you, and when he moved, it was hard to maintain. But I'll tell you, hearing that story dredges up so much of my own past. I told you, Cyd, I played with women's minds. I did whatever it took to get what I wanted." There was sorrow in his voice. "And I never once said I was sorry."

"But you've told God."

"I know." He dragged his hand across the back of his neck. A determination entered his eyes, and he tugged on her hand. "Can we pray together?"

"Of course."

"I don't want to fail you, Cyd." He paused. "I don't want to fail *us*."

Us. The sound of it made her jittery, more so after memories of

Gary had been awakened. Would this relationship fare any better? She'd known Cedric a fraction of the time. Should there even be an _us_ so soon? Should she be feeling this close to Cedric already? Was she in one of those whirlwind deals that would come crashing down in an instant?

His other hand reached across, and she took hold. "I'm not good at praying yet, but I'll try."

She squeezed his hand and bowed her head.

"God," he began. He waited a moment before he continued. "I'm just going to talk like I've been doing in my heart. I know You've put this woman in my life. I feel like she's the one. And I don't want to mess it up. Help us do everything just like You want us to." He looked up, then bowed his head again. "In Jesus' name. Amen."

"Amen." Cyd sat back and took in the sight of him. No, this wasn't a whirlwind romance. Their feet were firmly planted, their minds set on honoring God. Though she had to admit her _heart_ was doing a little whirl. The more time she spent getting to know Cedric, the more she dared to hope . . .

CEDRIC PICKED CYD up for church, and the minute they hopped out of his car, directly in her line of vision, she saw her parents.

Great.

Her mother in particular would have all kinds of questions. She had told Cyd a few days after the wedding—in her motherly warning way—that she needed to steer clear of Cedric. "His hands were all over you on that dance floor," she'd said, "like he wanted to undress you. With his girlfriend a few feet away, no less!"

Cyd was at once embarrassed and defensive. "How do you know that was his girlfriend?"

"Cyd, he brought the young lady to the rehearsal and dinner, and to the wedding. But then he ignores her at the reception and dances with you like he wants to take you to bed."

Cyd had assured her mother she had nothing to worry about, that there was nothing between her and Cedric. Now they were showing up at church together, early Sunday morning. Her mother took immediate notice, lifting her head their way, but thankfully, she and Bruce were engaged in conversation with others. Cyd tossed a quick wave and headed toward the main entrance doors.

Cedric slowed behind her. "But I wanted to meet your parents."

Cyd kept walking. "Didn't you meet them at the wedding?"

"Yeah, but I wanted to meet them again. You know, now that we're getting to know one another."

"Oh. Well, maybe if we see them after church." Cyd hoped they wouldn't. She wanted time to explain that this was not the same Cedric.

She found herself in the same predicament at the pew. Everyone was present—Scott and Dana, Stephanie and Lindell, even Phyllis was on time. Scott and Lindell smiled with their eyes; the women questioned with theirs. Cyd knew she couldn't put it off. She needed to update everyone on the leaps her heart had taken in just the past week. When her mother made a beeline for her after the service, Cyd corralled all the women right then for a quick confab in the fellowship area.

The women poured coffee or hot water for tea from the carafes in the café-style section of the church. Once the five of them were seated at a round pedestal table with high stool chairs, Cyd addressed their waiting stares.

"Well," she said, "I wanted to tell you all at the same time that Cedric and I are seeing each other."

"That's pretty obvious," Stephanie said, dipping her tea bag. "I'm waiting to hear why. Like, maybe you flipped your lid or something."

"I wouldn't have put it quite like that," Claudia said, "but I must say I was rather surprised to see the two of you riding to church together this morning."

Stephanie's eyes got wide. "I didn't know you _rode_ together." She leaned in and tried to whisper, as if no one could hear. "Did he spend the night?"

"Oh, Stephanie, please," Dana said. She took a sip of coffee and sneaked a peek at Cyd, as if to make sure Stephanie wasn't right.

"Okay, that's why we're here," Cyd said, "to clear up all confusion. Here's the deal in a nutshell . . ."

Cyd told them about the Botanical Garden, the white roses on campus, the long conversations they'd been having, and their desire to do things God's way.

"I can't believe all that's been happening, and you didn't say anything," Dana said. "And I can't believe Scott kept it a secret."

Cyd smiled and looked a few tables away, where Scott, Lindell, and Cedric were having a confab of their own. "I didn't want to say anything at first. I had so many questions myself. But after this morning, I had to."

"So you think he's really changed, huh?" Stephanie sounded doubtful. "I guess it _is_ kind of interesting that he won't come inside your house since all this happened."

Cyd shared that when he picked her up and dropped her off on Friday, he said his hello and good-bye on the doorstep. Same this morning. For now anyway, he said he needed big-time boundaries and didn't want to come inside.

Dana held her cup. "But, Cyd, you always said you wanted a Caleb or a Joshua, a strong man of God. Cedric's a baby Christian. Not quite what you had in mind."

Phyllis had been quietly drinking her tea, but now she spoke up. "We have our own picture of what we want, but it's not always what God has in mind for us. I can tell you this. I would love it if Hayes were a baby Christian. At least he'd be in the kingdom."

"Well said, Phyllis." Claudia nodded thoughtfully. "Cyd, I wouldn't have chosen Cedric for you, but that goes to show how much I know. God had His own plan, and it's wonderful to hear what He's doing in Cedric's life. If He has a plan for the two of you, I believe that will be wonderful as well. I'll be praying."

Cyd's heart skipped with joy.

"I guess you can thank me," Stephanie said. "If I hadn't married Lindell, you wouldn't have met Cedric." She chuckled. "Wouldn't it be wild if we ended up married to brothers?"

Cyd held up her hand. "I'm not even going there. One day at a time is all I can do."

"I'm happy for you, Cyd." Phyllis got down from her stool and came to give her a hug.

Dana came around and hugged her as well. "I'm happy for you too. Cedric better act right, or he'll have me to contend with."

"I know that's right." Stephanie stood and shook a fist his way.

Cedric spread his arms and mouthed, "What?"

Stephanie laughed and waved him off, turning back to Cyd. "Honestly, Cyd, he does seem different. Just in the way he was looking at you today and deferring to you. I'm hoping it works out."

Claudia hugged her last. "We'll have to have him over so we can get to know him."

Two weeks later Cedric joined the Sanders family for Thanksgiving, arriving with two bouquets of flowers. One was a beautiful arrangement for Claudia filled with assorted colors, which she dressed immediately in a vase and set on the dining room table. The other was for Cyd, another dozen roses. "These," he told her, "are yellow for the close friendship we've developed. I don't know what I would do without you."

Cyd was beginning to wonder the same thing.

Twenty-six

IT WAS CHRISTMAS Eve and Phyllis wasn't in the best of moods, and not because of problems with Hayes. Things bordered on better between them. Since her trip to Chicago last month, she had put her focus on the one area she and Hayes had a shared love for—their family.

She'd made a big deal of instituting a family game night and a family movie night where they popped popcorn and ate other junk that made the evening fun. They also watched family videos, which made Hayes beam because he always said they never took time to enjoy all the footage he recorded. They wondered aloud why they hadn't, since these were funnier than any comedy movie they'd ever watched. They laughed so much their stomachs hurt at the antics Hayes had caught on film.

When she and Hayes were alone, she worked to keep the light mood by talking about the children, goings-on at school, things Ella was learning. She took a renewed interest in Hayes, too, asking about work and showing enthusiasm in whatever interested him. Hayes even commented that the getaway had done her good.

The mention of it had grieved her anew. When she thought of how close she'd come . . . Only through her time with God could she put it all behind her. And it was those early mornings that gave her renewed strength to press on in her marriage, come what may.

But now she was talking to Him for a different reason, trying to prepare her heart for her mother-in-law's visit. Evelyn would arrive today from Memphis. As close as she lived, they only saw her once every other year at Christmas, and in the years she didn't come for Christmas, she'd come for Mother's Day. They were always quick visits—three days tops. That was about all Hayes could tolerate. And while she was there, he was always on edge. Tense and moody.

It put a damper on Phyllis's spirits just thinking about it. She didn't want their home to have that cloud again, not when things had been going fairly well. But she knew it was coming.

Lord, I probably shouldn't pray this, but if Evelyn decides at the last minute that she can't come for whatever reason, let it be so. It would be nice to have peace this Christmas. That's what I'm praying for, Lord. Peace.

Evelyn called not an hour later to confirm her flight arrival time, and by midmorning Phyllis was negotiating airport holiday traffic. She pulled into the cell phone lot, and when Evelyn gave word that she'd landed and was leaving baggage claim, Phyllis headed to passenger pickup. She spotted Evelyn in a black wool coat near the curb and squeezed the van right in front of her. With the car in park, Phyllis jumped out to help Evelyn with her single piece of luggage.

"Hi, Evelyn!" She hugged her. "So glad you made it safely."

Evelyn's smile was kind. "Me too. It's good to see you, Phyllis." She handed Phyllis her bag, and Phyllis hoisted it into the trunk.

Phyllis hadn't seen her in more than a year, and it struck her that Evelyn looked better. Her hair was layered short, the gray alive and lustrous. And even with the coat, Phyllis could tell she was smaller around the middle. Even had on a touch of makeup.

Evelyn was never chatty. Phyllis had the feeling she held back on purpose. Maybe she thought Hayes had shared whatever caused them to be estranged—which he hadn't. The dynamic was always awkward.

Evelyn buckled in and faced forward. She glanced at Phyllis. "I can't wait to see my grandbabies. How are they doing?"

Phyllis pulled out into traffic. "They're fine, can't wait to see you. You won't believe how big they are."

"I couldn't believe the school pictures you sent me," Evelyn said. "Cole looks like a real young man now, and Drew and Sean have lost all their baby fat." She smiled. "You know I can't wait to see little Miss Ella. She was a newborn when I saw her last."

Phyllis felt a sadness upon hearing that. Evelyn had to want a closer relationship with her grandkids, maybe have them visit. But she would never ask.

When traffic stalled, Phyllis turned to her. "You're looking really good, Evelyn, like you lost weight. What have you been doing?"

"Thank you," she said, glancing politely at Phyllis. "I started walking. Nothing fancy. Just around the neighborhood."

"Really?" Phyllis smiled as she waited in a long line of cars to exit the airport. "Good for you. I like to walk myself." She tapped the accelerator to inch ahead. "Looks like you cut your hair a little different too. It's sharp."

Evelyn patted the back of her hair. If Phyllis wasn't imagining things, she almost blushed. "I do like it like this. I wanted to try something new."

"Wow. Exercise, new haircut. You don't have a boyfriend, do you?" Phyllis chuckled to let her know she was teasing. She hoped Evelyn wouldn't take offense.

Evelyn played with the gloves in her hand. "I might as well tell you now. I did meet someone." She gave the slight smile of a school-girl with a crush.

Phyllis snapped her head in Evelyn's direction. "Really? Oh my goodness!" She slammed on the brake when she noticed traffic had stopped again. "You mind telling me about him?"

"No, I don't mind," Evelyn said, still playing with the gloves. "I met him when he moved into the neighborhood to be closer to his children and grandchildren. He's the one I've been walking with." She looked over at Phyllis. "Might as well tell you this now, too, and get it out of the way. We're getting married."

"What?" This was too much information to handle at once. Phyllis turned left and headed toward the highway. What was Hayes going to say?

Evelyn was reading her mind. "I know Hayes won't really care." She was looking down again. "He doesn't care about much of anything I do."

Sadness settled again over Phyllis. They'd never discussed anything this personal, never touched on the rift between her and her son. Phyllis dared to go with the flow of the conversation. "I guess it's painful, the relationship between you two."

Evelyn stared out the passenger window. "It hurts more than you know."

Quiet engulfed the car as Phyllis veered onto 70 East and stayed in the far right lane to take the highway toward Clayton. There was so much she wanted to say, so much she wanted to ask, but she didn't know whether she should.

Finally she said, "Evelyn, I think I might know a little about how you feel. My own relationship with Hayes has been painful at times. I'm wondering if you can help me understand him."

Evelyn looked at Phyllis, clearly surprised. "I always thought things were fine between you two."

"They were, until a few years ago." Phyllis kept her eyes on the road. "When I became a Christian."

Evelyn stared in wonder. "I've been praying for you and Hayes for years, that you would know the Lord."

Though she was going top speed on the highway, Phyllis met Evelyn's gaze with shocked eyes. "You're a believer too?"

Evelyn nodded. "Nine years ago." She shook her head in disbelief. "How could we not have known this about each other?"

Simple, Phyllis thought. Hayes had said long ago that Evelyn didn't attend church, so when she came at Christmas, Phyllis and the boys stayed home for her and Hayes's sake. Because Phyllis avoided spiritual talk around the house, Evelyn never had reason to know. And neither had Phyllis known about Evelyn.

Evelyn turned toward Phyllis. "So tell me about Hayes."

Phyllis didn't know where to start. "It's been difficult because Hayes is so hostile to anything related to God. And he doesn't like to talk about his childhood much either. I just wondered if you might be able to shed some light on why he's this way."

Evelyn lapsed deep into thought, staring out the window ahead. Finally she turned back. "He hasn't told you why his father and I divorced?"

Phyllis shook her head. "No."

"I don't mind sharing this with you, Phyllis, because I know God worked it for good, but it's a part of my life that I'm ashamed of."

Phyllis gave her a quick glance that said she was listening, though she felt weird suddenly. She was about to get a window into Hayes's soul, one she'd never had. Her exit was coming up and she took it, but instead of going home, she headed toward the park so they could continue talking.

Evelyn was fidgeting with her gloves again. "I had an affair when Hayes was ten years old."

Phyllis felt sick suddenly.

"Harris and I had been having marital problems, and I had gone for counseling." She paused. "With the pastor."

Phyllis listened as she drove into the park, which looked festive with holiday decorations.

"Our church was small, everybody knew everybody. The pastor and Harris were friends; I was friends with Marla, the pastor's wife."

Phyllis had already parked, and she hated to interrupt. Quietly she said, "It's kind of cool out, but do you want to walk?"

They made their way to the water basin in silence and stood by the concrete retaining wall.

Evelyn continued, "On the second counseling session, he started making overtures toward me. I was as much to blame as he was. The affair carried on for months. Marla found out, and after that the whole church knew. I didn't know they knew until we came to church that next Sunday. People were calling me Jezebel and all kinds of names, right in front of Hayes. And the pastor preached about it, saying folk better beware of judging their pastor, that he wasn't perfect, and he could be tempted by an adulteress like anyone else." Evelyn spoke softly, staring out at the water. "We walked out of the service, and soon after, Harris walked out on me. The pastor remained in his position."

Phyllis couldn't take her eyes off of Evelyn. So much was becoming clear, even the episode with Hayes coming to Living Word to hear what Scott and Pastor Lyles had to say about what he'd guessed was adultery. She had to know. "Did Hayes enjoy church before that?"

Evelyn turned to her now. "Oh, Phyllis, he loved it. He loved Jesus. He knew his Bible stories like the back of his hand." She had tears in her eyes. "And after that, especially after we got divorced, his heart turned cold. He blamed me, he blamed the pastor, he blamed God."

All these years with Hayes, and she'd never known. Phyllis's heart ached for him. No wonder he felt the way he did, about God and about his mother.

Phyllis met her gaze again. "What did you do after that? How did you cope?"

"It was years before I could truly get my life together. It was hard raising Hayes when he had such an attitude with me all the time, understandably so. And Harris just disappeared. I paid such a high price, Phyllis. Infidelity is an awful, awful thing."

On the brink of tears, Phyllis watched a mother duck and her babies.

Evelyn leaned over the wall, following the ducks as well. "I was bitter about my life for the longest time. Knowing it was my own fault made it unbearable. But one day I got to talking to this woman at work. We both worked in data entry, and on our breaks she began telling me her story, how God had brought peace and joy into her life. It had been so long since I thought myself worthy of even thinking about God. But because of her, I found out He hadn't forgotten about me. Oh, it was the sweetest moment, falling into His arms." Evelyn paused. "But it's been bittersweet, too, because I want so badly for Hayes to experience that peace."

She sighed, and Phyllis was sure that sigh held a lifetime of pain.

Phyllis was getting cold, but she lingered in silence anyway. With all of this insight, she hadn't a clue what to do with it.

"Evelyn," she said finally, "would you mind if we prayed for Hayes?"

Evelyn put her arm around Phyllis, and they bowed heads as Evelyn asked God to move powerfully in the heart of her only child.

"GRANDMA, MOVE!"

Drew was leaning left. "You're gonna get killed! You can't just *sit* there! Go *that* way."

"Okay. I'm trying to get the hang of it." Evelyn was leaning left, too, but she didn't know how to make her ship do the same. Her thumbs were going crazy on the buttons, but they must have been the wrong ones because her ship hadn't budged.

Boom!

"That's it, Grandma." Sean looked sympathetic. "You're out of ships. That's the third game, and you haven't gotten out of Stage 1."

Phyllis chuckled. "Winner and still reigning champion: Phyllis Owens!"

"No fair," Evelyn said, still poised in front of the big screen. "I'm just learning. These are practice games." She pushed the green button, sure of that one. "Let's go again."

Ella bounced in place, doing a happy jig. She pointed at Evelyn. "Gandma."

"That's right, sweetheart," Phyllis said. "That's your grandma."

Evelyn bent down, giving Ella a big kiss on the cheek. "Sweet baby! Grandma's gonna get all those kisses."

Hayes walked past the family room toward the kitchen.

"Hey, Dad!" Drew called. "Let's see you play Grandma."

Hayes loved Galaga and rarely turned down an offer to take over the controls. But he yelled back, "Can't right now. Thanks, though."

Phyllis knew he wouldn't. He'd been avoiding his mother since she got here. He didn't get home until almost five o'clock from work, though the office was officially closed today, and at dinner he'd been reserved, letting the kids entertain Evelyn with their many stories.

After four more games Evelyn had finally gotten as far as Stage 3, and Hayes came and stood at the door. "Boys, time to get ready for bed. You've got to go to sleep early so Santa can come."

Phyllis kept from rolling her eyes. Every year Hayes talked up Santa; it was silly, since the boys didn't believe it and she preferred they focus on the real reason for the season.

"Daddy's right," Phyllis said, trying to find common ground. "Get ready for bed, 'cause you know you'll be up bright and early."

This was the only night of the year they didn't have to say it more than once. The boys kissed Phyllis and their grandmother, then Hayes on the way upstairs, yelling, "Good night!"

Phyllis stood and stretched. "I'll get Ella ready for bed."

Hayes bent to his knees and held out his arms so Ella would run to him. "I'll take her." His voice changed. "Come on, Daddy's girl."

Again, he was fleeing the scene. Ella held out her arms, and Hayes scooped her up and turned for the stairs.

"Okay, I guess I'll start on the dishes," Phyllis said.

She headed to the kitchen, and Evelyn followed behind. "Let me do the dishes, Phyllis. You were in the kitchen all afternoon cooking that big meal. I can still taste that delicious roast beef."

"Thanks, Evelyn." Phyllis put an arm around her as they crossed the threshold of the kitchen. "How about we work together?"

Evelyn smiled. "Perfect." She began to gather the plates, humming, "We Three Kings."

"That's one of my favorite Christmas songs," Phyllis said. She started singing, but she only knew the first six words by heart, so Evelyn chimed in, her singing voice strong and beautiful. They made it a lively tune as they moved about, and when they got to the chorus, they both stopped and sang loudly, "Ohh-ohhhhhh"—holding it ten seconds at least—then laughed and continued, "star of wonder, star of light . . ."

After "We Three Kings," Phyllis cried, "Joy to the World!"

They launched into song after song as they washed and began putting away the dishes. Evelyn handed her a platter to dry, and when Phyllis was done, she went to put it back in the china cabinet. From the corner of her eye, she saw Hayes standing to the left of the kitchen doorway, but he moved as if passing through.

The second she saw him, Phyllis dropped the chorus of "O Come, All Ye Faithful," but Evelyn continued. So Phyllis picked it back up as she put the platter away. She didn't know where Hayes had gone, but he was passing through again when she headed back to the kitchen. She paused. "Why don't you join us?"

To her surprise, Hayes entered the kitchen behind her and leaned against the counter, watching them. Phyllis tried to act nonchalant, even as they sang, "O come, let us adore Him, Christ the Lord."

Evelyn looked over her shoulder from the sink. "That used to be Hayes's favorite Christmas carol as a boy," she told Phyllis. "Remember, Hayes?"

He folded his arms. "You mean, back when we were pretending to be a Christian family?"

Phyllis eased a plate into the cabinet, holding her breath.

Evelyn shut off the water and pulled the dishwashing gloves from her hands.

Phyllis kept her head in the cabinet, rearranging bowls and salad plates as Evelyn walked over to him.

"Son, you're right," she said. "We weren't the Christian home we should've been. I wasn't the Christian mother I should've been. And it grieves my heart."

Phyllis pivoted slightly so she could see. Evelyn had her hip against the counter, facing him.

"But what grieves me more," she was saying, "is what you took away from it. I think you thought that's what Christians were about. That that's what Christian life was about. But no, that's what Evelyn Owens was about. It had nothing to do with God."

"It had everything to do with God. That man was a *pastor*."

"He was Otis Tillman the Third, with a title the powers-that-be gave him because his father had been a pastor and knew the right people. Titles don't make a person a man of God."

Phyllis closed the cabinet quietly.

"We were both a poor reflection of God," Evelyn continued, "and I hate that it diminished the glory of God in your eyes." She stepped closer to Hayes, though he was still looking down. "Hayes, you used to stand on a little stool and pretend you were preaching." Her eyes smiled at the memory. "You said the same four words every time—that was the whole sermon—but it said it all. 'Jesus died for you.' At bedtime you wouldn't let me pray. You'd say, 'No, I'll pray, Mommy. I'll talk to Jesus myself.' And oh my goodness, how you cried and carried on if you were too sick to go to church."

Phyllis didn't move a muscle, but she stole a glance at Hayes. His jaw set, eyes hard as steel, he was still staring at the floor.

Evelyn moved even closer to him. "Hayes, if you never listen to another word I say, I want you to know that the Jesus you prayed to as a boy is real. He hasn't changed. _I_ let you down, but He'll never leave you nor forsake you. It's true, son. He died for you."

Five of the longest seconds of Phyllis's life passed as the three of them stood there in silence. Without looking at either of them, Hayes pushed off the counter and walked out.

And it hit Phyllis. He had listened to every word without cutting his mother off.

AT FIVE THIRTY Christmas morning, Phyllis's alarm sounded and she popped up. She knew she'd have less quiet time before the kids dashed out of bed, so she didn't want to tarry. She would head to the living room, sit in her favorite chair, and sip tea as she talked to God and read her Bible. But as her legs hit the floor, she felt a hand on her arm.

She looked back at Hayes in the dark. "What are you doing up so early?"

"I couldn't sleep last night."

Phyllis could see him better now. He was on his back, his eyes wide open.

"You don't feel well?" she asked.

"I don't know." Hayes shifted to his side to face her. "I just . . . I need you."

As Phyllis stared at him, she could see the images Evelyn had painted. Hayes as a little boy, praying to Jesus. Hayes let down by the people he trusted.

She nestled close to him and they held one another. Tenderly he kissed her, and for the first time in a long while she looked forward to where it would take them. As they became one, Phyllis was almost sure she felt a dampness on her cheek, but she didn't dwell on it. If she did, she might get her hopes up that something was happening inside of her husband, because of this she was sure.

She'd never known Hayes to cry.

THE KIDS WERE all by the tree, the ruckus high, bells and whistles sounding as they tested gifts they'd just opened. Phyllis and Evelyn were right there with them on the floor, playing with a doll's hair, wielding a lightsaber, squeezing talking stuffed animals. Evelyn, in her robe, was in high spirits, despite the fact that Hayes hadn't said much more to her than "Good morning." After the revelry of opening presents, he had gone into the kitchen to cook breakfast.

Ella was bringing every gift to Grandma, even gifts that weren't hers, wanting to play with them, though she'd only play for thirty seconds, toss it down, and move on to the next. Now she handed Evelyn a board book Phyllis had given her of the Christmas story. Ella lowered herself into Evelyn's lap and excitedly clasped her hands.

Evelyn gasped with delight. "You want me to read it to you?"

Ella nodded vigorously and pointed to the book. "Read."

Evelyn made a big show of reading the title. "*The Story of Jesus' Birth.*" She smiled at her granddaughter. "Oh, this will be a wonderful story, Ella. I'm so glad you brought it to me."

The boys came closer, taking seats beside their grandmother.

Evelyn began, "'A long time ago, God sent the angel Gabriel to a godly young woman named Mary.'"

Ella tapped the picture on the page.

"Yes, that's Mary! Good girl!" She continued, "'The angel told her, "You will have a son and His name will be Jesus. He will be called the Son of the Most High and He will reign forever."'"

Phyllis heard footsteps and saw Hayes standing by the archway to the living room.

When they all looked up, he said, "Breakfast is ready."

"Can we hear the rest of the story first, Dad?" Sean asked.

Hayes hesitated, glancing at his mother and Ella on the floor. "No problem."

He stayed in the archway as Evelyn continued. After a couple of pages, Phyllis got up and took his hand, leading him to the sofa. He put his arm around her when they sat.

"'Nearby, shepherds guarded their flocks by night. An angel appeared and told them the wonderful news. "There is born to you this day in the city of David a Savior, who is Christ the Lord."'" Evelyn gaped at the children. "Can you imagine being the one to hear such news!"

Sean made a funny face. "I would have been like, *What?*"

Phyllis laughed as Evelyn continued.

"'Suddenly, many more angels appeared, praising God and saying, "Glory to God in the highest and on earth peace, good will toward men."'"

As Evelyn went on, that one word stayed with Phyllis. *Peace.* That was what she'd prayed for, and here she was, experiencing it. The last twenty-four hours seemed like a dream, as if God had suddenly entered into their circumstances, as if He were finally taking notice.

Yet there was nothing sudden about it. Years and years of prayer had looked to this, prayers from her and now she knew, from Evelyn. Hayes hadn't professed belief in Christ, but Phyllis was thanking God nonetheless. For the first time, they were celebrating together the reason for the season, the birth of Jesus Christ. A beautiful peace was raining down, a peace her home had never known. God was giving her that glimmer again, brighter than she'd ever seen it, and with all her heart she would be faithful to pray. She would pray until the heart of that little boy found its way back into the arms of Jesus.

Twenty-seven

IT WAS MID-MARCH, and spring had surprised everyone by showing up a week early. St. Louis had had one of the coldest winters
on record, with successive temperatures in the single digits in much
of February and only rising as high as the teens in the first part of
March. Just this past weekend, the high temperature was thirty-three.
But suddenly, in St. Louis's wacky weather way, a new season had
burst forth. It was seventy-two.

Cyd strolled across campus to her car, enjoying the feel of the
breeze, the warmth of the air. The onset of spring was her favorite
time of year, when nature was abuzz with newness and color and
fragrance. Her mind filled with things to do to take advantage of the
balmy weather—a leisurely walk through the St. Louis Zoo, a bike
ride in Forest Park, a stroll through the Garden to view the flowers
in bloom, a trip to Maggie Moo's to enjoy an ice cream cone outside
on the bench.

But she couldn't enjoy any of it like she wanted to yet, not without Cedric. He had left town Sunday evening on business, when it was still cold, and wouldn't return until Saturday. It was Thursday, only four days since he'd been gone, and they had talked every one of those days, but she missed him terribly. This was the longest they'd gone without seeing one another, and the time apart made her realize how close they'd become.

For the last three months they'd met for coffee first thing in the morning at a café they'd come to love near Cedric's condo. Rain, sleet, or snow, they were there. Prior to that, they'd done early morning phone calls, but it wasn't enough. They needed to get a hug, lay eyes on one another, enjoy the smiles, expressions, and gestures that accompanied their conversation, all of which made it hard to part when it was time for work.

During the course of the day they texted one another, and every evening they talked by phone, meeting at least twice a week for dinner. Those were her days, filled with Cedric, and she couldn't wait until he returned so they could do something fun outdoors—a sort of celebration of their first spring together as a couple. She'd already told him the weather had turned, and he, too, couldn't wait to get back. He suggested they pack a picnic lunch after church and take it to the park.

Cyd hopped into her car and opened the windows and the moon roof for her five-minute ride home. She planned to immerse herself in work this evening. Tomorrow Dana, Phyllis, and Stephanie would be coming over for a Daughters' Fellowship—Stephanie's first. Dana suggested they include her, and it seemed appropriate in this new season of their lives.

As she rode down her street, Cyd waved at several neighbors working in their yards and slowed in front of the house next door, where Ted was pulling weeds near the sidewalk. She stuck her head out the window. "Always nice to see everyone coming out of hibernation, isn't it?"

He grunted in his amusing way. "I guess. Wish spring didn't mean having to do *this*, though." He held up a clump, then threw it to the pile.

Cyd parked in the driveway and surveyed her own yard on the way to the front door. Time to call the guy who cut her lawn to make sure she was on the schedule.

She put her key in the front door and opened it. And froze.

Three petals—a lavender one, a white one, and a yellow one— lay by the door. And as she let her eyes travel forward, she saw a trail of them, all lavender, white, and yellow. Her heart was beating fast. Cedric's name was all over this, but how was it possible? And what was he doing back from Cincinnati already?

She let the screen door close behind her as she stared downward, taking tentative steps inside. She tossed her purse and tote bag on the sofa and came back to the trail. Petals were everywhere, as far as she could see on the hardwood floor that led into the kitchen, spring welcoming her indoors as well as out.

She picked up her steps along the trail, hastening to the kitchen, trying to step around the gorgeous petals, but there were so many it was impossible. The moment she stepped inside the kitchen, she gasped and froze again.

Red roses dominated the landscape. Bouquets of them in stunning crystal vases on several areas of the counter, on two windowsills, and on the kitchen table. Overwhelmed, she covered her face with her hands, but before she could ponder it further, Cedric emerged from the shadows and embraced her from behind.

She turned, and her head fell into his chest. That he was here with her was even more thrilling than the roses.

He held her for a few seconds, then leaned back. "Hi."

She laughed through her tears. "What are you doing here?"

He made a sweeping gesture with his hand as he looked around. "This."

"But . . ." She wiped a tear and took a breath. "What _is_ this? How did you get in? And you're supposed to be in meetings all week in Cincinnati."

He put a finger to her lips. "Shh." He walked to the windowsill and lifted a single red rose from the vase.

She noticed he had on the gray suit she'd helped him pick out and the red striped tie she'd recommended. The suit hung just right on his body as he turned back to her, smiling.

"I don't have to tell you what red is for, do I?"

Her tears came harder. He'd never said it.

"You've shown me life as I've never known it." He bent his head down so she'd look at him again. "Because of you," he continued, "I wake up in the morning with purpose and joy. I didn't need spring to make everything brand new. You'd already done that by introducing me to Jesus." He paused, sighing. "This sounds feeble after all you've done for me, but I wanted to tell you in a very tangible way: I love you."

Cyd took the rose he handed to her and gazed into his eyes. Her heart had been hammering this truth for some time, and finally she would tell Cedric. The butterflies swirled as she said it. "I love you too."

He only stared at her and took a step back. "Enough to be my wife?"

Cyd's heart was in her throat.

Cedric reached inside his jacket and produced a small box. He opened it, took out a velvet case, and set the box and her rose on the counter. Bending on one knee, he took her shaking hand.

"Cyd Sanders, will you marry me?" He opened the velvet case.

It only vaguely registered that this was the most beautiful diamond she had ever seen. Her eyes were on him, every handsome, wonderful, romantic aspect of him. How had the two of them gotten here? How could Cedric London have become the man of her dreams?

A thought flickered that they should give it more time. They'd only been dating for a little over four months. Didn't she need at least a year to be sure about such a big step?

Cedric was giving her a funny look with his eyes. "I'm _dying_ here."

She smiled down at him. "Yes, I'll marry you. A thousand times yes!"

He slipped the ring on her finger and stood, holding her close. "You just don't know," he whispered in her ear. "You've made me the happiest man in the world." He kissed her forehead and ran a finger down her cheek. Then he backed up, wagging his finger. "I knew this would be hard. I want to kiss you so badly."

Cyd wanted the same. "There's nothing wrong with kissing, Cedric."

"I know. It's just . . . a thing between me and God. This whole time we've been dating has been awesome for me, watching how God has changed my desires. I didn't think it was possible." He took both her hands. "I want to wait. I want to hear, 'You may now kiss your bride.' I want that moment. You know?"

Cyd nodded, her heart swelling all the more.

"So that's why I had a plan coming into this thing," he said. "We're not lingering here. We're going to your parents' house."

"For what?"

Cedric rubbed her ring finger. "For our engagement party."

"They know?"

Cedric smiled. "I asked your father for your hand last night. Had dinner and everything."

"You were in town last night? But I talked to you."

He had that mischievous look in his eyes that she hadn't seen in a long while. "On my cell phone."

She gave him a smirk. "What if I had said no?"

Cedric shrugged. "I guess I would've called over there and told the caterers and everybody else to go home."

Cyd shook her head, overwhelmed again. "Who's there?"

"Let's see," Cedric said. "Hayes and Phyllis went over there after they let me in and helped me get set up. Oh, and they took Reese to their house so the kids and the babysitter could play with her."

Cyd looked around suddenly, just now realizing Reese was gone.

"Stephanie and Lindell, Dana and Scott . . . Dana took over the guest list. Her sister's coming, that wedding coordinator, whole bunch of people. She said everybody would want to be there to celebrate with you."

Cyd wrapped her arms around him again. "I can't believe it. You're amazing, you know that?"

"Um, yeah, I kinda knew that."

She pushed him and headed for the stairs, gazing at her ring, walking on a bed of petals. "I need to get changed, but I won't be long," she called, then paused on the second stair. "Ced?"

"Yeah, babe." He walked over and looked up.

"Do you think we'll live here or in your condo?"

"I think it should definitely be here," he said. "I can sell my place, and we can do all the upgrades you've been wanting to do to this house."

Cyd beamed. "Seriously?"

He reached for her hand across the railing. "And we can walk our little one up the street on the first day of kindergarten."

She contemplated that. "You don't think we're too old to get started on a family?"

"Oh no." He gave her the eye. "We'll be getting started on those activities right away."

She gave him her own mischievous glance as she continued up the stairs, basking in a delirious giddiness from head to toe. She couldn't wait to be Cyd London.

Twenty-eight

ALL CYD COULD think when her eyes popped open on June 22—
her wedding day—was that she had to have lost her mind. She'd
given control of her pre-wedding hours to Stephanie—which was
enough to upend her mood for the entire day. She had agreed in a
weak moment, caught off guard by a surprise visit from Stephanie
and, even more surprising, an apology.

"You were there for me through all my wedding plans," Stephanie
said, "but I might not have been as appreciative as I could've been."

"You think?" Cyd laughed. "Long forgotten, Steph. No big deal."

"Well, still . . . you did so much for me, and I'd like to return the
favor. I want to plan your wedding morning for you. I've got some
ideas."

"Such as . . ." Cyd thought she'd wait a couple of seconds before
blurting no.

"That's the thing," Stephanie said. "I want it to be a surprise . . .

so you'd kind of have to trust me." Stephanie saw Cyd's expression. "Nothing *way out* or anything. It'll be fun. Memorable. Don't you think?"

Cyd had blurted it then. "No. It'd be ridiculous. I can't imagine waking up on my wedding day not knowing what to expect. It'll be stressful enough as it is." She shook her head in incredulity. "Besides, Cassandra's already helping to coordinate things."

"But I just wanted to coordinate a few hours." Stephanie looked dejected. "I thought it would be a great way to bless you. But I understand . . ."

Great. Cyd had sighed heavily. "Okay . . . fine. But nothing crazy, Steph. Basic stuff like go get hair done, come home."

Stephanie had flung her arms around Cyd's neck. "Oh, good! I'm so excited!"

That was a month ago, and every week since, Cyd had regretted it and tried to get a hint of the plans—to no avail. Now she was wide awake in bed at 6:00 a.m., wondering what possessed her to cede control of precious hours to her impetuous, often flighty sister.

She could barely sleep last night, though admittedly that part had little to do with Stephanie. She couldn't get her mind off of Cedric and all that lay ahead—both today and the rest of their lives.

He had called at eleven forty-five last night—after several conversations that day—and they'd talked until the clock struck midnight, their agreed-upon time to cut off contact until she walked down the aisle. After they'd hung up, she couldn't get his voice out of her mind, couldn't believe she'd be hearing that voice—and seeing his face—every night and every morning. She missed him even now, and thought of sneaking in a call—when the phone rang.

Was he thinking the same thing? Cyd smiled as she reached across a furry lump for the phone. Soon as Reese was potty-trained, she'd had freedom to roam about the house at night—and always ended up in Cyd's bed.

The handset glowed with the words _Stephanie London._ Cyd's countenance fell, but only slightly. She was eager for some answers.

"Rise and shine! How's the bride-to-be this morning?"

Cyd liked the sound of that. "Raring to go. What's the plan?"

"Your big day kicks off in a couple of hours." Stephanie sounded official. "We've got appointments at eight."

"Where? And 'we' who?"

"You, me, Dana, and Phyllis. Bridal party pampering at the Horizons Day Spa. I'm calling it Daughters' Fellowship—Extreme Edition."

Cyd laughed. "I have to admit it sounds like fun. I've never been to that day spa."

"Cyd, you've never been to a day spa, period. You never take time to treat yourself. But today you're getting the works—hair, nails, toes, and a massage."

"Massage? Who's got time for a massage? I don't think that's really necess—"

"Cyd, Cyd, Cyd . . . it's your special day. How long have you waited for this? We're gonna do it up right, girl!" Stephanie was relishing her semi-coordinator role. "We've got plenty of time. Wedding's not till four."

Cyd let the thought wash over her. It really was her special day. Finally. "Am I meeting you all at the spa?"

"No," Stephanie said. "Your chariot will arrive at seven forty-five."

CHARIOT INDEED. THE back window had been spray-painted with letters that read: _Bride on board—Honk to wish her well!_

Stephanie got a hoot out of the number of cars happy to oblige . . . and needled Cyd for slumping low in the seat. They arrived none too soon, and Cyd spotted Dana, Phyllis, and—She squinted. Was that her wedding photographer waiting in front of the spa?

"Here comes the bride," Dana and Phyllis sang as they greeted her with big hugs. The photographer clicked away.

Cyd waved for the camera. "Hi, Mr. Hughes. Um, what are you doing here?"

Mr. Hughes was a longtime member of Living Word who'd done photography on the side for years. Now that he was retired, he'd made it his full-time business.

He tossed a nod to Stephanie, camera still to his face.

Stephanie led them to the door. "He's doing a little side work for me—capturing DF Extreme in all its glory."

"Oh. Why?"

Stephanie sighed. "Okay, if you must know, I'm going to make a scrapbook of our time together to give to you as a gift."

"That's so nice! But . . ." Cyd frowned slightly, and Mr. Hughes caught it. ". . . you don't scrapbook."

Stephanie winked at Phyllis as she opened the door. "A little bird's gonna teach me."

Inside, a host awaited them and carted Cyd off to her massage. When she rejoined the others—wonderfully wobbly at the knees—they sank into four comfy chairs in the pedicure room, pausing the chatter only long enough to vote on the polish for Cyd's toes and ham it up for the camera. After nails and hair, the ladies—and Mr. Hughes—climbed into their cars and moved out.

"Steph, that was awesome." Cyd was so refreshed she forgot to slouch down. "Where to now?" She checked her watch—eleven thirty—and wondered what Cedric was doing with his side of the wedding party—Lindell, Scott, and a childhood friend.

"You'll see soon enough," was all Stephanie would allow.

The caravan found itself at Cyd's house, and Cyd noticed Stephanie, Dana, and Phyllis carrying garment bags from their cars.

Hmm . . . guess we're getting dressed here.

When Cyd pushed the door open, a delicious aroma greeted her, and a moment later her mother appeared, with Reese in tow, and led them to the dining room Cyd rarely used.

"Okay, I didn't expect this." Cyd looked from Claudia to Stephanie to a table laid with fine china, fresh-cut flowers, and place cards with their names whimsically written.

The camera registered her surprise.

"This is incredible. How did you—?" She didn't bother to finish. "I need to figure out how many of my house keys are floating around out there."

They ushered Cyd to the head seat and showered her with funny memories and even funnier marriage wisdom while savoring spinach quiche and assorted fruit.

When a bout of laughter settled, Dana's voice drifted in. "Not trying to get too serious here, but since we're offering wisdom . . ."

Cyd and the other women waited to hear what she had to say. Mr. Hughes had taken some candid shots and left to give the women privacy.

"Right now," Dana said, her eyes on Cyd, "you're living a fairy tale. And I know it's awesome. But every day won't be a fairy tale." She took a breath, her eyes glistening. "But I can tell you this—every day, God is faithful."

Cyd was already tucking Dana's words into her heart.

"Who would've thought God would use Stephanie and Lindell to help heal our marriage?" Dana was saying. "But He did." She smiled at Stephanie. "Hanging out with you two—double dating and acting silly—has done so much for Scott and me." She turned back to Cyd. "My 'wisdom' for you today is to keep the faith, so that when you don't see the fairy tale, you'll still be able to see the beauty of God working."

"_Keep the faith_—that's beautiful, Dana," Claudia said. "Bruce and I are about to celebrate forty-five years, and you can imagine we've had our share of bumps in the road."

"*I* can't imagine," Stephanie interjected. "You and Daddy?"

Cyd chuckled. She was thinking the same. Even though Cyd knew her parents had to have issues, those issues rarely manifested openly. What showed was their love and respect for one another.

Claudia was nodding big for emphasis. "Yes, your daddy and me. Every marriage has difficulties. But looking back, I can say God was in the midst of each and every one, working it out. That's a lot of faithfulness."

"I guess when I think about it," Stephanie offered, "God's been working in my marriage too."

The women couldn't help but show amusement.

Stephanie joined them with a chuckle. "Okay, maybe I'm the last to see it," she said. "Dana, you said Lindell and I helped you and Scott, but I don't know where we'd be without you two. No telling what I'd be up to."

"I'll add my amen to 'keep the faith,'" Phyllis said, "which I failed to do for a while." Despite her words, Phyllis had a peace about her. "For the longest time I thought God had forgotten about us. I wondered what was the use of praying."

Cyd's heart went out to her friend. She wondered herself why God hadn't answered years of prayers regarding Hayes, yet her own husband-to-be had become a man of faith. It didn't seem fair.

Phyllis continued, "But even though God hasn't answered in the way I would like, I've been able to see that beauty Dana talked about . . . in the love Hayes shows for me and the kids. *And*," she added, "I've caught him reading my Bible a couple of times lately."

"Woooo," Cyd exclaimed, the others in chorus with her. "Why haven't you mentioned that? Girl, that's a praise update!"

Phyllis smiled. "Believe me, I did praise God. And if I have any wisdom to offer, it's to *look for* His faithfulness in your marriage. There will be times when it won't be packaged with bright bows, but it'll be there."

"This is so good." Cyd held their faces in her gaze. "Being able to spend meaningful time with you all on my wedding day, reflecting, sharing . . ." She got up and hugged her sister's neck. "I have to give it to you. Things didn't turn out too badly after all!"

"Told ya!" Stephanie hugged her in return, then checked the time. "Ooh! But they will if we don't get moving. Cassandra'll kill me if we're late."

ALL THE TALK of marriage made Cyd's insides a jumble—a wonderfully expectant jumble that built and swirled and didn't seem near real until she was staring at herself an hour later in the bathroom mirror, tears threatening to spill on her freshly made-up face. As Stephanie fussed with the zipper and messed with the train, Cyd was corralling the moment. Just last fall she thought she'd never see this day, and here she was. A bride. Cedric's bride. As incredible as the day had been thus far, she hadn't lost sight of the main event. She was about to marry the man who'd captured her heart . . . in only a matter of hours.

Thank You, God. She let the tears fall. _Thank You._

Stephanie dabbed the wetness in a flash and gave her a look as she applied some powder. "Okay now, there'll be time for all that later."

Cyd smiled at her sister.

"I think we're good," Stephanie said. "Oh, wait a minute." She did something with the back of the gown and stood back. "Wow. You look really good."

"Thanks, sis."

"Okay, come on."

Stephanie opened the door and Cyd stepped into her bedroom, where the others had been dressing and waiting for them. There was silence when they saw Cyd. They walked forward and took her in.

Tears started in Dana's eyes. "Oh, Cyd, you're absolutely beautiful. I'm so happy for you. So, so happy for you." She hugged Cyd and pressed the tears in the corners of her eyes. "That dress is amazing."

Phyllis was taking in the view all around. "You would've looked good in just about anything, Cyd, but nothing would've been this perfect. You're a vision." She smiled at Claudia. "Pretty special, huh?"

Claudia fingered the embroidery, her emotions stifling an immediate response. "Cyd wanted to surprise me, so I haven't seen it on her till now." She brushed her watery eyelids, embracing her daughter. "I could've never envisioned this."

"Me either," Cyd said. The dress swished as she walked to the full-length mirror, feeling every bit the princess. "It was better than I envisioned."

She'd only had three months to prepare for her wedding, and the gown was high priority on the list. But she'd just gone bridal boutique hopping with Stephanie last fall, and the pickings were fresh in her mind. Many were gorgeous, but only one stuck in her mind, and she hadn't seen it in a store; she'd seen it on the mantel of her parents' fireplace. Maybe she still saw it with the eyes of a young girl—and maybe it had everything to do with who had worn it—but it always seemed to her the dress of her dreams.

When she inquired, Claudia handed it down with a heart of joy. She'd preserved it well. The dilemma was the season, since the dress was suited to fall, the time Cyd's parents had married. The solution was simple, for a seamstress at least. The long sleeves were shortened and restyled with cutout lace, and the high neckline recut to a graceful scoop. As a special touch, the seamstress hand-beaded the bodice, leaving the balance of the lustrous satin sheath untouched.

"Turn around so I can get some pictures." Dana was filling in for Mr. Hughes, who had returned and was waiting for them downstairs. "So you've got your old," she said between clicks of the camera.

Cyd looked confused.

"You know, something old, something new . . ."

"Oh, I forgot about that." Cyd thought a moment. "My shoes are new." She lifted a foot. "Does that count?"

"I don't see why not." Phyllis was double-checking herself in the mirror. The bridal party wore ankle-length champagne-colored dresses, and they all looked fabulous. "What about something borrowed?"

Cyd moved her hair behind an ear. "Momma let me wear her diamond earrings."

"Those are gorgeous!" Dana said, turning an impressed look to Claudia. "You've got two bases covered, Ma Claudia."

"I just need something blue." Cyd wasn't big on the tradition, but since she had three out of four, she figured she might as well try.

"Girl," Stephanie said, "didn't you see me pin that little piece of blue fabric to the inside of your dress? I did the same thing with my own wedding gown."

Cyd kissed both of Stephanie's cheeks Euro-style. "Cassandra better watch out. You might be able to really run with this coordinator thing."

Stephanie laughed. "I don't know about that, but I _do_ know we need to get out of here—'cause Cassandra's already called twice to check up on us." She put her hand to the doorknob. "Ready, ladies?"

CYD'S ROSE-STUDDED WALK down the aisle was flanked by faces from every facet of her life, though mostly from Living Word—and most of _them_ seeming on the verge of outright applause. They were on their feet, grinning, half waving, easing into the aisle to get a good picture, apparently as awed as she that this was actually happening.

Hand looped inside her dad's arm, her eyes bounced naturally among the familiar faces, but always landed again squarely on Cedric, whose gaze remained fixed on her. As they took in the sight of one another now, she felt their love to her very core. This man, this moment, was ordained for her. Her heart echoed the day's refrain.

Thank You, God.

Mackenzie gave a tiny wave from up front and Cyd tiny-waved her back, then aimed one at Mark for good measure. Like Stephanie, Cyd had thought them indispensable to her wedding—and the kids loved that it was a family affair this time, since their parents were also taking part. Their aunt Trish had gotten them ready and brought them to church, where they'd hung out "backstage," as they'd called it, with the wedding party.

Cyd took her last steps to the front, where Cedric drew her by hand and leaned to her ear. "I'm never going this long again without talking to you," he whispered. "We should've had a morning wedding."

Cyd smiled, her heart on overload, filling with his presence. She tucked her arm inside his. "I missed you too."

Cedric sneaked his head close to hers once more, though Pastor Lyles had begun his opening remarks. "You're the most beautiful woman on the planet," he whispered. "There's no way I deserve you."

Cyd closed her eyes against his arm. Not a good way to start; emotion was already building. She kept her composure, though, through most of the ceremony . . . till they got to the last song.

Cedric's sister, Kelli, sang and the whole church seemed riveted. Cyd couldn't believe Kelli had penned the lyrics herself. They spoke of love and sacrifice, and Kelli sang from the depths of her soul.

Pastor Lyles led them through the traditional portion of the vows, then cued Cedric with a nod.

Cedric eased the wedding ring onto Cyd's finger. "In the presence of everyone gathered here and in the presence of God, I pledge to be true to Him first and foremost. And I pledge to be true to you, Cyd, to cherish and love you, and to grow in Christ with you through the years."

Cyd could barely see through her tears as she placed the band on Cedric's finger and repeated the same.

Pastor Lyles glanced at the guests. "Trust me, they've been waiting for this moment." He smiled at the couple. "I now pronounce you husband and wife. Cedric, you may kiss your bride."

Cedric looked into Cyd's eyes and twined his arms around her waist. Their lips touched lightly, then he kissed her again, holding her long seconds afterward. "I love you," he whispered.

She lingered in his embrace. "I love you too."

"I present to you," Pastor Lyles said, "Mr. and Mrs. Cedric London."

The guests really did erupt in applause now as Cyd and Cedric made their way down the aisle arm in arm. They strolled through the double doors of the sanctuary and continued to the outer doors of the church where a limousine awaited them. They would ride to the Botanical Garden, where the rest of the wedding party would meet them for pictures, and then on to the reception.

The driver opened the door, and Cedric helped Cyd inside. They settled in and snuggled close as the driver whisked them away. Cedric laid his head next to hers, their hands locked as one. "Did I tell you I love you?"

His whisper sent a sweet shiver through Cyd. She knew every day wouldn't be a fairy tale, but today was—and she would treasure every single second. "Um . . . I don't remember. Maybe you should tell me again."

He shifted so he could look into her eyes. "I love you, I love you, I love you, I love you." Their lips came together. "I can't say it in Greek, but want me to say it in French and Spanish?"

"I kind of like it when you say it this way." She brought her lips to his once more, then nestled back beside him.

Cedric brought an arm around her and exhaled. "This is nice—a few private minutes with my wife."

Cyd drank in his words. *"My wife."* She guessed she had a lot to get used to. She lifted her head again suddenly and stared at her husband, then kissed him slowly. "Can I do that whenever I want?"

He frowned an *Of course.*

"Just testing," she said. She could definitely get used to that. "Oh, hey—" She lifted her bouquet. "You haven't told me what these mean."

She'd thought she'd be carrying white roses, until the florist told her before the ceremony that Cedric wanted to surprise her.

"You don't know what orange roses mean?"

She wrinkled her face as if thinking about it. "Nope. Afraid I don't."

He chuckled. "I didn't either at first. I wanted something unique, and when I saw orange I just liked it; it was so vibrant. Then the florist told me what it symbolized." He gazed into her eyes. "She said it stood for passion and excitement and romance, and I knew it was perfect. That's what I want for the rest of our lives together." He leaned in for a kiss.

"Mmmm, sounds wonderful."

"Mm-hmm," Cedric said, their lips locked still. "Starting tonight."

"Sounds even better."

"Actually," he said, "let's just tell the driver to take us to our hotel suite right now."

Cyd laughed, her head falling on his shoulder. "Now, now, Mr. London. We can wait." She got a twinkle in her eye. "And it'll be worth it, because I have a surprise for you."

Cedric sat up a bit. "What?"

She stifled a smile. "All I can say is I got the idea from your brother."

"Lindell?"

Cyd nodded. "He's the man, you know."

Cedric sat up now, half frowning. *"Lindell?"*

"Yeah." It was all she could do not to laugh. "Wait till you see how he inspired me."

She leaned back in his arms and let him hold her. Something else she could definitely get used to.

Acknowledgments

I AM SO in awe of You, Lord. You are ever jumping from the pages of Scripture straight into my world, making Your ways known, showing Yourself strong. You are God, the Rock, the Holy One, the Most High . . . and You are *faithful*. Thank You for loving me, leading me, and teaching me. You are the vine, and I am the branch—apart from You, I can do nothing (John 15:5). I'm so clinging to You, Lord!

God has been *faithful* in providing an awesome support team that starts with my husband and children. Thank you, Bill, Quentin, and Cameron, for cheerleading me through, for believing in me, and for understanding when dinner's late (or, *ahem* . . . crisp) because the story was calling. To my mother, Edna J. Cash—thank you for being my personal prayer warrior, counselor, and editor. How many times did you read through the manuscript? I've thanked God a million times for you, so might as well make it a million and one. To my father and stepmom, Earl and Joyce Cash—thank you for loving and supporting me always, and for making me laugh. My life is richer because of you.

To Bridget Thomas, Anne Amado, and Tanya Harper—thank you for reading this story early on and sharing your thoughts and insights. And thank you for supplying the most needful thing—prayer. And speaking of prayer, I've got to thank Cheryl Bohlen for setting up a prayer team for me two years ago. Cheryl, I was surprised when you first told me you felt moved to do so, but who knew what God had in store? We've seen amazing answers to prayer. And, Anne, you know I've got to mention your Ephesians 3:20 signature e-mails. Only God knew what He would bring to pass . . .

To my "writing sisters in Christ"—Jenny B. Jones, Nicole O'Dell, Cara Putman, Cindy Thomson, Marybeth Whalen, and Kit Wilkinson—so thankful for the way God has knit this group together through blizzards of e-mails and the pouring out of hearts. Thank you for listening, advising, praying, and giving a needed kick in the pants.

God has been *faithful* in providing an awesome publishing team. To my publisher, Allen Arnold, my editor, Amanda Bostic, and my former editor, Jocelyn Bailey—you are gifts from God. Thank you for believing in me, and more than that, thank you for making me feel part of the Thomas Nelson Fiction family. Amanda and L.B. Norton, your editorial comments made this story immensely better—even that change in the ending I wondered about at first. ☺ It's been so enjoyable working with both of you. To Jennifer Deshler and Katie Bond (my Twitter friends), Becky Monds, Ami McConnell, Kristen Vasgaard, Andrea Lucado, Ashley Schneider, and Micah Walker—thank you for showing so much love on my first visit to Nashville. I had such a great time hanging out with y'all!

To Mary Graham and Lori Robertson—where do I even begin? Thank you for this incredibly amazing opportunity to be part of the Women of Faith family. My life has been enriched in so many ways because of you. Who knew therapy would be included? And to all of the Women of Faith speakers, musicians, and talented staff—thank you for lovingly welcoming me aboard. Your hugs were so appreciated!

To my agent, Tina Jacobson, and The B&B Media Group, Inc.— so thankful for all you've done. Talk about God being *faithful*. Tina, I'll never forget our first conversation—such a God-thing!—nor your belief in me. You bring such encouragement to my heart.

To my sorors of Alpha Kappa Alpha at the University of Maryland, College Park—our reunions inspired that aspect of the story. Thank you for special memories and laughter that reach back more than twenty years [gasp!].

And to the readers—this book is for you. I can't express how thankful I am that you would give of your time to read *Faithful*. You're the reason I do what I do. I'd love to hear from you. Contact me through my Web site—kimcashtate.com—or if you're on Facebook or Twitter, I'd love to connect there too (facebook.com/kimcashtate and twitter .com/kimcashtate). Praying God's blessings upon you!

Reading Group Guide

1. Cyd questioned God's promises because she had delighted in Him and abided in Him but had not received the desires of her heart—to marry and have children. Have you ever questioned God's promises? Did you look to God and the Bible for reassurance?

2. Phyllis told God, "Lord, I'm tired of trying to keep the faith." Have you ever prayed, believing for a circumstance to change, only to be disappointed time and time again? Did you admit to God that you were weary? Did you ask Him for strength to endure? Why or why not?

3. In her greatest time of need, Dana didn't think to pray right away. She turned inward instead of upward. Do you have a regular prayer life? Or do you find that your prayers can slacken, even in times of need? What tangible things can you do to increase fellowship time with God?

4. At the wedding reception, Cyd battled with the desires she felt for Cedric. At what point should she have drawn the line? Before the first dance? Before the second? Should she have agreed to go to dinner? Has the temptation of the moment ever caused you to move your boundary lines? What was the result?

5. Phyllis and Rod debated whether they could be friends. What do you think? Can a male and female believer maintain a Christlike friendship when one or both are married? If so, what safeguards should be erected in such a friendship?

6. When Scott addressed the congregation, he said they might be thinking, *I would never.* If you're married, do you feel you would never be unfaithful to your spouse? Discuss these verses in relation to the question: "Keep watching and praying, that you may not enter into temptation; the spirit is willing, but

the flesh is weak" (Matthew 26:41). "Therefore let him who thinks he stands take heed lest he fall" (1 Corinthians 10:12). How can you keep from falling?

7. The congregation's applause for Dana and Scott confirmed that it was okay for her to want her marriage. Why would she think it might not be okay to want her marriage? Does society give us that impression? Did Dana extend forgiveness too soon? Think about times you've been wronged in a relationship. Have you had difficulty forgiving?

8. Cyd told Cedric she couldn't follow feelings, that she had to let her mind lead, and her knowledge of what's right. Do you tend to follow your feelings or does your knowledge of what's right lead you?

9. The Intimacy Group tackled some tough questions. How would you respond to these: What is the path to adultery? How can it be avoided?

10. Cyd said she had to "pledge to be true" even if she never got married. How difficult is it for singles to honor God by remaining celibate? Discuss ways in which this goal can be achieved.

11. Curled up on a hotel bed, Phyllis wondered how she had gotten there. How *did* she get there, spiritually speaking? What had happened in her relationship with God? What lessons can you take away regarding your own relationship with God?

12. Read 1 Corinthians 10:13. How was God faithful in Phyllis's circumstance? What way of escape was given to her in the hotel? Can you remember times in your own life when God provided a way of escape?

13. On Cyd's wedding day, Dana told her that every day wouldn't be a fairy tale, but every day, God is faithful. Can you see God's faithfulness in your life? Do you remind yourself of that faithfulness in the hard times? Discuss the ways in which God has been faithful to you.

Coming Fall 2011

cherished

The new novel from

Kim Cash Tate

Author to Author

THE THOMAS NELSON Fiction team recently invited our authors to interview any other Thomas Nelson Fiction author in an unplugged Q&A session. They could ask any questions about any topic they wanted to know more about. What we love most about these conversations is that they reveal just as much about the ones asking the questions as they do the authors who are responding. So sit back and enjoy the discussion. Maybe you'll even be intrigued enough to pick up one of Neta's novels and discover a new favorite writer in the process.

A Note from Kim Cash Tate: About a year and a half ago, I picked up *The Yada Yada Prayer Group* and didn't stop walking with those women until—reluctantly—I had to part after the last of the seven-book series. I was moved in so many ways by the women in that prayer group, but the woman who intrigued me most was the author, Neta Jackson. It's not too often you can pick up a Christian fiction book and find such a rich rainbow of diversity in the characters. I knew she had to be a phenomenal woman, and the more I read about her, the more my suspicions were confirmed!

I'm so thrilled to be able to feature Neta Jackson in this Author to Author interview.

KIM CASH TATE: If I'm not mistaken, *The Yada Yada Prayer Group* was your first adult novel. After a publication history in nonfiction and historical fiction for the young, what made you shift to women's fiction?

NETA JACKSON: I had no intention of writing women's fiction! I had written several kids picture books—the Pet Parables and *Grandma Aggie and the Bless You Bike Ride*— and had a lot of ideas for more "Grandma Aggie" books. But meanwhile, "life happens," you know, and I'd been part of a racially and culturally diverse women's Bible study for several years that often met in our home, so my husband was privy to the dynamics and stories popping out of this group. One morning I woke up and he wasn't in the bed. That in itself was unusual—I'm *always* the first one up. But he wasn't in the house, either. I found a note on the kitchen table that said, "Got an idea for a story. Gone for a walk." When he came back, he handed me a tape recorder. "Now you go for a walk and listen to this. God gave me an idea for a great story during the night—but you'd have to write it." Ha! Guess what. It was basically the idea for a novel about a group of mismatched women from different races and cultures in a prayer group. Long story short—that's when *The Yada Yada Prayer Group* was born. It was supposed to be just one novel, but I was so naïve. Found out you can't put 12 feisty women in a novel and expect them to stay there. The stories just kept popping!

KCT: I have to tell you, after the first couple of chapters of *Yada Yada*, I was totally engrossed, inspired, and wondering . . . if you were a black woman! I thought, *Hmm, the way she captures the voices of the black characters, and there's no author picture on the cover, and well, the name "Neta Jackson" could be . . .* <big grin> When I looked up your website, my question was answered. But then I saw that you'd helped to write a book on racial reconciliation, and you attend a multi-ethnic church. You obviously have a passion for not only writing books that promote unity, but living it yourself. How did God work that into your heart?

NJ: Hmm. How long did you say this interview should be? Such a long, long story . . . which began way back in college when I attended a black storefront church on Chicago's west side. Talk about culture shock! Later my husband and I became members at this same church. It was the start of a journey God used to open our eyes to how divided the Body of Christ is—not only by denomination, but by culture and race and economics. Such a far cry from Jesus' prayer in John 17 that His disciples would be "one"! I have to admit, at first I thought we were "doing something great for God" by getting out of our comfort zone and relating to people across racial and cultural barriers. But the funny thing is, I began to learn so much about faith and worship and walking the Gospel from my brothers and sisters of color—especially the sisters in this women's Bible study that started over thirteen years ago—that I began to realize _how much I NEED them_. That passage of Scripture in 1 Corinthians 12 began to come alive in a new way—especially the verses about how much the different parts of the Body _need_ each other. In today's world, most Christians acknowledge that the Body of Christ is made up of many different cultures and races and denominations, but I think we're still a long way from owning how much we _need_ each other. You're right, this has become a passion in my life, to open our eyes to the blessings God has in store for us when we develop real relationships with our brothers and sisters across the barriers of denomination, culture, and race that so often keep us apart. It's my prayer that the Yada Yada novels are helping to do that in one small way. (Okay, okay, I'm getting off my soap box!)

KCT: Besides the black and white Americans in the prayer group, you included a Jewish woman, a Japanese woman, a Hispanic woman, and a Jamaican woman—all with authentic voices. Were those characters based on people you know? What caused you to want to cast such a wide net in terms of this rich tapestry of people?

NJ: Many of my characters were "inspired by" people God has put into my life, but I need to stress that all my characters and the details of their lives are fictional. The closest I've come to actually telling one person's story is Bandana Woman. (I dedicated *The Yada Yada Prayer Group Gets Down*, Book 2 in the series, to the real "Bandana Woman.") Otherwise, all the characters and many of the events are *composites* of real people and events God has used to teach and shape me. (Example: I've had a "Stu" in my life who seemed to do everything I could do, but always did it better . . . or first . . . or whatever, and I'd end up feeling small or late or all thumbs. So I wanted a character who made Jodi Baxter feel that way.) Another friend from Zimbabwe taught me so much about praying Scripture—so I created a character that brings that quality to the Yada Yadas, even though her life situation is fictional.

KCT: The power of prayer is, of course, central to the series, as is praise and worship and the Word of God. You show us how God can enter into ordinary, flawed lives and change them profoundly. Have you experienced a prayer group like this in your own life?

NJ: Yes, as I mentioned earlier. An African-American sister and I were in an intentional "racial reconciliation" group in our church, and we also sang alto together in a Gospel choir.

One day we confessed to each other that we got tired of talking about "issues" all the time. What we'd really like is a diverse group of sisters just to study the Bible and pray for one another, dealing with "issues" as they arose naturally from our life experiences. So we each began inviting others to join with us, committed to keeping the group ethnically diverse and keeping our focus on God's Word and prayer. We didn't really know what we were doing, but God has used this group to turn my life upside down (or maybe that's "rightside up"!). This is the group that inspired the Yada Yada Prayer Group series, even though we've had sisters come and go over the years—but we're still going strong!

KCT: I'm also loving your current series, the Yada Yada House of Hope, which features a new character, Gabrielle Fairbanks, with a sprinkling of familiar faces and places from _Yada Yada_. In the front of the book, it says Dottie Rambo's song, "I Go to the Rock," inspired the theme and the titles for the series: _Where Do I Go?_, _Who Do I Talk To?_, _Who Do I Lean On?_, and, upcoming, _Who is My Shelter?_ Could you tell us more? How did that song provide inspiration?

NJ: As you know from the Yada Yada series, I dropped a lot of gospel music into the story, which was one way of sharing how much God has used gospel and praise-and-worship songs to enrich my own worship life. As I was thinking about a new series, I thought it would be neat to use a gospel song as the theme and use phrases from the song for the book's titles. So the idea came first, the song came later. When I heard "I Go to the Rock" by Dottie Rambo sung by a local worship band—especially the phrase in the second verse, "Where do I go . . . when the storms of life are raging?"—I knew this was the song to undergird my story about a broken marriage and a homeless shelter. I got permission to use the song and was hoping to give Dottie Rambo copies of the novels in appreciation for her fantastic song—but she was killed in a tour bus accident in 2009. (However, I did meet Babbie Mason who also recorded that song, and was able to give *her* copies of the first two novels. Here's the serendipity part: we met at a fundraising banquet for a *homeless shelter* here in Chicago—the same shelter that inspired the House of Hope series. Babbie was the stage talent that night. Don't you love how God knits things together??)

KCT: What issues are you exploring in this current series? What do you want your readers to take away?

NJ: First of all, I didn't set out to write about a verbally abusive marriage. I simply wanted to show that life can fall apart for any of us—rich, poor, or in between—and that it's not just drug addicts and prostitutes who end up homeless and broke and in need of shelter. I volunteer at a homeless shelter and am amazed at some of the stories I've been privileged to hear, as well as God's redemptive work putting broken lives back together. Actually, the song says it all:

Where do I go . . . when there's no one else to turn to?
Who do I talk to . . . when nobody wants to listen?
Who do I lean on . . . when there's no foundation stable? . . .
When I need a shelter, when I need a friend
I go to the Rock.

("I Go to the Rock" by Dottie Rambo. Used by permission.)

KCT: I've got another suspicion about you, that there's so much more bubbling in your heart and ready to spill onto the pages for readers to devour. Care to share a sneak preview of people or themes you're planning to explore next?

NJ: If you only knew how scared I am to end these two series and tackle something brand new! It's hard to say goodbye to my Yada Yada friends. But . . . I'm thinking about writing a "stand-alone" novel next—which will be a challenge for me, since my one-book ideas seem to end up spilling over into a continuing, "episodic" story. But there's a character in the House of Hope series I'd like to write about—the old bag lady, "Lucy"—beginning with her childhood back in the late 1930s and early 40s as part of a migrant family following the crops from state to state, and how she ended up on the streets of Chicago. But that's still just an idea, not a promise of "what's next." My husband says writing Lucy's story would be good for me, because I'd have to cover decades of time—and so far my novels practically happen in "real time." (The Yada Yada series covers only two years in seven books. And the four House of Hope novels—I'm working on the finale now—cover exactly eight months! In all four novels! Sheesh. I need to learn how to write with a broader brush . . . you think?)

I'd like to connect with you! Drop me a line. Tell me how the book may have spoken to you. And I'd love to hear how God's been faithful in your life.

Here's where you can find me:

www.kimcashtate.com

www.facebook.com/kimcashtate

twitter.com/KimCashTate

A Note from the Author

Dear Friend,

I still vividly remember my first Women of Faith conference. The year was 2001, and a fairly new friend asked if I might like to go. I thought it would be a great opportunity to hear dynamic speakers who would make me laugh as well as cry, to experience amazing worship alongside thousands of other women, and to bond in a deeper way with my friend. The conference surpassed my every expectation.

I could look around that Dallas arena and know I wasn't alone. There were other women who were hungry to know God and walk out a life of faith, but who didn't have it all together. It was okay to be vulnerable, to laugh at ourselves, to realize we weren't expected to have it all together—that God's grace and love would see us through.

In *Faithful*, you find three friends—Cyd, Dana, and Phyllis—who endure struggles in their lives and look to one another for understanding and encouragement. With Women of Faith, you get to experience it yourself—real encouragement from women who understand your struggles and aren't afraid to reveal their own. You must go! And then I'm hoping you'll let me know just how blessed you were.

I'm so thankful to be able to share with you, through *Faithful*, the blessing of walking in close fellowship with God, and I pray you experience daily that fellowship and His faithfulness in your own life.

— Kim

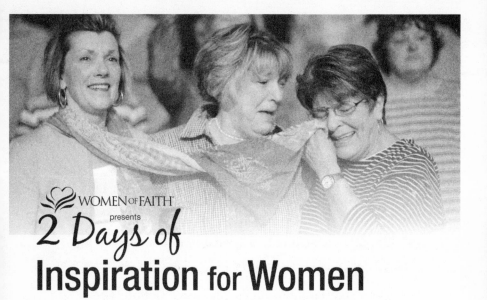

WOMEN OF **FAITH**
presents

2 Days of
Inspiration for Women

At a Women of Faith weekend, you'll join thousands of other women for a surprisingly intimate, unexpectedly funny, deeply touching 2-day event. Renowned speakers, award-winning musical artists, best-selling authors, drama, and more combine for a hope-filled event like no other.

> The music was incredible and each speaker's message either brought me to tears, laughing, or both! I have never had a more fulfilling, uplifting experience! You rehabilitated my soul! — *Debbie*

Coming to a City Near You
Schedule, Talent line up, and more at **womenoffaith.com**
Or call **888.49.FAITH** for details.

Join us at One of These Life-Changing Events!
It's the perfect getaway weekend for you and your friends — or a special time just for you and God to share. **Register Today!**

We'd love to hear your thoughts!

We hope you've enjoyed *Faithful* by Kim Cash Tate.

Your feedback as a Christian Fiction reader is extremely valuable to us. We'd like to invite you to participate in a brief on-line survey where you can share your opinions about Christian Fiction. The survey itself should take no more than 10 minutes.

For the first 500 readers who go online and complete the survey, we'll express our gratitude by mailing you a free full-length Christian Fiction novel as a thank you for your time. Visit www. nelsonfictionfeedback.com to begin the survey.

Thanks for believing in the power of story— and for helping us to create the stories you most want to read.